# The
# Frequency
# of
# Living Things

ALSO BY NICK FULLER GOOGINS

*The Great Transition*

# The
# Frequency
# of
# Living Things

*A Novel*

## NICK FULLER GOOGINS

**ATRIA** BOOKS

NEW YORK  AMSTERDAM/ANTWERP  LONDON
TORONTO  SYDNEY/MELBOURNE  NEW DELHI

**ATRIA**
**BOOKS**

An Imprint of Simon & Schuster, LLC
1230 Avenue of the Americas
New York, NY 10020

This book is a work of fiction. Any references to historical events, real people, or real places are used fictitiously. Other names, characters, places, and events are products of the author's imagination, and any resemblance to actual events or places or persons, living or dead, is entirely coincidental.

First Atria Books hardcover edition August 2025

**ATRIA** B O O K S and colophon are trademarks of Simon & Schuster, LLC

For information about special discounts for bulk purchases, please contact Simon & Schuster Special Sales at 1-866-506-1949 or business@simonandschuster.com.

The Simon & Schuster Speakers Bureau can bring authors to your live event. For more information or to book an event, contact the Simon & Schuster Speakers Bureau at 1-866-248-3049 or visit our website at www.simonspeakers.com.

*Interior design by Kyoko Watanabe*

Manufactured in the United States of America

1  3  5  7  9  10  8  6  4  2

Library of Congress Cataloging-in-Publication Data is available.

ISBN 978-1-6680-5606-6
ISBN 978-1-6680-5608-0 (ebook)

*For Mom, Dad, Ben, and Old Goat—the original pack*

Evolution is a science of connection.

—Lynn Margulis and Dorion Sagan
*Acquiring Genomes* (2002)

We have all known the long loneliness and we
have learned that the only solution is love.

—Dorothy Day
*The Long Loneliness* (1952)

Pray for the dead, and fight like hell for the living.

—Mary Harris "Mother" Jones

# PART I

# The Pack Is the Nucleus

# Chapter 1

# Josie

Josie Tayloe was a scientist. Had been a scientist. Was still a scientist? Let's see: there was MIT's science and engineering summer camp, there was a bachelor's in Developmental Bio at Tufts, there was four-fifths of a PhD in Ecology and Evolutionary Biology from Stanford. And don't forget the years of fieldteching the forests and beaches of America, the Fulbright Fellowship to Nicaragua, the EPA Star grant, the articles in *Nature* and *American Myrmecologist*. And so on.

And now what?

Now thirty-four years old at a gas station in central Maine, risking a potentially severe case of public plumber's crack as she inspected the casual insect holocaust of interstate travel.

Josie crabwalked between vehicles at the pumps, checking windshields, side mirrors, radiator grills. Mostly she found midges and gnats, some poor honeybees, but you had to sort the wheat from the chaff. Case in point: that very afternoon, an hour north of Boston, she'd collected a candy-striped leafhopper, murdered gracefully in a Mercedes hood ornament. Even Dean, never one to cream his pants over invertebrates, was impressed.

Midge, cricket, mosquito.

Thorax, wing, antenna.

She picked through the chitinous layers. Was this hard science? Probably this was not hard science.

Beyond the fluorescence of the gas station hung the great northern woods like a curtain. It was dusk. Saturday. Late July. The nocturnal phylums droned and swarmed the floodlights. Josie could see Dean inside through the big store windows, stocking up on energy drinks, snacks, antacids, beer. They were on their way to Acadia National Park for a week of oceanside camping, after which they would drive farther north—Canada practically—to the Mad Mountain Tavern. They would make the long drive because the Mad Mountain Tavern had a stage, and Josie's sisters were booked to perform on that stage. Not the most glamorous gig in America (or even Maine), but her sisters hadn't played live in almost a year, so Josie would be there.

"Can I help you with something?"

A fortysomething mustached man, presumable owner of the minivan before which Josie was crouching. Bucket-sized coffee in one hand, sleepy-eyed daughter over his shoulder.

"Just making a routine survey of hemiptera," Josie said.

"Sorry?"

"Bugs," Josie clarified. "Your vehicle has a dreamy front end. Killer surface area."

The man nodded as if he was used to the compliment. He buckled his daughter into her seat, unscrewed the gas cap, and filled up, leaving Josie to play with her bugs alone, as people usually did.

Midge, midge, mosquito, gnat.

Josie's knees popped when she stood. She inspected two sedans, a motorcycle, a Winnebago, then circled back to a maroon Saturn with California plates, parked next to Dean's 4Runner. Dean was now standing in line for the register. Josie watched him chat up a big woman in motorcycle leather, almost as tall as Dean. She threw her head back at something funny he said. Dean had that effect on people. He'd never bring home ribbons for Best Looking (lanky, no chin: an Abe Lincoln lookalike with worse skin) but the man could charm honey from the comb. He was a labor organizer with UNITE HERE Local 26, and—like all working-class heroes—hadn't allowed himself a true vacation in years. But as soon as Josie had mentioned that her sisters were gigging up north, Dean began researching campgrounds. He wanted to make a trip of it. He and Josie "needed" some time, just the two of them. They would unplug. No phones, no family. It would be relaxing! And didn't Josie deserve that, a little relaxation? One week without her heavy sash of worry?

Okay, she'd said. Okay, okay, okay.

She'd taken off work. She made sure her sisters were set with grocery money and spare keys and appointment reminders: She asked Ara if they'd be alright. She asked Emma if they'd be alright. She didn't believe either of them, but what else could she do?

"You can pack your bags," Dean had said. "We are going to have some fucking fun."

> OBSERVATION: Dean's never mentioned wanting (*needing*) to
>   get away like this.
> HYPOTHESIS: Getting away = excuse for alone time =
>   Dean prepping her for bad news.

Why did Josie expect the worst? Because the worst was what happened. Family history had been clear on that lesson. Even if Dean was sort of right about the trip so far. So far the trip had been fun. Relaxing. And a candy-striped leafhopper to boot.

Josie watched Dean crack another joke in line. The woman doubled over in laughter. He gestured outside. The woman waved. Josie waved back, then returned to the pulpy batter of thoraxes, wings, and antennae that plastered the Saturn's headlights.

Mosquito, gnat, beetle, gnat.

Josie missed the lab. One did not simply go years without access to a DNA thermocycler and feel like a fully functional human being. She worked now at a neighborhood reptile and insect zoo where she was overqualified by two academic degrees. Thank Darwin the place had a leafcutter ant colony. Josie loved ants. Obsessed over ants. In the past she'd observed ant colonies, extracted and amplified DNA, ran gels. Now she changed UV lights, dished out frozen mice and crickets, lectured groups of sticky toddlers and their hot foreign nannies. Not exactly hard science. But Josie, as a young girl, had fallen in love with science for the same reason she was in love with it still: science was everywhere, you just had to look. And look—

A moth.

A big honker. Wedged between the Saturn's license plate and frame. That hindwing patterning. That shade. She squinted and leaned closer.

A gas pump chugged behind her. A whiff of diesel floated in the air. She forbid herself from becoming too excited. She slid a bobby pin from her hair and gingerly pried the fuzzy body from the vehicle. She held the little bugger to the floodlights like an offering to the gods of good taxonomy.

**Wingspan:** two inches.
**Hindwings:** distinct white marginal banding.
**Forewings:** striated, wood camo patterning.
**Antenna:** white scaling on dorsal surface.

Oh my God.

It was impossible—a Kern Primrose sphinx moth, *Euproserpinus Euterpe*—and yet. Josie was certain. She was ninety-nine percent certain. She could not be one hundred percent certain because she'd never observed a Kern Primrose in the wild. Few people had. One of two moths on the Federal Endangered Species List, the insect's only known habitat was California's Carrizo Plain, where Josie had spent countless weekends, wading through those sharp grasses, head bowed, looking for egg, larvae, caterpillar, moth. You didn't have to volunteer to do these bullshit research favors for your dissertation advisor, but Josie had. The urge to please. That old story. Even now, she couldn't help but fantasize Dr. Lee's forgiveness should she, Josephine Tayloe, all-star mentee, the next E.O.-goddamn-Wilson (Dr. Lee's words, not hers), send news that she'd discovered a Kern Primrose light-years from its habitat. A complete specimen, no less. She turned the moth carefully in her palm. She pumped a fist. Darwin, she loved this shit.

———

Delicately, so delicately, she wrapped the dead moth in a casket of Dunkin' Donuts napkins and entombed the bundle in the glovebox where she and Dean had sequestered their phones, as demanded by the most sacrosanct of their Vacation Commandments:

*Check Not Thy Phone*

No Phones was more challenging than Josie would've liked to admit. It helped that Dean was family-cleansing with her. Dean's mother was used to calling daily, and Dean was used to picking up. But not today. Josie, in solidarity, had resisted the urge to check in with her sisters. Emma and Ara undoubtedly needed something—Dean agreed whole-heartedly on this point—but he trusted they could survive one week without her. Josie mocked his ignorance: What peer-reviewed studies, what data sets, what field notes supported his crackpot theory?

Josie did not worry because worry was the dominant allele of her emotional genotype (though it was), she worried because her family gave her so many brilliant reasons to worry. Which was why—glovebox open, phone *right there*, Dean busy dumping his haul of beer and snacks for the cashier to tally—she couldn't resist. She reached in. She turned on her phone.

Only the damn thing took forever to power up. Dean was paying now at the register. Walking out. She waited until the last possible second and—no luck—tossed the phone back into the glovebox as the gas station doors went *whoosh*.

Dean loped outside, his new friend in tow.

"Josie, meet Wanda. She's a fan—"

"—Fan doesn't cut it, I'm diehard, baby. Lost my V-card to Jojo and the Twins. Heard about the Caribou show and dammit I can't move my shift but I'll try to make the encore. How about a photo? Here sweetcheeks, you know what to do."

She gave her phone to Dean and threw an arm around Josie. These random fan encounters still happened every so often.

"Say cheese," Dean said.

Josie and Wanda held their breath, smiling.

"So your man here"—Wanda took her phone from Dean, grunting approvingly at the screen—"he says you're Jojo, and I'm like, 'Wanda Jenks you're paying those girls back.'"

Dean fanned the air with dollar scratch tickets. "Wanda got us a gift."

"Not a gift. I owe you fair and square. I downloaded your tunes for free, way back. A dog's age, but that doesn't make it right."

Jojo and the Twins was the name of Josie's sisters' band, and because

Josie never appeared onstage, fans like Wanda often assumed she was the quiet visionary behind the music—the Fifth Beatle, so to speak. This wasn't the least bit true, but Josie had stopped correcting the record a long time ago. After all, she was a crucial part of the band. Her sisters now earned about forty-three cents a week in streaming royalties. If not for Josie, they would be homeless. She covered ninety percent of their rent and one hundred percent of their Netflix and yoga. She was no George Martin making musical magic behind the Abbey Road curtain, but credit was absolutely due.

"When can I get my mitts on the new album?" Wanda said.

"Soon," Josie said, a line that had been getting old for years now.

"Good. We need you girls. This country is going worse to worse." Wanda gave engulfing hugs, kick-started her motorcycle, and ripped the night in two, yelling "Slay it in Caribou!" as she roared off.

Back on the road, Josie unwrapped the Kern Primrose to show Dean. She didn't want to make a big deal of it, not yet. "Morphological observation is no substitute for genetic confirmation," she said, but Dean whooped and honked the horn, so happy for her that she had to smile.

"So what's it mean?" he said.

"For migration patterns? I'm not getting my hopes up. The car had California plates. It probably collided somewhere near Carrizo and drove it across the country."

"Not for migration patterns, for your career."

"I don't have a career."

"This could be your ticket back!"

Josie envied his naivety. She knew all too well the pitfalls of open-faced hope. She turned on the radio. She scanned the static, the Christian rock, the sports talk. She scratched Wanda's lottery tickets, won five dollars, and celebrated by fisting a bag of Cheetos. She licked cheese dust off her fingers. She prepared to ask Dean (rhetorically of course) how he expected her to return to academia with her sisters—and her mother—more dependent on her than ever. Before she could ask, however, her phone rang from the glovebox. And, at nearly the same moment, her sisters came blasting from the speakers.

———

"American Mosh" was the 2002 single that had earned Jojo and the Twins a Grammy nod, a gold record, a Wikipedia page, a legion of diehard fans. Every so often you still caught some lone DJ playing it for Throwback Thursday. The bassy intro was epic. Then Emma's voice launched into the first verse with her trilling, operatic vault that still had the power to raise the hair on Josie's arms all these years later. Dean waited out of respect for the verse to end. Then he reached to turn off the radio. He cleared his throat.

"You broke a commandment." He nodded at the glovebox, where Josie's phone continued to loudly betray her. "You committed vacation heresy."

"What can I say, I'm heretical." Josie opened the glovebox. Sure enough: "I *knew* it. It's Emma."

"Don't pick up, Jo. Please."

"Something might be wrong."

"She's fine. Don't answer. You know you'll regret it."

But Josie couldn't help herself. First a freakishly rare Kern Primrose, then a nearly-as-endangered broadcast of "American Mosh," and, at the exact moment, her sister calling? The signs couldn't be clearer.

"You know she's going to ask for something. You don't have to pick up. You can put down the phone. It's your choice."

Since when had Dean mastered the tone and cadence of a hostage negotiator? Josie swiped, brought the phone to her ear, and exhaled.

"Em, everything okay?"

"Jojo! Thank God you answered."

Josie felt her heart plummet below the x-axis of her chest. "What's wrong?"

"The Mad Mountain Tavern changed dates on us. They moved it up. We're on tonight."

Josie took a breath. She was not her sisters' manager. "I wish I'd known earlier. We could have driven you up."

"Oh that's okay," Emma said.

"Well have you told them there's no way you can make it?"

"Huh? No. We're here."

"You're where?"

"Here. We flew. We're loading-in right now."

Josie clenched her jaw. "Ara's intake session was this morning. Please tell me she didn't miss it."

"Um . . ."

"*I told you*," Josie mouthed to Dean. "Em? Let me talk to her. No, you know what, forget it, I'll reschedule for her. I'll call tomorrow."

"Okay," Emma said, and then she asked, "Is there any chance you can make it tonight?"

Josie glanced at the dashboard clock. She ignored Dean, who was shaking his head violently and dragging imaginary blades across his throat.

"What time's sound check?" she asked.

"Nine," Emma said. "But we have to eat first. And we still haven't found anyone who can work the merch table . . ."

"I'll do it."

"Oh my God, really? I know you're on vacation. We were nervous to ask. We don't want to inconvenience you."

"You're not inconveniencing me. I'm offering."

"Honestly, it would be a huge help."

Help. The word was a skeleton key that opened every dopamine vault. Josie's brainstem began dumping huge quantities of the neurotransmitter into her amygdala, her prefrontal cortex, her hippocampus. She understood what was happening, at the cellular level, yet resistance was futile.

"Of course, Em. One hundred percent. I'll be there."

"Thanks, Jo."

"Put Ara on real quick?"

"I stashed the merch bag in the greenroom. Just go in and grab it if we're onstage. Love you, love you, kiss, kiss, kiss!"

"Wait, put on—"

Emma hung up. Josie made a big show of turning off her phone and returning it to the glovebox. "Their gig got moved up."

"So I heard," said Dean flatly.

"We need to go to Caribou. Tonight."

Dean's foot tapped the brake for no apparent reason. "I thought we were camping?"

Josie knew she pushed Dean, asked insane things of him. Ironically (sadistically?), the fact that he was incapable of saying "no" often made her push harder.

"They need someone to work the merch table."

"Your sisters need a favor from you. I am shocked."

"Dean. This is important. They haven't gigged in almost a year."

"Camping reservations at Acadia. Summer weekend. Not easy to get."

"We'll only miss one night."

"Why can't someone else work the merch table?"

"The merch table isn't the point."

"Then what is the point?"

Josie loved ants, in part, because they put other social organisms (like *Homo sapiens*) to shame. Ant colonies, as she never tired of explaining to anyone willing to listen, are complex social networks comprised almost exclusively of females. And not just females, but *sisters*, genetically speaking. Sisters who, thanks to the diploidic quirks of ant reproduction (of which almost nobody was willing to listen), share more DNA with one another than they do with their mother. Sisters who are ready to work and fight and sacrifice for each other without second thought. Even if their sisters are impulsive, washed-up rock stars who'd squandered a record label and a semi-fortune. Josie was one of a colony. *That was the point.* The point was to support Emma and Ara at this lowest asymptote of their career. The point was to check up on Ara, who Josie suspected of using again. A fear so deeply destabilizing that she couldn't air it aloud, not to Dean, not even to herself. The point was inclusion, for Josie, like every younger sibling since Zeus, hated being left out.

"The point is they need me," Josie said.

"You do know that you could be like a national spokesperson for unhealthy codependent relationships? I just want to make sure you're still aware of that career option."

Josie remained steadfastly unamused. They drove in silence.

Then Dean veered suddenly into the middle lane, shifted to accelerate, gunned the gas, and threaded a slot canyon between two tractor trailers. He punched the steering wheel. He punched the steering wheel again. "Alright. Alright. Let's go hear some damn music."

## Chapter 2

# Josie

The Mad Mountain Tavern was a bigger venue than Josie had expected, capacity one hundred–ish with an actual raised stage. Jojo and the Twins had gigged smaller spots ("The Den Sets") and larger spots ("Madison Square Garden"), but to Josie the air always tasted the same: burnt electronics, old beer, dollar bills.

Josie and Dean had driven nonstop to make it, and they may have failed if not for the Tavern's incompetent sound guy. Josie's sisters were onstage, urging the man to do his job. Ara's voice came over the speakers—"Little less on the kick drum, please?"—and then, when Sound Guy gave a thumbs-up without touching a knob on his board, Emma said—"Hey, Beefcake, work with us here, we sink or swim together"—and Ara machine-gunned her snare to reset his attention.

Ara sat behind her kit, dressed for comfort: yellow sweatsuit, chunky white sunglasses. Emma wore a tuxedo vest, white leggings, black high tops, her fingers sparkling with silver. Her hair was arranged in a complicated side braid, as long and flowing as Ara's was close-cropped. Josie waved. They didn't see her.

Dean, still upset about the U-turn in plans, peeled off for a shot and a beer at the bar. Josie let him sulk. She had work to do. She located the merch bag. She set up the table as she'd done so many times—T-shirts organized by size; posters, pins, and bumper stickers by color—and she purposefully did not dwell upon the fact that Ara was wearing sunglasses indoors. She also did not calculate the baggage costs of flying their gear from Boston against whatever pittance the Mad Mountain Tavern was likely paying. She did lay out the many iterations of *American Mosh* (cassette, CD, vinyl, flash drive, QR code) and tried hard to admire the variety not as a sign of her sisters' failure to produce a second album, but a testament to their marketing evolution. A piercing blast of feedback whined from Emma's monitor speaker.

"My bad," said Sound Guy.

Josie watched him adjust his knobs and levers while trying not to gawk too obviously at her sisters. His inability to multitask was understandable; Emma and Ara were gorgeous, in every hegemonic, Western, conventional twenty-first-century sense of the word. Adolescent Josie had consumed herself in envy, born only thirteen months after them, with half their nucleotide base pairs, and yet a cruelly divergent phenotype. The Punnett square lottery had not awarded her the gene for blemish-free skin, or a jawline you could cut yourself on, or hair that straightened naturally, or nails so healthy they kept their luster even in the depths of opioid addiction. As for the propensity toward worry weight, water weight, winter weight? The lucky bitches had escaped that fun little gene, adult Josie kidded. Adult Josie could kid with the lucky bitches (*kidding!*) because she was no longer jealous. She was only sometimes jealous. Like when she convinced Ara to jog mornings with her around Jamaica Pond (endorphins being excellent for recovery) and Ara, after a month, had to quit because she was losing too much weight. But genuine around-the-clock jealousy? Too exhausting in your mid-thirties. Plus, Josie had come to sincerely appreciate the dark wave of her hair, the splash of freckles on her cheeks and chest, her size. She felt solid. Serious. Womanly. Grounded. Unlike her sisters, who seemed as though they might fade and float away. And, of course, with great, conventional beauty came great, conventional cost. Josie had witnessed that for Emma and Ara both.

Ara waved and blew a kiss when she caught Josie staring. Josie shot one back.

"You know the Twins?"

A woman in lavish mascara and a polka-dot rockabilly dress plunked a cardboard box on the merch table. Josie picked up a copy of *American Mosh* (vinyl) and pointed to the middle of the three bird skeletons that made up the cover art. "That's me."

A flash of understanding. An unsolicited hug.

"You're Jojo! Oh. My. God. Your sisters are my heroes!"

Josie, if asked to create a public service spot for younger siblings of identical twins, could not have done better: You were special *and* you were in the shadows, usually within the span of a single breath. Or hug.

Rockabilly had a name, Yolanda, and Yolanda was with the Valley Women's Action Coalition: V-WAC. Emma and Ara played what some people called post–Riot Grrrl punk rock protest music, and although they privately disagreed with the label, they *did* enjoy coordinating with local social justice groups, offering free promotion and a cut of the door. Josie had left a portion of the merch table unoccupied for this purpose, and Yolanda set about filling it with V-WAC pamphlets, buttons, tank tops (**WHAT HAVE *YOU* DONE TODAY TO SMASH THE PATRIARCHY?**), the ubiquitous clipboard with sign-up sheet. Josie bought a tank top, earning karma points that she cashed in later, when Emma and Ara finished sound check and headed backstage.

"Cover for me, Yolanda? If you need help, shout for the drunk skinny dude at the bar."

————

The greenroom was a glorified closet. Cinderblocks and sofas. A loud minifridge stocked with High Life. Josie helped herself as Emma stepped into her stage outfit: cheerleading skirt, corset, Day-Glo wig, combat boots. She laced up while talking crowd size. "Pretty decent for last-minute notice, right? I'm feeling super good about tonight. I think we'll look back on tonight and be like, *Caribou, you were it!* Know what I mean?"

What Josie knew was that Emma was a pathological optimist. It was endearing. Also enraging. Looking back, they would more likely be like, *Jojo, those airline baggage fees were killer and we're dealing with some fairly grave credit card debt—do us a solid?*

"Mom might even be here," Emma added as she tightened her laces.

Josie scoffed. "Mom said she'd be here?"

"Well not exactly," said Emma.

"When did you talk to her?"

"We left a message," Ara said.

"They're about to set sail," Josie said. "I seriously doubt she'll be here."

"They don't leave till next week," Emma said.

"They leave in six days. She has a million things to do to get ready."

"Who knows?" Emma said.

"I do," said Josie. "She's not coming. Sorry."

"She never called to say she *wouldn't* make it," Ara said.

"That's very true," Emma said.

Pinpricks smoldered in Josie's vision. That she was the one who had sworn off talking to their mother, yet remained the one who tracked the irresponsible logistics of her life, was enough to push someone over the edge. But only if someone wanted to go over the edge, and—as a gift to her sisters, and herself—Josie decided against free fall. She chugged a High Life to cool her insides and did not ask whom her sisters had invited first to the show: Josie or their mother? She did not ask how Ara and Emma hoped to live successful, independent lives without Josie's help if they couldn't even caretake for themselves emotionally—if they were so naïve as to genuinely believe that their mother would inconvenience herself one iota to make their gig.

No, Josie thought. Not tonight. Tonight was about the band.

Celebration.

Rebirth.

Like the Kern Primrose moth, safely stowed in the glovebox. Chains of implausible events sometimes did in fact link together to make the impossible happen. The emergence of life on Earth proved that. Maybe Emma was right about Caribou—maybe tonight would be the night where they turned their ship around.

Josie grabbed another beer from the fridge, and sat cross-legged next to Ara, who was applying stripes of glossy face paint. Where Emma liked to chase the spotlight in minimal clothing, Ara preferred to hide behind her drum kit and costumes. She dipped her thumb in the paint pot and dotted Josie's forehead.

"Thanks for coming, Jo."

"You kidding? Of course. How are your wrists?"

"Fine."

"And you?"

"Fine," Ara said.

"Just fine?"

"Good. I'm feeling good."

The worry with Ara was that she felt *too* good. A number of unfortunate factors had led to pain, to Percocet, to OxyContin, to rehab, to a train wreck of SSRIs, to a horrifying fentanyl scare, to more rehab, and all throughout, to the fantasy in which Josie gunned down the family that owned Purdue Pharma.

"Should we open with 'No Doubt'?" Emma tore a paper plate in thirds to write out set lists for her, Ara, and the hopeless sound guy.

"I'm kind of feeling 'Cranberries,'" Ara said.

"'*Zombie*,'" they said at the same time.

Josie sipped her High Life. Her sisters were flushed with pre-gig glow. Always a joy to experience in proximity. But why was Ara still wearing sunglasses? If her pupils were pinned, game over. Then again, she wasn't picking at her cuticles, or wiping her nose, or running to the bathroom every five minutes. She wasn't drinking, or even smoking. None of the old signs. Josie felt like expensive NSA hardware, a highly-tuned instrument bristling with microphones, lenses, and unconstitutional directives. Was Ara using again? She had to know. She didn't want to know.

"Jojo, can you give this gal a drop-D?"

Emma handed Josie a guitar and tuner, freeing her to stuff the top of her corset with what looked like gauzy red scarves.

Josie's worry was that Ara had been distant lately. Off. Not herself. It could've been anything. But Josie felt in her gut that it was not anything. She'd been playing Nancy Drew, popping into her sisters' apartment (she paid the rent, she had the right), rooting through Ara's tote bags, pressing her ear to the door when Ara was in the bathroom, inviting Ara at unpredictable times to walk Jamaica Pond, noting behaviors and moods. Her sleuthing had turned up nothing. But—and this was key—it hadn't debunked her theory either.

So Josie almost wept with relief when Ara began rubbing her wrists with Tiger Balm.

*If Ara needed Tiger Balm, she was expecting her wrists to be in pain.*

*If Ara was expecting pain, she was not ripped on painkillers.*

*Q.E.D.*

"Get over here." Josie put aside the guitar and gooped Tiger Balm into Ara's ropey forearms.

Ara groaned. "It feels so good when someone else does it."

"Yeah that's oxytocin. Triggered by human touch. Evolution's way to keep us from becoming complete dickholes."

Emma was bouncing on her feet, humming, editing the playlist.

Josie lowered her voice. "Emma said you missed therapy this morning."

"We were so rushed," Ara said. "I had to pack."

"That wasn't an easy appointment to get." Josie employed the full spectrum of superhuman pressure required to calm her voice. "There was a really long wait list."

"I'm sorry," Ara said.

"Did you at least call to reschedule?"

"I don't have their number."

"You couldn't have looked it up?"

"Sorry."

Josie sighed. She'd enrolled both Ara and Emma in MassHealth. She'd found the Survivors' Resource Center, a provider for victims of sexual assault. She'd registered Ara. She'd scheduled Ara's intake session. She had not driven Ara, nor walked her in, nor camped outside the door. Next time she would. Josie had sat in enough Al-Anon meetings to know that managing another person's recovery wasn't an ideal route to success. But it was a hundred percent more ideal than no recovery.

"Hey, Jo?" Ara said.

"What?"

"You're hurting me."

Josie glanced down. She was squeezing Ara's wrists to the bone. "Sorry." She reminded herself not to go over the edge. But her feet kept shuffling toward the edge. They always did. "I just think it couldn't hurt to be more proactive. Just a smidge."

"I know."

"And I can help you. I'm *here* for you. Whatever you need, Ara. Whenever."

"Thanks."

"Hey I'd love to keep playing spa," Emma said, "but we're on in like, T-minus five."

Josie took her cue. She raided the fridge, grabbing as many beers as she could carry for Dean. Emma stopped her with a straight arm across the door.

"Wait. We have to tell you something."

"What? What's wrong?"

Emma smiled. "You're the greatest."

"Officially, Jo, you are." Ara opened her arms. "Band hug?"

———

Josie, in the eighth grade, had convinced Mrs. Enos, her science teacher, to donate a jar of iodine crystals for Josie's "crystal garden." But Josie was not growing crystals. She was conducting experiments, following the *Big Book of Mischief*, which she'd downloaded off the new World Wide Web:

1) Use coffee filter to strain ammonia through iodine crystals
2) Allow crumbly mixture to dry into nuggets
3) Toss nuggets against hard surface
4) Enjoy explosion and purple smoke

Ara had heard the blast, grabbed Emma's learner's permit, and driven Josie to the emergency room so a doctor could diagnose a perforated right eardrum. Decades later, Josie's hearing had never fully recovered, yet she could sense, within the first eight bars of "Zombie," that her sisters' show at the Mad Mountain Tavern was going to be painfully too loud.

The problem was physics: mass. There weren't enough bodies in the audience. Thirty humans, max. With so little organic matter to soak up Ara's cymbal crashes and Emma's operatics, the sound ricocheted off the walls and ceiling, harsh and desperate. Josie hoped she was being overly sensitive, but then Dean—sweaty and red from dancing—came over with twists of bar napkin in his ears and two more in his palm for her.

"No thanks," she shouted. Earplugs felt traitorous.

He jabbed a thumb at the stage. "They sound off to you?"

"They sound awesome. It's the venue. You know how it is with these local sound guys."

"You're glowing!" Dean touched her forehead where Ara had dotted her with what turned out to be black-light-activated paint. "That means you want to dance."

Dean was drunk and happy, the campground at Acadia a distant afterthought. His capacity for forgiveness, given sufficient alcohol, was inexhaustible, and Josie loved him for it. She followed him onto the dance floor.

They jumped in with the diehards crowding the stage. The diehards screamed along to Emma's every word, rocking faded T-shirts from the glory years. These people adored her sisters, and so Josie adored them. Tonight, however, the diehards were giving off a "rare-night-out" vibe that only enhanced the depressive atmosphere. More embarrassing were the activists with the Valley Women's Action Coalition: short skirts, dark lipstick, thigh tattoos, and all of them huddled by the bar, blue-faced in phone glow, ignoring Emma and Ara onstage.

OBSERVATION: Diehards aging out, youth unimpressed.

HYPOTHESIS: Jojo and the Twins will adapt or perish.

Her sisters, if they noticed, didn't care. Ara smiled from behind her kit, layering in vocals, her face streaked in glowing paint. Emma was looping guitar with bass and keys and lyrics, stomping pedals and running the stage, dancing over wires and cords while keeping the diehards happy on their toes. But Dean was right: Something sounded off. And it wasn't the sound guy.

Josie put her finger on it during "Irishman," when Ara, instead of landing on the final downbeat like she had a million times, came in a ghost-beat late. Josie saw a flash of horror cross Emma's face. As quickly as it appeared, Emma swallowed it and introduced Yolanda, drawing the loudest cheer of the evening.

Yolanda leapt onstage. She pitched V-WAC, inviting everyone to a sit-in at a state senator's office next week. Then, in an odd reversal—

usually the band pimped the cause, not vice versa—she said, "The Tayloe sisters rock. The Mosh for Women's Lives? That was all them. And *that's* how we fight, in the streets. Because no election is gonna save us. So support your sisters in the struggle. If you love the Twins, share their music. If you don't, pull your head out of your twat and buy their album now."

Emma rode the applause, launching into "Round Two," and there— *right there*—Ara was off again. Late in silencing a cymbal. Then rushing the kick drum. Now that Josie was actively listening, the mistakes were glaring. But she was too busy for prolonged observation because Yolanda's plug had drawn folks off their stools. Josie called Dean to the merch table to handle the credit card purchases. She was restocking medium T-shirts when the crowd went wild, stomping the floor in time with Ara's kick drum.

"American Mosh." That epic intro. Even the youth recognized it.

The bass thumped Josie's chest like grapeshot. She caught the rabid faces of the diehards—there was Wanda the biker chick!—and the hot lights and the artificial fog. Her sisters were putting on a show. Emma belted the chorus, her voice vaulting into a haunting, soulful ache that always seemed impossible, coming from an instrument so slender. She held the last note, on and on and on, casting red scarves from her chest in handfuls, sharing her heart with the world.

———

Josie was so buzzed with adrenaline, and the post-show merch rush, and Wanda muscling through the crowd for a sweaty hug, that she almost missed Emma bolting from backstage, her face red and puffy.

"Em! Wait up!"

Emma ignored her. She grabbed Sound Guy and pulled him outside.

Josie followed, leaving Dean to manage the table.

"Emma! Em?"

She turned the corner to find Emma and Sound Guy smashing face in the alley. Josie cleared her throat. Emma slapped Sound Guy on the ass, telling him to wait in his car.

"How'd we sound?" Emma's voice was raspy, her eyes red.

"What's wrong?" Josie said. "Have you been crying?"

"No." Emma wiped the corner of an eye.

Josie cut right to it: "Ara sounded off."

"Off? You thought she was *off*?"

It was like Emma was new to the word. Alarm bells clanged in Josie's head. She had a question. She wanted an answer.

"Shoot," said Emma.

"What the hell is going on?"

Emma said, "What are you talking about?" but her face gave it all away.

Josie felt her insides split like a milkweed pod.

"Is it pills? Tell me, Em. Is she using again?"

Emma crossed her arms. "Ara is not using pills again."

"You sound like you're on the stand. What is it? Talk to me. I'm her sister, too."

Emma looked over her shoulder. Sound Guy gave a thumbs-up from a red Jeep. "I'm tired, Jo. I need to get laid. Stop worrying for once. I got this."

Josie grabbed her wrist. "What does that mean? What's there to *get*?"

Emma opened her mouth like she was about to say something, but Sound Guy honked the horn. She twisted free from Josie's hand.

"Thanks for tonight, Jojo. You rocked the merch."

Josie walked a calming lap around the parking lot, vowing to be gentler with Ara. She found her smoking with Dean and Yolanda and some others at the side entrance. The V-WAC crew wanted to go skinny-dipping in a quarry. Josie sent Dean with them. She wanted to talk with her sister in private, she said. She asked Ara to hang back.

They sat on the hood of Dean's 4Runner, feet on the bumper. Ara smelled like sweat, Tiger Balm, tobacco. She lit a new cigarette. She was bubbly on what Josie hoped was post-gig adrenaline, describing the flight from Boston, the cute little prop plane, the tiny airport, the dream she'd had again, where all three of them were holding hands on the roof of their old house . . .

Josie half listened. She was more interested in the fact that Ara was still wearing her sunglasses. And babbling. Slurring, one might say? No, not slurring. Possibly slurring? Josie couldn't decide. And why wasn't she icing her wrists? Her wrists were usually killing her, post-gig. Maybe Tiger Balm was enough? Josie wanted to ask, had to ask, could not bear to ask. That muzzle of denial.

"Is everything okay with Em? She seemed upset."

Ara rested her head on Josie's shoulder. "Tonight wasn't my best performance."

"You sounded great."

"Ha."

"Well, you haven't gigged in a while. Maybe you're rusty?"

"Maybe."

Josie squeezed Ara's hand, her palm calloused and blood-blistered from a lifetime of keeping the beat.

"It's probably a good thing Mom didn't make it," Ara said.

Josie took a deep breath. Deeper. Deepest.

"I don't understand why you get your hopes up with her."

"It doesn't hurt to hope."

"I so completely disagree." Josie could not talk another minute about their mother. "Want to see something crazy I found on the way up here?"

"Duh."

Josie hopped down. She opened the passenger door and reached for the glove compartment.

"Dean and I can take your gear back, by the way. Save you baggage fees. Or we could all drive home together—or, hey, what if you come to Acadia with us? That would be so fun!"

"Emma hates camping."

"Emma doesn't have to come."

"Maybe."

"Come on! Get outside, stare at the ocean, skip some rocks, hug a tree—it always makes me feel better, being in nature."

"You don't have to worry about me all the time, Jo."

Josie's hand froze on the glovebox latch. "That's a little difficult for me to hear, Ara, if I'm being honest. You skipped therapy. Do you have any idea how much time I spent navigating MassHealth to get you that appointment?"

"I messed up. I said I was sorry."

Josie could feel her ribosomes vibrating in frustration. She reminded herself to be gentle.

"You're in their system now. It's all good. I'll reschedule. I can drive you next time. We can get lunch after."

"Jo. Stop worrying."

"I'm not worrying, I'm helping."

"Well you can't."

"What's that supposed to mean?"

"Nothing. I'm just . . . Sometimes I'm, like—I can't do this anymore."

"Can't do what?"

Ara waved her cigarette like a lasso.

"Can't do what, Ara?" Josie meant to sound concerned, not condescending, but her voice had that unfortunate jab.

Ara looked at Josie. She took a drag from her cigarette, shot an arrow of smoke from the corner of her mouth, and smiled. "Nothing. I'm just tired. Honestly, I feel pretty great."

And Ara, speaking honestly, did feel pretty great. For although Josie didn't know—couldn't know, would've spontaneously combusted right there in the parking lot like a white-hot coil of magnesium ribbon if she *did* know—Ara had enjoyed three modest bumps of heroin that evening.

**Bump #1:** precisely measured by Emma before the show.

**Bump #2:** snuck in haste before going onstage.

**Bump #3:** consumed flamboyantly, post-encore, in the
    greenroom as Emma screamed and cried her face off.

All bumps had long since immigrated past Ara's blood-brain barrier and metabolized into morphine, where they continued to hug every grateful opioid receptor in her skull.

"I'm glad you feel great," Josie said. "But if you need help, you'll ask, right? You'll let me know? Right?"

"Yes."

"You promise?"

"Cross my heart." Ara rubbed her face. She smiled. "Know what I thought, looking out the window, on the flight here?"

"What?" Josie said, wearily. She felt weak, defeated. She opened the glovebox and took out the bundle of napkins.

"How we'll be sisters longer than anything. We'll know each other longer than Mom, or Dean, or if we have kids. Pretty wild, if you think about it."

Josie thought about it. Her eyes blurred. Her sisters had control of her neurochemistry like few others. One little compliment, a band hug, the chance to help. Talk about a shot of oxytocin to the mainline. She was woozy, drowning in the stuff as she unwrapped the Kern Primrose. And so she was shocked, but perhaps not as shocked as she should've been, when the moth shuttered in her palm.

She gasped and cupped her hands. The moth fluttered its wings, a brush so light against her palms that Josie almost believed she was imagining it. Was she?

She cracked her hands. The moth was still.

"Ara, did you see that?"

"I saw it." Ara had pushed her sunglasses onto the crown of her head. If Josie hadn't been so sideswiped by the Kern Primrose, she may have noticed her sister's pupils, pinned to the size of mold spores.

Josie gently blew on the moth. It didn't move. But it had. *It had.* Science, Josie had discovered long ago, was a lifelong exercise in humility; the more you learned, the more your ignorance grew. How to explain that certain species of forest mushrooms have thousands of genders? Or the evolutionary discontinuity between simple prokaryotic cells and complex nucleated life? And what the fuck was going on with black matter? Or quantum entanglement? Or caring about your sisters so deeply that you sometimes hated them? She laughed in disbelief.

OBSERVATION: Dead Kern Primrose resurrects.
HYPOTHESIS: Omen of fresh starts, life, new things to come.

For what is life if not a four-billion-year-old recycling program? A continual renewal, a turning over. A moth is an omen like a sunrise is an omen. Big changes, they are always—*always*—coming. Josie could count on that.

# Chapter 3

# Emma

Emma crossed Blue Hill Avenue, hiked through Franklin Park, and summited Centre Street. It was Monday morning, the disastrous Caribou gig two days behind her. She needed caffeine.

Back when Emma and Ara were freshmen at Berklee and rode the Orange Line out for shows, The Fountain was a biker bar meets Kurt Cobain mancave meets Mass Art meat market. The stage used to be in the corner where a barista with a leather apron was now designing a swan in the oat milk froth of Emma's latte. The one time Emma and Ara had gigged here, their set ended abruptly when an eighty-sixed customer backed his Harley through the door and burned rubber, filling the place with tire fumes. *Memories.*

The new Fountain was exposed brick, Edison bulbs, a server with cheekbones and biceps that Emma wanted to lick. A display of local beets and basil advertised the name of the farmer (Gregory) who'd harvested them. Gentrification, if you could afford to live within hiking distance, was an unjust, beautiful thing.

The server walked over with her latte. While waiting for it to cool, Emma popped in her earbuds to review the Mad Mountain Tavern set. A band ritual of theirs, listening together to critique live shows, the way professional athletes might review game film. But trying to parse the set alone, without Ara, was like attempting a G-chord without a middle finger: she couldn't make the root note she needed. She swiped over to check her messages again.

*Sister, Sister, where art thou, Sister?*

No word from Ara in almost twenty-four hours. The Caribou gig, looking back, had been one drawn-out fight, interrupted by an all-too-brief set making music onstage. They'd fought before the show. They'd fought after the show. They'd fought on the Ikea sofa bed at Yolanda's house, where they spent the night. They'd fought across the aisle of the tiny prop plane as it buzzed into Boston. They'd fought in the backseat on the ride from Logan.

They'd fought because Ara had broken the rules. She'd gone behind Emma's back to get high. She'd embarrassed Emma onstage. And Emma had registered her disapproval, as any bandmate would. In retrospect, she could've practiced a little more diplomacy. Words had been said that couldn't be unsaid. Ara had run off and not come home. To someone as chemically dependent as her sister, Emma knew this could mean one of two things. Either Ara had copped, or she was suffering terribly.

Other scenarios were possible, too, of course, but Emma refused to follow them into the D-minor darkness. Instead, she called Josie. Again. Her responsible younger sister had chosen the worst possible time to unplug and disappear into the woods. Her phone went to voicemail. Again.

"Hi Jojo. Um. Call me—"

"—Sorry, I never do this, but do you know you have the most gorgeous hair?"

A woman was standing behind Emma, palming a lock of her hair. Strangers said they didn't often do this, but they did, touching Emma's hair as if it were a public good. Yes, her hair was long and extraordinarily well-conditioned. Yes, folks meant well. Still. Boundaries, people?

Emma hung up, and air-groped the woman's chest. "Sorry, I never do this, but you have the most gorgeous tits."

The woman mumbled a thank-you and retreated to her table.

Emma shrugged at the server, who had come to check on her. "What? She does."

Emma was wearing her leather moto jacket over a lacy sundress, and Ara's espadrilles. She'd caught the server staring when she walked in, and watched him until he knew he'd been caught, then continued watching him until he felt sufficiently encouraged, which, he finally did.

"Sorry, I never do this," he said, refilling her water, "but can I get your number?"

After settling her bill, she bought an avocado at the Yuppie Bodega and spooned bites in line at the bank, waiting to make her deposits: their earnings from the Caribou gig, a very late payment for performing "American Mosh" at a Ritz-Carlton Bat Mitzvah (clearly for the parents and parents' friends, not the bored middle-schoolers), a DistroDude payout for a documentary on celebrity kitchens that had used "American Mosh" in the opening credits. And the latest batch of royalty checks. The trick in depositing royalty checks was waiting until enough accumulated. The shock still walloped, but with less apocalyptic flair.

**PayMe:** $150.21
**Awesong:** $101.35
**WePlay:** $4.07

WePlay paid four-one-thousandths of a cent per stream. Four-one-hundredths if the album streamed from beginning to end. Awesong was less mercenary, taking ten percent of sales, but they sold downloads exclusively. The problem with downloads was that nobody bought them anymore but diehards, who either owned your music already, or had the decency to get it off your website (where PayMe took its pound). Jojo and the Twins—in the spirit of the peer-to-peer file sharing that had made them famous—let fans pay what they wanted. Most everyone paid something. That was the good news. The bad news: the same technology that had launched their career was now delivering them into poverty. Emma didn't need to be rich. She'd been rich. This was humiliating.

Another question strangers often felt the need to ask: *Can you read your twin's mind?*

If only.

―――――

On the walk home, Emma turned down a marriage proposal, flipped off a guy who suggested she smile, recorded a voice memo of a melody that popped into her head, and replied "Amen!" to an elderly man's

"Gracias a Dios!" She and Ara lived across Franklin Park, in Mattapan, a distant Pluto in the solar system of urban renewal, just now experiencing the first bleeps and bloops from the hungry inner planets. When Emma said *goodmorning* to neighbors, her clear white skin screamed: "Breweries are coming! Displacement is near!" Living in Mattapan made her feel guilty for being alive. Not an ideal situation, but until they finished their next album, they'd live wherever Josie could afford to pay their rent.

Emma let herself in. She called Ara's name. No response. She closed the door. The sound of the latch catching torqued her gut with worry. She boiled water for tea, played some Le Tigre to cloak the silence, and checked the piano bench. The piano bench was where she kept their old gig tapes, including one beat-up jewel case (*Paradise Lounge, 2001*) that hid a plastic baggie with Ara's heroin. All drugs were accounted for.

Emma was Ara's bagman. She bought for Ara, hid from Ara, double-checked with fentanyl test strips for Ara, measured precise doses at precise intervals for Ara. For months now, Emma had done this. It was terrible. Nauseatingly, hallucinatorily terrible. At times, Emma couldn't believe what she had agreed to. A surreal feeling, similar to dreaming. But Ara had overdosed once before. If she'd been alone, she would've died. Emma understood the stakes. Plus, Ara had asked her. Begged. Cried. Told Emma she was scared, needed help tapering off, couldn't do it alone. She called it harm reduction. She said that Bob Weir had been bagman for Jerry Garcia.

"Remind me again how that went for Jerry."

"Forget it," Ara had said, "I'll ask Roman."

Roman—Ara's ex—was unsuitable to Emma in almost every way. So Emma accepted the job. She took the job seriously. Because the job was extremely serious. Required megawatts of attention. She had to balance Ara's wrist pain versus Ara's band obligations, while factoring in variables like sleep and how much she'd eaten and the desperation with which she made her case for more. When Emma got the balance right, Ara was surprisingly functional with her beats, her harmonies, life in general. But too far one way, and she got dopesick. Too far the other way, and she was nodding off. She hadn't written new lyrics in forever. And then there was hiding everything from Josie until Ara could taper off. If Jojo found out—Emma and Ara agreed—it would be nuclear winter for all.

Emma sliced some celery and opened a jar of peanut butter. She left another message with Josie. She plugged her favorite headphones into her favorite amp and looped pentatonic scales on her favorite guitar until the steel of the strings bit pleasantly through her calluses. She decided to be officially worried. Worried and pissed. They had work to do. A band to run. An album to write. Ara had to pull her shit together.

She left another message with Josie. And another with Dean. She called the Dorothy Day House, hoping one of the Catholic Workers would pick up and connect her with their mother, but the phone just rang. She even called Roman. The full round robin. Was this an Emma boycott? She wondered if she ought to be widening her net, calling hospitals. Did people really do that?

Right then a slag of sound-absorbent waffle foam seized this symbolic moment to peel off the wall in a slow rip. Emma watched as it knocked over an aloe plant, scattering soil across the floor. Their apartment, a shifting marsh of cardboard boxes, some still unpacked, reeked of squalor. Emma kicked a box in the ribs. It coughed up a CD: *American Mosh*. She used her thumbnail to slice the plastic wrap, then she opened the jewel case and snapped the CD in half. Ten years ago, she and Ara had occupied the top floor of a warehouse-conversion by the Brooklyn Bridge. Rooftop patio, statement-piece chandelier, afternoon light like you wouldn't believe. Now their bedroom was a home music studio with a mattress in the corner. It smelled faintly like cat from previous tenants. The one window had a curtain that was not a curtain but a black velvet Elvis tapestry from a local thrift store named Boomerangs.

She called Ara again. She called Josie again. She shuffled to the record player and put on *Smiley Smile,* which wasn't the Beach Boys' best album, but certainly the most chill (allegedly engineered to help the listener come down from an acid trip). This particular record, under usual circumstances, had a soothing effect on Emma. But these were not usual circumstances. Her nerves wouldn't loosen. She put her face in her hands. She had to stop pretending this wasn't an emergency. She moaned. She had to start calling hospitals. She couldn't. Instead she booted up her monitor, minimized Logic Pro, and maximized Ara's email, trying variations of their birthday, their childhood address, and so on, until she remembered the password (GoodV!brations) in six tries.

Ara's inbox was unhelpful. Three library hold-notifications (*Herbal Healing for Addiction*, *Even Cowgirls Get the Blues*, *The Dispossessed*), an offer to join a clinical trial, a bunch of social media notifications, and a message from the Survivors' Resource Center: Ara had missed her intake session. They wanted to reschedule but couldn't get ahold of her.

Join the club, Emma thought. And then her phone rang.

She slipped on the soil of the aloe plant, banging her shin on a crate of XLR cables as she scrambled for her phone. A number she didn't recognize. She swiped.

"Ara?"

"Um, this is Ian."

"Who?" She knew a thousand Ians. "Are you with Ara?"

"Is this Emma?"

"Listen, who—I'm kind of extremely busy right now."

"This is Ian, from the Fountain? You gave me your number this morning?"

She rubbed her knee. She'd never been so disappointed to hear from such a good-looking man. "Right. Sorry. I'm waiting to hear from my sister."

"Oh. Want company while you wait?"

———

Ian from the Fountain. He'd moved from Connecticut two years ago, he said. Jamaica Plain was way less manicured back then. Condos were ruining everything. When he finished college he'd played a season of American football in Italy. He'd hopped freight trains with buddies. He had a memoir in him, he believed, but worried people wouldn't take it seriously, because of his age.

"How old are you?" Emma asked.

"Twenty-three. How old are you?"

Emma laughed. She got him off her mattress with a playful kick to his butt and said she'd tell him if he made her a cup of tea. She watched him tiptoe naked through the debris field of her apartment, and calculated that he'd been in elementary school when she and Ara had led the first Mosh for Women's Lives.

"So you're in a band." He set the kettle on the hot plate with a clatter. "What kind of music do you play?"

She pulled on his T-shirt, walked across the room, and plugged her phone into her workstation. She was showing off, but whatever—she'd earned the right, and it worked, every time. She hit play. "American Mosh" boomed through the apartment. Ian spun.

"Shut up! This is you?"

"Me and my sister."

"I *know* this song!"

Emma laughed. Ian's excitement was so genuine that she briefly considered breaking her no-boys-sleepover rule. Not since Ara was last in rehab had Emma spent more than one night by herself. The apartment was too quiet. She had to fill the void with something.

She turned down the music when Ian brought her a cup of tea. This was his first time to Mattapan, and he couldn't understand why everyone didn't live over here, he said. Did Emma realize what people would pay for this much space? He shared a two-bedroom unit on Centre Street with three college buddies; it was the only way they could afford rent. To him, Emma's apartment did not reek of squalor. He found it great they had room for their amps, mixers, looping pedals, guitars, keyboards. Their costumes, shoes, drumsticks, capos, picks. Their tuners, Fast Fret, harmonicas, and backstage lanyards from defunct music festivals. He thought the high ceilings were great. The molding. It was all really, really great.

He explored, picking and pawing through her belongings with the delicacy of a toddler archeologist. It felt invasive, but as long as he wasn't wearing clothes, Emma wasn't complaining. Not until he flipped open the record player and lifted *Smiley Smile* from the turntable.

"Put that down!" she yelled, jumping off the bed, spilling tea on the floor.

He flinched, almost dropping the record.

"Careful!" she said, taking it from him. Not only did *Smiley Smile* have the unique power to soothe Emma's nerves, it also happened to be the last remaining record from their father's collection. She couldn't relax until it was safe in its cardboard sleeve and propped up behind her workstation monitor.

"That's off limits," she said. "You can play with literally anything else."

"Like this?"

*Presented to Emma and Araminta Tayloe to commemorate RIAA Certified Gold Sales and Streams of more than 500,000 copies of the GhostTrain single "American Mosh."*

Ian had picked up their gold record. It was framed, and still in the original bubble tape packaging. "Why isn't this on your wall? I didn't even know these things were real."

Emma shrugged. "It was a long time ago. I don't care that much about the past. I'm all about the future, you know?"

"I do," Ian nodded. His sincerity, in conjunction with the way he was holding her record, at dick height, produced a jarring image that felt emblematic of Emma's career in a way that she did not wish to put her finger on.

"What else have you recorded?" He leaned the gold record back against the wall.

Emma closed her eyes. There was no question that she'd answered, and hated, more.

"Not every musician is Dylan," she said. "We don't just release every shitty thing that we make. Music is like sex. You can rush it, sure, but why not take your time?"

The truth was that after the success of *American Mosh*, their sophomore album had to be as good, if not better. And with each year that passed, the expectations had grown greater and greater.

The truth was that Ara was the beating, creative heart of the band, yet she had not been her beating, creative self for a very long time.

The truth was that although Emma had every right to make music without Ara, her one solo project—*Tigress*—had proven that she should never try anything like that ever again.

The truth was that Jojo and the Twins were en route to becoming one-hit wonders.

But Emma refused to accept this label. It would mean they'd made their best music as teenagers, which was too depressing. Worse, a one-hit wonder could only become a one-hit wonder retroactively, and if their career was over, that meant Ara was broken and Emma would never be able to put her back together.

"Anyway," she said, "we're about quality, not quantity. Look at Lauryn Hill. She only made one record, and it was perfect."

"Lauryn who?"

Emma laughed. She shook her head as she flipped through her crate of vinyl, looking for *Miseducation* so she could blow his young dumb mind. Just then, however, her phone lit up. Since it was still plugged into her workstation speakers, her ringtone chimed through the apartment.

Another unknown number, this one from Bogastow. She couldn't swipe fast enough.

"Hello?! Ara?"

*This is a collect call from the Massachusetts Department of Corrections . . .*

A beat of silence—no more than a sixteenth-note, but enough for Emma's blood to rush to her head and her hand to glance against the mug on her workstation desk and the mug to shatter on the floor and the tea to slosh and mix with the dry soil of the aloe plant—and then Ara's shaky voice, at full volume, through the speakers.

"Hey Sis. It's me . . ."

"Ara! Are you okay? Where—"

*Do you accept the charges?* said an automated voice.

"Yes!" Emma cried. "Yes! Yes! Yes!"

# Chapter 4

# Josie

Their third day at Acadia, Dean declared that he couldn't take another ocean cliff view, another mossy hike, another goddamn warm breeze across another drop-dead-gorgeous lake. He needed civilization, or he was going to lose his mind. By civilization, Josie knew, he meant a cocktail, and likely plural.

"I'll go with you." She put down a winter issue of *Nature* that she was finally catching up on. "Nobody should drink alone on vacation."

They climbed into Dean's 4Runner, the backseat still jammed with musical equipment. Hardcases rattled as they rolled out of the camp-ground. When Josie had insisted they haul the gear back to Boston, Ara hadn't complained. They'd hugged goodbye in the parking lot of the Mad Mountain Tavern, after which Josie and Dean had driven three straight hours to Acadia in a rush of adrenaline, sugar-free Red Bulls, and worry. She'd felt it when she hugged Ara goodbye. She felt it when they pulled into the campsite, her ears still ringing from the show. She'd felt it when she shook awake Dean so he could blow up the air mattress while she found somewhere to pee. Something was wrong.

"Of course something's wrong," Dean had said with a yawn. "Something's always wrong. That's what vacation is for, to pretend life's fine for a few days."

And pretend they had. They stashed their phones back in the glove-box with the dead Kern Primrose and set out. They hiked mountains and made fires. They dunked in waves and gaped at stars. They napped on slabs of sun-warmed granite. Elemental stuff. They'd even made friends, Meghan and Sylvie, a couple on their honeymoon who they'd met in line at the campground bathroom, bonding over the fact that they appeared to be the only four adults in the entire park without children. They'd grilled together on their second night, when one of those inevitable questions came up about kids, leading to Josie punching Dean playfully on the shoulder and saying, "We're just old friends," at the same time as Dean reached for her hand and said, "We haven't ruled it out," which led to Meghan and Sylvie graciously changing the subject to boardgames, of which they had brought an astonishing quantity. The four of them played Settlers of Catan, then brushed their teeth, put out the fire, and said goodnight.

Only Josie couldn't sleep. She blinked in the dark of their tent, trying to assess whether Dean was also awake. Their air mattress held all the firmness of a carnival bouncy house, but Dean was suspiciously still. Josie couldn't even hear him breathing. Had they been a couple in the traditional sense, this would've been the time for one of them to roll over and say something like, "Are we cool?" But, as they had made awkwardly clear to Meghan and Sylvie by the grill, they were not a couple in the traditional sense. They were a couple in the shared-history sense. The family-catastrophe sense. When Dean's mother, a fugitive darling of the countercultural left, had turned herself in to the authorities almost twenty-five years ago, Josie's mother was the lawyer who'd negotiated the terms of surrender. Dean stayed with the Tayloes for the summer so he could visit his mom, and he'd returned every summer through middle and high school. He and Josie had spent their most formative, most unstructured, adolescent months together. Naturally, bonds had formed.

Decades later, they were living together under the same roof once again. They had separate bedrooms in the top floor of an outer-Boston triplex, walking distance from Jamaica Pond. They shared rent, chores, library books, a PlayStation 4. Sometimes they slept together. Sometimes they slept with other people. They went as partners to author readings at the local bookstore, Al-Anon meetings at the Congregational church, excruciating toddler birthday parties of mutual acquaintances. They vented to each other about politics, traffic, weather, family. They could've been parents when Josie was seventeen, but she'd decided against it. Dean had gone with her to the clinic. He'd moved with her to California when she started at Stanford. He'd come with her back east when Ara first needed rehab. Josie never once asked him to pull up stakes and follow her around, but she was glad he did.

She was so, so glad.

Dean understood her demented family like nobody else. And vice versa. Theirs was a co-evolved, symbiotic relationship.

But symbiotic did not mean perfect. Like this third day in Acadia, when Josie had made excellent spinach and goat cheese omelets on the camp stove. She'd brewed strong coffee. She'd led an invigorating hike around Jordan Pond where she spotted a milk snake, a great crested fly-catcher, three tiger swallowtails, *and* a peregrine falcon making grocery runs to her nest on the cliffs. They ended at the Jordan Pond House restaurant. She'd wanted to surprise Dean with the popovers that every-one wouldn't shut up about, but she only got laughed at by the teenage server who explained no, they could not walk in and expect a table, and no they could not sit at the bar, and no, they did not sell drinks to go.

Dean was quiet on the shuttle bus back to their campsite. Josie chose not to remind him that this vacation was his idea. This week was sup-posed to be relaxing. Why then, as they left the Loop Road and crossed into the cool shadow of Cadillac Mountain, did Josie feel a pit of dread?

Because she knew what was coming: Dean wanted his mom to move in with them. Her twenty-five-year prison sentence was up this winter. Dean hadn't formally proposed the idea, but where else does a senior jailbird go? This was the serious news that Josie knew was about to drop. Yet they had been in Acadia for seventy-two hours, and Dean had not once mentioned his mother. So what was wrong?

Maybe nothing was wrong?

Ha. Haha. Hahaha.

Josie thought of her phone in the glovebox of the 4Runner. If they got back to the campsite before five, she could call the Survivors' Resource Center to reschedule Ara's appointment. She took a breath. She was un-accustomed to doing nothing. How did people do it? Vacation was hard.

And so, later that afternoon, when Dean said he needed some civi-lization, Josie acted as though she was doing him a favor, keeping him company, when truthfully, she could've killed for a drink herself.

———————

"Martinis. Two. Gin. Please. Olives. Please. Two. No, three. As many as you can fit in the glass?"

They'd followed the signs into Bar Harbor and pulled over at the first option, a breezy outdoor place with white rocking chairs on a deck overlooking the harbor. They ordered. They rocked. They made obligatory comments about the setting sun, the pink-hewed clouds, the metallic ocean waves. When the martinis arrived, Dean downed his in a few big gulps, chewed the olives, then turned to face Josie. He put his hands flat on the little white table between them.

"Yes?" She braced herself. Here it came.

"I can't believe you told them we're just friends."

Josie needed a moment to register what he was talking about.

"But we are," she said. "You are literally my best friend."

"Best friend is different from *just* friends."

"Well what should I have told them?"

He rocked his chair aggressively. He was smiling, but it wasn't his friendliest.

"Honestly, Jo? At this point, I don't know."

The summer Dean had initially stayed with the Tayloes, he'd given off an unhinged first impression. Josie knew teenage boys—she'd been forced to go to middle school with a great number of the species—but rarely had she observed one in its natural habitat. One vivid memory included a branch, the oak tree in the front yard, and Dean, red-faced and swinging until the branch splintered. Josie watched, aghast, with Ara and Emma from the kitchen as their mother sorted prisoner mail at the counter and told them to stop gawking. He's angry, she said. Imagine what he's going through.

Josie had kept her distance. Only when she'd run into Dean wandering the woods—*her* woods—did she dare approach with confidence. She'd shown him her favorite spots: the salamander homes she'd built under rocks, the ancient maple where the snowy owl lived, the edge of the marsh where you could almost always catch something, just watch—she'd kicked off her shoes, sloshed around, and come up with a painted turtle that she thrust into Dean's hands. The turtle stuck out its head. Dean smiled and softened. Josie relaxed. She'd recruited her first field research assistant, and he'd stayed by her side for over twenty years.

"Is that what you tell people?" Dean said. "That we're just friends?"

Josie waved down the server to order another round of martinis that couldn't come fast enough. "We're more than just friends. Okay? Can we talk about something else? We came here to unwind. I don't want to talk about serious things. Not tonight."

"Then when?"

"I don't know, Dean. Later. My mom is basically homeless. Your mom is about to get out. My sisters are one royalty check away from total poverty. We have a lot going on. So please forgive me if this doesn't feel like the best time to focus on us."

She dunked her fingers and popped an olive into her mouth.

Dean snatched her wrist and brought her hand to his face. He licked her fingers. He smiled. It was like that moment with the painted turtle at the marsh—everything would be alright. Josie laughed. She pulled back her hand.

"We're more than friends," she said.

"I knew it!"

Josie laughed again as the server arrived with fresh drinks. One sip of martini number two and she was voluminously drunk. But it wasn't just the alcohol. The last sun rays glittered off the waves. Flecks of mica sparkled in granite. The ocean lapped the shore. She put a hand on Dean's hand. Vacation was hard, but life was harder. She felt almost weak with gratitude, to have him as a partner.

"I want you," she said.

Dean chuckled, then saw she was serious. He stopped rocking.

"Like, now?"

"Do you have a condom?"

He nodded. He fumbled for his wallet. He checked. He nodded again.

She hopped off the deck toward the water. "Well come on then. Let's go."

———

Their chairs had hardly stopped rocking before their pants were already zipped back up and buttoned. They'd found a crevice between two granite slabs. Rockweed and barnacles underfoot. Waves sloshing their ankles. They were quick. No time for romance. Not a remote chance that Josie would come, but orgasm wasn't the goal. The goal was being as close as possible as two human beings who were more than just friends. They'd washed off with ocean, then run back giddy and flush. They settled back into their rocking chairs. Josie caught the server's eye and ordered another round.

The semi-public sex, combined with martini three made for a fun effervescence that lasted until they paid their tab and climbed into the 4Runner. Dean said he was good to drive, and Josie believed him, but neither could remember the way to the campground. He nodded at the glovebox.

"You sure?" Josie asked.

"Might as well. We've already sinned."

And so, for the first time in three days, Josie took out her phone and turned it on. Before she could pull up a map, the notifications started.

Texts from Emma. Voicemails. Dozens.

"Someone's popular," Dean said.

"Something's wrong." Josie felt every molecule of alcohol evaporate from her bloodstream. She couldn't dismiss the notifications fast enough to read them. More texts kept coming. And then her phone rang. Emma.

"Em! Hi. Is everything okay?"

"Jojo! Why haven't you been answering?"

The ocean, somewhere out there, was making its dark static. But all Josie could hear was Emma, sobbing. She reached out and clenched Dean's forearm. She squeezed and squeezed, as if force could somehow prevent the news that she had most expected and feared, coming true.

"Emma," Josie said clearly into the phone. "What happened?"

"It's Ara."

A sudden, shaky inhale. "Is she okay? Is she with you?"

"She got arrested. She really fucked up."

Josie shook her hand free from Dean and gestured for him to put the 4Runner into drive and get moving already. What was taking him so long?

He mimed drinking from a bottle.

*No*, she thought. They weren't just drunk. They were three-martini drunk. Driving a mile to a campsite was one thing. But five hours on the interstate? She punched the glovebox. She should've stayed sober. You never knew when an emergency was on the horizon. You never knew when the people you loved might need you most.

"Josie?"

"I'm here. I'll be there as soon as I can."

# Chapter 5

# Ara

So my roommate Kyla has this theory on pain and the human soul. Not hand-on-the-burner pain, but the nuclear stuff: withdrawal, childbirth, loss of custody. The human soul, Kyla says (will not stop saying), has the power to soothe the memory of pain. For most people it's a blessing: a way to get up each morning and start over and live well. But for the rest of us—Kyla spreads her arms to include all however-many-hundreds of us here—it's a curse. Our souls help us forget our pain, and so we never learn. We keep making the same dumbass mistakes again and again and again.

---

My recent dumbass mistakes include most from my Greatest Hits album: dope, coke, ketamine, Roman. Sister and I had just flown back from Caribou where we got an 80/20 door-split and Josie sold $500 in merch and we didn't even break even. I'd warned Sister that Caribou would be a monster waste of time and money. We were in the cab, heading home from the airport, when I mentioned how right I'd been.

Sister said she wouldn't fight with me until I was sober.

I said I wasn't trying to fight, just stating facts:

We are 36, eligible for food stamps, our sister paying our rent.

My wrists and back feel like broken glass.

My ears won't stop ringing with tinnitus.

My pain management routine is unsustainable.
Sister's voice is losing its upper range.
Our last gig, before Caribou, was a Bat Mitzvah.
Our last stage diver was how many years ago?

Sister's only response to my many facts was that stage divers don't matter.

"We stay greased. We show up. We bring our best. We're ready when opportunity strikes."

She couldn't even look at me as she spoke. Because she was (has long been) withholding what she knows is truth: opportunity is like lightning, it never strikes twice in the same place. We played some big, bouncy crowds. We sold some records. We walked the red carpet. That was then. Now?

"It's time to put the band out of its misery," I say.

"I'm not talking about this when you're high," she says.

The problem with Sister is that she only hears what she wants to hear.

The problem with Sister is that she has nothing besides the band.

The problem with Sister is that she needs to diversify her life.

I share with Sister the intersectionality of her problems.

"How have you diversified your life?" she says. "Bumps instead of lines?"

I say, "Yes as a matter fact," and mark the occasion by ripping away her handbag, then turn my body to block her as I dig around for a celebratory Amen.

Sister responds by throwing my dope out the window to what I'm sure was the utter joy of the Tremont Street pavement. "You want help quitting? There. You're welcome. Stop using behind my back. You were awful last night. You embarrassed me."

"Embarrassing," I tell her, "is flying to Nowhere, Maine, to play for ten people."

She clenches her jaw and says there were fifty-six ticketed audience members and anyway it doesn't matter because one's all we need. "One fan shares us with their fans who share us with their fans. That's how it works now."

Back in the day, Sister's motivational speeches invoked the hypothetical A&R rep from a major record label, watching from the bar. Now her greatest hope is to impress some teen influencer. I wondered, aloud, if she could hear just how fatally pathetic we'd become.

Sister hiccupped. "If you want pathetic, find a mirror. An aging rock star with a heroin problem. You couldn't be more of a cliché."

She asked if there was a script I'm following. She asked when she could expect to find me dead on the bathroom floor with a needle in my arm. (She was being dramatic . . . she knows needles freak me out.) She asked if I'd considered how selfish I was being: the tens of thousands wasted on rehab. Forcing her to lie to Jojo all these months. I can waste my life, she says, but not hers.

"Your choices affect me," she says. "You're part of a band."

"I think that's the problem," I say.

Again, she doesn't hear me. She asks why we haven't finished a second album all these years. Why Mom lost the house. Why Josie quit Stanford to come home and work at that shitty zoo. And you may think this was all the blood she could draw. But no.

"You know what I think?" she said. "I think Dad was the lucky one. At least he got to die before you had the chance to ruin his life, too."

The driver had been following our exchange with interest in the rearview mirror. Catching his eye was easy. I told him to pull over. Now.

I ran back along Tremont, cars honking as I searched for my bag, my chest tight-tight with every complicated knot which only that one thing can loosen. I backtracked once, twice. Couldn't find it. I called Roman.

Roman and I hadn't spoken in months, but three cigarettes and one alleyway-pee later, his exhaust pipes fill the air. That's Roman for you. Since we were kids. Always there for me when nobody else is.

He pulled up on his bike. He was on his way to a "business meeting" at the new casino in Revere, meaning he had exactly what I needed. He gave it to me, then fitted me with his spare helmet, slipping a finger under my strap to make sure it was snug. Lifted me onto his bike. My thumbs remembered their holds in his belt loops like it was yesterday.

He got us a suite with a Jacuzzi because he thought a Jacuzzi would be relaxing, and it hurt him physically to see me so stressed and upset.

Roman's greatest dream in life has always been to become a big-time gangster, but his biggest obstacle to his dream is himself: he's got too big a heart.

He unpacked his saddlebags, let me have another Amen, then texted his client as I undressed and slid into the warm champagne water. From there, the night spiraled.

Roman might not be a gangster, but to his credit he did sense that something was off. That was why he encouraged his client to sample the merchandise. But Roman did not lay out a generous line of cocaine as advertised. Instead, he gave the guy ketamine. Knocked him right out.

I watched with luminous eyes from the Jacuzzi as Roman rifled the guy's pockets. We thought about running. But if the man snoring on the floor was indeed an informant, the cops were nearby, if not watching. And a casino, with all the cameras. Also, I'd sampled that very ketamine myself. I was feeling perhaps the greatest a person can feel, meaning I didn't care for running because it was difficult—*impossible?*—to believe that anything bad could ever happen to me again. And then Roman got naked and slid into the Jacuzzi. "Our last stand," he said. We high-fived. Am I proud of what happened? I'm not proud. But the important thing to remember—the point I keep returning to when my stomach is pierced in shame—is that nobody got hurt. The guy who thought he was sampling a fat line of cocaine? People would pay thousands for the transcendental experience he probably enjoyed. Plus, he should've known better. Ketamine and coke look nothing alike.

———————

Most people I'm sure remember their first days in jail clearly, but mine are totally fractured by withdrawal: bioluminescent liquid shits, shakes, sweats, one long hallucinatory moan through tiled-linoleum hallways, clanging doors, blaring intercom, the never-ending nightmare-fluorescent lights. Somewhere in the horror show, as the dope festered from my body, there was a cell at Suffolk County, a courtroom, a bumpy van ride out here to Bogastow, a psychiatrist in a suit, a promise I wouldn't kill myself. A hot eternity in Health Services. Finally a guard shuffled me to my room (nobody here says *cell*). Bunkbeds, metal sink, ceramic toilet (no seat). A steel door with a square of scuffed plexiglass at eye level for a killer view of the glazed-tiled wall across the hallway. And my roommate, Kyla, fluffing my pillow.

"Welcome to Room 13," she said with a smile.

———

Four times a day we have to stand by our beds for count. If you are a delicate husk of a person, this is harder than you might think. Kyla helps me down from my bunk, lets me lean against her until they've checked off my name, then hoists me up. As it turns out, she was also with me in Health Services, pushing a mop and holding my hair while I shat myself green and sprayed puke through my fingers. She has nobody on the outside to deposit money in her canteen, so she scrubs all the disgusting places for prison wages. Health Services. Psych. Even the shit-smeared rooms in Max. She buys Crunchers crackers with her earnings. Also paper, pens, envelopes, and stamps.

As soon as the guard locks our door, she lays her hands on my shoulders. "Be real with me, you want to stay clean or not?"

"Yes," I tell her. "I do."

(True confessions, the urge lapped my insides right then as I said it.)

"Then you got to rehab your soul. That's what's happening here in Room 13. I've got a project going. We're here to remember our pain."

"I'm remembering it right now," I say, the taste of bile creeping up my throat.

"You're just kicking. I'm talking long term. You got to stay busy. You have to keep on your toes." She gifts me two sheets of stationery and a little rubber stub of a prison-issued pen. "You have to write it out."

That is Kyla's project: She writes. She writes to Mothers Opposing Mandatory Minimums. She writes to Crunchers, thanking the company for "lifting her spirits." And she writes to her girls, though in the four months she's been here, she's never gotten a response. She thinks their father moved them. "It doesn't matter," she says. "Writing's what matters. Getting it down. It's how we heal our souls. It's the only way we'll learn."

Her advice isn't new to me. The rehab crowd calls this "recovery journaling." Narcotics Anonymous has its own "12-Step journal." Britney, my peer recovery coach at New Pathways, called it her "sobriety diary." And while it's true that some people can journal their way to lifelong recovery,

I have shoeboxes crammed with old diaries and notebooks that prove it can't work for everyone. I've journaled my way through life. Wrung out my heart. Poured it into my music. Look where it's gotten me.

But Kyla was standing eye-level at my bunk and putting out strong "Not-taking-no-for-an-answer" vibes that didn't care much for my "Still-feeling-extremely-dopesick-fried" vibes.

I said, "Thanks," and picked up the little rubber pen.

So here we are again. Me and you. You and me.

—————

This isn't my first rodeo. Sister and I got arrested playing a Mosh for Women's Lives at the RNC in 2004. Disturbing the Peace. We Disturbed the Peace again, during the bombing of Gaza, in 2008, when Mom would've disowned us all if we didn't join the sit-in at the Israeli consulate. I'm not bragging, just saying that I'm familiar with the routine: rolling my fingers on digital ink, peeing in front of strangers. Anyone can do a night in a holding cell. But Room 13 of Barton Unit is no holding cell. Other than Suffolk County (where Kyla says I'm lucky to have spent just a night) there are no jails for women in Massachusetts. It's MCI-Bogastow for all. Those of us awaiting trial live in Barton Unit. We wear hunter green. Across the yard are the convicted. They wear navy blue. I'd been Kyla's roommate for a few short hours, moaning in and out of the sorriest sickest fug, my body reeling like a medieval shipwreck, when it surfaced in my mind who one of those convicted felons might likely still be. I asked Kyla.

"Janice Clancy?" Kyla repeated the name. She frowned.

"She robbed some banks in the seventies," I told her. "With the Weathermen? A cop died. She was on the run for decades—"

"Oh, JC!" Kyla laughs, slapping me on the knee. "Fuck yes, I know JC! Everyone knows JC. JC's our Queen Bee!"

—————

Dean's mom was like a distant aunt I'd heard about my whole life, but never met. I guess I've been something similar to her, because she shrieked when Kyla brought me to her this morning in the yard.

"Nobody told me you were out of Health Services! I would've had a care package ready. Dolores, Mary, Nancy, everyone—get your buns over here! This is Araminta Tayloe! Bertie's girl!"

Janice has short silvery hair. Big breasts, big belly. Dean's same oak-colored eyes. She wears those round glasses that nobody's pulled off since John Lennon. She stroked my hair, yanked me in for a hug until a voice from a guard tower warned her to let go.

"You poor thing, going coldturkey. What would help? What do you need?"

I knew better than to ask for the one thing I needed most, so I requested the runner-up: "Can we smoke here? I'd die for a cigarette."

Janice said I was decades too late. "The state banned tobacco in the nineties. How about ibuprofen? Candy? Something to suck on? They say that helps."

Kyla played guard dog, trailing while Janice and I walked the yard. I started in with my story involving Roman, only to have Janice raise a hand. "I've heard enough arrest stories for two lifetimes. What happened happened. I only care about now. How are you doing, hon? Really?"

"I'm fine," I tell her, but tears run down my face as I say it, which sort of undercuts my case.

She pulls me in for another hug. Rubs my back until a guard warns her again.

She steps off and I cry into the gap between us. I wipe my face and tell her plainly that I royally fucked up.

"Great, so you're a human being," she says.

"Not a very good one."

She says drug charges aren't what they used to be. "Plus you have your mom. With Bertie on the case, you'll be fine."

We walk toward the perimeter fence. I ask her to slow down so I can catch my breath. As I lean over to let a wave of nausea pass, she explains that she tried calling Dean as soon as she heard I was here, but he and Josie were on vacation and impossible to reach. She left a message. She asks how everyone else has taken the news. Did I need help setting things up for tomorrow?

"What's tomorrow?" I ask.

"Visitation. It'll save time if you put them on your list beforehand. Your mom didn't tell you?"

"I haven't talked to her."

"Who'd you call? Emma?"

I shook my head. Looked at the grass, thousands of blades bending beneath my feet.

Janice stopped walking. "Araminta. Who knows you're here? Who did you call?"

"I've been sick. I am sick. I haven't had time."

Roman and I were arrested on Sunday. That night, at Suffolk County, they'd given me my phone call, but I was still high, and mad, and so I said thanks but no thanks. Now two days have passed and coldturkey heroin withdrawal never killed anyone, sure, but what about shame?

I guess I shouldn't have been surprised, because Janice has been here long enough to see everything, but she did surprise me: she read my mind.

"You're ashamed," she says. "Well, I'm here to flat-out tell you: put that baloney away. Is there harm you need to repair? Sure. You will. Step one is reaching out. They love you, they're worried sick about you, they need to hear from you. You've got to call them as soon as you can. If you don't, I will. Better they hear from you. Let them hear your voice. Got it?"

"Got it," I mumble, not feeling like I have much say in the matter.

"I'll put money in your account. Dolores'll show you how to use the phones."

A stocky woman in gray jogs over to ask Janice if she has any lemon body sprays.

Janice tells the woman to meet in the dayroom after lunch. She calls her hon.

We continue our slow lap, eventually rounding the yard, bringing the marsh into view. Lone dead trees. Smell of skunk cabbage. Across the marsh, on what used to be Sunrise Farms, is a construction site. Plywood whale ribs of a housing development. The faint pop of nail guns. The whine of a buzz saw. A group of women clusters by the fence, waving and hollering at the workers across the water.

"We used to have a softball league," Janice says. "Now this is what passes for entertainment."

"That used to be a cornfield," I say. "We used to sneak down there to wave when we were girls."

"I remember," says Janice. We stand at the fence, staring into the past. Then Janice says, out of nowhere, "You're not asking for advice, Araminta, but I'm an old lady who can't help herself. You're sick with regret. You think they're going to be mad at you—"

"They're going to be so mad!"

She holds a finger to my lips. Reminds me that she's been where I am. Knows all about disappointing the people we love. "Family will amaze you with how deeply they can forgive. You just have to let them."

I was so grateful for Janice and her warm welcome, that I decided not to remind her that we'd just met. That she didn't know me. That she's not my mother. That she'd hardly been a mother to Dean.

She hugged me.

I hugged her back.

A guard yelled at us to separate.

———

Dolores taught me how to use the pay phones. I called.

"Hey Sis. It's me . . ."

Janice was right: she wasn't mad, just worried. She said they'd all be there tomorrow, and then she cried into the phone until I felt sick with guilt. That night I dreamt again that we were standing on the roof of our old home. Me, Josie, Sister. Sometimes in this dream we just stand there. Last night we shuffled to the edge. I heard our feet scraping on the shingles. I held Sister on one side, Josie on my other. Their hands were weightless. Like feathers. And then we jumped. I woke and scrambled for the toilet. Kyla got up to rub my back as I vomited. My body felt like I really had fallen three stories to the ground. Honestly, though, I think I was just bracing for the storm I knew was coming at visitation.

# Chapter 6

# Ara

I couldn't stand still as Janice and I waited for them to shuffle through the metal detectors and pat-downs. I drummed the air-snare. Stretched my quads. Cracked my knuckles. On our American Mosh tour, before opioids, I used to puke backstage from nerves. That was me now. Janice put a hand on my hands. She reminded me of the first summer Dean stayed with us. How angry he was.

"You'd think these walls would push family apart. But, hon, they can also make us stronger."

A buzzer rang. A door clanged open. There they were.

Sister jumped into my arms. Josie barreled forward and turned it into a band hug. Regulations permit "a brief embrace" at the beginning and end of visitation. We pushed the definition of *brief*. Lots of tears.

Dean and Josie had circles under their eyes. They'd driven nonstop, abandoning a prime campsite, but it was fine, Josie said, as long as I was okay. Sister was wearing my white romper. Hair unbrushed. Crusts of sleep in her eyes. She wouldn't stop staring at me. Everyone was exhausted, mental-looking. I glanced behind them, and asked, "Where's Mom?"

Josie threw her hands up, joyfully almost. "Gaza? Middle of the Atlantic? Who knows?"

Janice's jaw dropped. "Who's spoken to her?"

"I've been trying," Josie said. She asked Sister, "What were you doing?"—but didn't give her time to answer—"She was with some random guy. Surprise."

"I was waiting in case Ara called," Sister says. "At least someone had their phone on."

"Are you trying to make me feel guilty for taking one vacation in my life?"

"Girls, please," Janice said. "Bertie has to know. She's on the Lawyers Guild's national board for goodness' sakes—"

"Used to be," Josie interrupted. "Just like she *used to be* a lawyer who *used to be* permitted to practice law in the Commonwealth of Massachusetts and *used to* own a home."

Dean touched her arm in a way that suggested she take a breath. She sliced him in half with a look. He spun on a heel to visit the vending machines. I decided to examine the cracks between the floor tiles. We'd been visiting for approximately five minutes. These walls are not making us stronger.

"Bertie still knows people," Janice said. "I've seen her work her magic in here. Believe me. A few strategic phone calls—that's what Araminta needs." Then she muttered to herself, "One hundred thousand dollars. Outrageous. For a simple drug charge."

"Not that simple," Josie said.

Shame isn't something you can hold in your palm, but that doesn't mean it's not real. Just like a heavy bass note can vibrate your ribs and rattle your lungs, shame has real weight, too. I know because it buckled me over. I couldn't look up. Couldn't see anything but the floor cracks as Josie told everyone in visitation that $100,000 for bail isn't that surprising considering the quantities of drugs in the hotel room, and also $100,000 isn't really $100,000: "Nobody pays full bail. We only need ten percent for a bondsman to post the rest. I talked to your lawyer—"

"I have a lawyer? Is it one of Mom's friends? Marjorie?"

Apparently this was the totally wrong thing to interrupt with, because Josie pinched her eyes and said that the saddest part wasn't that I lied to her about using again (not technically true) or that I was still fucking Roman (definitely not true), but that I believed Mom would inconvenience herself in any way to help us.

Dean returned from the vending machines with a Diet Coke. He wiped the rim with his sleeve before giving it to Josie. We all watched her take a thirsty glug. She burped. Said she was so stressed out. Had quite possibly never been so stressed out.

I reexamined the floor again and said I was sorry.

Josie shrugged and said maybe I was, maybe I wasn't. "I can't tell anymore. I know it's not your fault. It's a disease. I know. But you've lied so many times that I've lost the ability to know what to believe. That goes for both of you. I don't trust either of you anymore."

I told her she could trust me now. She could believe me.

"Why?"

"Because I'm clean."

"You've stopped using before."

"This time is different."

"You *promised* to call me if you needed help."

"You were camping," I said. "You couldn't have helped if you'd wanted to."

"I'm sorry for taking time off. I'll never make that mistake again." She crushed the empty Diet Coke can in her hand.

"Relax, Jo," said Sister. "Getting angry won't help."

"I'm not angry. I'm just worried. And you don't get to tell me what to do ever again, so please spare the advice."

"Enough girls," Janice said. "There's no point arguing. We need to focus. Bertie has to know what happened."

"Why?" said Josie. "Why is it so important to you that she know?"

"Because she's your mother! You're her babies!"

Josie took a patronizing breath and lectured something along the lines of "reproduction and parental investment are different biological behaviors, *Janice*, and although reproduction is universal among organisms, *Janice*, parenting is unique to a few species of reptiles, amphibians, birds, and mammals. And not *all* mammals, *Janice*."

That made Janice go quiet. She'd turned herself in when Dean was a kid. We were all thinking it.

Now that Josie had silenced everyone, she took over, explaining that "unless this is all some secret brilliant plan you two hatched to record a jailhouse-fucking-special from behind bars and start finally selling records again" it was on her to find $10,000 for my bail bond, so she was making some executive decisions.

"First thing, Em, you're moving in with me and Dean. I'm going to sublet the Mattapan place and start generating income as fast as possible. Second—"

But Janice couldn't drop it. "What if someone drives up to Maine to tell Bertie in person?"

"I still have days off," Dean said. "I can swing back up."

"No you cannot," Josie said. "Our mother is not your problem."

"We *have* to get word to her before they set sail," Janice said.

"We really don't," said Josie.

"I'll go," said Sister.

"You need to start packing up and moving," Josie said. "Did you not just hear me? You have one job."

"Then who'll go?" Sister said.

Josie sighed and rubbed her forehead. Sometimes I wonder if she loves being in charge as much as she hates it. "I'll go. I'll do it. I still have vacation days, too—since our trip got cut short."

"I'm sorry," I said.

Sister started hiccupping. "Go easy on her, Jo. She's the one in prison. Not us. Relax."

Josie stood. "Either you get to buy her heroin, or you get to tell me to relax, but you do not get to do both. This is your fault as much as anyone's."

"You think I wanted to? What would you have done?" Sister stood so they were face-to-face. "Let her overdose again? Let her die?"

"Um, rehab? Therapy? There are options between doing nothing and enabling a heroin addiction. Which I would've happily explained if you'd just told me." Josie put her face in her hands. "I can't *believe* you bought her heroin!"

"It's called harm reduction."

"It's called HER-O-IN!"

"Stop yelling!" I yell. "Both of you. Please!"

A guard came over. He told everyone to sit down and chill out. He called us ladies. A mistake in almost any situation involving my sisters, but here, with tensions raised to death-metal levels, it was lethal.

Josie suggested that *he* chill out, and she did not do so nicely.

"Yer outta here." He grabbed her wrist and hauled her toward the door.

Josie shouted over her shoulder, her voice cracking in the high range like Sister's, but not in a soulful way: "I can't take care of you forever!"

I yelled back that I was sorry. Which I really was. I am. But she was gone. The room was silent, all eyes on us. Janice put a reassuring hand on my shoulder—like Mom could've done if she were there—until a guard by the metal detector ordered her to let go.

Dean attempted to salvage the visit by telling Janice about Acadia. While they talked, Sister leaned close to me, her breath hot against my ear: "I have an idea."

I could tell she was trying to make me feel better, so I humored her. "Oh? About what?"

"How to raise your bail."

More humor: "How?"

"With our new album!"

No more humor left, I reminded her we don't have a new album.

"Not yet! We're going to record a jailhouse special!" She was smiling so widely that I got a clear shot of her wisdom teeth.

"Josie was being sarcastic when she said that," I said.

"It's a great idea! Think about it, you write a few songs in here, like about prison or addiction or whatever—"

"Or whatever," I repeated.

"Yeah. And I'll start laying down tracks, mixing, polishing . . ." She disappeared inside her head. "If we start tonight . . . even just one song—a teaser, we could be moving preorders tomorrow!"

One response would've been to indulge in her delusion. Instead, I reminded her that I was a hundred percent clean for just the third time in years. I'd kicked coldturkey. This was an important moment for me.

"Perfect!" she said. "People will eat that shit up. Your best stuff is always from the heart. We could even record over the phone . . . oh my God, call me when I get home, I'll link my phone right into Logic Pro. We're going to do this! I *knew* Caribou would shake something loose. I fucking *kn-ew* it. This could literally be the best thing that ever happened to us!"

The visitation room is bolted-down orange chairs, vending machines, bored guards, a glassed-in meeting room where people talk with their lawyers. I watched a woman bounce her diapered daughter in her lap.

I listened to another woman tell her teenage son not to cuss. Then I turned back to Sister, unable to believe that two people can be so close genetically, yet so far apart. I thought of everything I would've said in her situation. She hadn't apologized for the horrible things she said on the ride from the airport. She hadn't congratulated me on kicking. Neither had Josie. Instead, Josie plays family martyr and Sister pushes ahead with the band, even when she knows—she must—that it will one day kill me.

"So?" she asked, her eyes huge. "Are you ready to make some music and bust your fine ass out of here?"

If you have an identical twin, you get so used to seeing yourself in them that their blemishes become deformities. Sister has her gray hairs, the scar an ex-boyfriend left on her temple, the forehead wrinkle she pretends doesn't bother her. Her insane expectations of perfection. Her need for attention and emotionally unavailable men. This stuff can't touch me when I'm high. But with my veins empty, her flaws are neon going *blink, blink, blink.*

"No," I told her. "I'm not ready."

"Like you need another day?"

"Like I'm done with the band."

She paused. "You're still going through withdrawal. You don't mean that."

"Yes I do."

"Your chemistry's all off. I remember this happening before. You're not yourself. You'll feel better. We just have to get you out of here."

"I have to go." I stand suddenly, my eyes tearing up. "Thanks for coming."

I motion for a guard to let me back into the heart of the prison.

"Wait!" cries Sister.

Janice had warned me of the "cough-and-bend-overs," as she calls them, the mandatory searches after visitation. Strip, raise arms, lift breasts, shake out hair, show bottoms of your feet, open your mouth so a guard can run a finger along your gums. Janice said it was invasive and humiliating—and it is—but right then I didn't care what was waiting for me, I just had to get away.

"Call me!" Sister cried as I stepped through the security door. "I just need an hour to set everything up. You'll call? Ara? Right?"

I couldn't look at her. Both times at New Pathways I needed about four days to fully kick. But that was just the physical symptoms. It's the psychological withdrawal that gets you. So I decided right there to play it safe: one full week to detox from my sisters. Because family and opioids really aren't so different. Both can make you feel great until suddenly they don't.

# PART II

# The Pack Is All
# of Us

# Chapter 7

# Josie

Josie's landlord, Fabio Castro, was a man, not a monster, which was his way of saying he could be open-minded when it came to rent. He owned nine Centre Street triplexes in Jamaica Plain, one by inheritance, the others via leveraged equity and extraordinarily good timing. His parents had fled Brazil to escape the dictatorship; Fabio knew that life could be unpredictable. If his tenants were experiencing sudden misfortune, the least he could do was accept alternative payment. In this way he'd become the proud owner of a flask of holy water blessed by Pope John Paul. A set of coins from colonial Honduras. An antique chair from a Hyannis yard sale (rumored property of the Kennedys). And the love of his life, a lavender lucifer albino ball python that he'd named Linda.

Fabio enjoyed retelling Linda's origin story as part of his "Gem of the World" presentation, meaning Josie had heard the details ad nauseam: It was the winter of 1999, when Fabio had a family of Bulgarians two months behind on their rent. The youngest boy, the family's English-speaking ambassador, approached, his hands cupped with a butterscotch sundae of a baby snake: yellow on white, eyes like maraschino cherries.

"Albino," the boy said. "Very special. You like?"

"It'll do."

Fast-forward ten years, and Linda was fully grown, Fabio was engaged, and his fiancée was not thrilled at cohabitating with a six-foot snake. She offered an ultimatum: woman or snake?

Fabio chose woman.

The Franklin Park Zoo would "consider" taking Linda, they told him, but there were waivers to sign, veterinarian exams to schedule. They made Fabio feel like he'd offered them a headache, not a phenomenally rare lavender python. Forget about it, he'd said, and drove Linda straight to the Butterfly & Reptile World where, as Fabio said, "They haven't been able to get rid of me since."

Fabio stuck around first to ensure the staff knew how Linda liked breakfast (mice warmed with a hair dryer). Later, after his fiancée broke things off, he volunteered weekends. He joined the staff part-time. And then, just before his fiftieth birthday, the owner—a conservationist and busy chief executive of a Latin American supermarket chain—offered him a full-time position.

"To run the reptile room?"

"Fabio, my man, I want you to run my World."

As manager of the Butterfly & Reptile World, Fabio acquired new species, introduced walkthrough exhibits, rebranded (*At the zoo you get to see animals—at the Butterfly & Reptile World you get to be with them*). The owner gave him carte blanche as long as Fabio balanced the budget. The salary wasn't much, but the recession had ended and Jamaica Plain was the new South End, young professionals with fabulous teeth shoveling immoral sums at Fabio for one of his Centre Street units.

Soon, however, Fabio encountered the age-old plague of the managerial class: personnel. The Franklin Park Zoo hogged all the true zoological talent. So imagine his delight one bright March day when a woman interrupted him as he was removing the American cockroaches that had snuck, yet again, into the hissing cockroach tank. She'd moved back to Massachusetts for a family emergency, she explained. She needed a job, she was ridiculously overqualified, and Fabio would be sorry not to hire her.

"Overqualified how?" Fabio asked.

She'd handed him two issues of *American Myrmecologist* with articles she'd authored, screenshots of certificates for two ant species she'd discovered, and a résumé that read like a National Geographic expedition itinerary.

He narrowed his eyes. "Why aren't you applying to the Zoo?"

"They're not hiring."

He handed back her résumé and materials. "The job won't make you rich."

"I kind of figured that."

"If you need a place to stay, I got an open unit on Centre Street, great light, top floor, new carpet. Start here tomorrow, and it's all yours. I'll give you a hell of a deal."

———

Josie, as Director of Operations, had established herself as the nucleus of the Butterfly & Reptile World. She'd wrangled the placards into strict taxonomic obedience, and expanded the arachnid collection. She spared expensive veterinarian visits by personally administering antibiotic injections to the terrapins, sexing the baby snakes, removing a row of abscessed teeth from Crumpets, the adorable crested gecko. She applied for grants. And she took on the grunt work, like shoveling ant middens, which she was doing when Fabio let himself in an hour before opening.

Fabio did a double take. "You're supposed to be on vacation."

"I missed shoveling shit."

"The shit missed you too."

Josie blew a strand of hair from her face. "Family trouble."

Fabio grabbed a shovel. "What have the rock stars done now? Or is it Mama Marx this time?"

"All of the above." Josie swung hard with her shovel. Every morning the leafcutter ants greeted them with their middens—a mound of excavated dirt and waste that had to be removed from the atrium walkway. The middens smelled faintly of wet dog. Unpleasant to most, but Josie enjoyed the organic funk. The leafcutters were as dependable as the sunrise, and Josie, after the past forty-eight hours, needed as much predictability as she could get.

She'd hoped to leave for Maine the moment she, Emma, and Dean returned from visiting Ara. But then she'd argued with Emma (who refused to start packing—she had her equipment set up and was feeling "inspired"), and she argued with Dean (who asked if Josie was *sure* she wanted Emma to move in), and then she'd begrudgingly closed her eyes for a short rest, which turned into a long rest, which turned into morning and Josie berating herself for sleeping in while Ara was in prison. She'd chugged half an iced coffee Dean had left in the fridge, then biked down Centre Street to the World. She needed to breathe the sweet familiar rot of the ant middens, and she needed to ask Fabio for a favor.

They worked side by side, clearing the walkway. Fabio said, "So another collector comes in yesterday, says he'll 'take the albino off my hands.' Like he's doing me a service."

"What'd you say?"

"Told him to buy an annual pass and see Linda whenever he damn wants."

Josie smiled to be polite, then cut to it: "Fabio, I might need more time off."

"It's summer. Go ahead. Take it."

"Maybe a lot of time."

He waved a hand. "We got interns out the ass."

She plucked a soldier ant off her pant cuff, pinching the thorax to avoid the bite. "Also, Emma's moving in with me and Dean. She's not on the lease. I thought you should know."

"Just one? I thought they came as a pair."

"Ara's in jail."

Fabio froze, mid-shovel. "No."

His expression—concern, extreme and genuine—ignited Josie's mirror neurons. She blinked and looked away, digging aggressively. Her shovel scraped the walkway.

"How bad?" Fabio asked.

"Multiple felonies bad. One-hundred-thousand-dollar-bail bad."

Fabio whistled. "How can I help?"

"A one-hundred-thousand-dollar advance on my pay?"

"I could advance you two weeks."

"How about a month?"

It was a big ask, but last May, Fabio had texted his most vital employee (and quietest and cleanest tenant) at 3 a.m., obviously drunk and lonely.

is dean yorr boyfriend? i love u

Josie, in her infinite wisdom and graciousness, had neither responded to nor mentioned the text, and for this—they both knew—she could ask for almost anything.

She set some frozen chicks under a heat lamp to thaw. She drafted a to-do list for the interns (sweep husks from chrysalis wall, swap citrus plants from hot shed, exercise monitor lizards). By noon, fueled on a one-month advance and a bag of Buffalo Blue Cheese Combos, she was on her way north, heading to Maine for the second time that week.

Her phone said she was three hours from Griffinport, where she would attempt to find her mother. One upside to any long drive into the field was the opportunity it offered for preparation: refine methodology, visualize obstacles, plan redundancies, run a mental review of the peer-reviewed literature.

OBSERVATION: Bertie had never put the needs of her children
   above the needs of the less-fortunate.
HYPOTHESIS: Sure as hell she's not about to start now.

Yet Josie would try. She would go wherever she was needed most, do whatever was needed, for Ara, for the good of the colony. As she'd always done. Why?

Because she had to. Because nobody else would.          •

# Chapter 8

# Emma

Emma needed to be making music but could not. Half of her band was in prison and incommunicado. She called and messaged Dean until he finally got back to her with word from Janice, who promised Ara was fine.

"Fine?" Emma scoffed into the phone.

"That's what she said," Dean said.

"But what exactly did she say?"

"*She's fine.*"

"That's impossible! I went to see her and she didn't show. She hasn't even called."

"Maybe she needs a little space?"

"Space? From who?"

Dean was conspicuously quiet.

"Hello?"

"I'm here," he said, wearily.

"Ask your mom to ask Ara if the guards even told her I was there. Actually, it's easier if your mom just calls me. Does she have my number? Will you give it to her? Dean? Dean?"

"Sure," said Dean.

"When?"

"Next time she calls."

"When will that be?"

"Tomorrow?"

"I can't wait that long!"

Dean was a patient man, but Emma could sense his limits were being tested. When he said he had to go, she released him.

But either he was lying, or Janice was lying, because Ara could not be fine. If Ara was fine, she would've called. If Ara was fine, Emma would not have driven to MCI-Bogastow and gone through a pat-down, only to be told by a guard with neon blue press-on nails that the "resident" would not be coming out.

"What am I supposed to do?" Emma said, her voice climbing to an octave normally reserved for encores and orgasms.

The guard shrugged. "You don't have to go home, baby, but you can't stay here."

Emma did go home, however, because the apartment felt empty and eerily quiet, but it had her workstation, and work was the one thing she knew. Josie was driving north, getting their mom, and Ara was stuck in prison, so who else but Emma was going to keep calm and carry on, make some new music, and start raising her sister's bail?

After Josie had first suggested the frankly brilliant idea for a prison album, Emma had returned home in a mania of inspiration, sprinting inside to flip on her power strip and turn on her looping pedal and hum impatiently as her workstation took an eternity to boot up. When Logic Pro was finally ready, she planted herself in front of her keys, filled her lungs, and . . . the melody that had been sailing around her head crashed into the reefs of self-doubt, where it sank to join the graveyard of *Tigress* and Emma's every attempt at a solo project since.

Emma could play music in her sleep—she often did, melodies dancing with chords in her dreams—but playing music and making music were not the same. Fans had Ara's lyrics tattooed on their bodies, not Emma's. Ara wrote in a way that hit as sincere but not sad-girl sappy. The same went for producing—the famous intro to "American Mosh" had been Ara's idea. She "felt" these things in a way that seemed like magic to Emma. Which made it all the more glaring-slash-sad-slash-enraging when Ara was too dopesick-slash-depressed-slash-high to put her creative gifts into practice.

Emma found herself in an uncomfortably off-key situation: She had to make music to save Ara (and the band) but without Ara, she couldn't begin. The disharmony brought a film of frustration to her eyes. She blinked it away, exhaled loudly, and shook her hands. "No," she spoke into the silence. She refused to be discouraged. She needed inspiration.

She plugged in her Yamaha, slapped on some Fast Fret, put *Smiley Smile* on the turntable, and matched Brian Wilson, chord for chord, word for word, through "Good Vibrations." She sang along to Florence & the Machine. She stood at her keys and belted covers of Sir Elton ("Rocket Man"), the Pixies ("Where Is My Mind?"), and finally Alanis ("Hand in my Pocket"), whom Emma appreciated for her repeated insistence that everything would be "fine, fine, fine."

She closed her eyes as the last note faded, fingers resting on her keys. Her home project studio included a godly set of instruments: two keyboards, four guitars, a 16-track MIDI sequencer with nine synthesizer engines, a 16-track audio recorder, gigabytes of waveform sound selection. When Emma remembered how she and Ara used to cobble together their demo CDs back at Berklee, her digital audio interface felt like cheating. She had no excuse. What she did have, unfortunately, was history. She'd attempted to replicate Ara's creative talents without her once before, and she knew what everyone said about history: learn that shit so you don't repeat it.

She checked her phone. She took a deep breath. She wrinkled her nose. Was something rotting? The floor was gritty from the crash-landing of the aloe plant. She needed to sweep. She needed to eat. Her chest tightened at the sight of Ara's drum kit, neglected in the corner. Even in the depths of using, Ara always carved out thirty-or-so minutes a day to practice. She played along to No Doubt or Hole, anything with a high BPM. Other times she'd just play the "Amen break," the same famous four bars, over and over, until the sound of hi-hat, snare, kick drum drove Emma crazy. But Emma would've given anything for an Amen right now. She checked her phone again. She could not be alone for another second. She swiped through contacts and settled on Zach.

"Hey you," he answered.

"What are you doing?" she said. "Wanna fuck?"

---

Zach worked from home. He was in tech, tracking ads or customer traffic for car dealerships. Something like that. He himself was less boring than his job. He had a fantastically chiseled body and almost no body hair and always made fruit smoothies for them after sex. Best of all, his wife worked long hours at some financial firm downtown, meaning she was both morally bankrupt and always gone.

"You know how to code, right?" Emma asked.

She'd biked to his place, arriving sweaty and ready. They'd showered together, then fallen into bed. She was now wearing one of his T-shirts and stretching her hamstrings at the kitchen counter. Zach was pouring tiny blueberries into a measuring cup. He'd helped to facilitate two orgasms, and Emma felt infinitely better for each of them.

"Yeah I code." He dumped the blueberries into the blender. "It's my job."

Without getting into the messy details, she explained that she was in the process of recording a new album with her sister, and they needed a platform to sell it.

He said, "Isn't that what your label is for?"

"We're going independent on this one."

"I'd just use Awesong," he said.

"They take ten percent. That's why we need our own platform. To save on the fees. Any chance you could help?"

His eyes darted to her, then to the blender. "I'm sort of very busy with work right now."

Emma watched him add oat milk, then pick a few mint leaves off a stem. She knew she was deviating from the usual musical score of their relationship, which started at sex and ended with smoothies and included—at most—a few measures of small talk in between. But Ara was in trouble, so Emma had to improvise.

"Do you at least have any advice for me?"

"Not really. I'd just go with Awesong. Like I said."

They went quiet as the blender did its thing.

He poured Emma's smoothie into a glass. He sipped his directly from the blender. Emma said that she'd figure something out, and anyway they couldn't record the album until Ara would call. "We have this perfect idea for a new album and she won't even reach out, even when this is what *she* needs more than anyone. It's weird, isn't it?"

"So weird."

"Dean says she needs space. Like what have I ever done except try to help her exactly as she asked me to?"

"Totally."

"If she needs space from anyone, it's Josie. You've never met someone who loves ordering people around so much. Josie is helpful, don't get me wrong. But holy shit, she can be smothering. Which, now that I think about it, is the complete opposite of our mom."

"Interesting."

Emma saw his eyes flash to the microwave clock. She put her glass on the counter with a loud crack. "Am I boring you? I'm sorry. Next time I'll keep sucking your dick so I won't talk too much."

He pinched his eyes. "That's not what I was thinking."

"What were you thinking?" Emma said.

She'd first spied Zach at the Arboretum last fall. He'd been on a bench, eating lunch. Emma had eyed his bag, said, "Oh my God I *love* Chipotle," and the rest was history. Men were really that easy. But then they took advantage of Emma. They took her for granted. They drank, they cheated, they hit. Or, like her dad, they simply left, and died. Josie occasionally suggested that Emma date guys outside the music scene. But, as Zach proved, music wasn't the problem. The problem was men. They couldn't be bothered to listen, or care, or do you one small favor.

"I like hanging out with you." Zach reached for a laptop on his kitchen island. "And I want to keep hanging out. But I don't think either of us have the bandwidth to be each other's therapist."

Emma tilted his laptop to look at the screen. "You are not checking your email right now."

He grimaced. "I'm so behind."

She pushed the computer off the counter, where it met the tiles with a rewarding crunch.

———

In the thirty-six years since a single fertilized egg had split, Emma could count only a handful of stretches that she and Ara had been apart like this without contact. The first was the six minutes after Emma's birth, until Ara finally joined her. Then there was Ara's honeymoon drug binge with Roman at Old Orchard Beach (before Emma drove up to check on them). And, of course, both times at New Pathways, where visits weren't allowed. But just because they kept little space between them did *not* mean that they shared some sort of sick twin co-enslavement. It wasn't as if they actively choreographed the minutiae of their existence. They merely happened to arrive at similar conclusions independently from each other. A long string of synchronicity. Such was the pattern of their lives.

Back when they'd decided (independently) to go to college, for example, they'd applied (independently) to the Berklee College of Music. They didn't register for all the same courses (Emma studied composition, Ara songwriting), nor did they dorm together (separate rooms on adjoining floors). They did find themselves, however, for the first time, sleeping outside of whispering distance from one another.

They took to the phone, workshopping melodies, studying for their Conducting 1 midterm (a core class they both had to take), comparing good-looking instructors, pro-conning the new Ani DiFranco album. Or they didn't speak at all, merely went about their lives as far as the cord would stretch. When Emma had to go past the point of maximum tensile strength, she would rest the phone on her desk, maintaining a portal to Ara's world. Sometimes she'd pick up to the sound of her sister breathing on the line, for at that same moment Ara had picked up, too.

"Hey, Sis, what are you doing?"

"Plucking my eyebrows and contemplating the unstable center of the universe."

"I'm contemplating pancakes. Wanna eat?"

They'd throw on bomber jackets (same jackets, different patches) and leave breadcrumb trails of cigarette butts to the South Street Diner, hop the Orange Line to catch a show at the Fountain, then inbound and over the Mass Ave. Bridge for a set at the Middle East, an after-party jam session, back across the bridge under the blush of dawn, stopping to watch the Ken dolls and their crew boats slice the muddy mirror of the Charles.

Among such short episodes in life, when dorm assignments or men separated Emma from Ara physically, there had always been the phone. But now Emma was moping around their too-quiet Mattapan apartment, subsisting on one meager visitation-room hour. It was her turn to taste the bitterness of withdrawal.

She swiped through her phone for someone who might be less of an asshole than Zach. Dozens of men would be thrilled to hear from her, only none of them felt right. There was exactly one person she wanted to see. She walked across the room and sat at Ara's drum kit. She ran a thumbnail over a cymbal. What if she got herself arrested? Some victimless crime, like public nudity. Then she could be with Ara—maybe even share a cell?

But that was insane.

Wasn't it? Insane?

Yes, Emma told herself with a shake of her head. It was certifiably insane. She was running on fumes. Ara was like a phantom limb: always there, even when she wasn't. Sometimes she tickled, sometimes she hurt. Right now she hurt.

She stomped Ara's kick drum: *whomp, whomp, whomp.* Had she ever felt so alone? She texted Samson, a sociology adjunct at Northeastern who did in fact have a free hour if Emma could make it to his place right now, he responded. And she could have. But not even her two great lovers—music and sex with emotionally unavailable men—were going to dull this pain.

She picked up Ara's drumsticks. She had to talk to someone. Zach's comment ran through her head, how he didn't have the "bandwidth" to listen to her or be her therapist. But Emma knew someone who might. She was already sitting at Ara's stool, running her thumbs over Ara's drumsticks, the wood worn smooth from hands that Emma knew just as well as her own. So why not?

She looked up the Survivors' Resource Center. She dialed. She left a message. "Hi, I missed my intake session. I'm really sorry. I need to reschedule. It's extremely urgent. My name is Araminta Tayloe. Thank you."

# Chapter 9

# Ara

CO Lopez popped our door after morning count—"Visitor, Tayloe." I hopped down, then realized there was no way Josie could be back with Mom so soon. I asked Lopez, "Does she look like me?" and when she said, "an uncanny fucking resemblance," I said, "not worth the strip search" and climbed back onto my bunk.

That was yesterday. This is today. Sister Detox, Day 3, and going strong. I'm starting to hear again. My thoughts. My needs. The buried beats. Like the guards—when it's quiet, you hear the COs coming before you see them.

CO Roberts walks at 60 BPM with a short heel scrape (think stick-drag across a cymbal).

CO Lopez has a plodding 40 BPM walk (think holding a turd).

Shift Commander Connelly goes at 90 BPM (think cocaine hurry).

Kyla says I'll have to learn the rest as they come. Inner Perimeter especially. Inner Perimeter, she told me, works behind the scenes, searching for contraband, reading mail, listening to calls. Think detective versus beat cop. Learn their footsteps, Kyla says, and it'll buy me time to flush what needs flushing before they turn our room upside down.

"Those chucklefucks will bust you for anything that makes you happy."

She must have caught me scanning Room 13 for what makes her happy, because she said, "I got everything I need right here," and hiked up her sleeve to introduce me to her girls—Ruby, Crystal, Gemma— their faces a green-black totem pole on her wide upper arm. "They live with their dad now, but he's only been in touch once, to gloat that he'd filed for full custody," Kyla said. (She shot him. She's been wearing baggy prison green for three months, awaiting trial for attempted murder. When she first told me, she said, "I should've attempted harder.")

"But I'll be back, babies," she murmured, caressing their faces. "You hang on. Momma's coming. Momma loves you."

As soon as she said it, I turned all weepy. It didn't feel like that large a leap between the girls on Kyla's arm and me in my bunk, all of us wondering the same: Where's Mom? Also keep in mind I'm still pretty dopesickshaky at this point. Fragile. Haven't eaten much besides orange juice and saline solution in days.

Kyla rubbed my back—"First days are the hardest, you just keep writing it out"—and went on mothering me. Did I need a Cruncher for my nausea? Wanna watch TV? Try the bottom bunk for a night?

I told her she was sweet to dote on me, someone she hardly even knew. Especially when she had so many bigger problems.

"Problems are problems," she said. "We take care of each other in here. I got you now."

————

CO Lopez came by again after major count. "Tayloe, visitor."

"I'm not feeling social," I reminded her.

"You sure? It's your lawyer. They say she's a good one."

I hopped down from my bunk. Lopez escorted me to the interview room. My lawyer was waiting. Her name is Mylene Shin. She's very young. Very pretty. Very no-nonsense. Not a wrinkle on her nice lawyer blouse or skirt. She introduced herself and before I could even land my ass in the chair, she's explaining how the public defender who stood in for my arraignment could've (should've) fought for better bail terms, but she's already appealed to Superior Court, but don't get my hopes up, Superior Court never reverses, and anyway the terms of my bail don't matter because she's working out a deal with the DA's office.

We were meeting in the wired-glass room in the corner of the larger visitation area. Goldfish bowl privacy. On the other side of the glass, prisoners and family were chatting, laughing, lining up at the vending machines. I scanned the room, head hurting, body woozy. Praying my sisters wouldn't show up again to make me feel worse than I already did.

"Hey." Mylene snapped her fingers.

"Yes," I said.

"Yes, you're okay with the plea agreement?"

"What agreement?"

"Continuance without a finding. We admit the DA's office has a slam-dunk case, they send you home. Stay good for a year, they drop the charges. No trial, no more time, no record. Easy."

I felt my hands reach out and wrap around the cool legs of the table because there are times you just need something to hold. When I first got out of New Pathways, my sisters were waiting for me in the parking lot. Sister smiling like a lunatic, holding a "Happy Graduation" foil balloon. Josie with carnations that I remember for their aggressive shade of blue. They were happy for me. I was happy, too. The food at New Pathways was violently constipating, I couldn't wait for an effortless poop. But at the same time, I felt this drip-drip-drip of dread, like I should've re-upped for another thirty days. Like I'd left too early. Like the route that lay ahead, now that I'd taken that first step off the property, was already plotted and doomed. And sure enough.

"Hello?" Mylene said.

"I need to think about it."

She frowned. "I'm already in conversation with the DA. Don't mess this up. You could be out soon."

"How soon?"

"A week. Ten days, max. They'll send someone in to depose you—don't worry, I'll be here too—and then we present to the judge. Shouldn't be more than a couple of days after that."

In recovery you learn to identify your triggers and patterns and routines. You miss them and you fear them. I'd vowed to take a week away from my sisters, and I meant it. But now, up against the reality of getting out so soon, seven days felt like not nearly enough.

"Depose me for what?" I asked.

"So you can present testimony against—" She took out a stapled packet and ran a finger down a page. "—Roman Lang."

I almost laughed. "You want me to testify against Roman?"

"Me and the prosecution. Yes. As a minimum for any deal."

"He's not a bad guy."

"I don't care if he's Gandhi. This is how you get out."

I didn't bother telling her that Roman and I were married, or that we enjoyed a fun, extended honeymoon in Old Orchard Beach (before Sister crashed the party). I didn't tell her because it's complicated. Roman and I don't have any burning romance. We're just childhood friends who happen to share a love for curiosity, risk, and getting high. Every once in a while we take a stab at sex, but dope makes fucking a chore (you never come). What we're best at is sabotaging ourselves. True team players in that regard. Also he stuck a Narcan canister up my nose when my lungs needed convincing. So there's that, too.

"How is he?" I asked Mylene.

"How is he. I have no idea. He's not my client. You are."

I thanked her for her concern, but explained that my mom was a lawyer who'd happened to get the highest score in the history of the Massachusetts Bar, and ran her own legal clinic for years. "She's out of the state, but as soon as she's back, she'll know what to do. She has a little more experience. How old are you? No offense."

"Offense fucking taken. You think I sought out a lifetime of debt from Yale Law to be disrespected like this?" She slid the packet back into her bag and told me something like if I wanted another lawyer, the waiting room was ass-to-elbow with Boston's top criminal defense attorneys, all begging for a shot at a drug case for a repeat offender who qualified for public defense and was too smashed to stand at her own arraignment.

That made me laugh. I told her that she reminded me of my sister.

She asked if I meant the sister who'd been calling her nonstop.

I told her that sounded like Josie. I asked if she had any siblings.

She sighed dramatically and glanced at her watch and said that in the name of client-attorney relationship-building she would dedicate precisely sixty seconds toward chitchat. So yes, she had a sister in Charlotte, and a brother in Atlanta.

"Are you all close?"

"So-so. You two?"

"Too close." I told her about Emma and the band.

"Jojo and the Twins," she said. "Never heard of you."

"'American Mosh'?" I tried.

She shrugged. "I guess you were before my time. No offense."

"Offense fucking taken," I said.

She smiled, then tapped her watch. "Great chat. Now are you ready to take a deal?"

I saw myself in the faint reflection of the glass, sitting in prison green across from my public defender, and for the millionth time in the past few days, I couldn't believe this was my life.

But if it's your life, at least you get to do with it what you want.

"No. Sorry. I'm not ready."

She stood up. "Wrong answer. I'm getting you a plea deal. If that upsets your delicate morality I don't give a shit. You can be angry at me when you're free."

She left. I went through the cough-and-bend-overs. Now I'm back in Room 13, Kyla writing below me, me writing above. I'm sick. So sick. But also less sick. Because I'm here. And I'm clean. And I'm not leaving until I know I can do life differently. I'm freeing myself.

––––––

I gave the NA meeting a try today. In the past, whether at New Pathways or the basement of the Congregational church, 12-Steps has always felt like too much God. Too many wrong people. Too much temptation, in their all-or-nothing way. Today in the cafeteria, 12-Steps felt the opposite: too easy, like nobody was there to slay addiction, just bored, and glad for any activity out of the ordinary. But I'm not chasing false success. I'm after the real thing. And it's working. My chest isn't aching for another Amen every second. Also, my tinnitus isn't so angry at me. Music is the only (non-habit-forming) remedy I've found for drowning out the ringing. The thrashier and louder the better. But there's no music here, and so maybe I just needed some space and silence all along? Whatever the reason, my ears aren't ringing as much, and I don't miss it.

What I do miss is nicotine. I ask Janice again in the yard. Again she shakes her head.

"I'm not about to blow up my supply ring so you can get lung cancer. Sorry, hon."

Janice brings comforts into the prison that you can't buy at the canteen. Concealer, conditioner, eyeliner, moisturizer. On Mother's Day,

Kyla told me, Janice made sure all the moms get chocolate. If you get sent to Max, you'll find a sixer of Diet Coke on your bunk when you come back. Another thing she does as Queen Bee: she makes sure no hard drugs get in.

"You can't score behind these walls, so don't waste your breath trying. Araminta? You hear me?"

"I hear you."

They gave the same no-drugs talk at New Pathways, but that was rehab, where there were ways around it, and this is prison, where Janice makes it clear that her way is the only way. Realizing that she is serious—knowing that I truly cannot get high in here—it loosens a knot in my chest, causing this sudden drop in pressure, the way my tinnitus will sometimes crescendo into a soft crumble of an explosion, after which everything goes quiet for one tender blue moment.

Something else about Janice: She's led so many protests over the years for prisoner rights, many with legal support from Mom. When DOC lowered the number of sanctioned bathrobes from two to one, she led the women around the yard wearing robes and nothing underneath. She's won more bad behavior than anyone. Everyone adores and respects her. No wonder they call her JC. Yet even the savior herself can't get me a cigarette. She patted me on the back and said, "But tell me, Araminta, what can I get you?"

I gave her a list: floss, deodorant, Crunchers.

(I've heard Kyla complaining about her gums, and I can smell her armpits from my bunk. As for the crackers, I want to do something nice for her. For all that she's done for me.)

"No, yes, and yes." Janice ticked the items off her fingers.

"No floss?"

"Inner Perimeter will look the other way on little things—I'm getting out so soon, they've mostly given up on me—but they draw the line at anything we might use as a rope."

We were walking the edge of the yard. I pointed at the perimeter fence, crowned with bales of glittery razor wire. "They think a rope made out of dental floss is getting us over that?"

Janice gave me a pitying smile. "There's more than one way to escape with a rope, hon."

---

Yard time was canceled when a Code 99 (serious injury or self-harm) came screeching over the intercom. We went into lockdown. Kyla was pushing a mop somewhere. Room 13 to myself, I took out a sheet of paper and my cute little pen. I was still thinking about how my lawyer said she'd never heard of our band. Sister would feel butthurt from a comment like that, but I felt weirdly freed. So there I was, sitting cross-legged on the top bunk, humming, free associating, scribbling whatever popped into my head. And this is how I discovered an un-expected benefit of Sister Detox: writing sober, and without Sister over my shoulder—I'd almost forgotten it was supposed to be fun.

Sister is a musical genius and she's a perfectionist. We must have 5 LPs of material recorded since Mosh, and not ten bars she'll stand behind. We lay down something new, she tears it apart, says we can do better—*have done better*—sends us back for a beat that will fit better with a particular fade that we can never get right.

But we are a band. Meaning it's not just her. Opioids at first carve out this magical space to create with zero self-doubt. At some point, though, the balance tips. You can't finish a line. Can't decide on the right word. Or you find the right word only to watch it float away. Your mind goes cotton candy distant. But here in Room 13, detoxing on my own terms, I read over what I've just written and surprise myself. There, scattered in the garbage, are two lines I don't totally hate.

*The pack is the nucleus.*
*The pack is ~~the two~~ all of us.*

The second time I got out of New Pathways, there were no blue carnations waiting for me. No balloons. No Josie. Only Sister. She'd driven all the way up. She didn't get out of the car, just pulled up to the entrance and reached over to fling open the passenger door.

"Get in loser, we're going shopping."

The physical symptoms of withdrawal are hell, but they're short-lived. A million times worse is the shame, the remorse, the pain of hearing yourself mumble yet another meaningless apology. So when Sister turned out of the parking lot and asked how I was feeling, I said "Way better," and burst into tears. She squeezed my leg, turned on the radio and drove. We'd moved back home then, living again with Mom. The house was four hours away. Plenty of road time to get to the deep root of things— what had happened with us, the band, what I really needed—but then the first notes of "Like a Prayer" came on the radio, and Sister couldn't not sing along, and I couldn't not harmonize with her, and this is the story of our lives.

My impulse is to call her as soon as I can get to a dayroom phone. I swing my legs off the top bunk, excited to share the first lines of my new song. Then I stop. I remember my triggers. My patterns. My detox. I have to stop giving everything to her. I have to keep some of me for myself.

## Chapter 10

# Josie

Griffinport, Maine, a mid-coast city of 7,000, beloved for its granite cliffs and fall foliage, its whale watches and puffin tours, its picturesque downtown and harbor, its eateries and galleries, had come, by way of a new generation of back-to-the-landers, an influx of post-Recession millennials, and the death of a respected (but fiscally conservative) six-term mayor, to elect a city government so progressive that residents half-jokingly referred to themselves as the Griffinport Commune.

The city had a local currency (G-Bux, accepted at most Main Street businesses). They had rent control, a police department trained in restorative justice, a subsidized daycare. They had become a sanctuary city before sanctuary cities were in vogue. Their Millionaire's Tax (five percent on all property deed transactions over $1 million) paid for some of the social services, and tourism covered the rest. The Griffinport Harbor boasted the only wharf north of Portland that could accommodate voyager-class cruise ships, and docking and carbon-offsetting fees were priced with the advantage in mind. An archway spanned the main road from the highway:

WELCOME TO GRIFFINPORT
WHERE "ME" IS "US"

Josie drove beneath the sign, crested the hill into a charming brick-and-slate downtown, and parked on Main Street between two news vans. She ducked inside a café, in need of chemical reinforcements, for

Main Street sloped precipitously to the harbor, and Josie had caught a glimpse of the cruise ship bobbing at the end of the wharf, a giant blue cross on its side: the American Rescue Cruise. Josie exchanged her American dollars for G-Bux, slugged a double espresso, and marched downhill to find her mother.

The harbor buzzed with activity. A crane grinded and whirred, loading containers onto the *A.R.C.* People stomped up the gangway carrying crates and bags. Gulls cawed. Metal halyards slapped sailboat masts. The air smelled like French fries. A large man at the dock held up a hand.

"Badge?"

The man was dressed in black. A pair of black sunglasses squeezed his head. He had a walkie-talkie holstered on one hip, a Taser on the other.

"I'm looking for Roberta Tayloe." Josie peered over his shoulder.

"Nobody's gets on the ship without a badge."

"I'm her daughter."

"Nobody's gets on the ship without a badge."

Josie clenched her jaw and visualized the clean parabola of the man pitching backward, off the dock and into the harbor.

The man, perhaps sensing Josie's vision, offered to radio Bertie, but first he needed ID.

Josie handed over her license. He scanned it, and walkie-talkied someone. A moment later the someone crackled back: "She's coming out."

Josie texted a photo of the ship to Dean. The *A.R.C.* wasn't much by Royal Caribbean standards, but set against the dinghies of Griffinport Harbor, the vessel was gargantuan: three decks (four including the open-aired top), strings of lights connecting two fat exhaust stacks, and a large, windowed mess hall, where Josie could see humans meeting, eating, stacking boxes. Some retirees preferred winding down in their golden years with birding or water coloring. Josie's mother, as soon as the Massachusetts Bar had stripped her of her credentials and the People's Law Center disbanded, had taken an entirely different route. When Bertie had first mentioned the *A.R.C.* ("The most important act of international solidarity since the Spanish Civil War"), Josie had half dismissed it as her latest crusade. But now, craning her neck to take in the *A.R.C.* in person, this was clearly no run-of-the-mill symbolic action.

OBSERVATION: Seriously huge ship with armed bouncer
demanding ID.
HYPOTHESIS: American Rescue Cruise not fucking around.

The *A.R.C.* aimed to sail across two oceans to bring a shipment of baby formula, antibiotics, and other humanitarian essentials to the besieged Gaza Strip. Unlike the port cities from Savannah to New Bedford, which had bent to pressure and rejected the *A.R.C.*'s request for docking rights, the Griffinport city council had welcomed the ship by unanimous vote. Years had passed since the last international attempt to break the Israeli blockade. The *A.R.C.* was gunning to resuscitate the movement. But that was only half the mission. On the return trip, the *A.R.C.* would swing by Cyprus to take on hundreds of Syrian refugees, sail back across the Atlantic, and support them in applying for asylum.

"Josephine! My gosh. What a *wonderful* surprise!"

Her mother bounced down the gangway, beaming, flapping her hands like an excited sparrow. Her bones pinched Josie when they hugged. Behind her came Audrey, equally birdlike but of the tall, stork variety. Audrey was a Catholic Worker. She and Bertie lived together at the Dorothy Day House, likely in some sort of romantic capacity, though Josie had neither asked for, nor wanted, the intimate details. Audrey bent down, embracing Josie. Last in line was a young person with short blue hair and open arms, falling into Josie to complete the hug trifecta.

"Josephine, this is Max. Max just came from the West Bank. Max, show Josephine your battle wound—look at that! From a rubber bullet. Max is starting law school this fall."

"I'm going into civil rights law, like your mom," Max said. "Are you the one who works with ants? I *love* ants. Did you know they're almost all female?"

"Mom, we need to talk." Josie felt overwhelmed. But they were already on the move, chugging uphill, arms swinging, crossing a waterfront park bustling with newscasters and cameras.

"Talk, please! Have you met Rosario Dawson yet? Mark Ruffalo is here, too. They're very approachable." She stopped to flick a crumb off Josie's shirt, and then she gasped. "You could record a family testimonial here, with the ship in the background! Could we do that, Max?"

"We could one-hundred-percent do that, Bertie," Max said, squaring an imaginary shot between thumbs and forefingers.

"Max handles the tech stuff," Bertie said. "You should see all their electronic doodads."

"Mom, I didn't come here to record a testimonial. We need to talk. Privately."

"Absolutely, dear, after the civil disobedience training. I'm leading it, we can't be late."

They crested a hill and power walked up a side street. Josie felt the double espresso course through her blood and wondered if a more chillaxed chemical reinforcement would've been better. The last time she'd spoken in person with her mother was the April Blowout Weekend, after which Josie had vowed (as she had before) that it would be the last. She saw her future-self explaining to her sisters, Janice, and Dean, that Bertie hadn't even stopped to *listen* to Josie, never mind entertain the idea of returning to help Ara. The vision calmed her with a warm cocktail of serotonin and allopregnanolone, the brain's reward for knowing it was right. Josie would not argue with Bertie. She would merely present the scenario, calmly make a request for legal assistance, and report back. She would take the high road. She fished around her tote bag.

"Em and Ara had a gig last weekend, Mom. Their first in a year. They were really hoping you'd make it. I knew you were too busy, so I got you a souvenir."

"*What Have You Done Today to Smash the Patriarchy?*" Bertie checked the tank top's label (to make sure it wasn't sweatshop made, Josie knew).

"So kind of you, Josephine, but you know I don't need new things."

"I'll take it!" Max chirped.

Bertie tossed the tank top to Max.

Audrey tapped an invisible watch. "People. We need to hustle."

"By all means," Josie said. "Don't let me hold you back."

———

Two security volunteers scanned badges at the door, confiscated phones, wanded Josie and the group for hidden cameras. Sabotage had ended a Danish effort to break the Israeli blockade in 2013, with the *Håber* mysteriously sinking at a Greek port. The *A.R.C.* was taking no such chances.

"They will come at night, they will come fast, they will come hard—"

"And despite what we tell the media, we are never armed with blanks."

Tal and Uri were *refuseniks*, Israeli Defense Force helicopter pilots who'd been dismissed and jailed for their opposition to the Occupation. After jail, they'd moved to America where they could legally marry. They were tall, buff, dark, egregiously good-looking. They wore camo pants, tank tops, and boots, and Josie suspected she wasn't alone in visualizing their sex life as they grappled in mock combat, modeling what the crew could expect as the *A.R.C.* approached Palestine and Israeli commandos boarded the ship. The training was being held in a refurbished seafood processing warehouse. Fluorescent lights hummed.

The *A.R.C.*'s crew was comprised of a hundred-odd doctors, teachers, clergy, artists, and engineers. Bertie split them into affinity groups and began with role-playing exercises.

"Tal and Uri will act as the commandos. And when they land, we will do what?"

The crew lifted their arms and chanted: *"Unarmed civilian! Don't shoot!"*

"Good. Now again, in Hebrew."

Bertie, afterward, led a Q&A on extradition and the Israeli judicial process, then Josie found herself speedwalking with her to a press conference on the wharf, and from there back uphill to Griffinport Unitarian, where Bertie and Audrey had volunteered to cook curry for forty. If Josie wanted to chop veggies, Bertie said, she and Audrey could get started on peeling peaches. She'd decided to "throw together a cobbler" for dessert.

"When did you become such the cook?" Josie tried not to sound out of breath as they trudged uphill.

"Oh, there's nothing to a cobbler."

"We *love* Bertie's cobblers," Audrey said.

Josie, who had prepared roughly one hundred percent of their non-frozen family meals through middle and high school, bit her tongue.

She hadn't come here to argue. Also, she was winded. Griffinport felt like one big hill.

The Unitarian kitchen smelled like the inside of an old cookie tin: not terrible, but you knew it had once been better. Josie quelled a kink of nausea as she chopped onions while Audrey conjured a bottle of wine and poured Josie a glass. Cheers. Josie began grating ginger. Bertie and Audrey, at a parallel counter, were laughing as they mixed sugar, milk, and flour in a giant pan. Josie's kink of nausea melted into a pad of twisted satisfaction: her mother had completely dismissed the important thing that Josie had come to discuss, exactly as Josie had known she would. She took a generous swallow of wine and moved on to the potatoes. She was cutting them into cubes when Bertie announced from across the kitchen that Max could set up cameras tomorrow for Josie to record her testimonial. It was too late tonight, she said. They'd lost the light. If only Josie had called ahead . . .

Josie wiped the blade of her knife and set it down. She prepared her words carefully so there would be no confusion, and also because some sick part of her was going to enjoy this.

"I did call ahead, Mom. I called many, many times."

"You should've tried Audrey. You know how my phone is always acting up."

Josie smiled calmly. "I don't have Audrey's number."

"Well you're here now, that's what matters. And Max can set up—"

"—I came here to talk to you, Mom, not to record a propaganda video."

"Proactive messaging," Max corrected, appearing out of nowhere. "In case the Israelis attack again."

"No," Josie said simply. "I will not be doing that."

Bertie unwrapped a stick of butter. "You girls are so silly. I don't see what the big deal is. It's just a video of you talking about your mother. Araminta had no problem doing it."

"That's because she was high, Mom. She's been using again. Heroin. And now she's in jail. She got arrested. That's why I'm here. That's what I've been trying to tell you."

Bertie's hand slipped, sending the stick of butter to the floor with a splat.

Josie observed the complex neurochemical plumbing in her brain. On the one hand, the red wine was siphoning her cortisol to the basement storage tanks, relieving pressure on her aggression conduits. On the other hand, her androstenedione gland was sump-pumping the basement storage tanks back into the control room. The hydro-engineering left her oddly calm on the surface, while inside, the hot water tank was rattling, about to blow.

"She was arrested with Roman. They have her at MCI-Bogastow on trafficking charges. They drugged an informant. It's bad. She relapsed. She's an addict and her bail is outrageous. She needs your help."

Bertie stooped to pick up the butter. "I don't think we say 'addict' anymore, dear. The term is 'substance use disorder.'"

"I know that," Josie said.

"The war on drugs is such bullshit," muttered Max.

———

Bertie, after learning that a daughter had relapsed and ended up in prison, jumped right back to work. People were hungry, she said. The crew needed to eat. First thing first. She prepared and served dinner, sat down for a few bites, then leapt up to wash dishes.

Josie watched, incredulous with fury, yet also incredulous with disappointment in herself, for after a lifetime as Bertie's daughter, why did she expect anything else?

Her mother had missed Josie's high school valedictorian speech to work as a legal observer for a Zapatista march on the Mexican consulate. She'd missed Emma and Ara's first headlining gig to represent a group of nuns who'd been detained protesting the U.S. Army's School of the Americas. She'd forgone Emma and Ara's Grammy ceremony to participate in a citizen's arrest of Donald Rumsfeld. And she'd been absent for the bad stuff too, like after Ara's assault, when Ara (and all of them) could've used a mother most.

Given the choice between helping her daughters, or helping strangers, Josie knew where Bertie would land. What she didn't know was why, after thirty-four years, it could still trigger in her immune system such an anaphylactic response.

To counteract the onrush of inflammatory mediators (histamines, hydrolytic enzymes, rage), she shoveled back a sagging paper plate of curry, then excused herself to wretch violently in the bathroom. After dishes were washed, Bertie announced that she had a security shift with Audrey. Josie jumped up and grabbed her mother's bony wrist.

"Excuse us, Audrey, my mom and I need to talk."

She dragged Bertie outside and downhill, toward the bay. The tide was rising. Sailboats bumped against their slips. Josie stopped by the wharf and presented the data. She told Bertie what had happened, and handed over a photocopied arrest report, along with a sheaf of court documents.

Bertie squinted. "I can't read in the dark."

Josie walked them to a lamppost, and waited impatiently for her mother to riffle through the papers.

"Well?"

Bertie sighed. "That was a big mistake, assaulting the informant like that."

"They didn't assault him, they drugged him. And Roman did it, not Ara, and why are we even discussing this? Obviously it was a mistake. What can we do to fix it?"

"Nothing."

Josie sputtered. "There must be someone you can call. One of your friends at the Lawyers Guild?"

"The Guild represents activists, not drug dealers."

"The ACLU?"

"What does this have to do with free speech?"

"Maybe you know the judge?"

Bertie shook her head. "Even if I did, I'm afraid those bridges are still smoldering."

During her disbarment hearings, Bertie had taken the Massachusetts legal community to task. *Dereliction of duty to moral law.* She'd prepared speeches. She'd named names.

"Please, Mom. You're not even trying. If Ara was your client, what would you tell her?"

"I'd tell her to plead. Cut a deal. Mandatory minimums are no joke."

Josie breathed a sigh of relief. They were getting somewhere. "Great. So how should she do that?"

"Claim duress. Coercion. Testify that Roman forced her to be there."

Josie deflated. Ara had a twisted loyalty for Roman that defied logic. "And if she won't?"

"She'll go to trial. But juries usually side with female defendants."

"Usually? That isn't good enough, Mom. It'll be weeks before her trial even starts."

"More like months. I've seen pretrial detention last almost a year."

"Ara is not spending a year in prison!"

"Have you considered it might not be the worst place for her? Sometimes people in her situation—they need to hit rock bottom. At least we'll know where she is. And Janice is there, don't forget. Janice runs a tight ship."

"It's not rehab, Mom! She is in prison! How are you so calm about this?"

"Because getting upset won't do a bit of good. I wish it would. Believe me. If there's one thing I've learned in life, it's to accept the things we cannot change."

Josie, who had heard and mumbled the Serenity Prayer at too many Al-Anon meetings to count, could not bear the hypocrisy of her mother leaning on it now.

"Oh like racism? Like the prison-industrial complex? Like the Israeli Occupation? You've literally spent your entire life trying to change things that can't be changed."

Bertie stopped walking to give Josie a look. "I feel sorry for you, dear, if you are truly that nihilistic. People said feudalism would never end. Slavery. Monarchy. Human history points to the fact that regular people always—"

"No, no, we are *not* doing this." Josie caught herself before falling into one of Bertie's conversational booby traps. "We're not talking about human history, we're talking about you coming down to help your daughter get out of prison."

"I'm sorry, dear. There's no secret legal loophole for something like this. There's nothing I can do."

"But you haven't even tried!"

Josie's voice echoed metallic off the steel hull of a tugboat lashed to the dock. Bertie continued walking. Josie trailed a half step behind, feeling like a child. Faint bass thumped from a car somewhere far off.

"I thought she quit that awful stuff," Bertie said, stopping at the end of the wharf. "How on earth did this happen?"

Josie had been asking the same question of herself. She was the biologist, after all. Ninety percent of her job was observation. Had Ara really grown that skilled at hiding her addiction, or had Josie become that oblivious?

"She'd be out already if we had the house to put up for collateral. I told you, Mom. I *told* you we might need that equity at some point. I told you there could be an emergency. Remember me saying that? I told you. And look!"

"Enough, Josephine. If I didn't know better, I'd say you were almost happy about this."

Josie, who was in fact happy—a dark gloating happiness to which she would never admit, not even to herself—said, "You could at least come down to see her. It would mean a lot."

"Hundreds of Syrian families are counting on us. They are waiting for us. Their lives are in our hands. Not to mention the families in Gaza, cut off. I can't do a thing for Araminta, but I can for them."

"Why do they need *you*? It's not like the ship can't sail without you."

"If everybody made excuses like that, justice would never have a chance."

"Ara's not an excuse! She's your daughter! She asked for you first thing, when we walked in. *Where's Mom?* she said. Those were her first words."

Bertie turned to face the shimmery bridge of moonlight on the harbor. "All I ever wanted was to make the world a safe and just place for you girls. I don't know if you and Dean are planning on children—that's none of my business—but Palestinian families are suffering every day because of an Israeli occupation that our tax dollars fund. Syrian families are scattered, grieving, and desperate. What kind of mother would I be if I was fine leaving this sort of world behind for you all?"

"I know another family that needs your help. And you don't have to sail halfway around the world to be there for them."

Bertie's thin shoulders rose and fell. An acidic, smoldering part of Josie almost hoped something bad would happen to Ara—a terrible thought that she banished the moment it popped through the surface tension of her mind—for how else would Bertie ever learn her lesson?

"So to be perfectly clear, Mom, I should tell Ara that you've decided not to help?"

"To be perfectly clear, Josephine, I'm sailing halfway around the world to help."

There was a reason Bertie had been such a formidable lawyer. The woman could argue with a stop sign.

# Chapter 11

# Ara

Writing in my bunk after morning count, when Dolores stops by.

"JC says to call your sister because she won't stop calling JC's boy and everyone's driving everyone crazy and you're the only one can put an end to the madness."

Dolores has been awaiting trial for something like nine months (she's representing herself), making her a senior resident of Barton Unit, and, I guess, Janice's messenger.

I tell the messenger: "Nope. Can't. Won't."

"What should I tell JC?"

"Tell her I'm not done detoxing."

"Okeeydokie." She turns to head back, then stops and says there was something else. She snaps her fingers. "Oh, your momma's not coming. She left on a cruise, I think?"

"Gotcha, thanks," I say and go back to writing, because what else am I supposed to do?

But true confessions, I was not writing. My pen was just tracing the same circle round and round and round. Opioids, for all their harm, do defend against a wide range of emotional sucker punches. Defenseless, I was stretched out on my bunk, shrugging to myself like I didn't care about my mom. Then I shrugged again, like okay maybe I care a little. Maybe a lot. Maybe I'd very much counted on her coming back for this one thing. For me.

That's when Kyla returns from her cleaning duties. Her hair is plastered to her scalp from working down in the heat of Max. She had to mop up dried blood. The Code 99. A girl had tried to kill herself, opened up her wrists with a paper clip . . .

She trails off, because as hot and disgusting as she feels, I can't hide how I'm feeling, and she can't help dropping into mom mode.

"Talk to me." She passes me a Cruncher. "What's going on?"

"Nothing. In the scheme of things, Kyla, it's nothing."

I was thinking of her, so desperate to see her girls. I was thinking of the blood she'd mopped up in Max. The Code 99. That poor girl who'd decided she was done, done, done.

"It's never nothing." Kyla pops another Cruncher into her mouth, holding a hand underneath her chin to catch every precious crumb.

I shrug again. "I guess I just want my mom."

"I hear you." Kyla puts a hand on my knee. "And I'm here for you."

I bite into a Cruncher. It might be the driest thing I've ever swallowed, but I force it down. The intercom crackles to life, announcing major count. The sound of locking doors cascades down the hallway. Kyla reaches up. I take her hand and hop down. Mom's not coming for me. Okay. But that doesn't mean I'm alone.

———

Dining hall. After count. A woman approaches me in line. Big chested and big thighed like Josie. Birthmark like war paint on her cheek. I'm seeing that fangirl look in her eye, like she recognizes me and wants a selfie. I couldn't be more wrong.

"Rich bitch. Jojo and the Twins blow ass."

Before I can say, "No shit, please tell my sister," Dolores slaps her hard enough to knock the ID tag off her shirt. The slap earns Dolores a night in Max.

I feel bad. Nancy tells me not to worry: Dolores will sleep it off, she says. Mary agrees: "That woman needs all the beauty rest she can get. Any one of us would've done the same."

Nancy and Mary are Lifers. They remember Mom's legal work from back in the day. They invite me and Kyla to sit at the Lifer table. They chat me up. Nancy asks if my name is a family name. I explain how Mom named us after famous radicals. Araminta Ross was Harriet Tubman's birth name.

Nancy points her plastic spoon at me. "So you're tunneling us to freedom?"

Mary grunts. "Too old to be crawling in the dirt. You dig your tunnel, Harriet, then you come back here with a bottle of Southern Comfort for me."

"And a rotisserie chicken," says Nancy.

"And a man with a grade-A tush!" someone else says.

"And some goddamned dental floss!" shouts Kyla, pounding both fists on the table.

Everyone goes silent.

"What? Gum disease is no joke."

Everyone nods, like, *Of course not, no joke at all.* Then Nancy, or maybe Mary, someone snorts, and we all burst into laughter, Kyla, too.

Know how long since I laughed like that? Me neither.

---

Back in Room 13 for afternoon count, Kyla and I are writing in our bunks (Kyla to her girls, me inching into what might be possibly a chorus, possibly a verse)—

> *Wanted thunder, got rain*
> *Prayed for holy, met pain*
> *No father, no mama, all ghost*
> *What you don't have hurts most*

—when we hear footsteps.

"Roberts?" I tilt my head.

"Lopez," Kyla says.

She's right. Lopez pops our door. "Lawyer time, Tayloe."

I jump down and step into my slippers.

Lopez walks me to the interview room where Mylene is tapping a pen against the table.

"Continuance without a finding and time-served in exchange for two years' probation, community service, financial restitution, Narcotics Anonymous," she says, before Lopez has shut the door.

"I'm doing okay," I say. "Thanks so much for asking. You?"

She doesn't even smile. "This is the best deal you're going to get. You should take it before they withdraw it, or transfer you to federal prison."

"I'm not turning on Roman."

She purses her lips and stares at me for two bars . . . four bars . . . eight.

"What?" I say.

"The evidence is overwhelming. You'll have no chance at trial. This is a good deal that the DA's office could withdraw at any time. Don't be an idiot."

"I just need to talk to him. Please?"

Her jaw muscles bulge like two pretty buttons. She says that prisoner-to-prisoner communication is forbidden. I say that's not entirely true.

I tell her about my mom's three-way mail service. When we were growing up, Mom would sit us at the kitchen counter, helping her open and sort letters from her clients, rewriting illegible portions, addressing and stamping envelopes with her special attorney barcodes. It was how she helped her incarcerated clients keep in touch with their lovers, friends, and comrades. Using her legal privilege to evade the Inner Perimeter censors.

Mylene presses her thumbs into her eyes. "I work seventy hours a week if I'm lucky. Most women here, they can't even get their lawyer on the phone. It's not unusual for us to meet a client for the first time in court. And then you're lucky if we have twenty minutes to review everything. So I just want you to know what you have here, before you burn it all down. I'm a fucking catch."

Then she sighs and rips a blank sheet from a notebook. She hands me a pen. No limp-dicked prison-issued rubber pen, but the real deal. "I'm operating on negative time," she says. "Hurry up."

*R—*

*Safe and weirdly happy. Hope you are, too. They want me to testify against you. Says they'll drop my charges. What are they telling you?*

*6 Days Clean,*
*—A*

*PS: Use me as a reference if you apply to any gangs.*
*PPS: (No racist gangs, obviously)*
*PPPS: I'm really sorry all of this happened.*
*PPPPS: xoxo*
*PPPPPS: I'm writing again.*
*PPPPPPS: Remember the cornfield across the marsh by the*
*railroad tracks? From the yard, I can see us there. Teenage Roman*
*says hi. He's cute.*

Mylene reads my note over, folds and slides it into her bag, then pulls out a Sharpie and a CD. *American Mosh.*

"It's not for me," she says flatly. "My aunt. Apparently she's a big fan. Her name's Jen. Her birthday's next week. An autograph would mean a lot."

I sign the cover, adding a cartoon skull with hearts for eyes, and a thought bubble. Inside the thought bubble, I draw a smaller skull, smiling—"*Happy Birthday Jen!*"

"Thanks." Mylene stashes the CD in her bag.

"Sure thing. Can you do me a solid back?"

Her smile disappears. "You mean in addition to the illegal mail?"

"This one's for my roommate. Like you said, she can't even get her lawyer on the phone. She needs help. Her ex won't let her daughters talk to her."

"I have literally no experience in family law."

"Yeah but everyone around here keeps saying you're such a catch."

"You're unbelievable," she says, but in a way that tells me she's already calculating how she'll cram Kyla into her schedule.

"You're the best," I say.

"I know," she says.

# Chapter 12

# Emma

Emma was no stranger to playing the part of Ara. April Fool's Day, in the fourth grade, they switched classrooms. Their teachers, bless their hearts, played along. Freshman year at Berklee, they traded boyfriends for a night. A joke. How long would it take them to notice? When boyfriends didn't notice—when moves were being made, clothes about to come off—it felt somehow both insulting and comforting at once; confirmation, for better and worse, that nobody would ever know them as well as they knew one another.

So now, entering the white-noise-machine hush of the Survivors' Resource Center, Emma expressed minimal anxiety, checking in as Ara. Even when the cheerful receptionist asked for her insurance card, Emma simply reported that she'd lost it (which was true). It didn't matter anyway; the receptionist did a bit of typing and found that someone (Josie, obviously) had filled out the forms ahead of time.

Emma sat in a plush love seat in the empty waiting room. She leafed through an old *Us Weekly*. She dismissed a text from Josie (you need help packing?). She examined a potted plant by her elbow—a rubber tree—which seemed fake at first glance (too healthy, too shiny) but upon closer look appeared to be real.

"Araminta Tayloe?"

"Right here!" Emma jumped—ran almost—to follow her sister's name.

The therapist was late-fiftyish. White pants, striped shirt, camel-colored blazer, leather sandals, lime-green toenail polish. She introduced herself as Kimberly Pine, and invited Emma to call her Kim. She radiated the pleasant scent of an essential oil (sandalwood?) and an air of such calm authority that Emma had only plopped onto the couch, and already she felt her desperation lower an octave.

"You're going to get sick of me saying this, but there's no timeline when it comes to healing from trauma," Kim said. "There is no 'right' way to feel. Okay? So I hope it's alright with you, but I really want to make this clear up front. I'll never pressure you to discuss anything you don't feel comfortable discussing, got it? What's important to me, Araminta, is making sure you feel safe, and to help you become the author of the life that *you* want to live."

"Thanks!" Emma said, her leg jittering.

Josie had taken Emma to a few Al-Anon meetings, which felt therapy-ish, but this was her first one-on-one therapy session. The novelty, along with the deception, produced a blend of nerves and anticipation that she recognized from backstage, when a show couldn't get started soon enough.

"Many people find it helpful to start by telling me what brought them here today," Kim said. "So Araminta, would it be okay for me to ask—what brings you here today?"

Emma opened her mouth, closed it, and burst into tears.

She spent the next minute toggling between crying, laughing, and pulling wads of tissues from a box that Kim handed her. She apologized for being such a mess. She apologized for blabbing. She apologized for apologizing. She was so used to people (men) not listening to her, that she felt an immense gratitude when Kim assured her to take all the time she needed before continuing their conversation.

"Blabbing is my love language," Kim said. "I want to hear about anything and everything that's important to you. You're the expert in the life that is Araminta Tayloe. So please, whenever you're ready—blab on!"

Emma took a breath. She wiped her eyes and told Kim that she and her sister were in a fight. That was what brought her here today. They weren't talking. It sounded so stupid, she knew, they were grown women, but ugh, it was the dumb truth, and it was tearing her apart. "Estrangement runs in our family. I never met my grandparents. What if she never talks to me again? Did I mention that we're identical twins? I don't know if that matters."

"It matters if it matters to you. What's your twin's name?"

Emma didn't miss a beat. "Her name is Emma."

"Would it be helpful to tell me a little more about Emma?"

Emma shrugged. "Maybe. What do you want to know?"

"Whatever you'd like to share. What's she like? What kind of things does Emma like to do?"

Emma interlaced her fingers in her lap. "She's a musician. I am, too. We're in a band. Jojo and the Twins?"—the hint of a scrunch around Kim's eyes made it clear she didn't know them, so Emma steamrolled on—"We recorded this one album. It did pretty well. We were nominated for a Grammy. So Emma—she's always trying to get us there again. She believes in us. That's why she's demanding. She knows what we're capable of. *And* she knows it will help me, if we make another great record. Because when I'm greased—when I'm on—we're really good. There's nothing Emma loves more than playing together, just the two of us. It's her favorite feeling in the world. Even more than sex."

"Do you have similar feelings about making music with her?"

Emma could hear Ara at visitation, claiming she was done with the band. "I love making music. But the problem is there are other things I love more."

"Oh. Would you mind if I ask what?"

Emma glanced at the door. "I can tell you anything here?"

Kim nodded.

"I use heroin," Emma blurted. "I don't shoot. No needles. And pills. Oxy. Percocet. Vicodin." She spread her hands helplessly. "So. Yeah."

Kim leaned forward. "First of all, thank you, Araminta, for sharing this part of your life with me. I don't take it lightly. Secondly, Christ—let's be honest here, you don't need me telling you that there are all these ideas out there about substance use. People are quick to judge, aren't they? Quick to give advice, quick to tell you what to do? Well I want you to know that I'll never judge you. My job is to help you live the life you want. If that life includes a relationship with substances, I'd love your permission to help you use as safely as possible. And if you don't want to use substances anymore, we can talk about that, too."

"Oh, I'm not using. I quit. Sorry, I should've led with that. I haven't used in"—Emma worked back from Ara's arrest, then double-checked her math, incredulous so much time had passed—"eight days."

"Eight days! That's wonderful! How have those eight days been for you?"

"Terrible," Emma answered truthfully.

"I'm sorry to hear that. What's felt terrible?"

If Emma had been randomly selected from the audience at a Twins tribute show to join the band and cover "American Mosh," that may have approached the sense of disorientation she was riding. But hadn't that always been the case? A blurry twilight zone, where Ara ended, and she began?

"Withdrawal," she answered. "That's the hard part. Everything I'm missing."

Kim nodded. "Cravings are a beast. There's no denying it. If you'd like, we have some great recovery services here at the Center. Would you be okay with me connecting you with a peer recovery coach? And I could send you home today with naloxone. Narcan."

"No, no, no, I don't need any of that, I'm good." Emma felt guilty enough, posing as Ara, taking Kim's time and emotional concern. She wasn't about to sign up for resources that someone else might genuinely need. Plus, she had Narcan: a box in her tote bag, and another in her bike bag. Josie, long ago, had made sure they all kept it at hand. It was because of her foresight that Roman had been able to bring Ara back to life.

"Oh, I'm not saying you'll need it," said Kim. "Or that you'll use again. It's just good to have around. Maybe it will be for a stranger, or a friend? You never know."

"Thanks but I'm doing this on my own. Really, Kim. I got this."

Kim pursed her lips. She'd promised no judgment, but judgment was what Emma felt. If she insisted on giving her Narcan, or signing her up for services, Emma would walk.

But Kim backed down. She smiled. She asked Emma to tell her more about the band. "I get the sense that you and your sister have enjoyed some real success as musicians?"

Emma relaxed, relieved to talk about anything else. "It's been a while since the 'success' part."

"Do you have an idea that you're not successful now?"

"Oh yes. Very much so."

"Why do you feel that?"

"Our highest-paying gig last year was a guest DJ spot at a club in Providence? After *American Mosh*, we were opening for Hole, Rage Against the Machine. We had a road crew of ten dudes who'd set up our monitors and gear. And now . . . I haven't been able to make new music on my own in, I don't even know how long. The magic's gone. We were given a career on a silver platter, and I wasted it."

Kim uncrossed her legs and recrossed them the other way. "What does success mean to you?"

Emma shrugged.

"I'm no musician, but I imagine some bands might see success as the number of albums sold? Or being on the radio? Or making music you're proud of?"

"That," Emma said. "Making music that doesn't suck."

"And you have made music that doesn't suck, right? Did I hear you right earlier—you and your sister won a Grammy award?"

"Coldplay won. We were only nominated."

"Do you consider a Grammy nomination a success?"

"It's no Grammy."

"Are most bands nominated for a Grammy?"

"No. Not really."

"Okay, I'm going to level with you here, Araminta. You're the author of your life, but I'm reading the pages, and I see a musician who experienced enormous, early success, and although her band has suffered a downturn, despite her assault *and* the resulting trauma *and* the illness of substance use disorder, she remains committed to her art."

"Yeah. I guess." Emma had never *forced* Ara to stay in the band and work on a second album all these years. But she had pushed her hard to make better music. Why? Because she knew what Ara was capable of. Because she knew Ara better than Ara knew herself.

Because she would never leave her alone again. Because she owed her, and could never pay her back for what had happened, but she would keep trying.

"Can I share with you, something I've learned about trauma, talking with people over my years doing this? Would that be okay?"

"Sure."

"Trauma invades the creative spaces in our brain. It makes it incredibly difficult to access our imaginations. So it doesn't surprise me one bit that you've struggled making new music."

"Then what's Emma's excuse?"

"Has your sister also felt stuck creatively?"

"Ha. If only."

Kim raised an eyebrow, like, *Blab on,* so Emma blabbed: She told her about *Tigress,* the solo album she'd recorded when Ara was there but not there, hazed out in depression and opioid experimentation. She told Kim about the cringy album art she never should've okayed (Emma riding a tiger, the tiger riding a missile). She told Kim about the reviews she never should've read.

*The shocker is that anyone would voluntarily listen to* Tigress *when there are decades of recorded human music to choose from.*

*If I wanted preachy, I'd go to church.*

*The only disappointing thing about* Tigress *is that you feel like a bully, mocking something so feeble.*

*If this is Tayloe attempting creative independence from her sister, she should beg her twin to conjoin at the hip and never leave her side again.*

Their diehard fans may have long forgotten and forgiven, but Emma could not.

"That's the kicker," she told Kim. "Not only was it a total embarrassment that set our career back, but she can't get over it. Like, say she feels a creative spark? She just remembers *Tigress* and *psst,* the spark dies.

She wishes she could go back in time and undo it. But that's Emma's story—everything she touches turns to shit."

"Would it be okay, Araminta, if I asked you—"

"I just want her to stop ruining my life. And I don't mean just the band. I mean everything. Like our last show? Emma scheduled this gig in Maine. She thought it would be good for me. But I wasn't ready. I had a bad set. I embarrassed her. She was mad. We fought. And here we are."

Kim nodded. Emma couldn't bear the empty silence, so she filled it.

"And I guess you should know that she's my bagman. Was. Which I only mention because she fucked that up, too."

Kim said she was unfamiliar with the term, so Emma explained the job of buying, hiding, weighing, testing. She scanned Kim's face for judgment—almost wanting to be screamed at, as Josie had, told that she'd done something terrible—but Kim only asked about Emma's relationship with substances.

"Oh Emma doesn't touch that stuff," said Emma, who'd consumed nothing stronger than a quad latte in the years since Ara had been raped.

"Except when she buys for you," said Kim.

"I asked her to. Our mom lost her house in April. We were living with her. We had to find a new place. Moving is stressful. Everything was so unstable. I don't know. I just needed help. I asked Emma to keep it from me, give me a tiny bit less each day. I could've tapered off. But she went too fast. She wanted to get me clean sooner. That's what I mean. She ruins everything."

"Can I ask how long you and Emma have lived together?"

"Well, forever, pretty much."

"Do you ever play with other musicians? Other bands?"

Emma, just last month, had been invited to participate in a show with Carrie Brownstein and some old music friends who'd moved to the Northwest. When she'd asked if Ara could join, she was told they already had a drummer.

"Only if they include both of us."

"Why's that?"

"Because we're a band. That's what bands do. They band together."

"Not all bands."

"Our band."

Emma took a breath. She knew what Kim was insinuating. "People assume because we're twins, we're the same person, we don't do anything apart. It's not like that. We just care about each other. I love my sister. A lot."

"I can feel that love, Araminta. I can. And I can feel that it goes both ways. Would it be okay if I shared with you, something I've seen in loving families like yours? Sometimes, when our loved ones really care about us—say they know about a sexual assault, or substance use—it affects them, too. Sometimes they want to help, but they have their own ideas how, and those ideas aren't always helpful. Are you familiar with the term, 'survivor's guilt'?"

Emma felt her neck flush. "Yeah. I know a little about that."

For the Bogastow Junior High talent show, Emma and Ara had played "Stairway to Heaven," and all these years later, Emma could still slide a guitar into her lap and nail the ending solo, note for note. The music resided deep in her body, coiled like a spring, ready to launch into action. Ara's rape was like that. It lived in Emma's chest, ready to emerge at the slightest of invitations.

She told Kim, "In orchestra, in high school, our conductor, Ms. Martel, she always said the secret to a great orchestra isn't the notes, but the rests. As a drill, she'd have us count two, four, eight, sixteen bars of silence and then the entire orchestra would come in together on the same downbeat. My sister and I kept up that drill for a long time, the two of us. Twenty, fifty, a hundred bars of silence, and then—*boom*, away we go. When we were in synch, we were *so* in synch. But then it happened. And we weren't. And we aren't. And what if we never are again?"

Kim handed her the tissues. Emma was crying again.

"I know this is difficult, Araminta, no matter how much time has passed. There's no 'right way' to be, or feel, even years after your assault. Those decisions are yours and nobody else's."

Something—a power surge in the building?—caused the white-noise machine to momentarily dip in frequency. Emma stared at Kim's green toenails. She didn't like how she kept using the term "your assault." It wasn't only Ara's. It was Emma's, too.

She wiped her nose. Her throat ached. It was now or never.

"Emma made me go to this stupid Halloween party. And Emma, she made us dress like sluts—like literally, she wrote *slut* on our stomachs in lipstick, to make fun of the self-objectification of women on Halloween. Big surprise, zero dudes got it. When I had bad vibes, Emma told me to loosen up, let her get her kicks, and so Emma got wasted and Emma left me all alone to go fuck some guy and so Emma was not the one who got raped. So, yeah."

It was the first time she'd spoken the words aloud, and even in a bizarre roundabout way through her sister's avatar, she couldn't quite believe she'd done it. Kim asked some follow-up question.

"What?" said Emma.

"Is there a name or a phrase that comes to mind when you think of that experience, being left alone by your sister?"

"Um. Pissed. Resentful."

"Have you ever voiced this sense of resentment with her?"

"It's implied."

"Why do you think it's implied?"

"She thinks I still hold it against her."

"Do you?"

Emma fought back the tears. She dug a thumbnail into the back of her hand.

"Sometimes I'm like, *Fuck you Emma* for leaving me alone . . . and *Fuck you Emma* for pushing us so hard with the band . . . and *Fuck you Emma* for pretending to know what I've been through. Because she doesn't. When you're in it together, forever . . . you say dumb things, you make promises. If something bad happens to one, the other will follow right behind. You'll never be apart. You'll never leave each other. But life happens. And you can't go back."

Emma let out a ragged breath. She ripped a tissue from the box and blew her nose. She let out another big breath. She laughed. "That felt good. Thanks."

"Thank you for sharing."

"So what do I do now?"

"This. Being here, holding space, sharing what you've shared—you're well on the path to recovery. You might not get there today. You might not get there tomorrow. Other people will chime in, family and society will chime in, cravings and trauma will chime in. But you, Araminta, are the author of your life, and you get to take as long as you want to decide how you will write it."

Emma leaned back into the couch. She looked up at the ceiling. "I think I already know."

Kim smiled warmly. "I can't wait to read."

---

Back when Emma and Ara recorded the demo tapes that would eventually become *American Mosh*, they'd rented a sound studio in Cambridge that charged half price between midnight and 5 a.m. Emma could remember walking into the dawn after playing through those hours: delirious, ravenous, yet fulfilled, for they'd created something new that had never before existed.

Biking home from the Survivors' Resource Center, she experienced a similar feeling: wrung-out, but revitalized. The relief of speaking certain combinations of words aloud to another human being who was listening, actually listening, to those words—it was the difference between humming solo in the shower and singing with a band. She knew it was just one session, and one hour couldn't "fix" everything, whatever that meant. Still, she couldn't deny the warmth in her lower abdomen—an almost erotic exhilaration that she rode all the way back to Mattapan. She was supposed to be packing up to move into Josie and Dean's place, but there was no way she was about to disassemble her studio now.

In one take she laid down the minor chord progression that had been bouncing around her head for days. She ran it back through the synth engine, looped it, top-loaded the loop to 98 bars, and adjusted the tempo. She plugged her guitar into the mixer, and added power chords. Then she slipped her glass slide over her ring finger and repeated it. From here she practically dove over to her workstation where she added some reverb. A little more reverb. Plopped down on their mattress to listen. She cringed in anticipation.

It wasn't bad.

A fusion of electric slide guitar, layered strings, some plush synths. Echoes of *Mosh*, yet also fresh, new. *Good?* It surprised without overwhelming. Not too precious. Just one thing missing, the only feature in her workstation that she'd never explored.

"Sorry," she whispered to Ara's kit across the room, and then proceeded to build a custom drum track setup from scratch. A little embarrassing, how easy it was.

What her home studio could never replicate, however, were Ara's lyrics. Emma ransacked their moving boxes until she found a tote bag crammed with Ara's old journals and diaries. By piecing together scraps of poems and jots, she cobbled two verses and a chorus that she didn't completely hate. She plugged in her mic and laid down vocals, no words at first, just nonsense humming, then toying out the melody, working her way into the lyrics until she found an opening line that felt right. She doubled the vocals. Triple them? Yes. When *Tigress* chimed in, warning that she couldn't make music without Ara, that she was ruining their one chance at a jailhouse album, the same way she ruined everything she touched, she told *Tigress* to go fuck itself. She was sick of the story of herself as a one-hit wonder in progress. She continued stacking tracks until she'd built a chorus worthy of the Sistine Chapel. Then she mixed them down, isolating, taking out the breaths, deleting the background hum of the fridge.

By midnight she had a rough cut that got her more excited each time she listened. How many years since this had happened? She named the track: "When the Amen Breaks You."

She was ready to bounce it and start selling preorders. If only Ara would call.

It was a quandary. Emma could not publish without Ara's consent. They were a band with ⁵⁰⁄₅₀ splits on their catalogue. But Ara had created another quandary with a $100,000 price tag. The next visitation hours weren't until tomorrow afternoon, and who was to say that Ara would even show?

Quandaries-within-quandaries.

Unless Emma rewrote the story. She hadn't been there when a frat boy got Ara drunk and carried her to a bedroom. She hadn't been there when Ara overdosed. But that did not mean she would abandon her sister again.

She uploaded a thirty-second teaser to Awesong, then sent out a social media blast to make the album official. She even had a title that she liked: *Jailbreak*. She made green tea. She made toast with almond butter. She harmonized with the hum of the refrigerator as she chewed. She took a shower and conditioned her hair. When Josie called to pester her again about packing, Emma told her to check online.

*Jailbreak*, in two short hours, had already logged thirty-six preorders. She was doing this!

By 5 a.m. the *Jailbreak* count was eighty-eight and she was twelve bars into a second song, adding a reverb tail to a chorus she wasn't mad at, stacking tracks with the vocals. The power of creating music, spinning something from nothing, bending a note exactly to make it sing that perfect pitch. When else could you enjoy such control? She slipped on her headphones and flipped on her favorite amp. It hummed awake with that warm brassy smell. She nestled her guitar in her lap and experienced a manic lightness, as if the right set of notes, played just so, could make any story come true.

## Chapter 13

# Ara

Janice asks me to walk with her after morning count. We do a lap, passing a cluster of women by the perimeter fence, then Janice faces me and says I should listen to my lawyer.

"Take the deal, hon. Get out of here."

I tell her I need to hear back from Roman and get my mom's legal opinion. Also, hello client-attorney confidentiality?

"Your mom's gone, hon."

"She's not dead, Janice. Jesus. They're coming back."

"In a month? You want to be out by then, trust me. Take the deal."

The women next to us erupt in hoots and hollers. Across the marsh a worker in construction orange is hip-thrusting a safety cone. I hook a finger on a link in the fence and remind Janice that she *chose* to be here. "You could've been free the rest of your life, but you turned yourself in. You had to be here. You know what I'm talking about. I know you do."

"I could've gotten away with it, sure, the FBI took me off their list," Janice says. "But a human being died because of what I did. And Dean, he had no idea who I really was. Who *he* was. That's why I turned myself in. For me and for him. I was exhausted. I was anxious. I was depressed. I couldn't go on like that. That's why I had to be here. But you don't."

I tell her how crazy it can make you to have an identical twin. "You have no idea what it's like to share the same space—not just physically but mentally, emotionally, everything—with someone else for your entire life."

Janice holds up two fingers. "I spent two decades living a double life. For twenty years my name was Rose Peters. I know exactly what it's like to lose yourself in someone else."

"That's not the same. You had a fake identity to hide behind. I don't. You're not the only one who gets to have a break."

"And you've had a break. Good. Great. Now take the deal. Do you know how many anxiety meds I'm on? All of us are here. Get out while you can. Be with the people who love you. They're worried sick. This isn't fair to you, and it isn't fair to them."

*My mom doesn't seem too bothered,* I thought, but didn't say.

———

Kyla and I were zoning out after morning count, watching *General Hospital,* when CO Roberts rapped the door. Mylene—bless her young, ambitious heart—had set up a meeting with Kyla. Kyla ran a hand over her head to smooth her fly-aways. She looked at me. I wished her luck.

Room to myself, I turned off the TV. Did some writing. Napped. Started on yoga. I was in Down Dog when the intercom screeched Code 99. Locking doors cascaded down the hall. A minute later my door popped open. Kyla would've known who was coming, but to me the footsteps could've belonged to anyone.

He stopped in my doorway. Short cop hair. Big arms. Not bad looking.

"Hello," I said.

"Lieutenant Andrews." He introduced himself in a way that wasn't fundamentally creepy except that he smiled huge, and guards never smile. Something was different about him. His uniform had more patches. One on his chest: *Inner Perimeter.*

"Hi, Lieutenant Andrews." I smiled back, but my smile did not last long, because he was staring at me with this wolfish look as he stepped into my room and casually unbuttoned his shirt, first the top button, then the second.

The reason some people don't defend themselves, or run, or scream for help, is because fear floods the prefrontal cortex with stress chemicals that make us freeze, become sleepy, sometimes even black out. Survival by disassociation. Josie, back after it happened, made sure I knew that it wasn't my fault I hadn't fought. It was science. Okay, but I was never going to let it happen again. Next time I'd override my brain's fear circuits. I wouldn't freeze and do nothing. But nothing is exactly what I'm doing as he undoes the third button on his shirt, the fourth, the fifth. I couldn't move. Couldn't breathe. Felt myself fading.

I shot a hand to steady myself, finding the steel frame of my bunk. My pen was on the mattress. I grabbed it as he peeled off his shirt.

"No," I said, pathetic-sounding, and hating him for it. "Please. Don't."

He connected the look on my face to how I was holding the pen, like a tiny dagger.

"Oh my God. No. Ara, yo, I'm a fan!"

He hiked his undershirt. A tattoo on his torso: three bird skeletons. Our album art.

"My wife's got the same one!" He laughed, lifting his shirt higher and twisting to reveal a date in gangster-diploma font. "We were there when you opened for Rage, at the Centrum! I proposed right after!"

He flashes his wedding band, reuniforms himself, crisps his collar. All the while ticking off our early shows that he caught back in the day: Buffalo, Syracuse, North Hampton, Providence, Springfield. "Next time you tour, don't be surprised if Becca leaves me and the girls to be your groupie!" He laughs again.

I force a smile. "Super fans."

He shakes his head. "What a trip, Araminta Fucking Tayloe. Becca is going to flip her lid."

I force another smile. I'm trying to act casual as if this is any fanboy doing his fanboy thing, when inwardly, my body is reeling. Trembling with adrenaline. And fear. And anger. Angry at my stress chemicals for making me freeze. Angry at him for having no idea what he's just done.

So when he makes apologetic gestures at the cinderblock walls and says, "Sorry about the digs," and asks if there's anything I need, anything he can do for me, I don't have to think about it. He'd taken something from me, now I wanted something from him.

"Cigarettes," I said. "And dental floss."

He rubbed his head. Said he was thinking more like a real pad of paper, some actual pens? And then he gives the game away: "You know, to help you with *Jailbreak*."

"*Jailbreak?*"

He slips his phone from his pocket. "Isn't that what you're calling it?"

Sister Detox has been such a success that I hardly hear them in my head anymore, but a few taps of his screen and out pours Sister, her cathedral voice overcoming the tinny speakers.

> *Sometimes the Amen takes you.*
> *Sometimes the Amen breaks you.*

My words. I recognize them right away from a recovery journal I kept at New Pathways. Sister had stolen and published my private thoughts, without my consent. Then I hear something even more offensive. *She used a fucking drum machine.*

"Amen is right!" Andrews said. "Becca could not be more amped. We preordered the second it was up. Two copies!"

We share an awkward four-count of him smiling at me. I know what's going through his mind because I've seen it in a thousand fan-boys: he wants recognition, as a dude, for supporting a female musician. But all that's going through my mind is rage at him and Sister and everything. I ask for his phone.

A serious breach of protocol. Obvious by the way he steps out and glances down the hallway. I hold out my hand. He gives me what I want.

> *Jailbreak: an album of recovery and resistance, years in the*
> *making and more urgent than ever. Preorder for only $10 to*
> *FREE ARA NOW!*

A ticker shows 217 preorders. Pathetic compared to numbers we used to move, but that was with a label and a manager and a Top 10 song and—key, very key—a record. *Jailbreak* doesn't exist. Sister's selling an idea. An idea of me, wretched junkie drummer, who is "songwriting in her cell, thankful for the opportunity to stay sober and focused, and grateful to our fans during this difficult time."

*Barf.*

I swipe down to a not-terrible photo of me, from one of the Lollapaloozas. Another swipe brings me to the teaser-track, "When the Amen Breaks You." I hate-listen to it again.

The thing about Sister's voice is that it is very good, objectively so. Doesn't matter if she's onstage or entertaining herself in the shower. Even with *Tigress*, where there was plenty to cringe at, nobody could argue with her range. So although I hate to admit it, and although she could've used a less peppy chorus, and some delay on the verse vocals, and the bass is a little muddy, the song isn't bad.

Andrews grabs his phone and moves in for a selfie.

"No pictures," I say, stepping back.

"Come on, Becca will freak. Or how about a shot of you writing? You can pose like I caught you in the middle of your 'creative process.'"

His air-quotes rub me the wrong way.

"No. No pictures. I look like shit."

"You kidding? You look incredible, Ara. You've always looked incredible."

He was getting too comfortable. I reminded him that to fire up my "creative process," my brain needed nicotine. And floss.

He winced. "What about paper? Pens?"

"Listen, dude, I'm not feeling great. If you can't help me out, can I at least get some peace and quiet? Give me some space?"

"Watch your tone," he snaps. He taps a patch on his sleeve. "You're new. Take some advice—talk to lieutenants with a little respect." He turns to glance into the hallway, and the shift of shadows on his face makes him look deformed, almost. Old. Scowling. I tense, my prefrontal cortex flooding all over again.

Then he steps back in, and the shadows break. He smiles. "Relax. I'm just saying it won't kill you to be a little more polite. Let's not give anyone reason to think I'm playing favorites."

His walkie-talkie squawks. A door clangs somewhere down the hall.

He says, "You're welcome," and waits for me to respond. When I don't, he says, "Alrighty," with a little shrug. He leaves, giving a double-tap to my window after he closes the door. The bolt slides home.

The moment they let us out, I power walk to the dayroom (running's not allowed) to be first in the phone line. Hands still shaking, I dial my account and punch in Sister's number. Listen to the ring. Then a voice in my head whispers that this was her plan: she *wants* me to call to complain about the drum machine and my stolen lyrics and the whole stupid album.

Fight, play, fight.

Beat, rest, beat.

Love, hate, love.

Use, quit, use.

People in group are always saying that they've never felt so good as when they are on Vicodin or coke or crystal or whatever. I would tend to agree. The first time Roman introduced me to heroin, every pleasure neuron in my brain blinked the same neon message: *amen, amen, amen.* What people don't always share in group is that the darkness between the blinks is just as good—the absence of feeling. The bliss of nothing. No pain. No loss. No fear. That's the real black magic, and the craving for that darkness guts me so deeply as I'm standing in the dayroom, phone to my ear, that I know I'll do anything to get it back. Apologize to sisters. Beg for their help. Sell Dad's last record. Tell them whatever they want to hear.

Or I can honor my soul, remember my pain.

I hang up the phone, while I still have the choice.

# Chapter 14

# Josie

Josie lost her Quietest and Cleanest Tenant crown not long after Emma moved in. Three trips from the Mattapan apartment had transformed Josie and Dean's place into a poorly curated roadie museum: amps, power cords, looping pedals, guitars, road cases, mic stands, Emma's monitor and tech gear, Ara's kit. Dean wasn't thrilled to have a third roommate with so much baggage, Josie could tell, but he helped with the move anyway, doing most of the major lifting. He and Josie carried Emma's heavy keyboard, then he chugged a glass of water over the sink, and took off for a union meeting. All that remained back in the Mattapan apartment was the foam soundproofing, which, in retrospect, they should've grabbed, for soon after Dean left, Josie and Emma went supernova.

The catalyst was Emma's suggestion that Josie move into Dean's room so she could convert Josie's room to a home project studio. Emma walked through Josie's space like a Realtor, envisioning the potential of so much wasted square footage. "If I stripped your closet, it would make a *perfect* vocal isolation booth. What couple needs separate bedrooms anyway?" She started grabbing handfuls of Josie's clothes on hangers and tossing them onto the bed.

Josie answered by picking up Emma, carrying her into the living room, and shutting her bedroom door to keep her out. Emma could try using Ara's addiction to sell records, Josie said through the door, but if she thought she was getting a private room out of the situation, she could think again.

Emma accused Josie of always needing to be in control, which was true.

Josie accused Emma of enabling Ara's addiction and lying about it, which was also true.

Emma said that Josie cared more about being the one who helped Ara than she cared about Ara herself, which wasn't a hundred percent true, but a hundred percent hurt.

"Even if *Jailbreak* does sell enough—" Josie started.

"We're already at two hundred seventy-seven!"

"—what then? Ara gets out, you go on tour? Take a wild guess where that will land her. She needs help, not another album. You're setting her up for failure."

"Don't go writing the story of her failure. She can write her own story when she's out."

"You, my sweet neurodivergent sister, wrote that story for her the day you started buying her heroin."

"Would you please stop yelling at me for once?"

"You call this yelling?"

"Shut up." Emma went quiet. "I hear my phone. Where's my phone?"

The buzzing was coming from Josie's room. Emma barged back in and together they pawed through the heap of clothes on the bed. Emma found it. She glanced at the screen, wailed, and flashed it at Josie's face.

Missed call. Massachusetts Department of Corrections.

"Look what you did!"

"Me?" said Josie. "Me?"

Emma fell to her knees and slammed a fist onto the floor. She slammed it again. The outburst startled Josie. She put a hand on Emma's shoulder—"Hey, calm down, you're going to break a finger. I'm sure she'll call right back"—when there came a knock at the door. A deep voice: "Everything okay in there?"

Josie opened the door, expecting Fabio, or a cop. It was one of the bros from apartment 2C.

"Ian?" Emma got up from the floor. "What are you doing here?"

"I live downstairs. What are you doing here? Are you okay?"

"I am now." Emma pushed Josie aside. "Let's go."

Josie watched her sister lead her neighbor down the hallway, and then she grabbed the Volvo keys off the counter, ready to drive to MCI-Bogastow. Emma might run off, but Josie would not. Then she remembered that visitation hours would be over by the time she arrived. Also, Emma had driven all the way there the other day, only to have Ara ghost her. Who was to say it wouldn't happen to Josie? Her phone pinged. Dean. He'd be out late. Drinks with the union crew.

Josie messaged back that they'd missed a call from Ara, could he ask his mom to tell Ara to try them again?

Dean responded with a thumbs-up.

Josie stepped over a snake's nest of guitar cables, and made for the fridge. She felt bloated and a twinge nauseous, yet also somehow hungry. She ate a snack of peanut butter and apple slices, then emptied her stomach in the toilet. The Griffinport curry had done lasting damage on her GI tract. Of course it wasn't just the curry. It was stress, for she'd failed to convince Bertie to come back, and she couldn't understand why Ara was avoiding them. It was regret, for taking it all out on Emma. It was loneliness, for although Josie knew she could never compete with a bond between identical siblings who'd spent nine months hanging out in utero, it still hurt that Ara had called Emma and not her. It really hurt.

Josie held the sink. She rinsed her mouth, looked in the mirror, and told her reflection what needed to be done: cut off the supply of cortisol to the bloodstream, now. Yoga, or a jog, or a pint of mint chocolate chip. Her body decided for her, sending her back to the floor.

This time, the post-vomit endorphin rush allowed for a ray of lucidity that cut through her bruised ego: the most important thing was bringing Ara home. And as much as Josie knew that *Jailbreak* was a risky plan that could send her sister on another spin through the recovery-relapse ringer, at the end of the day, she was a scientist who respected the evidence.

THE EVIDENCE:

1. *Jailbreak* was a better plan than Josie's best plan, which was maximum credit card cash advance ($2,000 at 30% APR)

plus maximum loan from Fa$tCa$h payday loan ($1,500 at 350% APR), plus Kelly Bluebook value of their Volvo ($1,900), which got them nowhere near $10,000.

2. Her sisters' success as a band had proof of concept. A bit outdated, but solid.

3. The principle of Occam's razor worked equally well for solutions as it did for problems: the simplest was almost always the best.

To this list, she added one more: *Jailbreak* had been her idea originally, even if she'd first mentioned it sarcastically.

She plugged in Emma's turntable and brushed her teeth to the one record that Ara had not sold from their dad's collection. Much of it was experimental stuff that didn't do much for Josie, but the first song on the B-Side, "Good Vibrations," always left her feeling better, upbeat, a little tingly. When the song ended, she switched off the turntable, rinsed her mouth, and got into bed. She was obsessively reloading the *Jailbreak* page (307 preorders . . .), and the *A.R.C.* feed (international waters, 15 knots, seas calm), and researching in-state rehabs that would accept MassHealth, when she heard Emma return. Sound of sandals kicked off. Vinyl sliding into cardboard sleeve. Springs groaning from the pullout couch.

The couch was a behemoth, impossible to set up alone. Josie put down her phone. "Get in here. You're sleeping with me."

Emma came into the room. Josie flipped back the covers. Emma took off her shorts and let down her hair and crawled in.

"I found subletters," she said.

"Already?"

"I can be convincing."

Josie asked, "Did Ara call you back?"

"No. You?"

Josie shook her head. "We'll go to visitation tomorrow."

Emma was quiet. Then she said, "I'm scared, Jo," and Josie felt her shudder. She curled herself around Emma, spooning her from behind.

Leafcutter ants, when threatened with torrential downpour, work heroically to plug entrances to their colony. Josie, during her Fulbright

Fellowship in Nicaragua, had observed the feat many times in the neotropical rainforests, and it never got old: thousands of ants (sisters) rolling balls of dirt between their mandibles, sealing their home to protect it from flooding. Josie was one of them, her colony under attack. All remaining (non-incarcerated) members had to band together under one roof. Yes, she would resent picking blond hairs from the shower drain and tripping over power cords, but as long as Emma was here, she was safe. And safe felt good.

"Did you eat dinner? I can make you something."

Emma didn't answer. Her body twitched, already drifting to sleep.

Josie nudged her. "Em? You can have my room. I'll move my stuff out tomorrow."

"I'll help you."

"No. You have an album to make. But you can go take a shower. You smell like sex."

# Chapter 15

# Ara

Good news bad news.

———

Good news: returned from afternoon yard time to find small mound of gifts on my pillow.

> 2 real pens (blue, Bic)
> 1 yellow legal pad (*Rock On* scrawled on top page)
> 100 unwaxed yards of dental floss in white plastic container

Bad news: should've warned Kyla that Public Defender Shin doesn't pull punches.

What I gathered was this: Mylene had told Kyla that she has zero chance of custody, and Kyla blacked out at the news, cracking her head on the table. Hence the Code 99. They rushed her to Health Services where she spent the day. Now I'm taking care of her like she did for me. Rubbing her back, feeding her Crunchers. Have never seen someone sober so vacant and numb. Her girls are growing up without her, she says. She's missing everything, her life's a sad joke, they'd be better off without her . . .

I rub her back and say it'll be okay, even as I look around, a little desperate for something to make it okay. Then I remember. I reach onto my bunk.

"Ta-da!"

She turns the floss in her hand and says she can't use it. "I have tight teeth. I need the ribbon floss. This stuff hurts my gums."

"Oh."

"But thank you!" she brightens. "Listen to me, whining. I'll make it work." She sticks the plastic container under her pillow.

"You don't have to, Kyla."

"I want to, it's so kind," she says, and I don't argue, because she's tearing up, and I'm just glad she's feeling something.

————

A long night in Room 13, Kyla quietly weeping below me. Her mental health was the first thing I brought up with Mylene when we met.

"I warned you I don't do family law."

"You couldn't have let her down easier?"

"No judge is giving custody to someone who shoots her spouse in front of her children. In my professional legal opinion."

"She said it was self-defense."

"I'm sure it was. But that comes with her prior record, and child endangerment, and what seems like some not-unserious mental health concerns."

"That sounds complicated."

"Welcome to my very fun life."

"Mental health concerns?" I ask.

"She smashed her head on the table," Mylene says, running a hand over the rounded edge.

"I thought she blacked out."

"Three times?" Mylene said.

Neither of us say anything for a moment. Then she unclasps her bag. Passes me a note.

*A-*

*Wish I could roll over for you but they have me with charges on charges. I'm looking at time. I have to fight. But you do what you need to do. Say what you need to say. I'll be okay. Get out of there and have fun for both of us.*

*Rage on,*
*-R*

*PS: Gangs rejected me. Too baller.*
*PPS: Country club in here. Cake.*

I read the note twice. Then I folded it in half and said, "I can't do it."

Mylene slammed her fist. "He's giving you the green light!"

"Should you be reading my mail?"

She pulled a planner out of her bag, flipped a page to September, and jabbed at a date in the late teens. "And that's just deposition. Your trial will be later. Are you ready to stay here until then?"

Outside, in visitation, someone was microwaving chocolate chip cookies from the vending machines. The fresh-baked smell made its way through the glass.

"Roman saved my life," I say.

"And you think he wants you to throw it away now?"

"I'm not throwing anything away. My sister and I have a plan."

She rolled her eyes. "*Jailbreak?*"

"You know about it?"

"My aunt is excited, to say the least. But I'll tell you now, raise ten grand, raise a million, you'll still have to go to trial and put your future in the hands of twelve people who lack the fortitude and guile to evade jury duty."

"I'll be fine."

She shoved her planner in her bag and waved to the guard. "Call me when you're ready to let me do my job."

I went through the cough-and-bend-overs with CO Jenks, who seemed particularly irritable, jamming her latex-gloved fingers around my mouth until I gagged. I dressed, then walked back to Room 13, hoping Kyla was still at her cleaning shift so I'd have a moment alone. But the room wasn't empty.

Lieutenant Andrews was sitting on Kyla's bunk, reading my journal. Reading you. He tapped one of your pages and looked up, grinning like he'd won a raffle.

"*Not bad looking?* Alrighty. I'll take it."

I felt drunk, I was so mad. I lunged. He stood, quickly, and held me back with a forearm to my chest. With his other arm, he raised you overhead.

"Give me that! That's mine!" I tried to move him. He was laughing.

"Technically nothing in here is yours, and *this* is contraband." He waved a pen in my face, then lowered his voice. "But between us, I'm happy to see that you're putting my presents to use."

"Give it back." I heaved, willing myself not to cry.

He lowered you, then snatched you away just as I reached.

"I'm sorry!" he laughed again, like it was a game. "I was just dying to see how *Jailbreak* is coming along. There are some killer lyrics here! You're so talented, Ara. Seriously."

I could've turned and walked to the dayroom—my door was wide open—but this was my room he'd invaded. Those were my words in his hands. My vision went blurry with rage.

"Free advice—don't write about your arrest. You're implicating your-self. You should flush all these pages. Though it did sound like a *very* fun casino night. I've never done ketamine. What's it like?"

I held out my hand. "Give it back to me."

"Can I get a please?"

Four measures of uncomfortable silence. Then he smiled and handed you over.

"Not even a thank-you," he muttered. "*Tsk-tsk.*"

I clasped you to my chest and turned sideways for him to leave.

He walked to the doorway, but didn't step out. He crossed his arms, lingering like a fanboy after a show who can't take the hint. "What about the floss? Is it what you wanted?"

"No."

"No?"

"That cheap shit hurts my teeth. I need ribbon floss."

His smile wavered. His bulk took up the entire doorway.

"Excuse me?" he said.

122 - NICK FULLER GOOGINS

The back of my neck tingled. "Nothing. Forget it."

"No. Please. What else can I do for you?"

"You can get me some ribbon floss—"

Two fast steps from the doorway. One hand around my throat, the other around my wrists, cuffing my arms at my waist. All your pages went fluttering to the floor. My mind stopped working. Pixilated with fear.

"This isn't a fucking hotel." He spoke through his teeth, his breath hot against my face. "I can make your life miserable. Do you have any idea what some of the COs do here? And here I am, a fan! Bringing you *presents*. Chipping in to fund your fucking bail. And you can't even give me one please? Not even a single thank-you?"

Aftershave rolled off him in waves. His hand tightened slightly on my throat.

"Say *thank you*."

"Thank you."

"*Thank you, Lieutenant Andrews.*"

"Thank you, Lieutenant Andrews."

Sister dropped out of college with me after my assault. We'd just signed our record deal with GhostTrain, so there was no reason to stay at Berklee. Josie took a semester off, too. We all moved home. I wanted to take scalding baths, and buzz my hair so nobody could ever grab it again, and sleep and sleep. But Josie made me eat, go for walks, and recondition my brain.

Soldiers can train to stay calm in battle. Boxers can drill away the flinch reflex. Anyone, with patience, can rewire their synapses to circumvent the stress chemicals. Jedi Mind Training, Josie called it. Pressure points. Breathing exercises. Getting the tiniest bit stoned. Repeating the mantra: *Next time I scream, next time I run, next time I fight, next time he's done.* Fans will recognize this as the bridge on "Round Two," a song that isn't our most popular, but one of my favorites. I've played it thousands of times and I'm proud to say it finally stuck: the moment he released my throat, my training overrode my stress chemicals. My prefrontal cortex hurtled back from the land of fear and into the land of keeping Ara alive.

I screamed my goddamned head off.

The noise jolted him. He let go of me and practically ran out. He stopped in the hallway and looked both ways. Our unit wasn't in lockdown. Anyone could've walked by.

I picked up the pen he'd dropped. I grabbed the other pen where I'd stashed it under my pillow. I held them like drumsticks. Like swords. My chest was heaving. Big moaning rasps. He held out his hands like I was a wild animal. Which I was.

"Calm down! Holy shit, just shut up. Be quiet. I'm only trying to help you. Why do you have to make everything so difficult?"

"Go. Away." My voice like low brass in my throat.

What he said next I couldn't make up if I tried. His voice went all whispery, basically talking to himself: "I have a wife. I have two daughters. I'm a feminist."

Then he nodded and he left.

All those stress chemicals I'd overrode? They came surging back. Levees shattered.

I shook and shook. Tears and snot.

But believe it or not, this might not be the worst thing that happened today. Still shaking, I picked your pages off the floor, then lined up our shampoos and conditioners, stacked Kyla's packages of Crunchers like logs in a woodpile, squared the TV. Your basic manic tidying to keep from losing your shit. I went to remake Kyla's bed. As I stretched her sheet over the mattress, my knuckles glanced something hard. I felt around. A slit in the mattress. Inside, the container of floss she said she couldn't use.

But she was using it. She'd woven 3-ish inches. The remaining strands were splayed. I fished them out of the mattress and saw that she was weaving a rope. Not nearly long enough to get her over the perimeter fence, but plenty enough to hitch on the top rail of our bunk.

I slumped to the floor, my back against the toilet privacy wall. Exactly where I'd been during my first hours here, Kyla mothering me. I saw those first hours unfold backward into my life as one long string of people taking care of me, cleaning up my shit, and losing something of themselves in the process. Sister. Josie. Roman. Janice. Kyla. All the peer recovery coaches. All the therapists. Even my dad, who I hardly remember. He was a photographer, always behind the camera, so we have almost no pictures of him. All we had were his records. Janis Joplin, Jefferson Airplane, Otis Redding. Zeppelin, Bowie, Dylan, Hendrix. The Who, The Beach Boys, The Beatles, The Stones. A great collection, in pristine condition, worth enough to keep me and Roman high for weeks. After I got back from New Pathways, I spent months combing thrift stores, posting online, trying and failing to find the vinyl that his hands had touched. That one window we had. How do you make up for something like that?

My legs were still spasming. I could feel Andrews's hand on my throat. I wanted my dead dad. I wanted Mom. Sisters. Roman. I wanted to take the deal, any deal, so I could get out of here and slide back into my old patterns and a never-ending Amen. No. I decided right there that I couldn't just leave and let Kyla hang herself. I couldn't turn on Roman. I couldn't let Andrews get away with what he did. I'm done sitting around, waiting for other people to fix everything while I burn down their lives and waste their money and destroy their souls. It's time for me to fix things on my own. I'm a survivor. I don't have to run from trouble. I can make trouble myself.

So

    let's

        fucking

           go.

# Bertie & Walt

# Chapter 16

# 1964–1965

*Lyndon B. Johnson, Executive Order 11241, August 26, 1965: Married men will no longer be eligible for 1-A draft exemption.*

The order, signed at noon, will not take effect until midnight. Word spreads. Single men have twelve short hours to get married and avoid the draft. The deadline is a coalition builder like none other. Maoists pool gas money with Trotskyites. SDSers loan cars to hippies. They speed over the Bay Bridge. East Coasters are out of luck. No courthouse east of the Rockies will issue a marriage license without a waiting period or blood test. But those on the left bank of America have a chance. They have Las Vegas.

Grooms are married in blue jeans. A shared veil is passed between brides. The county courthouse is two blocks from the neons of the Strip. Newlyweds emerge, the crowd erupting in hiphiphoorays. Some couples have been casually dating before tonight. Some happened to be engaged. Most, however, are like Roberta Tayloe and Walter McCannis: New Left acquaintances. Bertie is eighteen. Walt, twenty-two. They have failed to stop the carnage in Vietnam, but now, on this warm Nevada evening, clock edging toward midnight, the line inching up the courthouse steps, they can do something. They will deprive the American war machine of one more soldier.

The court clerk approaches with a clipboard. Bertie prints her information, deciding to keep "Tayloe." Walt scuffs his sandals on the sidewalk, itchy with unexpected joy. Bertie is a small firecracker of a woman. Impassioned, golden-haired, brilliant. He snaps a blossom from a bougainvillea to fix in her hair. She does the same for him, pinning a splash of pink above his ear. They laugh, nervous, excited. They are not waiting for the future. They are making it.

———

They first met on the day of the Savannah Yacht and Country Club Ball. Bertie had run away. Debutante satin hanging in her closet, she'd hitch-hiked to St. Augustine to see the Reverend Dr. King. She had marched the same streets as the great man, she watched a waterfront motor lodge turn from serving hamburgers to violence, she choked on tear gas.

As she was coughing, a photographer stopped to ask if she was al-right. He gave her a handkerchief. He poured water from a bottle, and offered to flush the sting from her eyes.

Shaggy, broad-shouldered, muttonchopped. He was visiting on assignment, he said, and hadn't seen many white girls supporting the struggle down here. "If you want to fight the good fight and really get your kicks, come to the Bay. California's birthing a whole new world." He asked permission to take her picture. She said yes.

"I'm Roberta, by the way. You can call me Bertie."

"Right on. I'm Walter. Walt."

She went to touch up her hair, but he told her to stop. He brought his camera to his face. "Don't change anything. You're perfect. Just like that."

*Click.*

She hitchhiked home, returning late, tired but electrified. She climbed the sycamore into her bedroom and slept. Her father was at the breakfast table the next morning, shoveling grits. Her mother had Bertie's diary, the lock pried open. She cleared her throat.

> *I just finished the* Diary of a Young Girl. *It was amazing. Anne Frank doesn't hold anything back. If father was Jan Gies, he wouldn't have hidden the Franks. He would've turned them over to the Nazis. He probably would've been a Nazi. He and mother both. They don't care about anyone who's not in the Yacht Club. I was born in the wrong time and into the wrong family.*

Roberta was a Tayloe, her mother said, and she ought not to forget it. She was a lady. Not a Bolshevik. She'd disgraced them last night, skipping the Ball—the most important night of the year. Poor Jonathan Landry, the young man who'd pinned her. "You will make your apologies, foremost to your father who *fought* the Nazis, with medals to show for it."

Bertie would not apologize. Not to people who considered the Ball the most important night of the year. Tell that to the students at Woolworth's. To Dr. King. The Vietnamese. Anyone with a heart. "How can you call yourself Christians when—"

Her father reached across the table, hit her with the back of his hand, then returned to his grits. Last month he'd burned her copy of Dr. King's *Strength to Love* in the sink. It shocked Bertie, then it didn't. This was what the Tayloes did. They owned slaves. They captained the Confederacy. They fundraised for George Wallace. They took. They destroyed.

Meanwhile Jan and Miep Gies risked execution to hide the Franks. Harriet Tubman returned thirteen times to the South. Dr. King continued to march despite the threats.

The weak, if they wanted, could show the strong they were not weak. Her cheek still stinging, Bertie spooned a lump of strawberry jam from the jar, and sent it over the breakfast table in a neat arc that ended at her father's face.

He knocked back his chair. He circled the dining room in slow strides. Bertie saw herself a Gies, a student at a Woolworth's counter, anyone but a Tayloe. Her father could hit her. Her family could disown her. Nothing mattered. Bertie had discovered the strength to love.

---

Mills University was a compromise between The Briarwood Preparatory School for Girls, where her mother wanted Bertie to follow in her footsteps, and Mississippi, where Bertie wanted to register Negro voters. That Mills was in Oakland, 3,000 miles from Savannah, seemed to relieve Bertie's parents as much as it relieved her. When Bertie wasn't studying, she joined marches, walked picket lines, supported every spark that might leap from the embers to ignite a new world.

Her roommate Tess had taken her to a Free Speech Movement rally at Berkeley when Bertie saw him: the photographer from St. Augustine. A student leader had climbed on a commandeered police car in Sproul Plaza, waving his arms like a conductor to the sea of demonstrators. History was being made, but Bertie was only trying to get the photographer's attention. What was his name? His camera lens turned her way, then lowered.

"Bertie! It's you!"

"Hello Mr. Handsome?" Tess whispered.

Bertie suddenly remembered. "Walt! Hi!"

Walt pushed through the crowd just as the riot police came stomping in with their nightsticks. He took the press badge off his lapel, stuck it on Bertie's blouse ("My First Amendment shield"), and grabbed her hand, whisking her and Tess to safety.

They crossed paths again at a Berkeley Draft Board march, Walt photographing through the smoke, then adding his draft card to the flames. A month later, Tess had tickets to the Beach Boys at the Coliseum, and Bertie could've sworn she saw him, dancing near the stage. Then a Vietnam Day Committee meeting, Bertie collecting signatures and money, Walt threading the crowds, camera to his face. Bertie watched him shoot Jerry Rubin, Abbie Hoffman, Norman Mailer. He had a way with people, a knack for drawing smiles. Even grouchy Mailer cracked up.

He caught up to her on Telegraph Avenue after the meeting. Could he walk with her? She hid a smile. Yes. He asked about school. She'd declared prelaw, she told him, on track to becoming a "people's lawyer" so she could unlace the knots of hatred and supremacy that men like her father had tied. She hadn't told many in California about the Tayloes of Georgia, their plantations, the Confederacy, her terrible inheritance. Strolling with Walt, it so easily tumbled out.

Walt, in turn, told her about the McCannises of Ireland, slave masters of a different ilk, he called them. Exporting beef during the potato famine. Enough misery for a hundred generations. Walt was from Maine. He'd accidently fallen in with the Portland Catholic Workers, mistaking their soup kitchen for a diner one hungry afternoon. He joined a radical lay study group, completed classes for Baptism, received the Eucharist, chipped in when an IRA representative passed a hat at a teach-in at USM. To Walt's Catholic-hating father, this was the final insult, arming the very hoards whom the McCannises had spilt blood fighting.

Walter could be a McCannis or a papist, his father declared, but not both.

Walt traded his blue jeans for robes. Took his vows. Two years of novitiate study at the Shadowbrook Seminary in the Berkshires.

Bertie turned to him in surprise. "You were a priest?"

Walt laughed. He'd joined the Jesuits for a theology of revolution. Vatican III. The Jesus he loved was the Jesus who overturned the tables in the temple. Although the Jesuits were the most open-minded society in the Church, the Master of Novices told Walt after his second year, perhaps they were not quite open-minded enough for Brother Walt?

The Jesuits, in addition to teaching Canonical Law and Biblical Archeology and Gregorian Chant, had also trained Walt in shutter speeds and aperture settings. He took his photography skills to San Francisco, as far from New England as he could get. He found a room at Oakland's Catholic Worker House and lucked into a job with the *Chronicle*, shooting protests and marches.

"And concerts?" Bertie said. She thought she'd seen him at the Beach Boys concert at the Coliseum, she said.

"Yes! What a show! Is there anything better than live music?"

They continued chatting as they turned from Telegraph Avenue, the blocks of colorful houses. A trail led into the hills. The spicy scent of eucalyptus. A grassy overlook. The smokestacks and shipping cranes of Oakland. The foggy mirror of the Bay. Walt lit a loose joint.

They smoked. They laughed. About Abbie Hoffman's hair. About Norman Mailer's breath. Bertie pointed out that the Vietnam Day Committee was led by men who did all the camera mugging, and run by women who did all the envelope stuffing. Walt agreed, and asked her opinion on how they could reform leadership. He asked again for her permission to take her picture. Bertie was used to Southern chivalry, but this was different. She tilted her chin to the sun. "Shoot away."

*Click.*

But then he overstepped, inviting her that night to see the Warlocks, local legends—Jerry Garcia, Bob Weir—and when she said she was busy, he said Jefferson Airplane was playing Thursday at the Fillmore with a musician from Texas—Janis Joplin—"you *have* to hear her voice, Bertie, I'll get us tickets."

Bertie stood. She brushed grass from her pants. She'd immigrated to the Bay to work for the struggle and a 4.0, not an MRS, she said. She saw where this was going. First a show, then dinner, then Walt pinning her like Jonathan Landry at the Yacht Club. She saw Mr. and Mrs. Walter McCannis, their pleasant comfortable life while Negroes were beaten and Vietnamese napalmed and—no, she had a history term paper, an SDS meeting, a volunteer shift with the NLG's Legal Referral clinic. How could they birth a new world by getting stoned and going to shows? LBJ was about to double the draft call, for fuck's sake.

The pot was speaking. Bertie never swore.

Walt just nodded and said she made a good point.

They watched the Bay turn gold in the setting sun. Young and angry and enraptured in the urge to right ancient wrongs, Bertie would soon return to the Mills library, and Walt to the darkroom, and they may have parted ways forever, martyring this seed of happiness before it had a chance to sprout.

Fortunately, LBJ.

Fortunately, Executive Order 11241.

Fortunately, Las Vegas.

———

They share their first kiss before a bleary-eyed judge who tells the love-birds to wrap it up already; he's been marrying couples for seven hours straight, and midnight's drawing near. But they linger. There is no guilt here. They are doing right. Under such circumstances—and only such circumstances, they believe—happiness is allowed.

## Chapter 17

# 1965–1969

Bertie is a wife. She moves from the Mills dorms into Walt's room at the Catholic Worker. Walt uses a thin mattress for a bed. Alphabetizes his records. Works three breakfast shifts a week, helping to feed Oakland's hungry. The Catholic Workers live in voluntary poverty. Bertie finds it strangely appealing, the clutter-free life of a monk. This past summer, Watts rioted, Pakistan invaded India, Johnson doubled the draft call. But here in Walt's room—*their* room—there is order. Bertie hangs her portrait of Dr. King above the record player. She adds her books to the shelves. All 200 square feet of the room make perfect sense.

They attend a United Farm Workers rally one afternoon in the Mission, then honeymoon in North Beach. A touristy Italian restaurant. Checkered tablecloth, plastic flowers, serenading mustached server: so tacky it's entertainment. After dinner, they walk the crests and troughs of Russian Hill, fantasizing where they will someday take a real honeymoon. Cuba, they decide. Walt's arms go around her waist. The views of the Bay. The lights of the city. Then shouting, a sudden high-pitched cry. Walt bolts. Bertie runs after him.

A man holds a woman by the wrist, yelling at her to get into a car. His haircut says military, high and tight. The woman's dress strap is broken.

Walt pulls up, short of breath. "Everything alright here?"

"Mind your own business."

Walt asks the woman, "Do you know this man?"

"She's my wife, faggot. Get lost."

"Miss, do you need help?"

Bertie turns the corner just in time to see the sucker punch. Walt collapses. Bertie leaps onto the man's back. She pounds his head, screams for him to leave her husband alone. *Husband.* She's not alone in screaming it—the other woman is yelling at Bertie to leave *her* husband alone. The woman claws at Bertie's hair, clubs her with a purse. Walt staggers to his feet, barrels ahead. It's a brawl, Bertie's first. She and Walt lose badly.

They shuffle away, clothes torn, lips swollen, Walt's eye already bruising. They are battle-weary but changed, for Bertie has learned something tonight about Walt: He will abandon her to help a stranger in need. *Whoever needs love the most.* This may have troubled most young wives, Bertie knows, but she is not most young wives. Walt's selflessness only increases his attraction. She stands on tiptoes, kisses his swollen cheek. He winces.

"Wouldja look at these two wayward soldiers of the night!"

A whistle of appreciation from the alley by City Lights bookstore. Two men smoking. One thickly bearded with glasses. The other skinny, boyish, a polka dot shirt.

"Whodja lovebirds kill today? LBJ?"

Bertie laughs. "We got in a fight—"

"With another couple," Walt says quickly. "Not each other. Tonight's our honeymoon."

The bearded man howls with laughter. "You see, Bobby? This is why we stay alive and grow old! Because everything weird will happen and it will be good. Blessed be the peaceful. Blessed be the blessed. May your two hearts beat together as one revolutionary cell."

The boyish man strikes a set of finger chimes. "Om Shanti Shanti. Caw, caw, caw."

Walt, when they're out of earshot, whispers that the bearded man was Allen Ginsberg, and the other was Bob Dylan. He's starstruck. Ginsberg and Dylan just blessed their marriage!

Bertie fixes Walt's collar. It was very sweet, she agrees, but they don't need any blessings. They'll be just fine, making their new life together.

———

They don't need blessings, but they decide to ask anyway. A bottle of wine before calling, to settle their nerves. Their parents will be upset,

Bertie predicts, but ultimately supportive. She is an only child, after all, as is Walt. The strength of their love will heal old wounds. She believes this wholeheartedly. She could not be more wrong.

Walt and his father haven't spoken in five years. His father makes it clear this conversation will be the last. He calls Walt a coward for hiding behind the skirts of a girl to avoid the draft. The only sin worse than fighting for the enemy, he says, is dodging the battle altogether.

As for Bertie, if her marriage announcement is an olive branch, the disappointment from her parents is a woodchipper. Eloping is one thing. Eloping with a Yankee-commie-draft-dodger is another. Roberta will come home at once, or they will cut her off.

Cut me off, she says. She doesn't want their blood money. She doesn't need them.

She slams the receiver. Walt puts his arms around her. They are kneeling by the bed, as if in prayer. Bertie breathes hard. The past is collapsing, the future expanding. There is sadness in separation. But there is something exhilarating in it, too.

----

They demonstrate against the troop trains. They rally to free Huey. Bertie leads the Mills SDS chapter with her friend Tess. She staffs the Lawyers Guild's equality center. She and Walt host big meetings at the Catholic Worker House, arguing and dreaming and smoking until the birds wake. So many causes. So much work. Where to focus? Where to serve? They ask themselves, again and again: *Who needs love most?* They chase exhausting days with nights at the Fillmore, the Avalon, the Longshoreman's Hall. Jefferson Airplane, the Dead, Janis Joplin. They sweat and spin. They pass Kesey's acid test with flying colors.

Walt is sent on assignment to shoot the rebellion in Newark. The rebellion in Detroit. The march on the Pentagon. Bertie's typewriter keys go quiet in his absence. She listens to his records, skims his worn, dog-earned copy of Dorothy Day's autobiography. She stubs her toe on the bed frame when the phone rings. It's not Walt. It's Tess, wondering why Bertie missed tonight's meeting. They voted to send $100 to the Panthers. Groovy?

"Groovy. What're you doing?"

Bertie adores Tess. Tess throws "Political Orphan" parties, as Bertie and Walt are not the only forsaken Bay youth. Tess's father works for Dow Chemical, manufacturer of napalm, Agent Orange. As much a war criminal as McNamara, Tess says. Tess's parties have jugs of wine. Pot. An excellent sound system. A backyard firepit. A swimming pool. Many ways to forget. Which Bertie needs. She scares herself with how much she craves Walt's evening call, an assurance that he is safe. A young wife with no income of her own, unable to concentrate on anything but the phone on the wall. She laughs at herself: What would Betty Freidan say? She declares herself the worst feminist in Berkeley. She would never ask Walt to stay out of trouble. She loves him because he can't. She needs him. They are a revolutionary cell of one.

---

Spring break, Bertie's junior year, Walt is sent to Memphis to cover the Poor People's Campaign, the sanitation workers' strike. Bertie joins him. She drinks beer on Beale Street, holds her nose at the mounds of garbage, sits in a pew at the Mason Temple while Walt kneels up front, shooting roll after roll of film.

"We've got to give ourselves to this struggle until the end," Dr. King bellows from the pulpit. "I'm happy tonight. I'm not worried about anything. I'm not fearing any man."

They're eating grilled cheeses at a diner the following day when from the kitchen comes the crash of dropped dishes. Someone turns up a radio. The terrible news. Walt grabs his camera bag. Bertie throws some bills on the table, catches up to him as he hails a cab. From all directions, the cry of sirens. Gnarled vines of smoke climb the clean blue sky.

---

With Dr. King's assassination, the weather shifts. No more dancing at the Fillmore, no more merrymaking with the Pranksters. Too much work to be done. Too many causes to serve.

*Who needs love most?*

Everyone. Everything.

The urgency is a room of broken glass that pops underfoot, nowhere safe to step.

They debate tactics of Che Guevara and Ho Chi Minh. Could the Berkeley Hills sustain armed revolution? Tess talks about building pipe bombs, raiding National Guard armories. Groups in Chicago and New York and Boston are prepping to go underground. Bertie remembers spooning a lump of jam into her father's face. There is something seductive in reflexively striking back. Satisfying, but short-lived. Juvenile, she thinks.

Walt is more enamored with going guerrilla. The helplessness of the moment is eating him. Bertie wakes one morning to find him on the floor, radio by his ear, listening to the body count. What if he enlists? he says. He could organize servicemen overseas. A revolt of the rank and file to return from Vietnam as an Army of Liberation. "Tess is right. We need to bring the war home, overturn some tables in the temple. I'm done turning the other cheek."

Bertie switches off the radio. She puts her hands on her hips. Did he already forget Las Vegas? That Bertie chose him? *Saved* him? He's not enlisting. He's not joining crazy Tess in the hills. She searches the bookshelf for his copy of Dorothy Day's autobiography, and opens to a dog-eared page. She points to his own underlined passage:

*No one has a right to sit down and feel hopeless. There is too much work to do.*

He's not sacrificing himself on the cross because he doesn't know what else to do. The revolution is coming and he's not leaving Bertie to dance alone on the barricades when the dust settles.

"Got that? Stand up. Off your butt, mister. Time for us to get to work."

# Chapter 18

# 1969–1975

Bertie graduates with invitations to six of the nation's best law schools, and although Walt hates the idea of returning to New England, he understands that Harvard is Harvard.

They pack their sparse belongings, bump over the Sierras, skirt Lake Tahoe, cruise the flat desert. Walt's record collection takes up the entire backseat. He worries about the vinyl warping in the heat, so insists on driving with the windows down. But the Nevada sun is so strong. He asks Bertie to take the wheel as he reaches back to cover his crates with a sheet. Bertie smiles as he fusses. Unlike Walt, she takes little with her. Her typewriter. Books and clothes. After some debate, she left behind her framed portrait of Dr. King. She has no space for the dead, she's decided. She and Walt are fighting for the living. The future. They are looking ahead. The road, it stretches on forever.

———

Cambridge. A light-filled, top-floor apartment five minutes from the lazy Charles River. Walt hits the ground running, landing a job with the *Boston Gazette*'s foreign bureau. He joins the International Coalition of War Correspondents, calls home from Belfast, Johannesburg, Saigon. Bertie misses his touch. She craves his evening call. She worries, but knows that his work is important. As is hers. She is happily swamped like never before.

To her Harvard coursework she adds an organizing role for Moratorium Day, coordinating buses and lodging. She organizes a sit-in when

Nixon invades Cambodia, and a walk-out when soldiers open fire at Kent State. She volunteers for the National Lawyers Guild. When the Boston Black Panthers attempt to block a highway expansion through Roxbury and Jamaica Plain, she offers to help. The Panthers have constructed a plywood shack in the bulldozers' path. The People's Free Health Clinic. They ask if she's a nurse.

"I'm a law student."

"We don't have a legal clinic."

"All I need is a table and two chairs."

They defeat the highway expansion. Walt is in Beirut, shooting an Israeli attack on PLO headquarters. Bertie is at their kitchen table with a cup of coffee, studying. The director of the Massachusetts Lawyers Guild has floated the idea of launching a legal clinic in a few years— The Baystate People's Law Center—and wants Bertie involved. First, though, Bertie must graduate and take the Bar. The phone rings. She jumps up. It's not Walt.

"Bertie?" The voice is familiar.

"Who's this?"

"An old friend. A political orphan."

Tess. Bertie hasn't heard from her since she went underground with the other Berkeley militants. Bertie wonders if the line is tapped. Tess clearly wonders the same, her voice clipped.

She needs a favor. A safe house. One night.

Bertie hesitates. She does not say no.

While Bertie has been studying law, the Weathermen have bombed the Bank of America headquarters, the New York City police department, the Pentagon. They've robbed National Guard armories. Bertie isn't willing to do these things, but she's grateful that someone is. After all, despite the many marches, the war has only spread. It has nagged at Bertie since she and Walt settled in Cambridge: how they live in simple comfort, sacrificing so little, while others risk so much. Yes, Walt is documenting the ravages of war, and Bertie is defending the defenseless, but it is so much easier—*safer*—to document and defend than take the offensive. She thinks of Dr. King and Harriet Tubman. Emma Goldman. Josephine Baker. John Brown, Jan Gies, Jesus Christ. Can you have real justice without real sacrifice?

Tess gives Bertie a date and time.

Bertie says she'll be ready. The least she can do. She'll be glad to see Tess again.

"I won't be there," Tess says after a pause.

"Who will?"

"Thanks, Bertie," Tess says, and hangs up.

———

Bertie's phone rings once after midnight. She turns off her lights, as instructed. It's raining hard. Two figures stand beneath an umbrella in the downstairs doorway. One disappears, the other slips inside. Bertie recognizes her immediately. A big woman with large brown eyes and an attractive, heart-shaped face that Bertie has seen on TV, in the newspaper, on the wanted notices in the post office. Janice Clancy.

While Janice dries and changes, Bertie takes the foil off the baked macaroni she's kept warm in the oven. Janice walks barefoot into the kitchen, appreciative for the food but not hungry. All people do is feed her, she says. How's she supposed to keep her figure? Got any wine?

Bertie uncorks a bottle. Janice gulps and sighs. She robbed three banks in Greater Boston with the Weathermen. An off-duty cop at the third bank died. Janice drove the getaway car. She's something of a local celebrity. An undergraduate group has been distributing pins on campus—*I am Janice Clancy*—the joke being to throw off J. Edgar Hoover and his goons. Bertie has one, pinned to the lapel of her coat, which happens to be draped over a kitchen chair. Janice sees the pin and smiles. "Bitchin' name. All yours if you want it."

They laugh. Bertie relaxes. She pours more wine.

Janice tours the apartment, trailing her hands over Walt's records. Bertie thinks about fingerprints. She thinks of the federal statute for harboring fugitives. She thinks of Jan and Miep Gies, risking everything for Anne Frank and her family.

Twenty-four hours. A small sacrifice.

Janice asks if Bertie has seen *A Clockwork Orange*. She misses going to the movies more than anything. "Well, not *anything*. I'm praying my next safe house will be with Paul Newman." She asks if Bertie has any games. Bertie unpacks Scrabble and they select tiles, but Janice uses her first turn to ask how Bertie met Walt, and the game fizzles out. Bertie takes her through St. Augustine, Las Vegas, Berkeley. Janice groans with envy. She pours more wine, slides the bottle to Bertie.

Soon dawn is leaking through the shades and the morning delivery trucks are making their throaty starts. Janice yawns. Bertie offers her the bed. She'll take the couch.

"Don't be a stranger," Janice says. "Plenty of room for two."

Bertie climbs into bed, her head spinning with wine. Warmth radiates from Janice. Their legs touch. Janice is pillowy, her body luxuriously soft. Bertie nestles into her and asks how she would've lived if born in a different time. No war to stop, no injustice to fight. What would she have done?

Janice sighs. "Find a comfy bed. Someone kind to share it with. Go to the movies. Get a large popcorn soaked with butter."

What would Bertie do? She considers it while falling asleep. Janice is right: In a perfect world, this life with Walt is enough. This really ought to be enough.

———

Bertie rushes out for morning classes. When she returns, Janice is sweating to Led Zeppelin in her bra and underwear.

"It's called aerobics!"

*Step Touch, Step Out, Heel Back, V Step, Straddle Down, T Step.*

When Walt calls from Beirut, crackly and long-distant, Bertie says she's studying, and covers her mouth to keep from laughing at Janice, who's prancing around the room, hands on hips, shimmying like a Rockette. Bertie wishes Janice didn't have to leave. They enjoy a second evening of drink and music and conversation. In another world they become fast friends. In this world, the phone rings once after midnight. They hug in the doorway.

"Good luck, Janice."

"Have a bitchin' life, Bertie."

Bertie promises she will.

———

Ten years of marriage. Time to finally celebrate.

They fly into Havana for their long-overdue honeymoon, sidestepping the travel ban by way of Mexico. The week is perfect. White sand squeaks underfoot. Waves thrum the Malecón. Men straddle the seawall, playing brass instruments. Kids dive for coins. The country smells like warm diesel and tobacco and citrus and rum. Bertie and Walt don't romanticize the Revolution, but they do romanticize the Revolution. They volunteer to cut sugarcane with a student brigade. They tour a healthcare cooperative, a senior center. Bertie is handed a baby boy during one of the big parades so a young mother can dance.

Increíble, the mother says afterward, scooping her sleeping boy from Bertie's arms. Tienes niños?

No kids, Bertie answers. I'm not a mom. Just a lawyer.

She and Walt agree that this world is no place to bring children. Too many people already. Too much work to do. For the same reason they waited a decade for their honeymoon. Look at all they've accomplished: Walt is assistant editor at the *Gazette*. Bertie has earned the highest score in Massachusetts Bar history and co-founded the People's Law Center. With each courtroom victory, she beats back the Tayloe family legacy an inch. Each day with Walt, the hereditary guilt recedes. They are forging a new path. And what better place to celebrate than Cuba, where things are not perfect, but the people are trying.

Their final night they swim at twilight, sky going pink with the sun. Bertie wraps her legs around Walt, floating free, light-headed. Maybe it's the rum. Maybe it's the soft Caribbean waves. Maybe it's the spirit of revolution. When Walt kisses her collarbone and wonders if maybe it *wouldn't* be the worst thing to consider children, Bertie doesn't file her usual objection. The world is rife with injustice, cruel and overpopulated, but floating on her back she sees the many shades of possibility. She and Walt could raise children right: toughminded, tenderhearted, ready to continue in the footsteps of justice. She and Walt have divorced their families, after all, so why not start their own? Walt takes Bertie by the hips, gives his lopsided smile. "Why not start tonight?"

# *Chapter 19*

# 1979–1982

They move from Harvard Square to leafy Bogastow, an hour west of the city. The house, an old colonial on a hill, bordered by marsh and forest, is palatial compared to the monkish room they once shared at the Oakland Catholic Worker. Extravagant, yet when they move in, Bertie allows herself a starburst of pride: the home is theirs, purchased without a penny of Tayloe blood money. And soon they will need the extra space.

Soon, however, takes longer than expected. Three years and two miscarriages, over which time Bertie becomes executive director at the People's Law Center. Walt works his way up to director of photography for the *Gazette*. They fill their big home with warmth and laughter, friends and colleagues. They throw parties that double as Sandinista fundraisers. Right when Bertie has accepted that life with Walt will be just as meaningful and expansive without children, it is Halloween and they are driving into Boston for a no-nukes rally on the Common. Walt is dressed as Muammar Gaddafi. Bertie is a Magic 8 Ball.

*Without a Doubt*, her round belly says.

She is bursting with twins.

———

People say it gets easier after the first months. People are wrong. People don't have colicky twins born five weeks early. Emma and Araminta have Bertie's light eyes and fine hair and last name. She loves them. Of course she does. But love only makes them slightly less difficult.

Sleepless nights, chafed nipples, perpetual laundry. The emptiness when Walt leaves for work. The flare of anger when the girls wake, crying. The stab of envy when he returns in the evening, flushed with purpose, affection, and an eagerness to help.

At first, Bertie's friends and Law Center colleagues stop by to gush over the girls. Five short months later, however, the trickle of visitors has squeezed to a drip, then a drought. Sheila Whitney walks over from next door, but when she knocks, Bertie pretends to be sleeping. Which she should be, she knows, banking as much rest as possible before the twins wake and fill the house with their wet, needy cries.

But sleep is difficult, too. It's February. The old house leaks warmth. Bertie's chest is damp, heavy. She worries that she and Walt have fallen into the gendered, privileged patterns they once scorned. She worries she's no longer a radical, but a hypocrite. She's stopped reading the paper. She worries for her mind. Where once grew a crystal garden of razor edges now lives a dull, rounded mound. She forgets words, thoughts, the reason she walked into the living room. She worries that she's becoming her mother. She is a civil rights attorney with the highest score in the history of the Massachusetts Bar. She is not a housewife.

Walt couldn't agree more. He wants them to hire someone to look after the twins while she returns to work. Someone to help with the cleaning and cooking.

Absolutely not, Bertie says. Her girls are *not* growing up entitled. There will be no nannies or maids. This is not debutante Savannah. She'll do it herself. She'll do everything herself.

Walt says she's being self-destructive.

Bertie says she's being a *mother*, screams the word loudly enough to wake the girls.

Walt helps as much as he can. He sweeps. He cooks. He plays his records until he finds the one record (*Smiley Smile*) with the one song ("Good Vibrations") that works some soothing magic on the girls, coaxing them to stop fussing and sleep. He straps them into the Volvo for an anti-Apartheid rally in the Common. He invites their friends for a Sandinista victory party, celebrating the guerrillas' march into Managua. He nods along when Bertie vows never to cook another meal or wash another load of laundry once the girls are old enough to do so themselves. He begs her to get out of the house, to spend at least one day a week in the office. She'll feel bad unless she's doing good, he says. It's postpartum blues. He says it will pass. He is wrong.

————

People say it gets easier after the first months. People don't have a third child thirteen months after giving birth to twins. Who knew it was a myth that breastfeeding suppresses ovulation? Not the brightest lawyer in the Commonwealth of Massachusetts.

Josephine, unlike her sisters, enters the world on time. A girl, she also gets Tayloe as a last name, but otherwise she is Walt's child. His wiry hair, his darker shade, his mellow temperament. She practices gymnastics with her face, works the room to win smiles. Sleeps often. Hardly cries. To Bertie, she's a beautiful miracle.

Still, three babies. Madness. Walt halves his hours. It's chaotic bunker exhilaration, leaving only for vaccinations, groceries, a protest at the El Salvadoran consulate. Bertie cooks hearty soups. Walt wears ruts in his records, sharing his music with the girls. Watching the four of them together in the living room, Bertie's heart is not big enough.

Finally, people are right: it gets easier.

The twins fascinate Bertie with their imaginative language, their capacity for memorization and mimicry. They sing to Walt's records, repeating choruses by heart. And then, when they begin nursery school, easy gets even easier. Walt returns to work full-time. Bertie is still lonely, still bored. But less so. She can feel her mind returning. She brews coffee, wraps Josephine peasant-style against her breast, and walks.

Josephine is a quiet, curious child. She spins her head like an owl, taking in the treetops, the clouds, an egret wading through the marsh. They walk the same route every morning: the woods, the train tracks, the fields of Sunrise Farms. Bertie nudges Josephine to crawl through the rows, play with earthworms, get as dirty as possible—every unladylike activity that would've scandalized her mother. She feeds her chewed up snap peas from the vines. Cherry tomatoes. Sweet corn. The girl loves everything. Across the marsh, buzzes the MCI-Bogastow intercom.

The women's prison has come to weigh on Bertie during these

morning walks. With Reagan in the Oval Office, the demand for radical lawyers has returned to Nixonian levels. *Who needs love most?* The incarcerated have fewer rights than anyone. Bertie wants the People's Law Center to establish a prisoners' rights clinic. She wants them to start immediately. She rings Marjorie Jevers, who has been acting director during Bertie's maternity leave. Marjorie agrees a prisoner rights' clinic would be perfect for the Center. When will Bertie be back to get it started?

"How does Monday sound?"

Walt is ecstatic that Bertie is returning. They celebrate with apple picking at Sunrise Farms. The twins totter behind, fall into leaf piles, run inside when they get home. Walt lifts Josephine from the Volvo. She's asleep, resting in the crook of his arm. Bertie holds his Nikon to her face.

"Show me those muscles."

Walt strikes a Popeye pose. Bertie centers him in the viewfinder. In the coming weeks, months, years, she will wonder: Why hadn't she taken more pictures? Recorded his voice on cassette? Had him write letters to the girls? Captured as much joy as possible from the life they had made together?

*Click.*

---

The Bay versus New England. Religion as opiate versus religion as liberation. *White Album* versus *Pet Sounds.* Bertie and Walt have argued about plenty these fifteen years, but no argument prepares them for their last.

Walt wants to go on assignment to Nicaragua.

Bertie says he must be joking.

The Sandinistas are under attack, Walt says. Their beautiful revolution. The Contras are slaughtering civilians, blowing up health clinics, hydroelectric stations. Everyone knows the CIA is arming them. Reagan's proxy war. If they could just turn public sentiment, perhaps involve Congress. He's convinced the *Gazette* to send a team.

"Wonderful," Bertie says. "You must have dozens of journalists without three young children."

Walt says he needs to be where it matters, with the people. Jesus didn't—

"Jesus wasn't a father. You have responsibilities the Son of God did not."

Walt is sitting on the counter. Bertie leans against the sink, arms crossed. The kitchen has become a courtroom. Josephine is napping in her crib. The twins, screaming and laughing, run laps through the house.

"I know I have responsibilities. That's the point. I have a responsibility to fight for a better world. For the girls."

"For the girls," Bertie repeats.

"For whoever needs love the most."

*I do!* Bertie screams in her head.

"Your girls do," she says.

Walt smiles sadly. Does Bertie want the girls to grow up in a world where their parents turn a blind eye to injustice? Doesn't she remember what that was like? The message it sent? To care only about your immediate family while the rest of the world burns?

The calmer he gets, the more Bertie boils. She hates him for putting her in this position. Philosophically, she agrees with everything he's saying. Physically, she's shaking.

He crosses the courtroom to hold her. She turns to the sink, pours a glass of water.

"You can't go," she says, knowing he will. She's known since their very first dinner date in San Francisco, when he fled—*sprinted*—from her to help a stranger in need.

"One week," he says. "Two at the most. I'll call every night."

Bertie's water glass explodes on the floor. The girls clatter into the kitchen, horrified and fascinated at the sight of their mother so upset.

Walt goes to her, touches her back. She flinches, pushes him away.

"I saved you." She picks glass from the linoleum. She can't look at him. At any of them. "They wanted to kill you. They wanted to send you to murder families and die. But I saved you. Me, Walt. Me. I chose *you*."

———

Bertie unplugs the answering machine. For four nights, the phone rings.

"Dadda?" Josephine frowns.

"Eat your dinner, sweet pea."

The fifth night the phone is silent. The next morning it starts up again and won't stop. Bertie decides he's learned his lesson. But it's not Walt. It's Roger Manch, the *Gazette*'s publisher.

"Mrs. McCannis?"

His tone gives it all away. Bertie has always corrected people who assume she took Walt's name. For once she doesn't have it in her to set the record straight.

## Chapter 20

# 1982–1983

The months that follow are bleached from memory. Somehow she sleeps, somehow she eats, somehow her girls are cared for. Her friends show up from the Law Center, the Lawyers Guild. A sympathy line without end. Until it does end. Sheila, bless her, still walks over to help in the kitchen, tinfoiling and labeling dishes. Her husband, Karl, mows the lawn. They bring the girls next door so Bertie can rest. She takes baths, scalding water that grows cold. A Contra land mine has unwound the cartilage and tissue that was her husband. She must remind herself of this three, four, fifty times a day.

For the first time in years, she nearly dials her mother. But Walt is not an olive branch. He is ash and bone in a cherrywood box that Bertie can't bring herself to bury. The associate from Full Circle Insurance explained that families typically set aside two to three thousand dollars for the service and a plot. Bertie wrote a $3,000 check in Walt's name to the Sandinista Junta of National Reconstruction. The remainder of the life insurance she deposited into an account for the girls' education.

The girls search for him. Under beds. In the shower. They revert to thumbsucking, bedwetting. Bertie cannot answer their one simple question. Eventually they stop asking. They transform back into toddlers: utterly delighted in the world or utterly distraught.

Bertie envies them for forgetting so easily. She walks the cherrywood box through the house, every room. She walks with the box through the fields, the forest. One afternoon, with the girls at nursery school, she rests with the box on the train tracks, laying her head against a cool steel rail until she feels that distant hum, growing nearer. She walks him through the sun, the rain, the snow. It's November. December. It's 1983. It's spring. Congress has increased military aid to the Contras. The lilacs are blooming. It's 3 a.m. The toilet is flushing. Josephine has trained herself to wipe, not through Bertie's instruction, but by observing her sisters. She speaks in full sentences. Life is happening. It hurts—so much—to notice.

———

Strange occurrences. Dishes are washed. Stairs swept. Clothes folded. Bertie asks if Sheila has been dropping by to do chores unannounced, to which Sheila replies, with a pitying smile, that she would be happy to take the girls if Bertie needs a rest.

One morning Bertie is staring at the phone, and it rings. "Hello?" The line hums and clicks, and then, with a burst, "Good Vibrations" crackles to life from the living room. She goes running, breathless, only to discover her girls have learned how to turn on the record player and set the needle. They can't understand what they've done wrong. Why is their mother crying, ordering them to their rooms?

———

She boxes his photographs. His clothes and photography equipment go to the Salvation Army. She wants to give away his books and records, but they are too heavy to move on her own. She keeps them in the living room for now. Sometimes, when the girls are at nursery school, she plays a record as loud as the speakers will tolerate. One afternoon, while folding laundry and matching tiny socks, she is listening to the Beach Boys album that Walt most enjoyed sharing with the girls. The record ends, the arm retracts. The silence is interrupted with a loud crack from the living room. Bertie jumps. She dries her hands on her shirt, and goes to investigate.

A book has fallen from the shelf. *The Long Loneliness.* The autobiography of Dorothy Day. Walt's worn copy. It lies open on the floor. Bertie picks it up. On the left page, a single underlined passage:

*No one has a right to sit down and feel hopeless. There is too much work to do.*

The hair rises on Bertie's arms. The back of her neck. She glances into the shadowed corner of the living room. "Yes," she says. There is work to do. The girls must be picked up soon. Lunch must be prepared. The cherrywood box must be stashed in her closet. The dead must be sealed away. She must look ahead, to the living. The future. Her girls. She must raise them to be strong and independent, ready for a day in which Bertie, too, could disappear in a blink. She must commit herself to forging a better world for them. For everyone. A brighter future for all.

After lunch, she will call Marjorie Jevers, who has stepped in again, this time for Bertie's bereavement. I'm ready, Bertie will tell Marjorie. I'm ready to put down my head and roll up my sleeves and get to work.

And for the next thirty-two years, she will do just that.

# PART III

# Family Loves

## Chapter 21

# Josie

Josie jolted awake to a whine of feedback.

"Sorry," came Emma's muffled voice through the wall.

Josie groped for Dean's side of the bed, which was now Emma's side of the bed, which was now empty. To make space for Emma's home project studio, Josie had disassembled her bed frame and emptied her closet. She'd pushed her dresser into the hallway and heaped her belongings in Dean's room. She'd slid her mattress into the living room, only to slide it back in when Emma said the acoustics were wonky with the studio *too* empty. So now Josie's bed was propped against a wall, for sound absorption, and the apartment as a whole had approached a vertical asymptote of maximum entropy. It wasn't hugely surprising when Dean decided to pack a bag and his PS4 and leave to crash at the empty Mattapan unit. Josie felt bad. Dean told her not to—his buddy from Local 26, Joey P, was coming over. They'd play FIFA, drink beer, eat tater tots, batch it up. She was glad Dean had somewhere to go, especially now, as the first rays of golden dawn angled through the window and Emma began a series of loud vocal warm-ups.

Josie sat up in bed. Someone in the building might call Fabio to complain about the volume at this early hour, but at least they couldn't be mad at Emma's voice. Even something as simple as running scales—the fullness of her sister's voice made Josie's ribosomes go tingly. She listened with her back against the headboard as a synth string section swelled. Emma added her voice, some words Josie couldn't make out. Then abrupt silence, followed by light cursing. The strings started again, from the top.

Josie pulled a blanket over her shoulders, stepped around the boxes in the hallway, and entered her former bedroom. Emma had set up her workstation in the center of the room. Keys, amps, guitars, and bass along one wall, Josie's mattress propped against the other wall, Ara's kit in the corner. A snake of XLR extension cords ran from the workstation, across the floor, and beneath the closet door.

Emma blinked like a surprised racoon when Josie opened the closet. She brightened, took off her headphones, hugged Josie goodmorning, and bounced over to her workstation.

"Want to hear what I've been working on?"

"I heard. Sounds great." Josie grabbed a tambourine and gave it a hopeful shake. "I'm up. What can I do? How can I help?"

Emma smiled in a way that felt just as intolerably patronizing to Josie at this early hour as it had been at age nine, when her sisters had called her to the garage because they'd formed a band (empty paint cans for drum kit, paper towel roll for mic, vacuum cleaner handle for mic stand) and named it, of all things, *Jojo and the Twins*.

To which nine-year-old Josie observed, correctly: "But I don't play anything."

To which ten-year-old Emma suggested, "What if you were the audience?"

To which ten-year-old Ara added, "Yes! Every band needs an audience, and—oh my God—there's a beach chair right here!"

To which nine-year-old Josie stormed off. She knew when she was being used. But her chromosomes had replicated and condensed and divided many trillions of times since then, transforming her into an adult who'd learned that the only thing worse than being used was being useless.

She sat behind Ara's drum kit, spun a cymbal, and reminded Emma that *Jailbreak* was her idea. "I want to be involved."

"Then get Ara to call. We're not a jam band. I need lyrics."

Josie flattened her palm on the smooth skin of the snare. Ara hadn't reached out again since that one missed call. Was she mad at them? Hurt? In pain, unable to call? Janice, via Dean, assured them she was fine, only taking some space while she detoxed. Which, okay. But for how long?

"I'll try," Josie said. "What about media? Could I help with outreach?"

"I've been posting," Emma said. "Speaking of which, this light is sort of perfect."

She handed Josie her phone and, in one practiced motion, peeled off her tank top, adjusted her sports bra, tied her hair into a messy bun, arranged her headphones around her neck, and posed behind her keys with an expression that Josie measured as one part concentration, nine parts seduction. "Anytime," she said through her teeth.

Josie took the photo. Emma had linked the *Jailbreak* page in her bio, and Josie happened to swipe over as preorders ticked from 449 to 450. Almost halfway.

"What about *media* media? Didn't you have a thing with a *Rolling Stone* editor?"

"He was just a photographer. I don't even remember his name." Emma frowned. "Gibran?"

"There has to be *something* I can do."

Emma looked up thoughtfully. "I wouldn't say no to egg whites with spinach."

By the time egg whites had scrambled and spinach had sauteed, *Jailbreak* preorders were 451. Just 49 more, then 500 after that, and they'd have enough to bring Ara home. Josie put a hand on the fridge to counteract a dangerous sway of hope.

> **OBSERVATION:** Nothing in the known universe escapes the thermodynamic suck toward disorder.
> **HYPOTHESIS:** This is too easy. Something must go wrong.

Or maybe not? Perhaps it was Josie's hypothesis that was wrong. Because after breakfast things continued sorting themselves into the taxonomic classes of easy, easier, easiest: first Josie found the online profile for the Deputy Managing Editor for Culture, Identity, and Social Justice at the *Boston Gazette*, then she pitched *Jailbreak* as a story of redemption (America's favorite genre) and got a nearly instantaneous response (*Would love to talk . . . quick chat this afternoon?*). Buoyed, Josie pitched *Pitchfork*, *Rolling Stone*, *Spin*, the *Boston Globe*. She updated her social media accounts, posting blanket requests for media contacts, spreading awareness the way a virus seeks to share its genome with the world.

Then she emailed a lease agreement to the bros in apartment 2C, at least one of whom Emma had seduced into subletting the Mattapan apartment. Finally, she dressed, said goodbye to Emma, and checked one more time before putting on her shoes and her helmet: 458 preorders. She floated down Centre Street on her bike, feeling less bloated and more optimistic than she had in days.

———

The summer interns, Fabio reported, had surprised them all by not burning the Butterfly & Reptile World to the ground in Josie's absence. Khalil had scrubbed every toddler handprint from the bearded dragon enclosures. Amar had dealt heroically with an inconsolable two-year-old who'd found a dying Malay Lacewing on the atrium walkway. "And Mimi was Mimi," Fabio said. "Our ball of radiant joy."

Mimi, a sophomore-to-be at Boston Latin, glowered and jacked off an invisible penis without looking up from the fish she was gutting.

Josie appreciated the unkempt irreverence that Fabio cultivated in the World. The World wasn't perfect. Exposed wires sagged from the walls, some hose always needed coiling, the scorpion tank's UV light had been broken for weeks. Josie often felt that her job consisted primarily of applying for grants, but this one grant for underrepresented youth in STEM education had really paid off. The interns were kids, meaning they never tucked in their uniforms, couldn't put down their phones, regularly forgot lunch, and wore nauseating amounts of body sprays. But they did what they were asked, they were eager to learn, and they loved every organism in the World, from the scaled to the winged to the thoraxed. The kids were alright.

Josie pulled on her gloves to give the cobras their antibiotic injections, then joined Mimi to deliver a lecture on the leafcutter ants to a Girl Scout troop. The girls listened politely until Mimi asked if they had any questions. Hands shot up.

"Where are the butterflies?"

"When do we get to see the chrysalis wall?"

"Bimbos," Mimi whispered as the girls ran off.

Mimi had zero patience for anyone who preferred the razzle-dazzle of the butterflies over ants that had *evolved to farm their own fucking snacks*, as Mimi phrased it. Coincidently, both Mimi and the leafcutters had come from Trinidad. Mimi had arrived at Logan International with her mother and brother at age six, following a harrowing journey originating in Eritrea that Mimi had alluded to just once (Josie had wanted to show the interns a shortcut through Franklin Park, and Mimi, grabbing Josie's hand, refused to take one step into the woods). The leafcutter ants had arrived by less traumatic means: international post. Fabio had mocked her—*nobody cares about ants*—and Josie had taken immense pleasure proving him wrong. She'd suspended a thin cable across the atrium, connecting the colony to a pedestal stocked with the vegetation that the ants used as fertilizer for their fungus farms. Result: The Ant Skyway, an eye-level procession of foragers commuting home, leaf clippings like parasols overhead. Mesmerizing on its own, but then they mixed in rose petals, daisies, and violets (Mimi's brilliant idea), turning the Skyway into a kaleidoscopic river *and* the World's most photographed exhibit, even more popular than Linda.

OTHER REASONS JOSIE LOVED MIMI:

1. Her eyes did not glaze over like honeyed hams when Josie recited the title of her incomplete dissertation (*Specificity of the symbiogenetic mutualistic association between leafcutter ants and their cultivar fungi*).
2. Her eyes *did* grow to the size of dinner plates when Josie took the Kern Primrose moth from the staff freezer, and explained how she'd spent years looking for them in California, only to find one at a gas station in Maine.
3. Her eyes narrowed in slits of fury when Josie told her *why* she'd spent years looking for Kern Primrose in California, at the behest of Dr. Lee.

"I'd never let a man order me around like that."

"Promise me?" Josie said.

Above all, Josie adored Mimi because she was unabashedly, aggressively curious. The girl asked the best kind of questions: ones that couldn't be easily answered.

*"Why didn't you kick Dr. Lee in the nuts?"*

*"Why can't you finish your research now?"*

*"Well then what can we research?"*

It was a timely question. With Ara ghosting them from prison, Josie had found herself thinking about colony communication, especially regeneration feedback loops in times of crisis. The different ant castes, she explained to Mimi, squatting down beside her—the soldiers, the foragers, the nurses, and so on—were determined by the quantity of fungus fed to larvae. But because the World's leafcutters lived without threat of predators, Josie suspected they raised fewer soldiers. Her hypothesis. If they wanted to know exactly *how* many fewer and *how* quickly the colony could adjust, they might reintroduce a perceived threat, like anteater pheromone, and observe how the colony responded.

A common response would've been: "Why would you want to know that?" but what Mimi said was, "How do we get anteater pheromone?" and because of a history of such Mimi-comments, Josie was dying to help the girl get into a good college, win a Fulbright, and crush a career in biology, ideally without need of praise from even one of her male superiors.

"We could order it," Josie said. "But first we'd need to mark thousands of ants, to establish our base numbers. It's painstaking work."

"When can we start?"

They moved to her cramped office. Josie slid a stack of grant applications off a chair so Mimi could sit. She flipped open her computer to order pheromone, a set of ultra-fine paint brushes, a tiny clay harnessing system, and nontoxic enamel paint.

"We'll need four colors, to mark the different castes. You choose."

"I don't give a shit which colors we use."

"You're the primary investigator, Mimi. You have to give all the shits."

"Sheesh. Alright. Anything but pink."

Josie completed the order, then degunked the fish filters, gut-loaded the life foods, stocked the gift-shop shelves, and took a shift at the front desk, selling tickets and greeting guests. Before heading home, she wanted to talk to Fabio. He was nearing the end of his "Gem of the World" presentation, showing off Linda to a group of summer campers with identical tie-dye T-shirts. Josie waited in his office as he finished. Photos of baby Linda, teenage Linda, and adult Linda adorned every inch of his office walls.

"What'd I do now?" Fabio walked in and crashed down hard on his chair.

"Emma's recording the new album at my place. I wanted to let you know, in case you get any noise complaints. It won't be forever."

"Anyone bitches, I'll make them buy the album."

When Josie had first told Fabio about *Jailbreak*, he'd immediately preordered five copies.

"Thanks, Fabio."

"Sure sure. Now get out of here before I change my mind."

"One more thing. Do you have any apartment vacancies?"

Josie was thinking ahead, for the *Jailbreak* page showed they were at 504, over halfway to bringing Ara home, and Josie was determined to keep her colony together and safe. If not under the same roof, at least on the same block.

Fabio kicked his feet up on his desk. "I'll tell you the same thing I told Dean. I got nothing free now, but any units open up, you two are my best tenants, you get first dibs."

Josie felt herself blink three times in rapid succession. "Dean asked?"

"About a new place. Yeah."

"When?"

"A couple of days ago?"

"Oh." She felt her face burn hot. She thanked Fabio and turned to leave before he might notice. She biked up Centre Street, wondering: How long had Dean been planning to move out? But then she got home, and there were real problems to worry about. The moment she walked in, Emma ripped off her headphones, and dropped them to the floor.

"Jojo! You're not going to believe it!"

She wrapped her arms around Josie. She squealed in delight. She stomped her bare feet on the floor.

Something had obviously changed while Josie was at work, and while this change may have excited a person who had not studied evolutionary biology at the genetic level, Josie knew full well that ninety-nine percent of all unexpected mutations tend toward disease, deformity, death.

"What happened, Em?"

Emma gripped Josie's shoulders. Her eyes were rapturous.

"Ara called! She's not mad at us. She's just been busy writing this whole time! *Listen!*"

Emma punched a button on her workstation:

*The pack is the nucleus.*
*The pack is all of us.*
*Family loves . . .*

Emma's voice made its usual magic, fragile, wavering, trilling into the heavens. Josie felt it in her ribs, her jaw and molars. The music washed through her, and although it was only ten seconds or so, it was possibly the best ten seconds her sisters had produced in years. She sob-laughed in relief.

"It's great, Em! It really is!"

"I know!"

"I love the beat."

"That's all Ara. She got it from the guards in the hallway. Their footsteps."

Josie leaned against the wall, weak with relief. "So she's really okay."

"Better than okay. She wrote two songs already and she's working on a third. I knew this had silver lining all over it. That's why we always stay greased, because you never know. Everything happens for a reason. Oh and we have to find her roommate's kids."

"Whose kids?"

"Her roommate, Kyla . . ." Emma shuffled through sticky notes and scraps of paper piled by her keyboard. "I wrote it down somewhere . . ."

Josie breathed slowly as Emma held up an envelope in triumph.

"Gemma, Ruby, Crystal. We have to bring them to visit. Then she'll let us bail her out and we're—"

"Let us? Em, stop. Who are we talking about? Kyla?"

"What? No, not Kyla. Ara. Our sister? Also, we decided to raise full bail, not some bullshit ten percent that we'll just have to throw away to a bondsman. I mean, Ara decided, but I one-thousand-percent agree. And it's a great narrative. It'll help move preorders."

The home project studio formally known as Josie's bedroom skipped before her eyes. So here it was: a deleterious mutation after all. She spoke slowly. "Emma. Her bail is a hundred thousand dollars. That's ten thousand orders."

"Actually eleven thousand. Awesong takes ten percent, don't forget."

Emma was smiling like a beauty pageant contestant: all teeth, unwavering.

Josie said, "I'm failing to understand your good mood."

Emma pressed a button and replayed the teaser track.

"Don't you hear this? Eleven thousand is the floor. This is our big comeback, Jo! This album is going to be huge!"

Josie said that she really hoped so. Then she ran to the bathroom and threw up.

# Chapter 22

# Bertie

Captain Tubbs had been born a red diaper baby into a long line of Wobblies, radical longshoremen, and merchant marines. His brief stint in Navy whites ended just after the Tet Offensive, when he earned a dishonorable discharge for coldcocking an admiral in the Bangkok Officers' Club. Forty years at sea, and Tubbs had faced down Vietcong snipers, Japanese whalers, and Exxon tankers. His beard was going white at the fray. He sang sea shanties, wore wool sweaters, smoked cigars while standing puff-chested at the bridge of the American Rescue Cruise. Boredom and fear were the two great threats to mission success, he was fond of saying. His most common order, when he caught you standing around: "Find a broom and start sweeping."

Bertie and Audrey rolled their eyes at the act—*boy could he play the part*—but they adored their captain. Everyone did. Tubbs kept the crew busy, he kept them safe, he kept them on course. After a week of chasing the sunrise, the *A.R.C.* was twenty-four hours from the Mediterranean. Bertie's body creaked and popped from the routine of light manual labor. She and Audrey had swept the galley, washed the windows, and scrubbed the toilets, a dozen times each. Mindless busy work, but work was purpose and work was distraction and work was penance, and plowing ahead for the Middle East, Bertie needed purpose, distraction, and penance.

Since leaving the Griffinport docks, she could not unhear what Josephine had told her.

*She asked for you first thing. Where's Mom?*

The words had braided a cable between Bertie's heart and Araminta's heart, and with each nautical mile the *A.R.C.* sailed east, the cable stretched tighter. Bertie had always strived to avoid coddling her girls. Better to foster independence. When she'd helped them in the past (and help them she *had*), she preferred to do so quietly, without their knowledge, and without making a big fuss. Returning with Josephine would've been just that: a big public fuss for nothing. She was legally powerless to help Ara. And Janice would care for her. The *A.R.C.* was the most important act of international solidarity since the Spanish Civil War, helping Syrian women who had lost their husbands, and Syrian children who had lost a parent—young families shattered from loss and war just like Bertie's young family. She knew these families. They needed her. That was enough, for now, to keep the cable between her and Araminta from tightening to the breaking point. She'd made her decision. This ship was not turning around.

The *A.R.C.* was a sturdy Belorussiya-class vessel as old as the twins. Built for the Baltic Sea Ferry Company, it had been retrofitted into a luxury cruiser during the Gorbachev years and later purchased by Greenpeace from a Hong Kong casino line that tanked during the Great Recession. Bar, lounge, library, theater, gift shop, dining hall, casino. Handsome, mahogany-brass spaces, now floor-to-ceiling with supplies for Gaza, would later be buzzing with Syrian families.

"Soon we'll see Morocco," Tubbs bellowed from the diving board. "From there, Cyprus. Then Gaza. Ready yourselves, sailors. War's coming."

General Assembly began every evening with Tubbs's briefing. It was always the same: half update, half pep talk, wholly entertaining. The crew gathered on the sundeck because the swimming pool made a natural amphitheater. The diving board was the speaker's platform and the pool (drained to reduce weight and fuel drag) could seat everyone. Max and the younger crew members perched on the edge, dangling their feet. Bertie and Audrey sat on the smooth bottom at the sloped 1-meter mark. They used lifejackets as cushions.

"And make no mistake," Tubbs went on, "this *is* war. If the Zionists don't rough us up, the red hats will be waiting for us back home. War's scary. And right up until that moment, it's boring as hell. You're allowed to be scared. You're allowed to be bored. You are not allowed to be an ass. Not on my ship. So if you find yourself getting on my nerves?"

He cupped a hand to his ear.

"*Find a broom and start sweeping,*" chanted the crew.

Tubbs beamed. "My lovely sailors."

Max's comm briefing followed. They took to the diving board, their blue hair a bun of cotton candy that bobbed as they relayed news from the mainland: the State Department had issued a travel warning to American citizens attempting to "provoke our ally" by approaching Gaza on boat. (Boos and hisses.) The *A.R.C.* Home Front Committee had enlisted its ninety-fifth Neighborhood Sanctuary to sponsor a Syrian family. (Cheers and whistles.) "*And,*" Max said, glancing at their satellite phone, "*Jailbreak* count is over six hundred. Give it up for Team Tayloe!"

Bertie forced a smile, then examined the wrinkles on the back of her hands until the applause dwindled. Everyone on the *A.R.C.* had preordered the new album, some more than one. Bertie massaged her knuckles. She wasn't ungrateful. Only people with far less privilege were arrested every day for so much less. All the fuss about Araminta plucked uncomfortably at the cable of her heart.

"Oh and one last thing," Max announced, "Kim and Kanye are rumored to be divorcing. Wanna know why? Me neither."

After comm briefing came Hopes and Concerns, or, as Audrey called it, Night Court. In the days since the Maine coastline had slipped beneath the curvature of the earth, the crew had debated smoking on the sundeck, sex in the staterooms (meant to be kept pristine for the refugees), and evening movie selection. Tonight's Hopes and Concerns focused on bathrooms. Marsha Rubin, a rabbi from Duluth, had scotchtaped "Women" outside a galley bathroom. A sign which Max had ripped down, only to find it replaced later.

Marsha stood on the shallow-end steps. "Call me old fashioned but I'm not comfortable throwing out my tampons in front of men."

"I thank you for sharing your discomfort," Max said, "but your modesty doesn't get to dictate the spaces our bodies occupy."

Max was as eloquent in gender politics as they were in JavaScript, one of many unexpected pairings that no longer surprised Bertie when it came to this new generation of activists. They rolled filterless cigarettes while gulping kale smoothies. Worshipped group consensus while absorbing themselves in their private screens. Bertie had represented Max and their friends during Occupy Boston. In some ways, she knew them better than her daughters. They were literary yet techy, funny yet uncompromising. Tattooed and pierced, yet religious about skin care. They hydrated obsessively. They were spunky paradoxes and they gave Bertie immense hope for the future.

"All I'm asking is *one* bathroom for women."

"Sure and we'll have one for white folks, one for straight folks, one for Christians."

"What about the return trip?" said Danny Noor, a firefighter from Dearborn. "Are we really going to require traditional Arab women to share bathrooms with men?"

"God forbid we risk offending people's gendernormative worldviews as we save their lives," Max said. "And why do you assume they're 'traditional'?"

Bertie, at seventy-one, had initially found the bathroom issue perplexing. All the new pronouns. But she'd learned in her role as elder not to lecture the younger generation. Instead to encourage, mentor, learn. She knew the importance of picking battles. You simply didn't have the luxury to fight for everyone. If it were that easy, she would've returned to be with Araminta.

People were climbing from the pool, lining up to speak their mind. The scene reminded Bertie of Occupy. They'd be debating for hours. Suddenly a siren blared. Captain Tubbs stood wide-legged on the bridge, a megaphone to his face.

"We're listing two degrees off keel. Cargo needs readjustment in the casino. All hands below deck. Move it!"

The crew clamored downstairs where they formed a fire bucket brigade to transfer rows of infant formula and powdered milk from the roulette corner to nearer the blackjack tables. Bertie took twenty-pound cases from Audrey and handed them to Max. Soon everyone was grunting and sweating, not a word about bathrooms. Bertie pinched Tubbs's elbow when he walked by.

"Off keel my rear end."

His eyes glittered. "Sailor, are you wisemouthing your captain?"

Bertie pushed a case of infant formula into his arms. "Yes, sir, I most certainly am."

# Chapter 23

# Josie

Dean texted to say that he'd left some clothes he needed for work. Also a belt. Also his phone charger. Josie found everything and drove it over to Mattapan. Dean was in the shower when she arrived, which gave her time to refit the sheet that had popped off the mattress, wrestle open the window, and search for a broom. The air smelled like alcohol and farts. Other than the mattress, the only furniture was a flatscreen and the PS4, the controllers like two sad tentacles splayed on the gritty floor. Josie searched the kitchen. Had her sisters seriously never had a broom? On the counter, next to a sickly aloe plant, was an empty pizza box with a grease stain like a planetary nebula. A pile of High Life empties in the sink, and an empty bottle of Jack Daniel's.

"You guys went pretty hard," she said, when the hiss of the shower stopped.

"What?" Dean called from the bathroom.

"Looks like you and Joey P had fun. I'm glad."

"Boys' night in." Dean grinned, stepping into the hall naked, toweling off his hair. His eyes were hangover red. He dried, then changed into the fresh clothes. He plugged in his phone. He thanked Josie for driving everything over.

"It's the least I can do. Thank you for living in a shithole while I manage the dumpster fire of my family."

"Any dumpster fire updates?" Dean asked.

"Yes, actually. Ara finally called."

"That's great! How is she?"

"Not good." Josie explained Ara's outrageous terms for release.

"I bet she just needs to be heard. She'll change her mind."

"She better. Even if we did raise a hundred thousand dollars, how are we supposed to find three random girls?"

Dean threaded his belt through his pants. "Want me to ask Seema? She's great with the private eye stuff. The union sent her to Dallas last year to trail executives and root through trash cans."

Seema worked for Local 26 as some kind of research analyst. Josie had never met her, but knew of her. She and Dean had gone on two dates. They'd made out once. Dean liked her, he said. She was fun, even if she wasn't his type.

"Sure," Josie said. "Ask Seema. Can't hurt."

Dean plopped on the mattress to put on his socks. His knees came up to his ears. Josie saw the slag of sound-absorbent foam, rolled into a tube by the head of the mattress.

"Are you using that as a pillow?"

"It's more comfortable than you think."

Josie groaned. "I'll bring you a real one. I hope this isn't for much longer."

"Make it up to me with dinner tonight?"

"Maybe. Let me talk to Em, see if she needs anything."

"Or we could do a picnic circuit tomorrow? Tomorrow is supposed to be beautiful."

"I'm visiting Ara tomorrow."

"All day?"

"Dean. I can't."

"Well . . . you *could*."

She bristled. "Please don't make me feel guilty for supporting my family."

He smiled, and pulled on his shoes.

"What?" Josie said.

"Nothing. Am I not allowed to smile?"

"Are you still drunk?"

"No. Not really."

She knelt and scooped dry soil off the floor with her hands. She carried the soil to the kitchen and patted it gently around the base of the aloe plant. She had to move beer cans from the sink so she could give the plant some water.

"Drinking so much isn't healthy for your liver," she said over her shoulder.

"Tell Joey P. I just had a few."

She let the soil drain, then soaked it a second time.

"Are you mad?" Dean called.

Josie was mad. But Dean had given up his room for Josie's family. Who was Josie to fault him for a night of drinking? Or asking Fabio behind her back about a new place to live? She turned off the sink and walked back in.

"I'm not mad. I'm just stressed. And a little sick. I haven't been feeling well."

Dean tied his shoes and reached up. Josie dried her hands on her pants, then helped him stand. Instead of letting go, he pulled her in for a hug.

"We've known each other a long time, Jo."

"I sense an *and* coming," she said into his chest.

"*And* I don't want to see you waste your life letting them stress you out and make you sick."

She squirmed out of his hug. "You think I'm wasting my life?"

Dean hesitated. "I think anybody can float along, putting out other people's fires, and poof, there goes your life, and you never got to decide what *you* wanted. Not for you, not for us."

"Dean. I appreciate you so much, for so many things. But now is a pretty shitty time to talk about this."

"Yeah. It always is."

They stared at each other. Josie swallowed. Then her phone rang. *Massachusetts Department of Corrections.* She held up the screen.

"It's probably Ara," she said.

"Probably."

"We'll talk later?"

"Sure." Dean grabbed his keys. "Tell her I said hi."

## Chapter 24

# Emma

Emma and Ara had been on a two-day creative bender, recording in bursts. The prison pay phones only allowed for twenty minutes, then the line would disconnect, and Ara would have to call back, assuming nobody was waiting behind her. Emma found the interruptions excruciating at first, but after laying down two full songs, and with another two in the pipeline, she appreciated the gaps as time to pee, drink water, eat whatever Josie had left her in the fridge, and prep for Ara's next call.

This morning, she had a longer gap than usual. They'd worked after breakfast, then Ara said she had lunch, yard time, afternoon count, and an NA meeting. She wouldn't have access to the dayroom phones again until three. This would've been a natural time for Emma to scroll her contacts, but she didn't need the distraction of sex. She needed fresh air and vitamin D. She sniffed a pair of yoga pants and pulled them on. She grabbed a tank top. Then she rummaged her moving boxes, stuffed a band T-shirt and a CD into a tote bag, and carried her bike downstairs to experience direct sunlight for the first time in days.

A ride around the pond and down Jamaica Way brought her to Boylston Avenue and the brownstone that was the Survivors' Resource Center. She'd only meant to pop inside and leave the shirt and album at the front desk, but the ever-cheerful receptionist told her that Dr. Pine had a last-minute cancellation, hold on, she'd be back in a jiff . . .

"That's alright—" Emma said, but the woman had already ducked out back, and here was Kim.

"Araminta! What a wonderful surprise. Your timing couldn't be better. Come in!"

"I don't want to bother you—"

"You're not bothering me. We'll just bill this as a regularly scheduled—can we do that, Yvonne?" The receptionist gave a thumbs-up. "Plus, Yvonne says you brought something?"

Emma followed her into her office. She gave Kim the copy of *American Mosh* and a Jojo and the Twins shirt. She'd guessed extra-large, to be safe, but now, seeing Kim, she doubted herself. "Shit. You're a large, aren't you?"

Kim held the shirt to her body. "It's perfect, thanks. You really didn't have to."

"Actually I did. My sister and I are talking again and everything's great and it's all because of you. You're an honorary member of the band."

Kim laughed. "Appreciated, but no way I'm taking credit for your work! You're the author of your life, not me." She folded the T-shirt and placed it neatly on a side table. She squared the CD on top of the shirt. "Please, have a seat. There are lots of ways for us to continue our conversation, but one approach that people find helpful is—"

"Oh no, sorry Kim, I can't stay. I was just popping in."

Kim reached down and flipped on a white-noise machine and said, "Not even a quick check-in?" and her calm voice, her pleasant scent, the white-noise hush—it settled over Emma like a heavy quilt. She'd been running on adrenaline for how long? She slid off her tote bag and slumped on the couch. She yawned. Ara wouldn't be calling for a few hours.

"I guess I can stay for a little while."

"Wonderful. Can I ask you, then, what brings you here today?"

"Honestly I just needed an excuse to get some fresh air. This is my first time outside in days if you can believe it. We've been in the zone, working, barely sleeping. We made up, and now we're like, it's just like . . . all these years I was so focused on perfection, and it got us nowhere. And now I'm laying down vocals in one take, recording everything dry, and the sound is *good*. All the little imperfections. This is the best thing that could've happened for us. That's why I always say to keep greased. You never know when opportunity will strike. Good advice for anyone. Which okay, that's sort of cheesy . . . but it's true. When something challenges you, and you rise to it. I guess I'm just happy! Ha. I don't know. You know?"

"I think I do. I'm thrilled that you and your sister made up. How did you resolve things?"

"It just happened. She called, said she'd been writing on her own. She wanted to finish our new album and get started right away."

"That's great to hear. Thank you for telling me about Emma last week, I really enjoyed getting to know her a bit. What about the rest of your family? Can I ask about your parents?"

"My dad's dead."

"I'm so sorry."

"It's alright. He died when I was three."

Emma often told herself that it was alright. And indeed, many months could pass without a single thought of him. She barely remembered him. But why then did she protect *Smiley Smile* at all costs? Because it was all she had left.

"Is your mother in the picture?"

"Sort of. She works a lot."

"Did she remarry after your father passed?"

"No. She raised us by herself. But mostly it was just us and Josie. Or that's how it felt. We were raised . . . feral? Not in an abusive way or anything. We were never hungry. I never felt unsafe. Our mom just worked a lot. She trusted us, to be independent."

"Who's Josie?"

Emma felt a stab of guilt. She hadn't mentioned Josie?

"Josie's my other sister."

"Are you two close?"

"With Josie you don't get the choice not to be close. She kind of makes it her mission to look after everyone. But it goes both ways. That's why we're *Jojo* and the Twins. Our band took off because we were taking care of her."

Kim raised an eyebrow, like *Please blab on.*

Emma blabbed on: "We were at Berklee, our freshman year. Josie was at home—she was still in high school—and she got pregnant. She wanted an abortion, so we drove her to the clinic on Comm Ave. It was good we went because the scene outside was hostile. One huge group shouting at the other. Cops parting the seas. We rushed Josie through the gauntlet. We were trying to be there for her, keep things calm, but you could hear the screaming from outside. Not exactly a relaxing environment. Dean—her boyfriend, sort of—he went with her when her name was called. And that's when my sister and I were like, "Should we talk to the people?"

"Talk to who?"

"To the nuttos outside waving their gross pictures and signs. We screamed at them, flipped them off. Which I highly recommend. Very cathartic. We wanted Josie to try on her way out. But she was in pain. She wanted to go home. Then Dean had to fly back West and our mom was at a conference or something, so we stayed home from college to cook and do Josie's laundry and drive her to school. We wanted to help. But Josie has a hard time accepting help. She never makes it easy. She said we were missing class. She said she'd be fine. 'I'm fine, I'm fine, I'm fine.' When people say they're fine that many times you know they're not. So we decided to get revenge for her."

"Revenge?"

"We went back to the clinic to scream our heads off. But it didn't feel as good as before. Diminishing returns, you know? Plus, I have to be careful of my vocal cords. I'll get nodules. So we lugged our band gear across the street. We'd put up flyers at the Fountain, Paradise. We would've been happy if ten people came. We got over a hundred. We called it the Mosh for Women's Lives."

"I remember that! It was in the news."

"Yeah! You might have heard about it later, after it got bigger and spread to other cities? Our first one was pretty small. But we still put on a real shit show in the streets. We were doing this punchy cover of 'Girls Just Wanna Have Fun' when the cops pulled up. We had to scatter so they didn't confiscate our gear. But it worked! The sidewalk outside the clinic got cleared for a whole day, not one fascist fucknut in sight. Sorry, I don't know how I got on this. What am I talking about?"

"You were sharing with me how caring for your sister Josie led to your band's early success."

"Yes. That. The Mosh got us our first gig. It was at the Middle East. We were nineteen, which is just wild to think about. Babies! We made this banner to hang behind stage—*Abortion: On Demand and Without Apology*—and half the door went to the Comm Ave. clinic. We packed the house. Then Napster came out. The timing was perfect. Free publicity. College groups across the country suddenly inviting us. We had a backward start: a fan base first, *then* a record deal."

"What a story! So exciting! Thank you for sharing."

Emma laughed. It *was* a good story. But that was the beginning, when anything was still possible. The sad middle of their career was the part that Emma had to prevent from becoming the sad end. And she was trying. She and Ara both. They were the co-authors and they were writing this new life of theirs together.

"I know you can't stay long," Kim said, "but if it's okay for me to ask before you go—how has the past week been? Have you experienced any cravings?"

Emma thought about her twenty-minute recording sessions with Ara. Ara had sounded more clear, more purposeful, than any time in recent memory.

"No. No cravings."

"No? Okay. Great. That's wonderful." Kim paused. "Can I level with you, Araminta? Can I share with you something I've seen over my years, working with people?"

"Sure."

"Thank you. And I know that you know this, so please, just consider it a reminder, but—let's just come out and name it: Addiction is a beast. You know that. And the most common thing I see is that people think they have it beat. But then something happens, and the temptation is too much, and if you haven't been using, your tolerance has dropped. You can't do the same amount. It's fatal. Some setbacks we can come back from, but not that. And again, please, I'm not trying to scare you, or tell you anything you don't already know, or claiming this will happen to you. I'm just saying that in my personal experience, I've seen it happen, even to people who've gone through long periods of sobriety. But we have tools. We don't have to cross our fingers and hope for the best. One of those tools is

Narcan, and another is a medication called buprenorphine. It's taken daily, to prevent relapse."

"Like methadone?"

"Lots of people like buprenorphine better than methadone. You can take it at home. It doesn't alter your behavior. People say it helps with cravings, and frees them up to, let's be honest—to help deal with all the other complicated shit that comes with being alive in this world."

Emma blinked away the surprise of tears. Ara had hated visiting the methadone clinic in Framingham. Waiting in line with the "real" junkies. Could it be that something as simple as a pill taken at home might put an end to her pain for good? And, if so, how had they not known about this before?

Kim asked, "Is it okay that I'm making this suggestion? I could connect you with our partner pharmacy in Hyde Square. They could fill a prescription for you today."

Emma knew she'd already committed Medicaid fraud, at the very least, sitting in as Ara. What was one more tiny crime? She had to think long term. Because bailing out Ara would be just the beginning. After Emma saved her, she would need to keep saving her, and saving her, and saving her. If there was a magic pill? Hell yes. She'd take all the help she could get.

Emma nodded. "Sign me up."

# Chapter 25

# Josie

The metal detector made Josie try three times before allowing her into the waiting room. She sat beside a young girl and a grandmotherly woman. The girl could've been dressed for Easter dinner: white dress, stockings, patent leather Mary Janes. She held hands with the older woman, who stared ahead, a deep frown creased into her forehead. When the girl turned abruptly to ask Josie, "Do you know my mom?" the woman snapped, "Quit bothering nice ladies, Bella," and yanked the girl onto her lap.

The intercom crackled: "Proceed to visitation."

Josie darted through the small crowd, finding Ara with the speed and force of an oppositely charged ion. A guard warned them to keep the hug brief. Somehow, impossibly, almost two full weeks had passed since Josie had occupied this same space with Dean, Emma, Janice, and Ara. Einstein may have deduced that gravity could bend light (and therefore time), but he hadn't known that a good family crisis could do the job nearly as well.

"Wrap it up," said the guard.

Josie released Ara. She couldn't afford to be kicked out again. Ara had called her, and explained that she'd told Emma she was going to an NA meeting, but truthfully she wanted Josie to meet her in visitation, so they could talk privately.

"It's great to see you," Josie said, "I'm really glad you called." They sat at a table by the vending machines and the microwave. "How does your hair look so good?"

"It's the conditioner. Janice gets me the best of everything."

Ara's hair was shiny, bouncy, luxuriant. It was everything else about her appearance that worried Josie. Maybe everyone looked equally corpse-like under the fluorescent lighting? Maybe Josie, too, had waxy skin and a badger, tunnel darkness to her eyes? She certainly felt that way. At the next table over, an inmate and her visitor exploded in laughter.

"So." Ara pressed her palms together, as if praying. "I want to apologize. I'm sorry I ruined your camping trip."

"Oh my God, Ara, that is in the distant past. It literally does not matter."

"It does matter. And I'm sorry for lying. And making you drop out of school and—"

"You didn't *make* me drop out of school, I've told you a million times, it was my choice."

"—and so much more. I'm just sorry, Jo. For everything I've put you all through. The money I've wasted. Dad's records. Ugh. It makes me sick. I can't say it enough. I'm so sorry."

"Apology accepted. We're just glad you're safe. Let's move on."

She had to cut off Ara. Otherwise the apology-a-thon might burn up their entire visitation. Back when she'd returned from her second stay at New Pathways, Ara came home armed with a ten-page list of every person, instance, and institution to which she'd felt angry, jealous, or resentful, along with a short consideration of *her* role in each—a sick self-flagellating meta-apology that made Josie flagellate herself for not more carefully vetting the methodology of New Pathways's "research-based methods." For the final step, Ara's counselors had directed her to read the list aloud to someone who'd simply listen without judgment, which turned out to be significantly less simple than Josie had expected when she'd told Ara to go ahead.

Josie had to put a stop to a new round of Rehab Reflection before it went too far. She'd come here to talk sense into her sister, not listen to her make amends.

"But I *am* sorry," Ara protested. "I have to make sure you know that."

"I do. And I'm sorry, too. I shouldn't have been so hard on you. I just wanted to help."

"You did! You do! Our whole lives. That's what I'm saying. And I'm so thankful, Jo. I really am. And now it's my turn."

It disturbed Josie that Ara's lines sounded rehearsed. It also disturbed Josie that the feeling of being disturbed, combined with the couple at the next table openly weeping with laughter, reignited the pilot light beneath the furnace of her anger. She twisted in her seat.

"I'm looking for a place in my building for you and Em. So we can all be together when you're out."

Ara smiled. "That sounds nice."

"Agreed. But first we have to get you out." Josie spoke carefully, testing the waters.

Ara nodded in agreement.

"One hundred thousand dollars is a lot of money, Ara. It could take months—"

"—and Kyla's girls, don't forget. We have to figure out how she can see them."

Josie clenched her teeth. She'd never admit it, but she was jealous of humans like her mother, who met conflict with action and seemed happy—*energized!*—for it. She was jealous of Dean, who'd exhausted his anger in adolescence and now sailed through life on an even keel, self-regulating with alcohol, class warfare, and FIFA. She was jealous of Emma, who could get over anything with a cry, a fuck, or an encore. She was even jealous of the couple one table over, laughing, gasping for air, clutching their stomachs. Then there were humans like Josie and the irritable grandma in the waiting room. Why was anger their default mode? Because someone had to be angry. The people they loved: someone had to make them realize the deadly seriousness of life.

"Ara. You and Em have done an amazing thing with *Jailbreak*. It's turning out great. You've sold over eight hundred preorders. That's incredible. You'll hit a thousand in a couple of days. We could pay for the bond and you'd be home with us next week. Think about that."

Ara glanced at a guard by the door. Her throat bobbed. She scratched the back of a hand.

Josie had become so attuned to her sister's mannerisms, any small signs of relapse. It was obvious Ara wasn't saying something. Josie asked, gently, "Is everything okay? Do you want to tell me anything?"

Ara caught Josie's eye. She blinked and shook her head. "No. We're not throwing away ten grand on me—"

"It's not 'throwing away'—"

"And we have to figure out how Kyla can see her girls."

Josie deflated. "Say we try to find your roommate's girls but they're in Alaska or—"

"Her name's Kyla. And I seriously doubt they're in Alaska."

"What if we can't find them?"

"Remember the moth you showed me? You said it was impossible to find, and you did. You said it was dead, and it came back to life. We *saw* that, Jo. We saw that together."

Josie closed her eyes. The parking lot of the Mad Mountain Tavern felt like a lifetime ago.

"Anything's possible," Ara said.

"False."

"We're *not* giving away ten thousand dollars to a bondsman. It's all or nothing."

"But what if we can't raise it? Don't you want to get out?"

She swallowed again. Her eyes watered. "I have to make things right."

"With who?"

"With everyone. With me. Myself. It's the only way."

"I hear you, Ara, and I respectfully reject your hypothesis. You can't just isolate yourself. What you do affects us. It affects me. I worry about you every second you're in here."

Ara leaned back. She crossed her arms. "This is exactly why I needed space. You always make it about you. This is about me. I have to make things right, Jo. I'm not fighting about it."

One of Ara's therapists in the past had prescribed Lexapro, making Ara a zombie, leading to Josie's suggestion of a new therapist, who put Ara on Wellbutrin, making her a speed freak, leading to Josie's insistence on yet another therapist, who prescribed Klonopin, leading to Josie calling to ask (scream) who the fuck gave benzodiazepines to an addict unless they were begging for a malpractice lawsuit, leading to the therapist dropping Ara off a benzo cliff, leading to Ara's psychotic, disassociated tailspin, leading her to Roman in search of something— *anything*—to take the edge off, leading to a knock-off Xanax laced with fentanyl, which was all it would've taken to stop Ara's lungs for good if Josie had not

A) insisted that Ara keep Narcan in her handbag, and
B) made sure Roman knew it was there

Ara had almost died, because Josie couldn't be everywhere at once.

What she needed was a Britney Spears–type conservatorship over her sister. Barring that, at the very least, she needed Ara to stop making it so difficult to help her.

"I didn't ask you to come here by yourself so we could argue," Ara said.

"We're not arguing," Josie said. "We're discussing."

"There's nothing to discuss. I'm not going anywhere until we raise full bail. And Kyla—she took care of me when nobody else could. She's not in a good place. She needs a win. I won't come home until I pay it forward."

"Is this a twelve-step thing?"

"It's the right thing."

"You can do the right thing from home!" Josie groaned. "With us! You're sober. You're clean. That's wonderful, Ara. You should be proud of yourself. Don't waste that clarity. Be responsible. Use your head."

"Please don't get mad at me."

"Who's mad? I'm not mad. I just don't want you to treat this like rehab. This isn't New Pathways. This is prison, and prison can be a dangerous place."

Ara's face darkened. "You think I don't fucking know that?"

The outburst startled Josie. She bent to rest her forehead on the table, willing herself to be calm, and less like the grandmother in the waiting room. Less like herself.

"They're *us*, Jojo," Ara said in a hush. "Kyla's girls. Imagine if someone pulled up the driveway when we were little and said they knew where Dad was, and we could see him? After we thought he was dead all those years?"

"He was dead all those years," Josie said into the table.

"Don't you ever think about how our lives would've been different if he wasn't?"

Sure, Josie sometimes did. But you couldn't account for variables in life. Not without a control element. No way of attempting the experiment again to result in a father who doesn't step on a land mine in Nicaragua, but instead lives to be sitting beside Josie in the visitation room, helping convince his daughter to please, for the love of Darwin, *come home, baby girl, come home.*

"So we find Kyla's girls, sell ten thousand albums and then what? You're back on tour, drumming through your pain—"

"I know."

"—and some dumbass bassist offers you a bump—"

"I know."

"—and Emma's off getting laid and—"

"Jo. Stop. I know. I have this last album in me. Then I'm done. I quit."

"Quit what? The band?" Josie lifted her head off the table, not even attempting to conceal her skepticism.

Ara nodded. "It's the only way I can stay sober. Put all my triggers behind me. A fresh reset."

"Uh-huh. And do what with your life?"

Ara drummed her fingers on the table. "I was thinking I could teach music. To kids."

"That's great. You do know you need a degree to teach?"

"So I'll go back to school."

"And pay for it how?"

"I'll stock veggies at the Yuppie Bodega. Who cares? Some dumb job. Anything but the band."

"Does Emma know?"

Ara rolled her eyes. "That's why I wanted you to come here alone. So you'd know I'm serious. Emma and I will finish the album. I need your help finding Kyla's girls. Please, Josie. I can't do it alone. *I need you.*"

Those magic words. No amount of sister-inhibitors could block so potent a drug. She scanned Ara's face. Maybe they did need to let her make amends in her own way, or at least try. Josie had driven out here to convince Ara, yet somehow the inverse was happening: Ara had convinced her.

She nudged her sister's foot under the table. "Okay. I'll try."

Ara beamed. "Thank you!"

Josie smiled weakly and groped for anything else to talk about.

"Em says you're really excited about this new song you're working on?"

"Yes. Very."

"What's it about?"

Ara's eyes sparkled. "Revenge."

# Chapter 26

# Ara

I'm through the cough-and-bend-overs and back in Barton Unit after visiting with Jojo. I almost cracked and told her what happened with Andrews. Almost said, "Of course I want to come home, Jo, bail me out. Take me home right now."

But I held strong and she agreed to help with Kyla's girls. Victory upon victory.

Andrews has not been back again to demonstrate his feminism. But every set of footsteps makes my heart beat faster. Every clanging door. I spend as much time as possible in the dayroom, but they send us back to our rooms for count, and if Kyla's at work, I'm all alone.

How do people live in fear while sober? Almost couldn't remember. You stay busy.

Making music helps. Writing helps. Helping helps. Revenge helps.

———

Writing revenge isn't easy. You've got your classics—"You're So Vain" and "Rocky Raccoon" and "Santeria"—but they all focus on the ex, or the dude who "stole" the ex. No blueprint exists for what I'm doing. I've got pages of attempts. Nothing quite right. Too spoken-word-whiney. Too vague. A Revenge Song must be accurate, lasting, popular. Not the sort of thing to rush.

———

We had another Code 99. Another woman in Max. She was on suicide watch. Nobody was watching. Kyla relayed the news in the same detached tone that she uses to catch me up on *General Hospital.* I'd flushed her DIY noose when I found it. But I remember Sister throwing my dope out the window to the Tremont Street pavement. I remember Josie confronting me with a dusty Percocet she'd found under my dresser. I remember Sister asking, "Hey, where are Dad's records?"

You can a hundred percent shame someone into becoming *more* secretive, *more* stubborn, *more* inventively florid in their using and their lies. You cannot shame someone into quitting.

Kyla's noose wasn't the problem. The problem is Kyla. She thinks she'll never see her girls again. We need to prove her wrong.

---

Sister and I got one more recording session in before afternoon count. She was in a rush, expecting a photographer to stop by any moment to shoot her home studio. A reporter had already interviewed her about *Jailbreak.* They want to interview me too, but there are a ton of forms to fill out. I said I'd ask Mylene next time we met. Sister was recording me directly into her workstation, layering my harmonies. I had to stop because someone was complaining loudly about the line for the phones. I turned and saw the woman who Dolores slapped in the cafeteria. She was saying, "Anyone can bang on a damn drum, I got actual musical talent, get off the phone already," to which Nancy said, "Go be talented somewhere else," and stood by me like a bouncer for the rest of our session.

I did another two takes. Then Sister said the track was done, ready to bounce. Our fifth song. Over 900 preorders. We have momentum. Sister thinks we can do $100,000 easy. Enough for bail plus lawyers plus a tour plus a new merch line. All without GhostTrain's neocolonial contracts and misogynist managers.

Could she hear me smile over the phone? When Sister gets excited, she's contagious. Almost impossible not to believe what she believes. To want what she wants. To remember why you were ever upset with her in the first place. To remember I have just one more song in me.

# Chapter 27

# Josie

In the liberated zone outside MCI-Bogastow, where one could hug at will, Josie walked into the hot sunlight, turned on her repatriated phone, and checked the *Jailbreak* page: 905. She felt suddenly sick with whatever she'd just promised Ara. She stopped in the middle of the parking lot and wondered: Could one bail out an immediate family member against their will? She looked it up. Seemingly, one could not.

Her phone buzzed with queued messages coming in at once: a sweet one from Dean (just saying hi, I'll swing by later) and a less-sweet barrage from Emma:

Gazette photographer coming over at 2 . . .

Maybe don't come home till you hear from me . . .

Where do you keep your fans it's SO HOT!!!

We need toilet paper.

Josie wandered the parking lot in a daze, unable to remember where she'd parked the Volvo, and feeling uncertain—for the $n+1$ time—about her role in her family. Ants, when confronted with an attack on the colony, release pheromones that tell their sisters *exactly* where to go, and *exactly* what to do. A positive feedback strategy, evolved over hundreds of millions of years, guaranteeing decisive action, and a quick return to social homeostasis. What a fucking dream. No guessing games. No wondering if Ara had wanted Josie to fight harder for her to come home. No doubting whether her attempts at helping her sisters over the years had made things worse. No worrying that her sole role at this most crucial juncture in her colony's survival was to . . . pick up toilet paper?

But that wasn't true. She had to find three little girls and bring them to visit their incarcerated mother. She had a role. The problem was that her role was covariably insane.

Josie found the Volvo, half-hidden beside a large black pickup truck. She drove away from the prison with a tightness seizing her chest and a growing pressure in her pelvis. She needed to pee. She needed to go home. But Emma was home, baking in the humidity, and possibly seducing a photojournalist.

Human beings, Josie often lamented, possess embarrassingly few instincts as compared to other charismatic megafauna. Her species had an innate knowledge to crawl, nurse, yawn contagiously, stare transfixed into campfires, and . . . that was about it. Humans are born learners, not born knowers. That said, Josie experienced what could only be classified as an instinctual urge as she approached the Mass Pike; instead of merging onto the highway to drive home, she flipped her blinker for the other direction: home.

---

As girls, Josie and her sisters could skip off their front steps, tromp through the woods to the train tracks, balance along the rails, cut through the cornfields, and arrive at the marsh across from MCI-Bogastow, all in about twenty minutes (longer if they had to search the railroad gravel for pennies they'd left to be flattened by the trains). Now, behind the wheel of the Volvo, the reverse trip from prison to home took Josie just over seven minutes.

She braked at the foot of the driveway where she, Emma, and Ara had spent some hundreds of mornings waiting for bus #18. The driveway, a long uphill S, had grown a shag of pine needles and forest detritus over the neglected months. A sign sprouted from the road's edge:

FOR SALE BY AUCTION

Josie turned in, then decided against it, yanking the wheel to continue down the road, only to mutter "screw it" and hit the brakes, pulling off just past the Whitneys' old place. She parked, stepped over the stone wall, and marched into the woods where she'd spent the best part of her childhood kicking rotten stumps to hunt for grubs, building salamander homes under rocks, waiting under the giant maple for the snowy owl to show. She ducked behind that very maple, pulled down her shorts and squatted, making eye contact with a chipmunk who chirped at her from a branch as she peed. She finished, buttoned her shorts, slapped a mosquito, and approximated her position as the midpoint between the road and her backyard, so why not? She crunched along through the dry leaves and underbrush, emerging at the tree line.

Her childhood home: large, white, colonial, old. Josie, the summer after fourth grade, had nursed an orphaned cottontail back to health, and when the rabbit developed a taste for wallpaper, Josie learned that behind the wallpaper was older wallpaper. Behind those patterns, still more. Squirrels scurried through the walls. Some pipe was always clanging. Stairs creaked, floorboards popped, the train shook the tracks behind the marsh.

Home.

Josie hadn't been back since the April Blowout Weekend, when she'd helped her mother pack up. The house looked the same, just darker. Empty. A black square of second-floor window marked her old bedroom. The backyard was unmowed, the lawn going to seed in that breathless, rewilding way. Shoots of black-eyed Susans and Queen Anne's Lace. Bees. No doubt teeming with ticks, but Josie cut through anyway, hands trailing at her sides to brush the soft tops of the flower heads and grasses.

She peeked around the corner to confirm that no real estate agents, federal marshals, or IRS officers were parked out front. Satisfied she could trespass in peace, she tried the door, and—finding it locked—made herself at home on the steps.

Home was no longer home, because Bertie, years ago, had stopped paying federal income taxes.

Was she sorry?

Bertie maintained that she was not sorry, no matter how vocally or violently Josie had pushed her to admit otherwise.

In Josie's opinion (delivered in a biting tone that became exponentially more biting the less it affected her mother), Bertie had made a purely totemic point that would have no effect on the world except to leave three-fourths of their family homeless and four-fourths of them without any hope of long-term fiduciary security.

In Bertie's opinion (delivered in a calm, authorial tone that impressed juries with the precise inverse power in which it infuriated her youngest daughter), she'd made as material a point as one could make in late-capitalist society: she'd deprived the Pentagon of hard currency—some tens of thousands fewer dollars to fund the Saudi bombing of Yemen, the billions sent to Israel every year, and so on.

War Tax Resisting, she called it, in the tradition of Henry David Thoreau, and, as with so much in their lives, she hadn't told her daughters. Probably she never would've told them, Josie suspected, if the IRS hadn't finally declared its intention to seize and auction the house, forcing Bertie to call Josie and say: if you want anything, come get it while you can.

Josie had worked feverishly to fix things, but it was too late: By April, appeals were exhausted, final eviction notices had arrived, and no amount of pleading with the IRS could help. That window, Josie learned, had closed six months earlier, when they could've still paid a twenty-five percent penalty, plus interest.

Bertie chalked it up to bad luck: only one hundred-ish people had actually had their homes seized for war tax resisting since World War Two. "Less than one percent."

"That's called a non-zero chance," said Josie. "Which, for some reason that defies the most generous parameters of responsibility, you decided to take."

"You can be complicit in endless war all you want, Josephine. I'm not judging your decisions. I'm simply done writing our government a blank check to kill innocent people."

"No, instead you gave them an entire house!" Josie gestured wildly to the rooms they were in the middle of packing.

Josie had assumed that she, Ara, and Emma would work as a united front over the April weekend, especially as Ara and Emma were currently *living there*, sleeping in their *childhood bedrooms*, and would've only needed to *come downstairs* to help. To give her sisters a modicum of credit, they'd agreed that they couldn't leave Josie alone with Bertie. But then Emma bailed in the most classic Emma fashion: at the last minute, for a guy (an old fling, a bassist, whose band was in town). As for Ara, she stuck around, but she was utterly unhelpful, sick with the flu (so Josie thought at the time) and spacey (so Josie thought at the time), spending the entire weekend in the living room, detangling a ball of Christmas tree lights with a committed inefficiency that drove Josie mad.

So Josie was left alone, trapped behind enemy lines, with her mother.

Two snipers, they traded shots amidst the rubble of cardboard boxes, packing tape, balled-up newspapers, and household odds and ends that nobody—not even Goodwill—would want.

"How could you have been so irresponsible? I feel like I'm talking to a teenager."

"Talk to me about teenagers once you've raised three by yourself."

"What if there's an emergency? What if you fall and break a hip? A house is equity. Everyone knows that. Who do you think is going to take care of you? We are, Mom. Did you even stop to think about us? Our futures?"

"Nuclear family inheritance is the single greatest driver of racial and social inequality. For all you know, I may have been planning to donate the house to Code Pink, or Veterans for Peace, or a refugee family."

"That would've been fantastic! Instead, you gave it to the U.S. Government!"

"They took it," Bertie corrected.

"What about you, Mom? Where are you going to live? With me and Dean?"

"I'd never impose on you like that."

"You can if you need to."

"Audrey invited me to stay with her at the Dorothy Day House."

Josie laughed. "You're going to become a Catholic Worker?"

"Why not? This is a rather exciting time for me. I'm trying to find the silver linings, treating this like a new exploratory phase in my life. You should try doing the same."

Josie's stress over her family's living situation would end up emulsifying in her gut, which explained why she did not enjoy a solid bowel movement that spring, not until she'd finally secured the Mattapan apartment for Emma and Ara. Her mother, on the other hand, seemed relieved—*gleeful*—to be moving on.

"Well I'm thrilled this is some fun adventure for you." Josie's thumbs had gone raw from the tape dispenser teeth. She watched her mother pack away tea towels and obsolete electrical chargers and a half package of coffee filters, and tape the flaps shut. Then Bertie stood and brushed back a lock of hair that had stuck to her damp forehead.

"You know, Josephine, I've dedicated my life toward making the world a better place for you girls and every other living person. I'm not sure why you seem so determined to make me feel guilty for that."

"Because you lost our house! Do you—"

"Enough," snapped Bertie with an unexpected flash of temper. "It's just stuff. Stuff doesn't matter. It's only a house."

---

A house that would have proven extremely useful, Josie thought now, sitting on the front steps and picking a tick off her right ankle. They could have sold it. Or taken a home equity loan. Or artfully, perhaps with Roman's expertise, torched it for the insurance. So many paths to $100,000, all of them now blocked by the tangled free fall of Bertie's recklessness.

Mentally replaying the April Blowout Weekend raised Josie's hemoglobin to just below its boiling point, even as she sat on the wooden steps where she'd enjoyed some of the most peaceful evenings of her life. She cracked her neck and pulled out her phone. The *A.R.C.* had crossed the Atlantic without sinking. Full steam ahead. She resisted checking the *Jailbreak* page again. Checking too often was bad mojo. Agreeing to Ara's demands seemed suddenly mental. What kind of spell had she cast on Josie in the visitation room?

A dog barked in the distance. A crow called out. Cicadas hummed. Photons that had traveled 90 million miles from the core of the sun warmed Josie's face and shredded her epidermal DNA.

She checked the *Jailbreak* page: 908.

Unless a miracle occurred soon, she would have to make one.

# Chapter 28

# Ara

It happened. He sent for me.

End of major count, quick footsteps in the hallway.

"Connelly," said Kyla.

Seconds later, CO Connelly appeared in our door.

"Hop to it Tayloe. Inner Perimeter wants a chat."

Inner Perimeter's housed in one of the old buildings. Damp slate shingles, gothic corners, bricks rounded with age. Connelly read my face as we were waiting for the door to buzz open.

"Relax kid. It's I.P. not the Gestapo."

Two more doors. A flight of stairs. Door of fogged glass and black lettering:

### LIEUTENANT BLAKE ANDREWS
#### ASSISTANT COMMANDER, INNER PERIMETER SECURITY

He was standing at his desk. His aftershave hit me. My heart threw rocks against the wall of my chest.

"Leave the door open," he told Connelly, then flashed his big smile when we were alone. "Have a seat. Want coffee? Water?"

I stood, silent. He swiped his phone. Sister's voice filled the air.

*She-wolf howling sunrise*
*More please more please*
*Call girl on the picket line*

*More please more please*
*Inmate on the barricade*
*More please more please*
*Soldier with the strip tease*
*More please more please*
*Housemaid with the AK*
*Yes please yes please*

Our newest, this fun call-and-response track that I'd enjoyed a lot more before Andrews put down his phone and said, "I am loving this so goddamn hard."

I looked past him, fixing my eyes on a yellow patch of water damage where wall met ceiling.

He leaned against his desk and invited me again to sit.

I didn't sit. I was priming my prefrontal cortex to run. Scream. Fight. Survive.

He followed my eyes to the water stain. "MCI-Bogastow, longest-running women's prison in the country. Built in 1866, and as we say around here, they haven't remodeled since."

I didn't respond.

"You're upset. Please. Let me clear the air. Have a seat."

"No thank you."

He shrugged and ran a hand through his hair. Office noises came from the hallway. Chatter. Bursts of walkie-talkie. Sister's voice was still streaming from his phone. The man who had attacked me, who'd grabbed my throat, who had our album art tattooed on his ribs, was bobbing his head to our music. The situation couldn't have felt more surreal.

Sister's voice finally faded. Then came me—a promo bit she had me record: "Live from MCI-Bogastow, this is Araminta Tayloe, sending you kisses and love."

I was not enjoying the sound of my own voice when he walked over to close his door. Click of the latch tripped my panic alarms. I let him know in no uncertain terms that I'd claw his face off if he came at me again. I could've fist-bumped my voice for sounding so smooth and confident when my insides were anything but.

He made a crucifix with his index fingers and told me not to get hysterical. "Attacking a ranking officer will definitely not help your case for early release. Stop being so dramatic. Calm down."

He sat at his desk and opened a file.

"Rough start here. Coldturkey. Ouch. How you feeling now? Withdrawal hits in stages, you know. You're likely to have another couple bumps ahead. D.O.C. won't allow methadone because they're bureaucratic eunuchs, but I could have Health Services send you Xanax, Ambien, Klonopin . . . generic of course, but pick your poison."

"No."

He smiled. "Ara. Come on! I'm just trying to help."

"You assaulted me. You almost strangled me."

"What?" He laughed and closed my file. He crossed his arms, fabric of his sleeves tight against his biceps. "I was trying to *help* you. That's all that happened. You were dopesick, confused. Maybe you still are?"

"I could not be more sober."

"You are suffering from substance use disorder, and I'm a ranking officer—a lieutenant—who took personal interest in the well-being of a resident suffering through withdrawal. But more than that—my God, come on, Ara, what the fuck are we doing here? I'm a fan! I'm literally paying for your bail! Can we show some civility? Talk to each other like two decent adults?"

"You are the worst kind of man."

He took a big yogi breath. Smiled his big wolfy smile. Then pulled out a set of keys, unlocked a drawer, and thumped a brown paper lunch bag on his desk. "You would not believe the kind of contraband that some knuckleheads think they can mail in here."

I stared at the paper bag. I could almost feel its heft. Could practically taste the bitterness in the back of my throat.

He smiled a row of straight white teeth. "Wanna see? You can hold it." I shook my head.

He held his smile for another beat, then said, "Suit yourself," and dropped the bag back in its drawer. Click of the lock. Jangle of keys. From his pocket came a pack of American Spirits.

"At least join me in a peace pipe? To officially bury the hatchet and start over?"

I shook my head again. I said I wanted to go back to my room.

His jaw muscles bulged. "I'm trying here, Ara. I'm trying to apologize."

I looked directly at him. "And yet you haven't."

His eyes flashed big. He smiled. "How about this—hard fucking reset. We try again, but this time you try your absolute best not to act like a spoiled cunt?" He cleared his throat and spoke in a high stage voice: "Hey Ara, really dig your tunes. Huge fan. My wife and I caught tons of shows. Really pumped for *Jailbreak*. Want a smoke? Not easy finding a smoke around here. Or a friend."

No way I was giving him a reason to believe he'd made peace, or done me a favor. But on the other hand, my fear circuits were blinking, warning me. And sure, I wanted a cigarette.

Hating myself a little, I held out a palm.

He stepped on his chair to twist a smoke detector off the ceiling. Cracked a window. Unwrapped the pack. Happy holy sounds of plastic and foil. Hadn't yet snicked the lighter and already I tasted the warm bloom of tobacco across my tongue.

I blew smoke signals out the window and fantasized about Revenge Song—on the radio, streaming from every car, every gym, peaking higher than "American Mosh" on the Billboard Top 100—while he told me how much he and Becca were digging *Jailbreak*. I lit a second cigarette without asking, but it gave him such a look of smug satisfaction that I killed it in the empty soda can we were using for an ashtray. My head singing with nicotine, I asked to go back to my room.

"Not empty-handed." He reached into his drawer.

I thought for one joyful terrible second that he was going for the brown paper bag.

"Waxed, unwaxed, *and* mint. All ribbon. The good shit."

He winked, and skated three containers of floss across his desk.

I skated them right back. Floss was the last thing I was bringing back to Kyla. "Thanks but no thanks."

Big surprise, this was not the reaction he wanted. He said, "Honest question, did your mother never teach you any manners? Or does being an uppity bitch run in your family?"

Britney, my peer recovery coach at New Pathways, loved to say that getting high doesn't magically happen, but results from a chain of isolated choices. You choose to beg your sister to cop for you. You choose an extra bump before gigging. You choose to insert straw directly into the bag to forgo the chore of cutting lines. And if using is a chain of isolated choices, that means any one link can be broken. Easier said than done, but I'm proud to say I made the choice not to rise to Andrews's douchebaggery. Instead I reached to scoop the floss off his desk, tucking the containers into my socks like a Bogastow pro.

"I'm sorry," I said. "You're right. Thank you so much."

"Ladies and gents! A thank-you from Araminta Tayloe! We knew she had it in her!"

He applauded, and I deployed my nicest smile, even as I'm fairly confident I've never hated someone so much.

The floss knobbed my ankles as Connelly escorted me back across the yard. A train whistle cut through the woods. The sun winked off the fuselage of a passenger plane. Three containers of floss. Forty-odd yards each. Enough for all of Barton Unit.

Want to know what my mom _did_ teach me?

_Never let the assholes get away with it._

# Chapter 29

# Josie

Emma was fitting clean sheets to Josie's bed, whistling when Josie got home.

"I take it the shoot went well?" Josie dropped a case of toilet paper on the floor.

Emma flipped her hair. "Daniel was a gentleman. The story's up tomorrow. Hi Dean!"

Dean walked in with a bike helmet on his head. He had a tire pump in one hand, a plastic grocery bag in the other. He put down the pump, pulled out a bottle of rosé, and held the bottle in front of Josie. A drop of condensation splattered on her shirt. "Time for a picnic circuit."

"I can't," said Josie. "I'm sorry. We're too busy for a picnic."

"That's exactly when you need one most."

He had a canvassing shift that evening, but was free until then, he said. They had a window, at this moment, and he was going to lose his goddamn mind if they didn't jump through it.

Josie looked at Emma. "The fridge is almost empty. What are you going to eat?"

"Get out of here! Go have a date!"

"I could make you a quick sandwich?"

"Can't hear you." Emma slipped on her headphones. "Bye."

Sandwiches from Yuppie Bodega
Rosé from Bottle Room
Gently sloped field by Jamaica Pond
+ Blanket, two mitts, two baseballs (in case the pond ate one)
Perfect summer picnic circuit

Josie and Dean, during a calmer season, had stumbled upon the formula, and, like Albert Hofmann after his enlightened LSD bicycle ride, there was no point in tweaking the compound ever again. Today, however, a contaminated test tube spoiled the chemistry. Josie caught a whiff of stone-ground mustard, sharp cheddar, and pickled green tomatoes, and gagged.

Dean sniffed her sandwich, shrugged, and took a bite. "You've been sick a lot lately. Are you sure it's just stress?"

"Family," she said. "Prison. Life."

"Rosé," Dean said, uncapping the bottle. "Drink. Now."

Josie took three big glugs and flopped on her back, inviting the alcohol molecules to bond as rapidly as possible to her GABA receptors. A plane drew a contrail across the sky. Ducks quacked. Two barefoot boys ran by, laughing, attempting to brain one another with sticks. As long as the alcohol muddied her neural pathways, she was almost capable of pretending that life was this simple and pleasant. She told Dean about her visit, how Ara seemed committed to her insane bail demands. She sat up. "She doesn't even know where the girls live. So first I have to find them, then convince their dad, or whoever's in charge, to bring them in? What if they won't? Or say they're in foster care? Or they moved?"

"I asked Seema. She's on it. I told you, she used to be a private eye."

"Thanks." Josie drew circles on Dean's knee. "For the record, I don't want to be someone who only complains about family. I'm sorry. I know it's not healthy. For me or for you. But I can't think of anything to talk about."

"How about this," Dean said, chewing. "You have to say one non-family thing, right now, or the Earth blows up. Right now! Hurry!"

Josie squeezed her eyes, clenched her teeth, shook her head. "Sorry, Earth."

Dean ate the last bit of crust. He finished the last drop of rosé. He helped Josie to her feet and tossed her a mitt.

"I'm so sick of hearing myself," she said. "Can you just talk to me? Tell me about work? When's the proletariat going to rise up, already?"

Dean spoke excitedly about a new campaign, recruiting undercover organizers to apply for jobs at the new Seaport hotels. He had to train them by giving mock interviews and doctoring their résumés. It felt like he was part career coach, part labor organizer, part spy. A lot of work, but UNITE HERE had run the same campaign in Las Vegas, and it had paid off.

Josie caught the ball with a satisfying *thwap*. "I feel bad you're working so hard while sleeping on a mattress in that shitty apartment. Are you having any fun at all?"

"I'm having fun right now."

*Thwap.*

"I mean real fun. Any plans to hang with Joey P again?"

"He's busier than me."

"Any hot dates?"

*Thwap.*

"One. Not that hot. Just a drink last night. With Seema."

*Thwap.*

"Seema. Cool." Her next throw went wide. Dean chased it down.

Josie prided herself on their channels of communication. Their open relationship demanded it. Monogamy wasn't bullshit, just narrow-minded. She and Dean enjoyed a healthier, more socially evolved relationship, she liked to think. Why then did she feel like telling him, as he ran back with the ball, that she *really* hoped he had fun fucking Seema's brains out while she'd been physically sick with stress, trying to save her family?

*Thwap.*

Instead, she said, "Fabio told me you were asking about an apartment?"

"He's got nothing. He said he'd let me know if anything opens up."

*Thwap.*

"Were you going to tell me you were looking for a new place? Or was that a secret too?"

Dean held the ball. "My mom gets out in four months. That's not a secret."

"I thought she'd stay with us till she got on her feet."

"I'm confused. Do you want my mom to live with us, or don't you?"

"I want us to be honest with each other."

"Honestly, I'm putting out feelers. The apartment's getting a little crowded."

"Sorry my sisters need help," Josie snapped, not sounding sorry at all.

"Hey, I'm glad Emma moved in. I know it's important to have her close. I'm just planning ahead."

"You're planning to leave."

"I was asking Fabio about a place for my mom. I'm not going anywhere."

"Well you can if you want. Move in with Seema. I don't care."

*Thwap.*

Dean held the ball. "Jo. What are you doing?"

And here came a phenomenon so rare that Dean had witnessed it exactly once, years ago, the summer in high school when Josie's rabbit had to be put down: Josie started crying, loudly, and without abandon.

The two boys fighting with sticks declared a bilateral ceasefire and stared. Dean dropped the ball. He ran over and held her tightly.

"I'm sorry. I'll stay, I'll go. Whatever you need. I know how stressful things are right now."

Her chest shook. The nicer Dean acted, the more hateful she felt. She did not make public displays of emotion. She was a grown woman who Kept Her Shit Together. Yet here she went, falling to her knees and punching the soft ground, denting the earth that she could've saved by saying one normal non-family thing and had not. A foursome on a blanket gave her disappointed looks for violating the Picnickers Creed: *thou shalt not make a scene.*

"How miserable are you going to let me make you?" she asked.

"You don't make me miserable."

"Why do you put up with this shit?"

"Because I love you, Josie. You know that. There's no other shit I want."

"Don't say that. You know it's only a matter of time . . . just get it over with. Cut your losses, man." Tears dripped into the grass.

"Okay, I have to be honest," Dean said. "I have no idea what's happening right now."

Josie couldn't look at him. Whenever the tree of life grows—whether it branches, buds, or inosculates back on itself—who knows what might evolve? Go in the other direction, however, into destruction, entropy, extinction? There was a calming certainty in that. Failure was safe. Predictable. Quite possibly the only outcome in a wildly chaotic universe that Josie could guarantee, each and every time.

"What's happening is that you're leaving me," she said.

"No I'm not."

"You will."

Dean rubbed her back. "I can't help with everything, Jo, but I can tell you the truth, and the truth is that I want to be with you. What signs have I ever given otherwise? Let's do this. Let's be together."

"You don't want that."

He whispered, serious: "I do."

Dean drank far too much, sure, and he played too many videogames, and he could've splashed less when washing his face in their shared bathroom, but he worked tirelessly for Josie and her sisters and his mother and the working class, and hardly asked for anything himself. Yet he was asking now. He dropped a knee and asked Josie to marry him. Just like that. The motherfucker.

She answered with her mitt, a broadside to his head. "Stop it! Stand up! Right now."

Now Dean was the one with tears in his eyes. "Why the hell not?"

"Because you just drank a whole bottle of wine and you're being an idiot and you're an alcoholic and you don't mean it and you literally could not have picked a worse time."

"There will never be a good time, Jo. That's life! So who cares? I love you."

"Shut up! Stop saying that."

She wound up and made a gorgeous parabola with her mitt into the pond. Ducks paddled to investigate the splash. The foursome packed baskets and rolled blankets in a hasty retreat.

Dean wouldn't shut up. "We can't do life alone. We're a social species, like you're always saying. So let's do this. Me and you. Let's make something. Together. What we have is good. You know that. Don't burn it down just because you don't think you deserve to be happy. Don't let what happened at Stanford happen all over again."

She had to mute him immediately, so she punched him in the face. It worked. A good portion of human DNA is viral, Josie knew, up to eight percent of our genome made from ancient retroviruses that invaded early cells, stuck around, and became us. In this moment, however, Josie felt viral through and through, a hundred percent sick with the desire to infect, hijack, and self-sabotage all that was good and healthy. Her breasts ached. Her pelvis hurt. She felt dizzy, dark, cruel. "You need to move out," she said.

"I think I already did?" The cracks between Dean's teeth were pink with blood.

"I mean for good."

"You don't mean that."

"I do!" Josie hit him with her fists. "I do!"

She spun and walked into Jamaica Pond to retrieve her mitt. She waded out, treading water. The force of her tears had created a syphon effect—she was done crying, but the tears wouldn't stop. If there was one thing Josie had learned in life, it was that other humans couldn't be counted on. Her father. Her mother. Her sisters. People always left. And sure enough, when she turned around, Dean had packed up. She watched him throw a leg over his bike and pedal off, wobbling a little, but not looking back. The picnic was over. He was leaving. As she'd always known he would.

# Chapter 30

# Ara

Called Sister after dinner. She gave me a preorder update (962) and played a track-in-progress. I gave notes. She said she needed lyrics, when would Revenge Song be ready? I said I was working on it. We said our goodbyes.

A group in the dayroom was watching *Judge Judy*, including the woman with the birthmark. I sat next to her.

"Heard you make music," I said.

"Heard right."

I asked if she ever wrote lyrics.

"Whack MCs write lyrics. I write poetry."

My defenses somehow subdued an eye roll. I asked if she wanted to help me with a song.

She said she'd been wondering when I'd ask.

Her name is Jules. Lead singer of Red Lipstick, an alt-femme band I'd never heard of but said I had. She's awaiting trial, picked up for writing bad checks, and if you can't admire her for trying to pass off bad checks in our modern times, you can admire her bluntness.

"You started the Mosh for Women's Lives and then you abandoned the movement," she said. "You opened for Rage, for fuck's sake! If I looked like you and your sis? If I had a hit like 'American Mosh'? Shit I'd have ten records by now *and* a revolution."

I smiled. Something fun about her abuse. An admiration behind her jabs.

"I'm having trouble with this one song," I said. "Maybe I'm overthinking it."

"Yeah that'll happen."

Judge Judy was hearing the case of a chicken farmer who'd accused a neighbor's dog of murdering his flock. The dog had gotten into the coop and killed every hen. The farmer was shaking his fist. Judge Judy banged her gavel. The wanton destruction, the farmer yelled. The senselessness. Somebody's gotta pay.

"So what do you do?" I asked.

"Stop overthinking it."

"That easy?"

"If you want it bad enough."

"I do."

"So go."

Okay, I did. Scribbled down a few lines right there.

"Who's Becca?" Jules said, reading over my shoulder.

"A fan," I said. "A diehard."

# Chapter 31

# Josie

Josie dried out on the grass by the shores of Jamaica Pond until the sun set and the mosquitoes started up. She couldn't go home. Dean was home. Or he wasn't. Both realities felt equally unbearable. She was shaky with anger at him, for getting drunk and pulling this shit now, when Ara needed her most. She wrung the last drops of pond from her hair, wearily straddled her bike, and pedaled down Centre Street in the opposite direction from the apartment. She secured her bike against the natural gas meter outside the Butterfly & Reptile World and unlocked the door.

One step inside, and already she felt calmer. Humans always let you down. Nature, never. It was why she'd spent her childhood running through woods and wading through marshes. Why she'd studied biology at Tufts. Why she'd done a year as a fieldtech after graduation: one fun summer at a Florida Panhandle Army base, tagging sea turtle nests and sleeping in '50s-era concrete barracks. Then southern Georgia, earning $100 a week to comb the remaining patches of wetland for flatwoods salamanders. A wet winter on the Oregon coast, catching brown bats with slingshot rigs and mist nets, banding wings, smoking pot on driftwood benches, nerding out with fellow nerds on foggy beaches.

She loved fieldteching. Everyone wanted to advance research and geek out about nature. Even the primary investigators, mostly PhD students, were relaxed (because they were the ones with funding, she later understood). There was casual romance. There was terrific Northern California pot. And, for the ambitious, the opportunity to make connections and climb the career ladder from the ground up.

It worked.

Fieldteching led to Fulbright Fellowship.

Fulbright Fellowship led to the discovery of two new ant species (*Pheidole araminta, Pheidole emmata*), and a theory about horizontal gene transfer, leafcutter ants, and their cultivar fungi.

Which led to Stanford.

Stanford hadn't been Josie's first choice, but Dr. Victor Lee wanted her, *needed* her, could *not fathom* his lab at the Department of Ecology and Evolutionary Biology without this Josephine Tayloe everyone was talking about. He recruited her aggressively, thanks in large part to Ilana Sanchez, the PhD candidate who'd supervised the Oregon brown bat study. Josie was entertaining other offers. But flattery, as usual, won.

Dr. Lee ("Call me Victor!"—Josie tried and could not) wore crisp suits with no tie. He buzzed his head. An athletic fifty, single, he was maybe asexual, maybe too committed a scientist to bother with love. He chaired the department, taught, published like a Gutenberg, leap-frogged the Northern Hemisphere conference-symposium circuit, and somehow *still* found time for lab pop-ins to ensure his team was eating, sleeping, having sex—

"Your boss asks if you're having sex?" Dean said.

Dean and Josie were throwing a Frisbee in Golden Gate Park when he posed the question. Dean had moved to San Francisco to be near Josie. He was organizing for the Service Employees International Union, representing airport workers. He and Josie got together once or so a month when their 8,000-hour weeks allowed.

"First of all, he's not my *boss*. He's the Principal Investigator, head of my lab. Secondly, sex is a biological need. You're just trying to make him sound creepy, phrasing it like that."

"I'd love to hear you try phrasing it in a non-creepy way."

What Josie couldn't articulate was that Dr. Lee simply wasn't like that. He believed (as Josie did!) that scientific knowledge was a collaborative project. While other principal investigators guarded their research, Dr. Lee proposed joint investigations into the sperm-storage capabilities of multiple moth species, offered to personally line-edit articles, brought to their attention a competitive DoD grant that could boost departmental morale.

Not that they needed morale!

Morale was another thing Dr. Lee took care of, hosting wine-and-cheeses at his Victorian overlooking Half Moon Bay. He feted a rotating cast of docs, postdocs, visiting fellows, the rare lay-expert deemed worthy. And then, just when you thought the man must sleep, he kept your inbox warm through dawn:

Could a spermatheca investigation be run in tandem with your ant project?

Can you sub my BIOSCI 101 seminar Thurs?

Any lab requests? How are new thermocyclers? PCR gods approve?

Dr. Lee was not creepy, as Dean seemed to suggest. Dr. Lee was ambitious, and his ambition rubbed off; three years in his lab, and Josie had two articles in *American Myrmecologist*, a gutsy dissertation topic continuing Dr. Lee's work on moth reproduction, and unimpeachable student reviews.

"Student reviews? I thought you didn't have to teach?"

Here Dean went again. This time he and Josie were working the merch table at the Greek Theater. Emma and Ara were onstage for the second of two sold-out shows.

"It's just a seminar," Josie shouted over the music.

Josie's EPA Star grant did technically free her from teaching responsibilities, but another trait she admired in Dr. Lee was his commitment to preparing "future citizen scientists," as he called the undergrads. And if his commitment required the occasional assist, well, knowledge was a collaborative project.

"Hold up, it's *his* seminar you're teaching?" Dean asked.

"Whose seminar? Dr. Lee's?"

"Yes. Dr. Lee's." Dean was smiling, enjoying himself. "Please tell me you're fucking."

Josie sprayed a mist of beer across the T-shirt display. "Gross."

"You're in love with him."

"You're jealous."

"Of course I'm jealous!" Dean laughed. "He's all you talk about."

"It's not like that. Dr. Lee's more like a—"

Josie blushed violently, for she knew that Dean knew what had nearly slipped from her mouth, and it embarrassed her to be a grown-ass woman who was ashamed at a word as common as *father*.

"—he's more like a *mentor*," she said. "Go get us more beers."

They sold out of T-shirts, her sisters crushed the encore, she slept at Dean's, they got pleasantly lost in Golden Gate Park the next morning. A good weekend by all accounts. Yet Dean's comment had induced a somatic mutation, and evolution, as Josie well knew, is irreversible.

That morning, driving the lab van back to campus, she felt blind to the spectacular views of Pacific and cliff. She could only think about Dr. Lee, but not in the good (*fatherly*) way. She was teaching his BIOSCI 101 seminar. Her dissertation had evolved from the role of bacteria in gene transfer between fungus and ants—which *she* loved—to the reproductive capacities of moths, which *Dr. Lee* loved.

The tape of her time at Stanford continued rewinding, and like "Stairway to Heaven" played backward, what had been a momentous, successful hit became a warped, minor-key tune with possible satanic influences.

Most shameful was the Kern Primrose. How many hours had Josie spent kicking around Carrizo searching for the doomed species? A thought struck her. A Crazy Thought: What if the Kern Primrose was not threatened, but extinct, and only Dr. Lee knew, yet sent Josie and the others as a loyalty test?

She brought up the Crazy Thought with Ilana Sanchez. They were in the lab, waiting for their thermocyclers to complete their PCR reactions.

Ilana swatted Josie's knee. "You're *so* funny, Josie!"

"You don't think it's weird he never goes to Carrizo?"

"With his schedule? When would he? But he better make time for my wedding."

Ilana wasted no opportunity reminding others of her engagement to John Wang, the hot lab supervisor. The diamond on her ring winked as she hit reset for another PCR cycle. She was amplifying a bat mite gene, and her primer required a long strand of non-binding DNA. She put a hand on Josie's arm and lowered her voice.

"Don't tell anyone—I haven't even told John—but I'm going to ask Victor to walk me down the aisle. He'll say yes, don't you think?"

"For sure," Josie said, swallowing an uncomfortable taste of envy. "Is your dad not in the picture?"

Ilana stuck out her tongue. "That prokaryotic piece of shit left when I was four."

Josie hadn't known this about Ilana, and although the commonality could've been a Petri dish of loss over which to compare notes, and perhaps even share a bond of grief, Josie instead felt a chill. Her father had died when she was two, her sisters three. As a girl, she'd insisted to Emma and Ara that she remembered him, but in truth, she did not. There had been a few photos (none prominently displayed) which offered a proto-memory sensation, but Bertie so rarely mentioned him that Josie and her sisters had grown up with the understanding that they weren't supposed to ask, even if their mother had never outright forbidden it.

So what?

Many young individuals from all kingdoms of life grew into fully-functional adult individuals under fatherless conditions. Only now, turning in her swivel chair, Josie gave the lab a 360-degree survey and wondered: How many of Dr. Lee's graduate assistants also happened to be fatherless women? And of these, how many had Ilana recruited? Josie watched Ilana fiddle with her thermocycler. Ilana had defended her dissertation the fall before. She was a postdoc who'd remained at her graduating institution. Which *nobody* did unless they wanted to commit career hara-kiri. Unless, Josie thought, someone cared more about her advisor than her career. Unless someone worshipped her advisor like the father she never had . . .

Ilana closed her eyes and murmured a prayer for a smooth PCR cycle. The thermocyclers were finicky. Everyone built silly altars to "appease the PCR gods" as Dr. Lee liked to say. Josie's altar had an ant key chain, an Ant Man action figure, one of Emma's guitar picks. Ilana's altar had a bat Beanie Baby and a little toy Batmobile. Leaning against the hood of the Batmobile was a small picture that Josie hadn't closely inspected until now. It was an author photo, meticulously cut, from *The Sex Lives of Moths*, by Dr. Victor Lee.

Holy shit, Josie realized. I'm in a cult.

Just then, as if Beloved Leader was watching, her email pinged:

Hey kid! Hope you had a blast at the show. Just downloaded American Mosh, what a tune! Lab calendar says you're free Friday? Can you swing by Carrizo? PS, take van, all yours. PS, send me your latest chapter, I know there's an article we can squeeze out of it. Keep on rocking, so proud. – V

Some cults operated on vulnerability, revealed secrets, shared pain. Others, like Dr. Lee's lab, operated on flattery and pride. Josie much preferred her sort of cult, and so it wasn't with total surprise (and tolerable levels of self-loathing) that she found herself exiting I-5 later that week for the Carrizo Plain. She waded fruitlessly through the sharp grasses for two hours, crossed that section off the field grid, then decided to treat herself with a Pismo Beach detour on the trip back.

It was prime monarch season, the heart of the northern migration. Butterflies fluttered through the eucalyptus grove, tinting the sky orange. Josie watched in reverence, not thinking about population decline (all signs pointed toward extinction within decades), nor Dr. Lee, nor her sickening urge to please him. As a girl, she'd raised monarch caterpillars on transplanted milkweed shoots at her bedside table. She loved monarchs almost as much as she loved ants.

Something caught her eye at the edge of the grove, where the trees edged into sand dunes: a man in denim overalls, shuffling along, head stooped in classic entomologist posture. Josie walked over.

"Hi there, you collecting?"

The man smiled, displaying two rows of catastrophic teeth. "Do not worry. Not your pretty butterflies. I'm only after heteropterans."

(*Heteroptera*, aka leaf bugs, Josie would've told her undergrads. Water bugs, flower bugs, plant bugs. Think: *Bugs*.)

He tweezered a green insect off a leaf and dropped it into a vial. He had wispy Beethoven hair, a tanned leather face with many malignant-looking moles, a vaguely Teutonic accent. His name was Moritz Crueler, German by way of Zurich, and he was collecting leaf bugs in Pismo Beach because it was downwind of the Diablo Canyon nuclear power plant, he explained. Last month he'd collected by the Hanford reactor in Washington. Before that, Three Mile Island. He'd already done the French reactors. Next up was Japan. He was documenting mutations caused by low-level radionuclide emissions. He collected heteropterans because they were so vulnerable to contamination. Josie was welcome to examine his biodata, if she was curious.

*If?*

The only way Josie could've been more curious was if Moritz Crueler had been a heteropteran himself.

She followed in her car to his rented bungalow, which doubled as his lab. He prepped a stereo microscope and invited Josie to look. She didn't need an advanced degree to notice wing parts emerging from eyes, the stumps sprouting from thoraxes, the partially-formed neck plates, the missing legs.

While Moritz took photographs of the deformities with a mounted microscope camera, Josie flipped through his binders, admiring the careful documentation from other sites.

"This is incredible," she said. "Why don't people know?"

"They do."

"Where have you published?"

Moritz sneered. "You academics and your publications."

"But this could be a monumental study! If you can back up the morphological data with genetic sequencing—think of the public safety implications. People need to know."

"I've been letting people know for years."

"For real, I mean. On a larger scale. A peer-reviewed study."

Moritz sneered again. He was a big sneerer. He checked his watch, then opened a bottle of white wine, and offered Josie a glass.

Josie didn't understand how he could be so cavalier. Her curiosity, in the span of forty-five minutes, had evolved into a multi-cellular growth of breathtaking complexity.

*This* was the work she wanted to be doing!

*This* was the maverick scientist she wanted to be!

She'd come to Stanford to learn how leafcutter ants communicated, how they responded as a united colony in the face of tragedy, and instead she'd wasted years on moth sperm. She'd been worshipping a person instead of nature. Fuck Dr. Lee's moths. Fuck Dr. Lee!

Her hands were shaking, she was so excited. She tried not to spill her wine as she followed Moritz to the porch. "Say your methodology controlled for mitigating factors, say you offered a comparative baseline, a reference habitat—"

He lit a thin cigarette. "Yes, yes, you think I don't know?"

"So you've already talked to experts?"

"I am an expert."

"Other experts."

Two surfers walked by, boards under arms. The sound of the ocean carried from the beach. Moritz flicked his cigarette. "Your *experts* say low-level nucleotide emissions are harmless, falling within safe levels of natural radiation from Earth's crust."

"And?"

Moritz extended an arm toward his bungalow-lab, his binders, his thousands of photographs of deformed bugs. "I conclude."

"You *hypothesize*," Josie corrected. "But if you completed a full statistical analysis, backed up by genetic—"

"I have neither the time nor the money. I collect, I document, I give talks at libraries when invited. This is my work." He spit over the railing.

"What if I did it?" Josie said, gulping her wine.

"Did what?"

"I have time, Moritz! I have funding! My lab has an electron microscope with tungsten imaging resolution. I have access to one of the most powerful DNA sequencers in the country!"

"Good for you."

"Is that a yes?" Josie said, blood rushing to her head. "Can I?"

Moritz flicked a nub of ash from his cigarette. "If you wish."

———

"*Low-level radiation induces genetic mutations leading to germline deformities in heteropteran insects.*" Dr. Lee ran a hand over his stubbled scalp. "I don't think so, kid."

"Sorry?" Josie hadn't expected a high five, but she had expected a discussion.

"You can't expect me to let you trash your research and start over on something so, so—"

*Unrelated to moths?* Josie thought.

"—reckless. Even if you could complete this kind of analysis, which is pretty ambitious, let's be real, the thing reeks of conspiracy theory." He rolled Josie's proposal into a paper tube and smacked it like a gavel in his open palm. "Put yourself in my position, kid—how can I, in good faith, allow you to defend something like this?"

Josie, for a nanosecond, blacked out. "Are you saying you won't let me defend if I revise my dissertation?"

"This isn't revising. This is burning everything to the ground."

"Are you saying you won't let me defend?" Josie repeated.

Dr. Lee paused, choosing his words carefully. "I'm saying that your dissertation committee will anticipate some grave challenges."

Ha! Grave challenges accepted. Josie wouldn't switch dissertations. *She would do both.*

She committed herself to proving Dr. Lee wrong and Moritz Crueler right. Her commitment required frequent collection trips to Pismo Beach and Yosemite (her comparative baseline habitat), all-nighters in the lab, interlibrary loan requests to catch her up on the latest literature on Hox genes, homeotic mutation, the mechanisms of radiological damage.

Eighteen-hour days became the norm. She was in the lab, or she was on the road. The lab van worked double-duty as a depository for potato chip bags, seltzer cans, energy bar wrappers. She visited university health when her constipation approached the event horizon. They gave her a stool softener. The stool softener relieved her constipation, but not her impulse to stress-eat. When she stepped on a scale, the data point confirmed her observations: acquired mass. But mass could be lost. The only nonrenewable resource was time. She had to take advantage of each minute of the day.

Everyone knew that radioactive contamination caused mutation, but Moritz Crueler hypothesized that radionuclide emissions were causing *germline* mutations, meaning the deformities could be passed to offspring. Scary stuff. Proving it was tiresome work, requiring two parallel projects: her Nineteenth Century project, and her Twenty-First Century project.

Her Nineteenth Century project was old-school naturalist observation. She collected leaf bugs to breed in the lab, propagating family lines to document mutations when they reappeared. It was essentially the same method that O.G. geneticist Gregor Mendel had made famous with his pea plants in the 1800s (the only difference being that Mendel hadn't enjoyed access to a $100,000 scanning electron microscope). Josie had to feed the bugs (cucumber, oat bran), clean the cases, apologize to Ilana and the others for the smell. Was it laborious? It was laborious. But it was fun, quaint—*joyous!*—compared to her Twenty-First Century project.

Her Twenty-First Century used CRISPR to isolate an offending Hox gene. Then she'd amplify the DNA, run a gel, send it to the DataHog GX for sequencing, and wait for the chromatogram. This she'd compare against an online database of genomes, pull anomalies, and repeat the entire process, many hundreds of times.

Like all state-of-the-art technology, the DataHog GX would become an obsolete relic in a decade's time, but at the moment, the machine was a crown jewel in the university treasury. Scientists sent subsamples from as far as Colorado. Despite its power, the DataHog techs could only sequence so many samples in a day. Fortunately for Josie, the techs were human beings, and thus not immune from petty bribery. Bribery, combined with her EPA grant privileges, got her subsamples bumped to the front of the line. But she had thousands of subsamples. After the techs emailed her the chromatograms, she still had to proof the damn things by eye. She began sleeping under her lab bench, a blanket draped to keep out the light. She dreamt of sine waves, the warm hum of the thermocyclers. She missed class for the first time since she'd blown out her ear drum in the eighth grade. She was running on fumes. She needed two hands to pipette a subsample, they shook so badly.

"You don't sound so good," Dean said, when Josie made the mistake of answering his call.

"I'm find."

"You're find?"

"I'm *fine*! It's fine, everything's fine."

In some ways, Josie was fine. Her body thrummed with purpose. She hadn't done a favor for her sisters or argued with her mother in weeks. Months! And she was making progress with her research. She sent Dr. Lee her abstract and preliminary findings. He did not respond with enthusiasm.

Can't hide disappointment that you continue down this path of self-destruction. Also, I'm getting emails. You canceled 3 classes in a row? Ilana says van is a mess. Van is a privilege. Come on, kid. Meet to chat?

Josie cherrypicked from the stages of grief (denial, anger), then added two new ones (rebellion, paranoia), and doubled her efforts. Nineteen-, twenty-hour days. That was when the paranoia really set in. Except that paranoia based on concrete observation wasn't paranoia, Josie decided. It was . . . reality? Because reality was that people were giving her looks. Reality was that her ID card didn't work one night, leaving her locked outside the lab. Reality was that someone had reprogrammed her thermocycler, ruining a batch of substrates, and when she asked Ilana if she was the one who'd fucked with her shit, Ilana looked at Josie like she was a failing undergrad begging for a C. She did not get an invite to Dr. Lee's January wine-and-cheese, nor a Save the Date to Ilana and John Wang's engagement party.

John nudged Josie awake one night. Her thermocycler had been beeping for twenty minutes, he said. He looked around, as if to double-check they were alone. "Josie, I'm telling you this not as your lab supervisor, but as your friend—you might want to take a shower."

She fired off an email to Dr. Lee: *What are you saying about me behind my back?*

He didn't reply. Too disappointed? Too busy talking about her over wine and cheese? Josie was going to prove him wrong even if it killed her. Which it nearly did.

She was returning from Pismo Beach when she fell asleep. The PCR gods were watching over her—fifty yards in either direction and she would've plummeted into the Pacific. Instead the van careened off the guardrail and flipped, landing with a sickening crunch. Josie hung upside down, her seat belt fastened, a comfort not enjoyed by the vat in back. The lid splintered upon impact. Liquid nitrogen sloshed, hissing and steaming. So too went the 171 cryovials of leaf bug samples collected that morning. Josie listened to the crackling of the upholstery going subzero, and worried that the accident would set her back days, possibly even a week.

"I'm afraid this is far more serious than a week," said the Dean of the Graduate School.

They were meeting in a conference room. The Dean, the Vice President of Student Affairs, and Dr. Lee. Totaling the departmental van wasn't the sole issue, Dr. Lee said. Josie had missed BIOSCI 595 three weeks running. Her BIOSCI 101 seminar was in open revolt. The DataHog techs had received threatening emails. Someone had melted Ilana's altar in her thermocycler, ruining a $2,000 piece of equipment.

"If you're trying to sabotage me, it won't work." Josie grimaced. Her ribs still ached from the accident.

Dr. Lee shook his head. "You're sabotaging yourself, kid. You need a break. Don't burn out. You've got a real future here."

"Stop calling me *kid*! You're not my fucking father."

Dr. Lee put his face in his hands.

The Dean piped up. "We're recommending a semester leave, followed by university counseling, if you elect to return."

"I reject your recommendation."

Dr. Lee spoke through his hands: "It's not that kind of recommendation."

She called Moritz from the lab. He was gleeful to hear that Josie wished to abandon the life of a pretentious academic. Yes, he'd happily pick her up. Yes, she could fill the trunk of his car with as much lab equipment as she could carry out.

The haul amounted to one set of micro-pipettes, a case of disposable pipette tips, a box of Erlenmeyer flasks, and a case of Taq polymerase enzyme that occupied most of Moritz's freezer along with the rack of 50 ml falcon tubes containing her buffer solutions (which wasn't *really* stealing, as she had mixed the solutions in the first place).

Soon after, Josie ran smack into the problem shared by rebel intellectuals since Socrates: without institutional support—without an electron-scanning microscope or a DataHog GX sequencer—you can only get so far. Her research sputtered. While she strategized on what to do next, she slept. She slept on Moritz's couch. She slept on the plastic chaise lounge on his porch. She slept with her head on her arms at the makeshift desk he'd assembled for her in the kitchen.

Josie knew she was depressed. Adrift. Numb. She observed a fascinating, obliterating sense of shame that grew in direct proportion to the variable $x$, which stood for the number of emails she sent Dr. Lee that went unanswered. Crashing on the Pacific Coast Highway had permanently altered her cell chemistry. Her messenger RNA only remembered how to deliver a single line of run-on code: *you are useless and will never fully succeed at anything so why even try.*

But Dean wouldn't let her wallow. He kept calling. She had to respond. He required approximately two seconds to conclude that he was immediately driving down.

"Don't," Josie said, monotone. She couldn't bear for him to see her like this.

"Too bad. I'm on my way."

"Well I'm in the field. I don't know when I'll be back."

Moritz, who overheard the conversation, later said, "You've not told your boyfriend that you were terminated?"

"I was suspended, not terminated. And Dean's not my boyfriend."

"I see," said Moritz, and that evening, after his 4 p.m. wine, he kissed her on the mouth and fondled her breasts.

Josie pushed him off. "No, Moritz. Dammit. You can't do that."

He looked shocked. "I apologize. I won't."

She'd done it again. Trying to make a father figure out of someone who didn't want the job. Why else was she sleeping on Moritz's couch, working maniacally to prove *his* theory, if not to win *his* approval? Why was she doing any of this? For the heteropterans? They'd existed millions of years before humans and would continue long after, radionuclide germline mutations and all. They didn't need her. Nobody did.

She moped for another week. She took up smoking. She rewatched every episode of *My So-Called Life*. What further paths of self-destruction may Josie have blazed into the map of her future, she'd never know, for one morning, as she was filling an Erlenmeyer flask to the 500 ml line with Pino Grigio, Dean walked in, came straight across the kitchen, and wrapped his long arms around her.

Moritz stepped in behind him. "I borrowed your phone. Apologies for the intrusion, but I felt the responsibility had fallen on me to let someone know."

"Let someone know what?" Josie asked.

Moritz's and Dean's eyes flashed to the Erlenmeyer flask of white wine.

"I'm not allowed to take a research break?" Josie said.

The men said nothing.

She pointed at Dean. "You're the one with the drinking problem. Not me."

"I'm worried about you, Jo. You got kicked out of school?"

Josie groaned. She was mortified to have been found by Dean like this. Yet she also experienced a twisted stab of pleasure at being seen in such a wretched state. At the same time, she felt embarrassed at this pleasure. She was angry at Moritz, for calling Dean. And angry at Dean, for arriving unannounced. Most confusing, she felt an immense sense of comfort that she couldn't understand—oh, because other people were finally worried about *her* for a change! The conflicting emotions bounced around her head like so many excited photons trying to escape the core of the sun. They'd take eons to sort out. As for explaining to Dean what had happened, she didn't know where to begin.

Fortunately, she didn't have to. That very morning, as she and Dean were walking Pismo Beach in silence, a small miracle occurred: Emma called with the terrible yet timely news that Ara's need for painkillers and Xanax had grown "problematic."

Emma didn't outright ask Josie to help organize an intervention, or research inpatient treatment centers, or find a trauma-informed therapist who knew about tapered withdrawal from benzodiazepines. But "help" was all Josie heard.

She'd drop out of school immediately, she told Emma, trying not to sound excited about it. She'd fly back East. She'd move home. She'd go wherever she was needed most, do whatever was needed, for the good of the colony.

———

Now, one unfinished PhD and five years later, Josie stood in the semi-darkness of the Butterfly & Reptile World, watching the leafcutters busy on the Skyway, hauling vegetation for their fungal gardens. Fabio and the interns had closed for the evening. Fluorescent light peeked through from the nocturnal room. Josie walked alongside the Skyway, taking in the sweet kombucha rot of tropical vegetation, the hum of the ventilation, the unceasing march of the leafcutters. Individual ants might rest periodically, but the super organism never paused. Twenty-four hours a day, 365 days a year, always at work for the collective good.

There was a saying at Al-Anon: "We're only as sick as our secrets." Josie had sat in enough circles in the Congregational church's basement to know the futility of blaming yourself for a loved-one's addiction. She hadn't caused Ara to start using. But allowing her to believe that she was responsible—even partially—for ending Josie's academic career? Could that have made things worse? She had to tell Ara every shameful detail of what had happened. And she would, eventually. First, though, she had to get her sister out.

Another thing Josie admired about leafcutters: They were incredibly strong—any one could carry a leaf fragment fifty times her weight—yet they knew their limits. None would ever think of attempting to lift an entire leaf alone. They carried exactly as much as they could bear, not a gram more.

She watched them until her bladder was about to rupture. She went to the staff breakroom, peed, and then, out of habit, checked the fridge after washing her hands. Other than some packets of soy sauce and a bottle of spicy mustard, it was empty. The freezer held more: three cases of frozen mice, an opened box of mango popsicles, and the Tupperware containing the plastic bag containing the Kern Primrose sphinx moth. Josie popped the Tupperware, opened the bag, and cradled the moth in her palm.

"What are you?"

*A Kern Primrose sphinx moth.*

"But we can't really know, without genetic sequencing."

*Morphological observation is vastly underrated in the digital age. Trust your gut.*

"I don't trust anything anymore."

*Why not?*

"Because it feels like everything is falling apart."

*It is. It's called the Second Law of Thermodynamics.*

"But can't we slow the rate?"

*You're so funny, Josie!*

"But seriously. Can't we try?"

*Go ahead.*

A bearded dragon hissed from the reptile room. Josie put away the moth, took a popsicle, and turned off the breakroom light. She checked on the dragons, then paused by Linda's enclosure. The snake's butterscotch sheen glowed. Linda truly was a beautiful animal.

A beautiful, fantastically valuable animal.

Josie's breath fogged the glass enclosure. How had she not considered it until now? She tapped the base of the popsicle stick softly against the glass.

*Don't.*

*Worry.*

*Linda.*

*I.*

*Would.*

*Never.*

Oh, but Linda knew she would. Every ant and butterfly and lizard in the World knew it. For the survival of the family—the colony, the species, the genome—what won't an organism do?

## Chapter 32

# Bertie

Europe was a dry strip of sepia. Africa, a fishing village barely visible through the hot haze that rested on the water. Ocean traffic merged into a multi-lane highway. Cargo ships, tankers, yachts, an iceberg of a cruise ship that eclipsed the evening sun as it gleamed past. From the mist rose the mountains of Morocco. The hump of Gibraltar. When the intercom buzzed—"we have officially entered the wine-dark sea, sailors"—the crew hooted and hollered.

As sun gave way to moon, Bertie saw that the Mediterranean was just like the Atlantic: the same bow of horizon, the same slipslapping waves, the same high-flying boredom. The lilt of the rolling ocean. The hot fierce sky. The hours to fill.

To fill the hours, Bertie led civil disobedience drills on the sundeck. Uri offered IDF calisthenics for those who wanted to sweat. Danny Noor and the Dearborn contingent gave Arabic lessons at the stern. Marsha Rubin dealt blackjack at a table excavated from the casino cargo hold. There was dinner to look forward to, General Assembly, evening movie.

Still, more than anything, there was time.

The crew's collective résumé boasted seventy-two post-bachelor's degrees, three MacArthur grants, two Pulitzers, two Nobels, and one Academy Award. The sailing was left to Tubbs, Tal, and Uri: the mechanically and navigationally inclined who knew radar blips and the dietary requirements of the Wärtsilä-Pielstick engines that kept the *A.R.C.* cleaving waves at a fuel-efficient 15 knots an hour. The rest of the crew was expected to fulfill one cooking, cleaning, and security shift per twenty-four-hour period. Bertie and Audrey, in the passage from New World to Old, had polished the sundeck railings, peeled potatoes, inspected fire extinguishers, shelled peas. They'd kept watch through every dull minute of the rocking night.

In four months, Bertie would be seventy-two. Audrey wanted to celebrate with a citizen's arrest of a Koch brother (it didn't matter which). Audrey was seventy-three. She hailed from a family of Alabama share-croppers, her grandfather an original Black Belt Communist. It wasn't impossible that Audrey's ancestors had once been property of Bertie's ancestors, which Audrey enjoyed reminding Bertie when it was her morning for breakfast prep at the Dorothy Day House and she didn't feel like getting out of bed.

Bertie was happy to take Audrey's breakfast shifts. She was grateful to the woman in more ways than one. Not until her disbarment hearings and the shuttering of the People's Law Center had Bertie realized how deeply her career had grounded her. Her final month as a lawyer, she'd argued a case against the Department of Corrections (they were cen-soring books on the Attica prison uprising) and settled a case requiring the state to provide attorneys to juveniles accused of violating parole.

After those last wins, she found herself disbarred, anchorless, adrift.

She hadn't been celibate since Walt's death, but moving into the Dorothy Day House had unlocked a secret of the post-menopausal: a totally unexpected sexual reawakening. Yes there was a decrease in valu-able bodily fluids, but there was also silicon lubricant, and vitamin E, and of course Audrey, whom Bertie couldn't yet say if she loved, but certainly loved being with.

Bertie hadn't planned on Audrey. But neither had she ever planned on becoming a wife, or a widowed mother of three young girls, or a woman openly in a relationship with another woman. She remembered what Allen Ginsberg and Bob Dylan had told her and Walt:

*This is why we must grow old, because everything weird will happen and it will be good.*

It had been good. But now Bertie was in knots; neither she nor Audrey had enjoyed a solid night's sleep since leaving Griffinport. Their cabin was a cramped windowless room in the quarters below deck. Audrey hadn't suspected just how intensely she'd dislike the open ocean. She tensed and reached for her lifejacket at every creak in the hull. Bertie tried to soothe her while also finding sleep herself. Troubling dreams kept waking her up.

She was a girl practicing her posture, floating across the polished Savannah Yacht and Country Club floor with a sandbag on her head, Araminta calling the steps.

She was a young mother, shouting Araminta's name in the marsh behind their house.

She was seventy-one, spooning Araminta in the sludgy dark of the A.R.C.

She'd wake, jaw clenched, sheets soaked. Finally, she and Audrey gave up and volunteered for the lonely midnight-to-3-a.m. shift. If they couldn't sleep, at least they could stretch their legs, try to identify constellations, and fill their lungs with salty night air.

They walked the rec deck, the sundeck, the promenade deck. Scanning the darkness for . . . Israeli zodiac boats? Orphaned shipping containers? The crew had agreed to take on all refugees spotted adrift, but Bertie couldn't even see where sea ended and sky began. They were rounding the sundeck hot tub when Audrey tugged her arm.

"This a race I don't know about? Take a breather. I got a surprise for you."

She squared Bertie to face the ocean. She then stepped behind her and fitted her with earbuds. Emma's voice suddenly swamped Bertie's head.

*The pack is the nucleus.*
*The pack is all of us.*
*Family loves, family kills . . .*

Bertie held the railing. Ghost vibrations from the propellers buzzed through the hull and into her bones. She listened until the song faded, replaced by Ara's voice, *Live from MCI-Bogastow, this is Araminta Tayloe, sending you kisses and love.*

She popped out the earbuds. "This is *precisely* why I didn't drive back with Josephine. See all they accomplished on their own?"

Audrey wrapped her arms around Bertie. "Sounds to me like mama bear's proud."

"Stop it. You know I can't stand that word."

Bertie smacked Audrey playfully with her earbuds. She loathed *proud* because *proud* sowed dependency and *proud* undermined self-worth. Parents these days caused irreparable harm with their coddling. Yet Bertie did have to admit that the new song was quite good. Haunting. Her girls were so gifted. And Josephine, could she cause a stink, but the mind on her! If only Walt could've lived to see the brilliant women their girls had become.

"I like that I can understand the lyrics," Bertie said. "Some of their old tunes are so loud I can hardly make out a word."

"You better like it! I got Max to download it off the satellite connection. Wasn't cheap. Cost a week of bathroom duty."

"That was silly. You didn't have to do that. But thank you."

"Don't thank me. Wasn't my bathroom duty I traded. It was yours."

Bertie smiled. She squeezed Audrey's arm. A satellite arced across the night sky.

"Play it again?"

They took an earbud each, and as Bertie listened to her girls, the cable connecting her heart to Araminta's loosened for the first time since leaving Griffinport. Not much—a quarter-turn at most—but any slack was relief.

———

Later that morning, after their shift, as dawn colored the clouds and Audrey's nervous moaning filled their cabin, the tension returned with a flare. Bertie gave birth to the twins. She was squatting in the living room of the old house. The girls slid out, naked, glistening, fully formed adults, but in miniature. The kitchen phone was ringing. Ringing and ringing. This time she would pick up. But she couldn't get to the phone. Emma held her down, craning her mouth for her breast. And Ara had crawled into the fireplace. She was stuffing ashes into her vagina.

*Get out of there, Araminta. Get out of that filthy place now.*
*I need this filthy place, Mom. I need this filth the most.*
*Om Shanti Shanti.*

*Caw, caw, caw.*

The girls were toddlers when Walt had left for good. What Bertie was doing on the *A.R.C.* was completely different, she told herself, awake and soaked in nightsweat, her legs dangling off the bunk. Her girls were grown women. They didn't need her. They *shouldn't* need her. It wasn't right to hold a child's hand forever. Janice was looking after Araminta, after all. And Bertie herself was disbarred—she wasn't allowed to help. She'd tried, the night before the *A.R.C.* sailed from Griffinport, calling three judges she knew. But it was as she'd warned Josie—people weren't jumping to be associated with Bertie after her disbarment hearings, especially for something as clear-cut as a drug charge. If she could've sucked the poison from her girl's veins, she would've, long ago. But she couldn't. Returning would've done nothing for Ara. The *A.R.C.* was important—extending a hand to widowed women and grieving children. Even if she wanted to, she couldn't turn the *A.R.C.* around. A person could go crazy trying to fix everything that couldn't be fixed. Driving back with Josephine when she had the chance would've been so easy. But being a good mother—it was almost never easy.

# PART IV

# Family Kills

# Chapter 33

# Josie

Josie was suffering a problem shared by gambling addicts, parents of ransomed children, and third-world finance ministers facing a visit from the IMF: she was desperate for money, she needed it now, and she had no way of getting enough.

*Jailbreak* preorders had rocketed by the 1,000 milestone three days ago, hit 2,000 yesterday, then flatlined around 2,500 for almost twenty-four hours. Stagnation was killer.

"We're almost halfway there." Emma looked up from her workstation. She rubbed her eyes. "We're doing this. Stop worrying."

"Incorrect. We're not even three-tenths there. And nowhere with the girls."

"So keep trying to find them?" Emma suggested cheerfully, slipping on her headphones and returning to her keys.

Josie pried the cup of Emma's headphones off her right ear. "I say we get the bond, and tell Ara we made full bail."

"You want us to lie to her?"

"She lied to me. You both did."

Emma gave Josie a look that suggested she was behaving like an organism of the phylum *heartless*. "We need to let Ara be the author of her own life."

"Great. She can write it *here*, with *us*."

Darwin, Josie hated the whine of her own voice! When had Emma become the calm, collected one who spoke like a therapist, and Josie the one in need of validation? A mutation had occurred in the genome of their relationship. Not since wallowing on Moritz's couch by Pismo Beach had Josie felt this thoroughly useless. It didn't help that she hadn't heard a peep from Dean in four days. He'd offered his heart on a platter, and Josie had sent it back to the kitchen.

Emma cleared her throat. She told Josie to stop hovering. "Ara and I got the music. You find the girls."

"Okay," Josie mumbled.

She dragged herself to the kitchen and dug a joyless spoonful of extra-crunchy peanut butter from the jar. The sum total of information that Ara had passed along included the girls' names (Gemma, Ruby, Crystal), their father's (Kevin Johnson), and an address (a Lowell apartment complex). Josie had burned half of Friday driving to Lowell to wait two hours for the property manager to return from a Home Depot run so he could tell her that he remembered the family but didn't know where they'd gone. Josie called the Lowell public schools, yet—surprise—the district was not eager to provide strangers with student information. She didn't even know if the family still lived in Lowell. Or Massachusetts? As for dad, there were thousands of Kevin Johnsons out there, and a few of them (a former NBA player, a mayor, a retired gangster with the Winter Hill Gang) were far more famous Kevin Johnsons who monopolized the online search results.

What more could Josie do?

She took the peanut butter to her room and registered for a missing persons database that was surely a scam for desperate people like her. She wondered about hiring a private investigator. She dialed a bondsman to ask how she might bail someone out against their will. The bondsman (a woman) hung up. She checked the *Jailbreak* page (2,558). She called Ara's public defender three, four, five times. When the woman finally called back, it wasn't to strategize on finding three minors, as Josie hoped, but to scold. "I don't have time for this bullshit. Call me once you've convinced your sister to take the plea deal."

Josie flopped on her bed, spinning, nauseous. Sick with fear for Ara, sick at the sluggish pace of preorders, sick with regret about Dean. Sick most of all at her need to control every situation, along with the Second Law of Thermodynamics, and her utter failure to do so.

Sick, sick, sick.

Her phone pinged. She jumped for it. Not Dean. Not the missing persons database. Not Ara. Just Fabio, wondering if Josie would be gracing the World today with her presence.

She looked at the time. Shit.

She hustled into pants and biked down Centre Street, barging in to find Mimi crouched over a small pile of dead ants, neon green paint splattered everywhere.

"This is harder than you said," Mimi said.

"You shouldn't have started without me."

"I had to. You weren't here. And I'm the primary investigator."

Josie rushed through her chores, then set up to teach Mimi how to mark insects. Josie hadn't done it in years, but her fine-motor muscle memory behaved like no time had passed: She showed Mimi how to pluck an ant with forceps, fix it beneath the thread of the harness, dab paint on the thorax, return her to her sisters to get kicked around for a bit for smelling so foul. Josie repeated with a second ant, then a third, until Mimi grew impatient and said she was ready to try again.

Mimi crushed the first ant in her forceps, then got the hang of it. When a soldier nipped her finger, she didn't lash out. When Fabio asked if he was paying Mimi to decorate ants, Mimi did not respond. She was in the zone, dabbing minuscule thoraxes in green. Her concentration was fierce. She reminded Josie of someone. Herself.

"Fuck." Mimi held up her forceps. "I murdered another one."

"You're learning."

They worked together until Mimi had to start on her closing tasks. Josie didn't want her to leave. Back at Stanford, she and the other lab rats could go hours without remembering to eat, pee, use their legs. Sometimes she missed that most of all: the work, meditative in its enormity, an entomologist nirvana where the betrayals of human social behavior couldn't touch you.

"See you tomorrow, Josie."

"Mimi, wait. Can you listen to something?"

Josie played the latest track off her phone. "What do you think?"

"It's alright. Who is it?"

"My sisters. You don't have to buy it, obviously, I mean you can if you want, we're just doing preorders—but maybe you could like, share the link? With your friends?"

Josie cringed at every desperate old-person word coming out of her old-person mouth.

Mimi raised a fist. "I got you, Josie."

Then Mimi was gone. Then Fabio was gone. Then there were only so many chrysalis husks to sweep and hoses to coil before Josie too had to leave the World she loved for the world she did not. She stepped outside, locked the doors, and it all came crashing back: Ara was in prison and refusing bail and would be there for weeks—months? years?—and the best Josie could do was beg a fourteen-year-old girl to *maybe, like, share the link?*

Unacceptable. Josie unlocked the side door and marched back inside the Butterfly & Reptile World. She beelined for Fabio's office, and under the glow of her phone, rifled through his file cabinet until she found his list of rare animal vendors: people he'd connected with over the years when he wanted to show up the Franklin Park Zoo by acquiring something special.

Everybody else left when you needed them most, but Josie did not. Josie fought for the people she loved. She fought for them like hell. And if you wanted to fight for something like hell, you had to do it yourself. This, she'd known forever.

# Chapter 34

# Josie

She was pacing the artificial twilight of the Butterfly & Reptile World, when her phone pinged with a message from Dean. She dismissed it. Anxious as she was to hear from him since their fight, she was more anxious to hear from Ivan Tabachnik, a dealer with particular interest in rare and endangered animals. She'd agreed to meet him behind the World at 11 p.m. He'd be here any moment.

Josie had located Tabachnik by calling through Fabio's lists, asking contacts for contacts until she found someone four degrees of separation from anybody Fabio might ever conceivably know. Ivan Tabachnik, a Russian ex-pat, owned three Greater Boston ambulance companies and would pay based on an examination. Money—he assured Josie in an accent so rich she would've accepted it as collateral—would be no problem.

This was not betrayal, Josie told herself as her phone lit up. She was merely being proactive to help her helpless sister. She opened the back door and let him into the World.

Tabachnik stank of cologne. He wore a leather jacket, jeans, leather loafers with no socks, a chunky pinky ring that dug into Josie's hand when they shook hello. In his left hand he held a black gym bag.

"The moth?" he said.

Josie handed him a glass display cube. Almost a decade since she'd pinned and mounted an insect, and she'd done a beautiful job. The Kern Primrose's wings were spread, showcasing all their glory.

Tabachnik rotated the cube in his hands. "A fine specimen. A pity it is only threatened." He put down his bag to take photos. His phone *whooshed* with an outgoing text.

He hadn't expressed interest when Josie first pitched the Kern Primrose. His clients only desired endangered species. But Josie convinced him to think of the moth as an Anthropocene investment; no Kern Primrose had been seen in years, carbon emissions were at an all-time high, insect populations were nosediving. When Fish & Wildlife next updated their lists, they would certainly upgrade the moth's status to endangered.

Tabachnik's phone pinged. He looked up from his screen. "We have a deal."

"Yay," Josie said, imagining for one sickening moment that the client was Dr. Lee.

Tabachnik placed the display cube in his bag and gave Josie an envelope. She riffled the crisp bills. She felt like she was in a movie. Was it bad form to count the money now? She didn't care. She'd wanted a meaningful reason to find a Kern Primrose a continent away from its habitat? She'd wanted a reason to sell off her ticket to an article in *Nature*, and possibly a return to academia? Here were 3,000 reasons. She nodded at Tabachnik.

He smiled. "And now? The pièce de résistance?"

"This way."

Josie led him to the reptile room. He shone a penlight over Linda and grunted in admiration. A lavender lucifer albino ball python wasn't endangered, but it was fantastically rare, genetically unheard of practically, and, as Tabachnik was now seeing with his own eyes, utterly stunning. He pulled on leather gloves, measured Linda from tip to tail, palpated her length, examined her eyes and ears, then pulled out a plastic speculum to observe her oral cavity. He quizzed Josie about medical history, provenance, temperament. He examined shed skin and droppings, then fixed a hanging scale on the enclosure. Josie was helping him hoist Linda into the nylon webbing when she heard what was, empirically, the worst two sounds she could've imagined at this moment: the back door opening, and Fabio's laugh.

"Scatter!" Josie blurted to Tabachnik.

"What?"

Too late. Lights flipped on. Josie squinted in the brightness.

"Josie?" Fabio stood with his arm around a woman in a shimmery green top. "What's going on?"

"Hey, Fabio."

"What are you doing with Linda? Who the hell are you?"

Tabachnik looked at Josie. Fabio and his date looked at Josie. Linda flicked her tongue at Josie, as if she, too, were eager for an explanation. Josie took a breath. The creativity required for a lie of this caliber demanded every synapse in her brain firing at once. She had nothing. She released her breath in a long sigh, the resolve running out of her like cytoplasm through a punctured cell wall. She hoped Tabachnik could do better.

"Fabio, this is Ivan." She mouthed to Tabachnik, "*My boss.*"

Tabachnik winked, as though he'd dealt with this situation before. He transferred Linda's full weight to Josie's shoulders, pulled off his right glove, and strode over to Fabio, hand extended.

"Ivan Tabachnik. Rare animal collector and dealer. Your institution has many fine specimens. To say I'm interested would be understatement."

"Your institution!" Fabio's date laughed, visibly drunk. "I like the sound of that, Fabs."

Fabio's upper lip twitched. "Vicky, babe, wait in my office."

"You said I could hold the snake!"

"Go to my office. Now."

Vicky's heels clicked across the floor. She slammed the door. The monitor lizards woke and began hissing.

"You. Leave," Fabio told Tabachnik.

"Beg your pardon?"

"Get out of here."

Tabachnik pointed to Josie, who was trying to hide behind Linda's thick middle as the snake slithered around her shoulders. "Your colleague invited me to—"

"I'm in charge here. Not her. Get the fuck out."

Tabachnik grumbled as he packed up. "You waste my time, big

joke? Do not call me again, I don't care if you have albino Tyranno-saurus."

Josie watched Tabachnik huff off.

"Fabio," she began. "Ara's bail—"

"—No. Don't even."

He glared at her for a long moment. He said "Fu-u-uck" like one long drawn-out sine wave. The UV lights reflected off his eyes. He was tearing up. Josie had known sad drunk Fabio over the years. Also, happy drunk Fabio. Never angry drunk Fabio.

"How could you?" he said.

"I'm sorry." She shifted Linda's weight. Her arms were getting tired.

Fabio walked over. Together they hoisted Linda into her enclosure. They stood shoulder to shoulder, watching as she resettled into her home. Josie smelled alcohol on Fabio's breath. She wanted to run away, but she didn't dare move.

"I'm sorry," she said again.

Fabio was quiet. Then he said, "How much did he offer?"

Not only had Ivan Tabachnik stormed off with possibly the last Kern Primrose on the planet, he'd also left with $20,000, the amount he and Josie had agreed upon for Linda, pending examination. But now, stand-ing next to Fabio, the glint of hurt in his eyes, Josie felt that $20,000 would be insulting for a betrayal of this magnitude.

"Forty thousand," she said.

Fabio shook his head. He walked into his office. Josie heard shout-ing, drawers slamming. Just as she thought she should slip away through the back door, Fabio came storming out. He wound up and threw a wad of paper at Josie. It missed her, and bounced off Linda's enclosure.

"Pick it up," he said.

Fabio Castro, with his seven triplexes on the golden mile, his swollen bank account and nobody to spend it on—no children, no wife, no parents, nobody besides a lavender lucifer albino ball python and two so-so dates with Vicky—had written Josie a personal check for $40,001. Josie smoothed it against her thigh.

"Thank you, Fabio."

He spat on the floor. "I want you out of my unit by the end of the month."

———

Josie wheeled her bicycle up Centre Street in a trance. She had a check for $40,001 in one pocket, and an envelope with $3,000 in the other. Fabio hadn't technically fired her, though it was strongly implied. Tonight was Saturday, and the people were out, enjoying the warm air, and Josie had won. She'd sacrificed the most for Ara. More than Bertie or Dean, both of whom left when things got tough. More than Emma, who was already warming her face in the spotlight of fame to come. More even than Ara herself, who seemed happier in prison than out, which was so deeply sad if Josie stopped to think about it, so she didn't.

She crossed the street, watching for traffic while observing the emotional reaction taking place in the test tube of her heart. The final synthesized compound was as simple as it was familiar: one-part grief to two-parts relief. The same compound she'd synthesized after Dr. Lee's committee "recommended" a leave of absence. The same compound she'd synthesized after terminating her pregnancy at seventeen. The same compound she'd synthesized when Dean threw a leg over his bike and left the picnic, pedaling off for good.

She locked her bike outside the Fountain, pulled a one-hundred-dollar bill from the envelope, and watched a redhead with a sleeve of anime ink pour her a celebratory rosé at the bar.

She checked the *Jailbreak* page. 2,613 preorders. $26,130. If they could just double those numbers, and if Fabio didn't cancel his check, and if Ara accepted that they'd made a sincere attempt to find her roommate's girls? Ara could be free, possibly by next week. The thought made Josie giddy. It also shunted tears to the front of her eyes. A lot of "ifs." And then what?

"Tough day?" said the bartender.

Josie nodded.

The bartender displayed her inner biceps and flexed:

*not everything will be okay but something will*

"I hope so." Josie rested her head on her arms.

"I know so," said the bartender, squeezing a lime.

Then Josie remembered the message from Dean. She sat up and pulled out her phone.

Seema found the girls. 514 Old Mill Road, Newfield. This is for Ara.

# Chapter 35

# Josie

Old Mill Road ran parallel to the New Hampshire border. The Newfield landscape, like much of rural Massachusetts, was idyllic, even if the homes themselves had known better days. Lots of saggy roofs. Lots of discarded satellite dishes, washers, tire rims, water heaters. In one yard, a man was circling an aboveground swimming pool on an ATV, a rope from his hitch towing a boy on a floaty. Josie waved as they passed. The man raised a hand with a beer.

"Now that's a party," Emma said.

A bee flew in the window, tangling in Josie's hair. She gently brushed it away. She and Emma had stayed up late discussing what to do, then debriefed Ara when she made her morning call. Together, they hatched a plan: drive to Newfield, meet Kevin Johnson, arrange a visit for his girls, bring Ara home by the weekend.

"*If* he lets the girls visit," Ara had said. "And *if* we get to a hundred thousand."

"I'm feeling really good about the next seventy-two hours," said Emma.

Josie hadn't told her sisters about Fabio's check, or her Russian mob cash. The reality of losing her job and their home didn't feel real, as long as she kept it secret. When she realized with horror that this was *precisely* what their mother had done, it was double the reason not to tell. Plus, she agreed with Emma: her sister's optimism, for once, had some grounding in reality; the *Gazette* article had gone semi-viral. Preorders, overnight, had spiked. Online alerts Josie had set up for *Jailbreak* and the band were pinging. Something was happening.

———

514 Old Mill Road had no mailbox, so it took them two passes to choose the most likely candidate: a yellowing single-family home with a heap of pink, tasseled bicycles in the yard. Josie pulled even to the driveway just as a rusty-haired man in a blue mechanic's shirt walked outside and tossed a water bottle through the open back window of a sedan. He opened the driver's side door, then noticed Josie and Emma in the idling Volvo.

"You ladies trying to get back on the Turnpike?" he hollered.

"We're looking for the Johnsons," Josie said. "Are you Kevin?"

He took four steps toward them. He stuck his hands in his pockets. "Who's asking?"

Josie and Emma could've written a full Choose Your Own Adventure based on the many scenarios they'd planned with Ara over the phone.

If you SAY YOU ARE FRIENDS OF KYLA's . . .
If you SAY YOU ARE WITH PRISON OUTREACH . . .

"We're with MCI-Bogastow outreach," Emma said. "We help keep families in touch—"

"And reunite families who've dropped out of touch," Josie added.

He looked at them for an uncomfortable beat. "That woman tried to kill me."

If you APPEAL TO HIS DAUGHTERS' WELL-BEING . . .
If you APPEAL TO HIS WIFE'S WELL-BEING . . .

"Mr. Johnson," Josie said, "we know that things have been difficult, but studies show that children benefit from contact with their mother, even in cases of—"

"How'd you know where we moved?"

If you CITE ADDITIONAL STUDIES . . .
If you APOLOGIZE FOR THE INTRUSION . . .

"Sorry, arriving unannounced like this," Josie said. "It looks like you're headed out. Is there a better time we can chat? This evening?"

"We'll bring dinner!" Emma offered. "Anything you want!"

"What I want is you off my property. Leave my family alone."

If you POINT OUT THAT YOU'RE TECHNICALLY NOT
   ON HIS PROPERTY . . .
If you DRIVE THE FUCK AWAY . . .

Josie tapped the gas, forgot she was in reverse, hit the brakes, shifted gears, and drove off.

This was not the outcome they'd been hoping for. The sad truth was that getting minors into the visitation room of a correctional facility in Massachusetts was nearly impossible for non-parents. Even with Kevin Johnson's cooperation, the process was a bureaucratic polypeptide chain from hell. Without his cooperation, there would be no visit. Fortunately, Josie and her sisters had planned for this, too. After driving country roads for fifteen minutes, after talking things over with Ara when she called to check in, after driving around more to make sure that Kevin would be gone and that they were *really, truly* up for this, they circled back to 514 Old Mill Road.

The driveway was empty. Their engine idled. A crow cawed. The bee that Josie had brushed from her hair buzzed feebly in the acute angle between windshield and dashboard. Josie felt the opposite, her pulse racing. She parked, turned off the engine.

If you KNOCK ON THE DOOR . . .
If you WAIT AND OBSERVE . . .

The choice was made for them. A girl in need of a haircut skipped from the backyard. She was wearing purple tights, yellow rain boots, no shirt. She licked her palms. She picked a wedgie.

"Say something," Josie whispered.

"I haven't talked to anyone under the age of eighteen in like, eighteen years. You're the one who works with kids all the time."

The girl saw them and skipped over. She stared slack-jawed at

Emma—"Your hair is *so* pretty!"—and suddenly they had one-third of the Johnson girls practically inside the Volvo, spellbound, along with the rest of the world, by Emma's hair.

"Thank you," Emma said.

"Can I brush it?" The girl spoke in the pitch of an excited mouse.

"No," Emma said.

"Are you Crystal?" asked Josie.

The girl laughed. "I'm Ruby!"

"Guess what, Ruby? Emma's just shy. Go ahead and give her hair a little pat with the back of your hand, palm up, like this. She doesn't bite."

The same speech Josie used to encourage kids to touch Matilda, the African centipede.

"Wanna know a freaky fact about life?" Ruby said, brushing Emma's hair with the back of her hand. "Gemma stuck a goldfish up her nose and it stayed there for two days."

"Gross," Emma said.

"Where is Gemma?" Josie said.

"Inside."

"With Crystal?"

Ruby nodded.

"Go get them. I want to show you all a magic trick."

Off Ruby went. Emma looked at Josie. Josie shrugged.

Front door opened. Front door slammed closed. The other two girls emerged, barefoot.

"Why are you talking to my sister?" asked the tallest. Early middle-schoolish, glasses. A vanguard rash of pimples. A baggy, floral-print dress. "Who are you?"

"I'm Josie. This is Emma. We're sisters."

"*Ohh*," said the middle one. She wore a large, faded Metallica T-shirt like a muumuu. "She *does* look like a princess."

"Shush, Gemma, no talking to strangers."

"*You're* talking to them."

"We're not strangers," Josie said. "We know your dad. We were just talking to him this morning." *This sounds bad*, she thought. *So, so bad.*

"Can I touch her hair too?" Gemma asked.

"She likes it like this." Ruby demonstrated, reaching for Emma.

Emma flinched. "Jojo, you had a magic trick?"

Josie took a mostly empty bottle of iced tea from the cup holder and poured the last drops into the cap, which she balanced on the hood. She plucked the exhausted bee from the dash.

"It's gonna sting you," Gemma said.

"She's too hungry to sting," Josie said.

"How do you know it's a girl?"

"Almost all bees are. Ants, too. And termites. They're all sisters."

"Nu-uh," said Ruby.

"Yes-uh," said Josie. "Now watch."

She dropped the bee in the cap. It circled around for a moment, then buzzed off, sugar-loaded and healed.

Ruby touched Josie's knee. "Are you a witch?"

"No such thing," Crystal said.

"I'm sort of like a nature witch," Josie said. "And Emma's like a music witch. If you ask nicely, maybe she'll sing you a song."

"I'm not doing Disney, so don't ask."

"'Let It Go'!" said Gemma and Ruby at the same time.

"What did I literally just say?"

"Come on, Em," Josie said.

Emma filled her lungs. A pitch-perfect Elsa came out.

Ruby and Gemma clapped. Even Crystal looked impressed.

"I was in the school play last year," Crystal said. "We did *Beauty and the Beast*."

"Crystal was Belle," Gemma said.

"No I wasn't. I was a candlestick."

If you OFFER THE GIRLS A CHANCE TO SEE THEIR
    MOTHER . . .
If you OFFER THE GIRLS A RIDE . . .

"Would you girls like to go for a drive?" Josie asked, incredulous that these were the actual words being projected by her actual mouth.

Crystal smirked. "So you can kidnap us? No thanks."

Emma scoffed. "Do we look like kidnappers?"

"They're witches," Ruby reminded everyone.

"Can we go to the pond?" Gemma said. "I know how to float on my back."

"I want to go to Dairy Queen," Ruby said.

"We're not going anywhere," Crystal said. "Get inside, both of you."

If you LEVERAGE LITTLE SISTERS AGAINST BIG
     SISTER . . .
If you REASON WITH BIG SISTER . . .

Josie told Ruby and Gemma that Emma needed a new hairdo. They looked at each other like they couldn't believe their luck. Emma sighed and gave the tiniest of nods. She turned in her seat. The girls ran over.

"You take good care of your sisters," Josie said to Crystal.

"I have to."

"Do you cook for them?"

"And make sure they go to bed on time, and brush their teeth, and don't run in the street. Ruby won't go to the bathroom alone. They are so annoying."

"I had to take care of my sisters, too. I still do. It's hard being the responsible one. But your sisters love you, even if they're annoying. Lots of people love you, Crystal."

Crystal adjusted her glasses.

Josie took a breath. "Emma and I have another sister. Her name is Ara. Ara is in jail. With your mom. They're roommates. My sister and your mom are friends."

Crystal's face went white.

"Your mom wants to see you. She asked me and Emma to take you and your sisters to visit. She misses you so much. And we can go see her. But we have to leave right now."

Cold emotional manipulation, yes, but also the warm bighearted truth.

Team Tayloe huddled up while Team Johnson ran screaming inside for socks, shoes, shirts, pants. Crystal had told her sisters they were getting Dairy Queen. Which they would, Josie promised.

"So we're doing this?" Emma winced, working a knot from her hair.

"I think we are. I mean we have to, right?"

"We absolutely do not have to."

Josie popped her knuckles one by one. "We told Ara. Their mom will be expecting them."

Off-key singing came from inside the house.

"We're not kidnapping them," Emma said.

"We're borrowing them," Josie said.

"We're borrowing them and buying them Dairy Queen."

"We're essentially babysitting."

"Essentially we should be getting paid for this."

As for the serious stuff? Like if Kevin Johnson found out? Crystal, with impressive thirteen-year-old reassurance, had promised Josie that their father never called from work to check in, not once all summer. Ruby and Gemma wouldn't tell him. And even if they did, he wouldn't believe them, not with all the imaginative stuff they made up.

Just in case, Josie gave Crystal her number.

"For what?" Emma said. "He starts slapping them around, we drive out here, say *Dude, stop?*"

"I don't know, Em. Call social services? You think I like this? Bad shit's happening everywhere, all the time, whether we involve ourselves or not. At least we're doing something."

"You sound exactly like a certain disbarred lawyer I know."

"Don't you fucking dare."

The girls, fully dressed, ran outside and climbed into the car. Gemma and Ruby had brought a brush, a comb, and an assortment of bedazzled hair clips. They sat behind Emma and got to work. Crystal slid in behind Josie. She had a book in her lap. One of the Harry Potters.

"Wanna hear a freaky fact about life?" Gemma said. "I stuck a goldfish up my nose—"

"—and it stayed there for two days?" Emma said.

Gemma shrieked. "How'd you know!"

"I have a freaky fact about life," Josie said, pulling onto the road. "There's a species of African termite that can blow itself up. It sprays its enemies with poisonous gloop."

"Poisonous poop?" Ruby said.

Crystal turned a page with a sigh. "Yes, Ruby, poisonous poop."

"I eat ice cream like this." Gemma stood, laughing, and wiggled her butt.

"I eat ice cream like that, too." Ruby mimicked her sister.

"Girls, please sit down and buckle your seat belts," Josie spoke to the rearview mirror.

Girls didn't listen. Girls laughed. Girls screeched.

Josie tried again. "Please sit down. Girls?"

Ruby crawled over the center console and poked Josie's belly. "Is that a baby?"

"Sit down and shut up!" Emma snapped.

The girls went instantly quiet. Ruby and Gemma sat back and buckled themselves in. They looked as if they might cry.

"Geez, sorry. I just need you to be quiet. So you can, um, concentrate on my hair."

Chaos slowly resumed, only Josie couldn't hear it. She was gripping the wheel, blood draining from her face, doing ninety in the passing lane, and not because they had to be at MCI-Bogastow within the hour. Little Ruby's comment had sent Josie's mental tape rewinding.

**OBSERVATION:** Nausea. Exhaustion. Cramps. Achy breasts. Mood swings. Spotting. How many days since her last—

**HYPOTHESIS:** Noooooooooooooooooooooooooooooooooooooooo oooo.

She'd blamed stress. She'd blamed spicy curry. Three weeks seemed too soon for sickness. But sick she was. She saw herself and Dean in Bar Harbor, martini-happy, ears still ringing from the Caribou show, sneaking down to the granite shoreline, waves splashing over her ankles . . .

Someone else might've gone into shock, denial, delusions of immaculate conception. Dean had used protection, after all. He always

did. Ever since their accidental pregnancy, they'd followed the pre-
cautions of a level 4 biosafety laboratory (after sex, he'd sometimes
fill his condom at the bathroom sink to double-check for leaks). But
Josie knew about life. She'd studied life. And the thing about life—the
really freaky fact?

That shit was relentless.

# Chapter 36

# Emma

Emma, in the interest of time, wanted to use the Dairy Queen drive-thru, but Ruby said she had to poop, settling the matter. Josie insisted on dropping everyone off while she parked.

Emma clamored out of the Volvo, suddenly responsible for three miniature women who were dedicated to making a simple Dairy Queen run as hard as possible. Gemma raided the drinking straw dispenser, while Ruby held her butt cheeks and looked at Emma with quivering, watery eyes.

"Crystal, little help here?"

Crystal was preoccupied, for she did not take her Dairy Queen lightly. She was interrogating the teenager working the counter on his professional opinions: To Blizzard or to Soft Serve? Sugar Cone or Waffle?

"I'm gonna go!" Ruby wailed, drawing looks from strangers, which was the last thing a kidnapper needed. What a kidnapper needed was a bathroom.

"We don't have one," the teenager told Emma. "People go to the DSW across the parking lot."

"You're telling me that you walk to DSW every time you have to take a dump?"

"Our bathroom isn't for customers."

"Dude, it's an emergency." Emma lifted Ruby by the armpits. "She's not a four-hundred-pound trucker. She won't destroy your toilet. She probably poops like a rabbit."

"I have poisonous poop," Ruby said. "I spray it on my enemies."

The kid rolled his eyes and opened the door. "If my manager asks, you snuck in."

———

Back on the turnpike, a few miles from the Bogastow exit, the sugar rush peaked. Gemma blew straw wrapper missiles, Ruby batted Emma's hair like a kitten, Crystal lectured on spells versus charms, blabbing to everybody and nobody like a coked-up Harry Potter fangirl. Josie, on the other hand, had grown conspicuously quiet, white-knuckling the wheel and staring ahead, biting the insides of her cheeks as her Blizzard devolved into a soupy mixture of cream and Oreo, untouched.

"You want me to tell them to shut up?" asked Emma.

"Sure."

"You okay?"

"No. I'm not."

Emma didn't push it. She spun in her seat and told the girls to shush. She hooked up her phone to the stereo, cranked the volume on their latest track.

*What you don't know can hurt me.*
*The man you don't know, he hurt me.*

The girls, for the first few bars, were stone silent. This was Ara's revenge song—"Track for Becca"—and Emma couldn't decide what was more horrifying, that the girls didn't seem to like what they were hearing, or that she cared so much for their approval. Just as she reached to turn it off, the drumline kicked in. Suddenly the girls were jumping around the backseat, smashing shoulders, screeching in delight. Then came the part Emma was really proud of, the bridge that kept building, momentum sneaking up on you until you were sixteen bars in and didn't want it to end, a bridge so good it could've been a stand-alone track (she'd debated it) but worked better as this punky interlude that—if her backseat focus group was any gauge—kicked some pretty serious ass.

"I think we got a hit on our hands," Emma said to Josie over the music.

"It's great," Josie said, evenly.

Emma squeezed Josie's leg. She squeezed her again. She wished her sister could take a page from the Johnson girls. Yes, life was heavy. But come on, Jojo, sometimes you have to let yourself lighten up.

———

It was Sunday, the construction site empty. Gaining access was as simple as getting out to swing open a chain-linked gate. Gemma and Ruby laughed in delight as the Volvo rolled down the gravel road, rattling and shaking over the bulldozer tread marks.

Josie parked behind a dumpster. They climbed out to the smell of plywood and overturned dirt. Skunk cabbage and duckweed. Across the marsh stood the prison, the razor-wired fence, a cluster of women. Somewhere in that crowd was Ara. Emma could feel her. Sheets of Tyvek house wrap flapped from the unfinished condos like sails on a ship.

"Here we go team." Emma clapped. "Everyone wave. Go ahead."

"Why?" Gemma shot a straw wrapper onto the ground.

"Um . . ." Emma trailed off. "Crystal, you tell them."

Crystal looked at Emma. Emma nodded.

"We're here to see Mom," Crystal said.

"Mommy's in jail," Ruby said. "She's bad."

"Don't say that," Crystal said. "You don't remember what she was like before. You were just a baby."

"I remember," Gemma said.

"No you don't."

Ruby hugged Emma's leg. "I wish you were my mommy."

"Oh my God you do not," Emma said. "Just wave. Please."

Gemma and Ruby wandered off to crouch by the marsh, examining the tadpoles and the muck. Crystal returned to the Volvo. She sat in the back and opened her book. Then she closed it.

"This is weird. You said we were going to visit her."

"We said you were going to *see* her," Emma said. "It's complicated. This is the best we could do."

"It sucks. I want to go home."

"Me too," said Ruby over her shoulder.

"Not me." Gemma was pulling reeds from the marsh. "I'm playing horsies with Mommy. Mommy loves playing horsies."

"You don't remember her!" Crystal said.

"I do too!"

Gemma chomped a reed to make a bit and galloped along the marsh. Ruby copied her. They whinnied and snorted, tossing their manes, stomping their hooves.

Emma turned to Crystal, desperate. "Just wave. Please! A few big waves, then we'll go back to Dairy Queen. We'll buy you whatever you want. Right, Jo?"

Josie nodded absently. She was staring off across the marsh, distant, checked out.

"This is really weird," Crystal said again.

Emma was prepared to drag the girls into the marsh and wave their arms for them. They weren't coming this far to fail Ara now. Thankfully, she didn't have to.

"Look," Josie said, pointing.

A woman was mirroring the girls along the inside of the fence, galloping like a horse.

Crystal whispered: "Mom?" She raised a limp hand.

"Try from here," Josie said. She climbed onto the hood of the Volvo. Emma helped Crystal up.

"This is so stupid," Crystal said, standing next to Josie. "How can I even tell who she is?"

"She'll see you, just try it." Josie waved her arms like an air-traffic controller.

Crystal tried, a little reluctantly at first, but then came a big cheer from across the marsh as one of the women waved back. Crystal smiled. She waved some more, then hopped down and chased after her sisters, waving and trotting along.

Emma sat with Josie on the hood. Three little girls at the edge of the marsh. Sunlight winking off razor wire. The nostalgia was a Dairy Queen Blizzard: thick thick thick. Emma squinted, trying to pinpoint Ara. Josie rested her head on Emma's shoulder.

"What am I going to do, Em?"

"What do you mean? We did it."

Emma felt Josie sob, just once. She put an arm around her and stroked her hair and sang "Good Vibrations" because "Good Vibrations" had always made them all feel better, and if Josie couldn't feel better now—helping a mom see her kids, one step closer to bringing Ara home—would she ever feel good about anything?

Emma couldn't say. She wasn't writing Josie's story. She could only write her own story, and she wasn't about to let her storm cloud of a younger sister end this chapter on a depressing note, not when Emma felt so radiantly positive. She raised a hand to wave to Ara across the marsh. A train whistled through the trees, a bright G-major 6th chord that brought tears to her eyes with that perfectly imperfect pitch.

# Chapter 37

# Ara

As a drummer, as a musician, as a human being with two eardrums, I do get tired of verse-chorus-verse. The overused ¼ time signature. The I-IV-V standard chord progression. That's why I love "Good Vibrations." The song is simply genius: three totally unique sections stitched together with these unexpected key modulations and counter melodies and tempo shifts. The key kicks up a full tone with each line in the first chorus as the cellos are swinging triplets, and the theremin does its eerie thing. Then, near the end, the key shunts *back down* the scale with each line, dropping you off where you began. There's nothing like it in the history of rock. Today was like "Good Vibrations." Started up up up. Ended down down down, with lots of key and tempo changes all around.

First, up: Kyla's girls. Sisters fucking did it. They found them. They got them here.

We almost blew it because Kyla wouldn't leave her bed. I had to toughlove her into the yard. We kicked around, walking slow laps as she complained about the heat. I was worried—there wasn't much time left—when a flash of Volvo gold winked from the construction site.

"Kyla!" I pulled her over to the fence.

She squinted across the marsh. "What?"

Three small figures spilled from the Volvo's backseat. My body was vibrating.

"Your girls, Kyla! We found them! Those are your babies."

Kyla's mouth did a little two-step. Then she fell to her knees. Sitting isn't allowed in the yard, so Janice and I yanked her up before a guard could yell at us to move along.

"Ruby! Crystal! Gemma! Momma's here! You hear me, girls?"

The girls couldn't hear her. But that didn't stop Kyla from giving it a shot. Her voice went raw trying to cross the marsh. Listening to her blubber, there was no way I was keeping it together. Quantifiably impossible. Same for others, when they drifted over. In the heavy minor chord that vibrates through MCI-Bogastow, children are the root note. Lots of women miss sex, dope, music, internet, floss, cigarettes, but there's exactly one thing that unites almost everyone, and that's what they'd do to see their babies.

Two of Kyla's girls were running, tossing their hair, galloping. Kyla waved. She sobbed and yelled.

"Horsies, they're playing horsies! I need a long piece of grass!"

We scattered like pigeons. Nancy found a long grass by the fence where the mower couldn't reach. Kyla clamped it between her teeth for a bit. She tossed her mane, stampeded off, skipped the inside of the fence. Her foals mirrored her across the marsh.

We were all crying and cheering them on, but I was also blowing kisses past Kyla's girls. I could see Josie and Sister by the Volvo. For the first time since arriving here, I was ready to be with them on the other side of the fence.

The buzzer marked the end of yard time. We moved the party inside. The scene in the dayroom was ecstatic, like we'd won a war. I waited for a pay phone to call Sister. I could hardly hear her over the racket. Kyla's girls were scream-singing in the background. Were they singing what I thought they were singing? Sister put the phone against the car speakers. My Revenge Song came blasting through. She'd finished it.

When I'd sent her the lyrics, I'd told her to spin some bubble-gum pop, an easy candy-hued track that could play at a Bat Mitzvah or the Super Bowl Halftime show. Instead, she built a song that is pure Holy Pop sacrilege: three-four time, a sort of thrasher-warp-waltz with this huge thundering bridge. But so, so catchy. My heart ran a victory lap.

"Bounce it, Em! Put it up. Let's sell some records, and get me out of here. I'm ready. I want to come home."

Hearing myself say the words made my throat ache. I yelled through the phone that I loved them, then I told Sister to put on the girls. I waved Kyla over.

Everyone in the dayroom was laughing, shouting, breaking off pieces of Ding-Dongs that Dolores passed around. We crowded Kyla when she got off the phone. She was in shock, laugh-crying when she opened her mouth. Two women fanned her with magazines while others retold the story for those who'd missed it, acting out the parts. And this was only partway through the very long song of this very long day. We were still going up the scale.

We had not yet begun the slide back down.

---

Dinner is usually a funhouse, chatter zigzagging off the walls. Not tonight.

"Somebody die?" Janice looked around. "Thought we were cele-brating?"

Dolores and Nancy deserve the credit. I'd only given them the floss and suggested they could redistribute the wealth. It was their idea to keep Janice out of it. Janice has led so many protests over the years. Fought to make everyone's lives a little better, a touch more comfortable, a scrap more dignified. This was a final homage to their Queen Bee.

The intercom screeched its orders for us to stand and bring our trays to the kitchen. A few women got up, including Janice, then saw the rest of us weren't moving. They sat right back down. And that's when it happened: a few hundred women, pulling lengths of floss from our sleeves, and cleaning our teeth.

The guards scrambled from the gangway. Intercom blared Code 82 for a riot, which was pretty funny because this is dental hygiene we're talking about. No chanting, no yelling, just our ticking and picking. Dolores sat across from me, giving her teeth all the love, smile threat-ening to split her face in two.

Inner Perimeter arrived. They went straight to Janice, and for the first time in twenty-five years they were dealing with a protest she hadn't planned. She seemed as surprised as them. Once in fifth grade Sister and I organized a strike at recess. Instead of going inside we convinced our class to stay on the playground. Josie rallied the fourth graders. Mom was called to come pick us up. I remember her walking into the principal's office with this look of intense pride. That was Janice at the head of the table, Inner Perimeter crowding her.

"Yes I'm glad to help, Officers. You see these uppity women? They're responsible. Every last one of them."

She folded her arms over her chest, and winked at us.

The action would've tapered off but Jules jumped on a table and burst into song: "We Shall Overcome." Classic case of Lead Singer Syndrome. No spotlight is safe. Maybe she expected us to link arms and join in. That didn't happen. What happened was Jules offered her body for the love of her ego and the guards accepted her sacrifice. Tasers crackled. Party over.

They confiscated our floss, then herded us out. Marching from the dining hall I spotted Andrews on the gangway. I'd been saving my most elegant middle finger for this occasion, and I delivered. He waved, smiling his big smile.

All evening we were in lockdown as punishment. I was sitting with Kyla on her bed so she could exhaust herself of tears and "thank-you"s. She wanted to hear again how my sisters had done it, how her girls had seemed, could we do it again? Suddenly she stopped mid-sentence, tilted her head, and lunged, reaching over me.

Then I heard what she'd heard: footsteps, coming fast.

"Inner Perimeter," she whispered. "Give me your journal. Now!"

She didn't wait. Hands shot under my pillow. She took you and slipped you under her waistband just as flashlights washed hotwhite over my eyes. Our lock popped.

"Hop down Tayloe everything stays where it is let's go."

Gruff voices. Male and female. I didn't recognize either.

"Where are you taking her?" Kyla's voice was hoarse from yelling across the marsh.

"Max."

Word hit me like a brick. "Why?"

"Protective custody." The man snapped my wrists in cuffs.

"Bullshit," Kyla rasped.

"Shut your mouth," said the woman. She was running her hands under my mattress, my pillow. Kyla pressed her back against the wall.

"Protection from what?" I asked.

"Other residents."

"For how long?"

"Till you're protected."

# Chapter 38

# Bertie

Malta was a clove on the ham of the horizon. Sicily, a band of green over the port railing. A fuzz of rain had driven General Assembly from the swimming pool into the mess hall. Bertie and Audrey shared a table with Danny Noor. The smell of sautéed onions from dinner hung in the air. Bo Leung stood on a chair and picked up from where the rain had interrupted. Bo was known for her documentary on dissident journalists in which she'd barely escaped China with her footage. In addition to documenting the voyage of the *A.R.C.*, she'd seized the title of Evening Movie Czar. The crew had responded well to her selections thus far. *Casablanca, Battle of Algiers, Catch-22*. For tonight's movie, however, she had something special, she said. She turned off the mess hall lights. A digital projector blinked to life.

"Sit back, relax, and enjoy the show. I present—us!"

"Oh no I look awful," groaned Max as they appeared on the wall, sandwiched between their parents, who were dressed in khakis and pastels, and posing before a picket fence.

> *We haven't always agreed with Max on everything but dissent is a bedrock virtue of our Republic and we're so proud—*(that word! Bertie cringed)—*of our child for standing up for the American beliefs of freedom and justice for all.*

Everyone on the *A.R.C.* had recorded testimonials before setting sail. Preemptive propaganda, recorded to counter the inevitable corporate-media slant and the Israeli lobby spin doctors. It would be one thing, for instance, to hear Israel's Minister of Defense describing Marsha Rubin of Duluth as a Hamas-loving terrorist, and another to hear her husband, Ted, on a faded plaid couch, lauding Marsha's vegetable garden, her work at the synagogue, the hotdish-cookoff fundraiser she'd organized to support arts in schools.

Bo had stitched the testimonials together into a bighearted, rapid-fire montage. Happy loving families, all of whom seemed miles more supportive than Bertie's. Araminta alone had agreed to record a testimonial. Bertie, at the time, had been grateful. Now, she didn't know if she could stomach what was coming. She pushed back her chair. Audrey stopped her with a hooked finger to her belt loop.

"Where are you going?"

"I need some air."

"Without your poncho? Take mine."

Danny Noor shot them an excited look: "My boys!"

Bertie, not wanting to be rude, sat back down.

The Noors were standing before a cherry-red firetruck. "I'm Kamal and I'm a person!" a toddler screamed. A smaller boy echoed that he, too, was a person.

The boys were dressed in firefighting gear to match their father. Helmets that fit like caldrons. Jacket sleeves brushing the ground. Danny's young wife, made up and hijabbed, blinked her dark mascara eyes.

*Anybody with a heart will help their family and neighbors, but a real hero is the man who helps those he's never met. That's Daniel.*

Bertie whispered to Danny, "What a sweetheart."

Danny rolled his eyes. "You know this is all for show. Israa was furious at me for leaving. Correction—*is* furious."

"She's just scared."

"You don't know Israa. I'm the one who should be scared."

"But you left anyway," Bertie said.

"I wouldn't have been able to live with myself if I didn't."

Bertie nodded. People like her and Walt and Danny Noor—they

couldn't help but consider the good of the human family. The species as a whole. Why couldn't Josephine—a biologist of all things—understand that?

Such an enigma, Bertie's youngest. A brilliant storm in a locked box. It took so very little to light her fuse. This was the reason Bertie hadn't planned on asking her to record a testimonial. In the end, though, she'd decided Josephine would be more offended if she *wasn't* invited to record one. So Bertie had suggested it, during the April weekend they were supposed to all come together to pack up the house. Josephine had not responded kindly.

"You want me to go down on record, Mom, as enabling your irresponsible behavior?"

"Forget it. I'm sorry I asked."

And Bertie was sorry. She'd hoped the testimonials might be a fun break from the serious work of packing up their old lives and saying goodbye to their house. But Josephine had refused. Emma had run off to meet a man. That left Araminita, who appeared suddenly on the mess hall wall, flashing to life before Bertie had a chance to flee above deck.

*Hi Mom! Oh my God, get that camera out of my face . . . I'm sick. Doesn't Emma want to sing something? What about Jojo?*

*Your sisters are being difficult,* Bertie heard herself saying. *I need you, Araminta. Please.*

In the video, Araminta was sitting cross-legged in the middle of the mostly empty living room. She wiped her nose with the back of a hand. She was wearing ridiculous sunglasses, yellow frames, speckled in rhinestones. A mess of Christmas lights around her. Her skin was pale. Off-color. Her face, puffy. She was getting over the flu, she'd said, and Bertie hadn't doubted her, because she wanted it to be true. She saw it clearly, larger than life—her daughter's disease—and the cable tethering them grew so tight so suddenly that Bertie thought it might wrench her heart from her chest. She reached for Audrey's hand under the table.

*What should I say?*

*Just talk about me, dear. Whatever comes to mind.*

Ara wiped her nose. She stared into the camera.

*Well you're the most committed activist on the planet. Remember how you skipped Josie's graduation to march with the Zapatistas?*

*I didn't skip,* Bertie said on video, laughing tightly. *What about a story growing up?*

Ara stared into space. Her words came out like molasses: *"You paid us fifty bucks each summer not to watch TV. Remember? That was a good idea . . . You must've saved us a billion brain cells each. We ended up running around outside, playing in the woods. Starting our band . . ."*

*"Araminta, dear, they want these videos in the third person. Pretend I'm not here."*

Bertie's face burned in the dark of the mess hall. Wasn't Bo supposed to have been an award-winning documentarian? She couldn't have done a *little* editing?

*"My mom . . . she lost . . . she had a difficult—she raised us by herself. She never complained. Our childhood was feminism in practice. We were girls and we could do anything. Be whatever. She never told us what to become. As long as we weren't Republicans.*

Laughter bounced around the mess hall. Bertie let out a held breath and smiled.

Ara was right. It had been difficult. Josephine's valedictorian speech. Ara's last-minute wedding. The twins' first show. Walt's absence in those moments was a ragged hole. Plenty big enough to disappear into, if she'd let herself. She could've let Walt's death become the defining event for all of them. She could've made big sappy scenes, made it all about her grief instead of her girls, their present and future. She'd found quieter, more dignified ways to support them: marches, protests, lawsuits, donations—investments in a better tomorrow, *their* tomorrow—which did not involve coddling or sacrificing the scrappy independence she'd raised them to embody. Life could've gone differently. Bertie could've let loss and bitterness swallow them all.

*You bought me my first snare when I was ten. You were a good mom, Mom. You are.*

Bertie squeezed Audrey's hand and swallowed a sharp jag in her throat. Emma tended to take up more than her share of oxygen in the room, and Josephine was always sharpening her blades, but Araminta had a calming soul. After the twins went broke and moved home, Bertie could sit with Ara, just the two of them reading, or listening to music, and it was *nice.* That's what Bertie had believed. It stabbed her to have missed then what was the truth: Ara had been in pain. A girl loses her father. A girl is raped. A girl is committed to slowly destroying herself. Why else would she have turned to those terrible drugs? If Bertie had just held her more. Shook some sense into her. Said something. Said what?

Ara wiped her nose on-screen. *And . . . this was our house. This was where we all grew up. You'll miss it. Won't you, Mom?*

Third person, Araminta. Please. Pretend I'm not here.

*Got it. Sorry. You're not here.*

Bertie, not wanting to make a scene, waited until the next testimonial before bolting.

She stood at the railing of the sundeck and gulped the salty air. The bulk of the rain had blown south. Mist beaded her arms. At every step she'd considered her own mother and tried her best to do the opposite. She never shamed. She never pried. Never hovered. Never used pride as a cudgel. Never showed dependence on a man. Never showed dependence, period. But maybe a little dependency wouldn't have hurt? Araminta, after all, had found it elsewhere. Perhaps they all had.

Footsteps on the sundeck. A poncho around her shoulders. Audrey's arms.

"You're allowed to feel lousy if you want to, but it's not your fault. You can't blame yourself for her disease. That's substance abuse 101. Your poor girl was dealt a bad hand."

The pitch of the ocean swung through Bertie. The wink of an airplane between two bright stars. "I'm not asking for pity, Audrey."

"Good thing I wasn't giving you any."

The engines hummed. The waves chopped against the hull. A round of faint laugher came from the mess hall. Then Audrey asked, "So what are you asking for, Bertie?"

*To turn this boat around. To do it over again. All of it.*

"Justice." Bertie blinked into the mist. "Peace."

# Chapter 39

# Ara

More colors in the prison rainbow than I knew.

Pretrial wears green.

Convicted gets blue.

And now there's my new uniform: red.

Red is Max. Solitary.

Concrete slab for a bed, thin mat, thin blanket. Meals delivered through slot in door. An 8 x 12 walk-in closet at what feels like 90 degrees. That's red. That's me. I am red.

———

My first hours in Max are cross-legged in the silence, back against the wall, breathing deep, sweating in the heat. Staring at the door. Waiting for the lock to pop. Waiting for him. I knew he was coming. Of course he was. Fifteen minutes? An hour? Three? Impossible, in the silence, to know how much time has passed. I thought about the tour-bus bunkbeds. Our third-floor attic. Roman's arms. There's comfort in being cocooned. Enclosed. I like to wrap myself in my bedsheets as tightly as I can. Small spaces never bothered me. What bothers me is silence. In Max there's not even hallway footsteps, and without sound—no intercom announcing count, no Kyla scratching out another letter, no toilet flushing down the hall—time turns flimsy. It doesn't exist. Without time, your hands turn inward. Worry-pick your toenails, cuticles. Roll waxballs from your ears. Without time, you start doubting that you exist. You feel the closeness of the walls. The residual buzz of every woman who was ever in here. Twisted bedsheets, dental floss, razor blades. All the tools of escape.

In what measure does the darkness jump from the faint backbeat to the brassy downbeat?

The one and the three, to the two and the four.

I know what you're thinking: pull it together.

I know. I scared myself, knowing, yet unable to stop. The unraveling. Fraying like the end of Kyla's floss noose. A minute is an hour. An hour is a night.

No anchor.

So you drift.

I didn't notice I was counting my heartbeat until it started working. Two fingers on my soft inner wrist. Slowed my breath. Dropped my tempo. Pulse dipped from 110 beats per minute to 80. Pretty impressive swing. Think Led Zeppelin to Otis Redding. Pressure in my face released a notch. Began singing along. Softly at first, then louder. And drumming.

Left thigh = snare

Right thigh = toms

Knees = cymbals

I wasn't playing randomly. I wasn't sitting eyes closed in Max, sweating. I was home. I was skipping through Jimi Hendrix, Janis Joplin, Brian Wilson. That's how I survived my first night in Max, dropping the needle again and again on Dad's records. The discography of my memory. Spinning in the whirlpool of the past, and drumming to the hi-hat of my heart. Song after song after song, until the door slot suddenly rattled, and I jumped out of my skin. It was breakfast.

Bran cereal, white toast, slushy orange juice.

I held the cold juice against my forehead. Drank it down, crunching slivers of ice. Didn't touch the food. When the door rattled again, two unsmiling female guards ignored my questions about phone calls and lawyers. Took me for a shower, a urine test, then the "rec pen," which has the precise feel and appearance of a dog kennel. I lay on the asphalt, hands behind my head, and followed the cloudhigh silhouette of a hawk while savoring the—

whisper of wind

hammering from construction site
whistle of train
coo of mourning dove

———

Room reeked of bleach and cleaner when they brought me back. Breakfast tray, gone. Sound, gone. I slumped against the wall and took a breath, prepping for the next stretch of stopped time in which I was not going to go weepy or pick my cuticles till they bled or wonder what would happen when Andrews came for me.

Closed my eyes. Dropped the needle. Returned to his records.

This time it didn't work.

How long since the guards had brought me from the rec pen?

Couldn't have been more than fifteen minutes.

Unless it was more? Much more?

Dolores had done a night in Max. Not to mention Mumia Abu-Jamal, Bobby Sands, Angela Davis. Assata Shakur spent months in solitary at Rikers. So many had it so much worse. People who weren't semi-filthy with privilege. Who hadn't flirted with Carson Daly on *TRL*. People know me. They know about *Jailbreak*. They know where I am.

My head congratulated me for each of my rational arguments. My heart called bullshit.

Look around, heart said. Look what you've done with your privilege and fame.

Pretty soon heart was drumming 130 beats per minute, close to the tempo of the original Winston Brothers' "Amen Break."

I put my mouth to the food slot: "Hello?"

Not even an echo.

My mind kick-drummed: fuckfuckfuckfuck.

Stink of bleach in my nostrils. Ache in my throat. My tinnitus came raging back, blooming until it did its soft explosion thing, which was a welcome break from the ringing. But then it went right back to its steady background whine. I must've drummed a thousand measures on my knees. I did some crunches. Push-ups. Warrior-2s. Cried pretty hard for a while. Drummed another thousand measures. Cried some more. Hands returned to attack mode. Picking picking. Cuticles of my thumbs went wet and coppery. Shivering, breathing in little gasps like my lungs couldn't rip enough oxygen from the air. That's when I pulled the blanket off my bedslab, to wrap myself tight, and there it went—a lone white moth, flying across the room.

I flinched, jumping back.

The moth hit the wall and fell to the ground, unmoving. I stepped over and saw that it wasn't a moth at all. It was you: a tight fold of thin canteen paper. I picked you up. Four glorious sheets. I pressed you to my lips. Inhaled your pulpy smell. Unfolded your wings.

### WRITE SMALL. MAKE IT LAST. KEEP ON YOUR TOES. THANK U.

When we were girls, for Christmas, instead of writing Santa, Mom had us write political prisoners in South Africa, Palestine, Louisiana. Same message, every letter: <u>You are not alone.</u>

Well let me tell you, something so small really does mean so much.

Kyla had scrubbed my room clean, shuttled out my breakfast tray, and smuggled you in, along with a rubber prison pen I found jammed in the ridge between bedslab and wall.

So here we are again. Me and you. You and me.

We are red. We are Max. We are not alone.

---

He came. Told you he would. I'd escaped—was dreaming my dream on the roof with Sisters, holding hands, about to jump—when the food slot rattled. Dinner, I thought, but no tray appeared.

"Sleeping well? Sleep's the trick in Max. Sleep as much as you can."

He was crouching in the hallway, face level with the slot.

"Heard your new song. 'Track for Becca.' Cool, cool. Very cool. What's the reception been? How's it working out for you now?"

My heart played timpani in my chest. A thought like clear black ice: this is going to be the fight for my life. I swung my feet to the floor and said, "I want to call my lawyer."

He said he was sorry it had come to this. Said it was his fault, never should've extended me privileges. The problem he did not foresee was that I am "a raging bitch who enjoys—*lives for*—making everything so fucking difficult for anyone who tries to help. You thrive on drama. You lack empathy. You have a disease." He spoke clinically, like these were the sad facts.

"I want to call my lawyer."

"I heard you the first time. Unfortunately, the Max phone—it's on wheels, rolls right up to the door, very retro—unfortunately it's broken. As we say: MCI-Bogastow, built in 1866 and they haven't remodeled since."

He was lying, probably. But what could I do?

The food slot swung, hinges squeaking as he pushed it with a finger. "You're scared, Ara. A little unsettled? Max is a scary place. That's why I'm here. I know you dislike it when I help—when I *try* to help—but I'm a super fan. What can I say, I can't help myself. I've ordered the good officers in Max to leave you alone. There will be no searches of your cell, no sweeps. You won't be disturbed. Think of this as your personal bliss retreat."

There was a long silence. Like he wanted me to thank him.

"You can't keep me down here. I demand to talk to my lawyer."

"Bon appétit."

The food slot swung open, and he pushed through a brown paper bag. My heart tumbled to the ground with it. The same bag he'd pulled from the drawer in his desk. I'd known then what was in it. I was right.

---

Thirty-six glassine bags. I've arranged them on the floor. My line stretches wall-to-wall. Someone in my position could be high for weeks solid if someone in my position wanted to be high for weeks solid. Naturally I must flush everything immediately.

Naturally I have not.

---

Flushed one bag. It was the least promising of the bunch—pretty jaundiced—so hold your applause. Watched it spiral and disappear. Thought about its lifespan from Mexican poppy field to drug mule to inmate-addressed mail to brown bag to leeching field to marsh to tadpole to wherever next. The loops we make.

Thirty-five bags left.

———

Arranged bags from purest-looking to questionable-looking.

A paint sample strip: Eggshell White to Daffodil Yellow.

I can palm the whitest of white, balance the heft in my hand, and put it back down.

I can do that.

I can lie down with thirty-five bags on my chest like my dreamcoat blanket, rising and falling like the ocean if you think about it and I do.

There's such a thing as tempting fate.

Also defeating it.

———

Can't defeat it. Tried flushing more. Tried slipping back into memory. Put myself back home surrounded by smell of old vinyl and dusty cardboard jackets and every good vibration. I'm fifteen. I'm eight. I'm three. Speakers are scratching with the Beach Boys. Smell of spruce. Stockings. Snow ticking against windowpanes, I shit you not. Real-life Christmas card. Father of Christmas past, at the fireplace. Striking a match. Singing along.

Mostly when I think of him over the years it's like sitting in an empty hole. Not bad. Just empty. A little cold. But then sometimes a memory with warmth.

At three years old, everything is perfect.

At thirty-six, nothing is perfect.

Thirty-five bags left.

Almost one for every year of the failure that is this life.

———

I needed something to happen so badly that I cried real tears when the slot rattled with dinner. Seafood Surprise.

Surprise, I ate it.

Full stomach made me sleepyeyed and great-great, nobody makes bad decisions when asleep, not even me.

I woke up to Dad at the foot of my bed. Humming to me like Kyla hummed to me on day one. Let's get you out of this place, Ara girl. He plucked a bag from my chest. Dropped it in the toilet. Flushed. He was humming "Good Vibrations." He flushed a second bag. A third. Without the weight of my dreamcoat I began floating, and it might've been the greatest feeling—a helium relief that I didn't even know I wanted—but I rose so quickly, through the ceiling of my bedroom and the roof of our old house and into the starlight clouds. Higher and higher, picking up speed, so fast that it scared me awake.

My jaw was sore from clenching. My uniform sour with sweat. I got on all fours crawling in the silentdark, collecting the bags that had slid from my chest.

Ten bags were missing.

I counted them again. Ran my hands along the floor.

I'd flushed them in my sleep. Must have. The alternative is too crazy. Too close to what people in Max start believing before they decide to escape for good.

I'd really scared myself. I shoveled all remaining bags into the toilet before I could think about it.

People say addicts have zero willpower.

Lies, lies, hideous lies.

You can't imagine what kind of willpower is needed to stand there sobbing with your finger on the button, and not flush. You can't imagine what kind of willpower is needed to sell all of your dad's records, but save one. You can't imagine. The problem is too *much* willpower.

My will is strong.

It's my *won't* that is weak.

———

There was some seepage. Some ruined product.

Salvage drying now like an altar in the corner.

This is where I'm supposed to confess how much I disgust myself. What it's like to scoop bags of stale heroin out of a prison toilet bowl. What it's like to examine a life that cannot possibly be yours, and still, still, still your heart beats on, betraying you with joy at the thought of one more Amen. I could describe these feelings in detail. I have before.

But I am writing small and almost out of paper. And maybe Kyla will get me more. And maybe she won't. And maybe Sisters will bail me out. And maybe they won't. And maybe Mom will come for me. And maybe and maybe and maybe.

———

So much of New Pathways = learning the science behind the thirst. Dopamine receptors. Pleasure neurons. The many ways your coyote brain will plot to trick you. We learned that we can heal. Synapses regrow. Thirst will slack. All we need is time. But how do you heal when time disappears? When you've wasted so much of it? I'm thirty-six. People by thirty-six have found a skin that's comfortable. Redefining myself now would be like drumming without a beat. Told myself I needed to break old patterns. Wipe slate clean. Told Josie I was done with the band.

True confessions?

Prospect of life without Sister or band = boring, bleak, panic-making.

What's that?

Word for word what junkies say about the prospect of a dope-free future?

What can I say. Nobody runs with arms wide open into a methadone life.

———

Opened one bag. Had to. Just a whiff. What if it was only baking soda? Bisquick?

Nope.

That Band-Aid, antiseptic smell sent me light-headed and weepy. Told myself to stop whining. May have said it out loud. May have been lecturing myself how symptoms of withdrawal are way overrated, no worse than the flu. How I could simply ration carefully. I could use it to help me through Max, then kick again at home. Easy easy!

The delusion is the most pathetic part. Sometimes even scarier than the itch.

The itch is chemical. Opioids, dopamine.

But the delusion? Delusion's all me.

———

How many hours until breakfast? I should've been counting measures to track time. I lost time again. Should've been sleeping. Can't. Where is everyone?

———

Mom didn't cook me big comfort meals when I could've used them. Didn't draw me hot baths. Didn't tell me lies like: everything will be alright.

What she did do:

> Gave me stacks of bedside feminist reading.
> Made me feel guilty for not pressing charges.
> Worked, worked, worked.

Sister and Josie will probably never forgive her for being absent then. But I do. Life's a string of addictions. We're all committed to something. Everyone needs an emergency exit.

———

I think about *Jailbreak*. The money. How I'll disappear it.
bail, court costs, rehab
how I'll ruin everything for one more Amen.
Not throwing a pity party
Just stating facts like—

> Josie drops out of school
> Mom blows dad's life insurance
> Roman goes to prison
> Sister could've been Courtney Love, Gwen Stefani, Pink, anybody.
> Josie says she can't take care of me forever, but she will try if I let her.
> they all will
> follow me off the roof

they can't help themselves
only me


Ever wondered how thirty-five bags get you to a smiley face? Wonder
no more you just go

> 27 bags for circle
> 2 for eyes
> 6 for the never-ending smile

During our American Mosh tour, we had a bathroom on the bus
but sometimes we'd still ask the driver to pull over.

Peeing in a prairie = delightful. Rippling fields, sheer expanse of
horizon.

Same thing peeing outside anywhere. A forest, a desert. Gives you
the shivers in that good way that happens when you feel small and safe.
I liked that about Roman. With Roman I'm
delicate protected

Same being high. This one tough-love therapist at New Pathways, I
can't remember her name, she kept suggesting that I was compensating.

What's your problem? she'd say.

Opioids, I'd say.

Wrong, she'd say.

Oxys, I'd say. Percocet. Vicodin.

Wrong, wrong, wrong, she'd say. Those things make problems go
away. What's your *problem*?

What did she want me to say? My dad died? My mom was never
around? A man raped me?

Now we're getting somewhere, she said.

But we didn't. We didn't get anywhere. Not then, not since.

———

> Pain of past = guilt
> Pain of present = depression
> Pain of future = anxiety
> Common denominator = time

The thing about the Amen, the truly magical denominator
    = it stops time
Stopping time = opposite of disappearing time

When time disappears it's a week since Seafood Surprise and your mind drums no-no-no. But when time stops you pin it to the wall like a prize ribbon and your veins run just-right.

I don't want my soul to remember pain. That's the difference between me and Kyla.

I want pain to stop.

————

In high school we threw exactly one big house party. Mom was in D.C. at some protest. Sister and I were talent-show famous. We had our band and a new set-list, just needed an audience. Half of Bogastow High showed up. We played on the flat roof outside the attic window. It was a solid show, but kids wouldn't go home. Climbing trees. Hurling in bushes. Plastic cups and cigarette butts in the grass. Roman kicking up the rowdiness. The last straw was when Josie found us. She was shaking. Some senior hockey creep had followed her into her room and wouldn't hear no until she made crazy eyes and said she was feeling murdery. Sister brought us back up to the roof and we stepped to the edge and shouted at everyone to leave. Promised we'd jump if they didn't go home. There was a little nervous laughter. Then we took a step closer. Toes wiggling in the air over the hard driveway. Things got quiet. Someone cut the music. Roman was telling everybody we were serious, scram. Kids shuffled to their cars, weirded out. We three sisters with the names of power. We who a week later would steal hockey creep's Jeep from the high school lot and leave it on the railroad tracks with veiny penises keyed into soft white paint. We who didn't need mother or father. We who had each other.

————

Pro-tip: roll your blanket into a pillow so you don't choke on your vomit.
    Pro-tip: roll a torn square of a paper diagonally for a tighter straw.
    Pro-tip: never use alone.
    I don't remember overdosing, and that's the story you'll hear at every

meeting: nobody who's returned remembers. Wasn't peaceful. Wasn't not peaceful. No bright light. Just waking up suddenly to the full-body vomit agony of Roman bringing me back.

Sister crashed my honeymoon. Dad played us his records in the living room. Mom organized a talent show in the holding cell after we were arrested at the big anti-war march in New York City. Josie collected snake skins on her princess dresser. Turtle shells and dragonfly wings. Owl pellets. Feathers by color, exoskeletons by size. A papery loaf of a hornets' nest. Mouse bones like sewing needles. Spring peepers playing like a synth chorus from the marsh.

I can glide through the rooms of my memory palace.

But there is no memory of almost dying in an oceanside motel room next to Roman.

There should be more to it. When you blink out for good. Shouldn't be painless, so easy. Like falling asleep. One second here and the next second time stops.

---

You have to wonder. Because you can't simply say it. Words don't work like that. You have to show it. Action. That's what makes love concrete. Love for family. Love for the pack. We love and we kill and we love and we love and we love and we love.

Free the animals free the pack.

Free yourself free the pack.

You just have to wonder.

---

In my dream the dream I always dream sometimes we fall. Sometimes I step off the roof taking sisters with me. Other times we fly. Sometimes I squeeze sisters' arms and they are not arms they are wings. Sisters are floating. Up away beautiful. They are rising. Unburdened. Free.

I can see that now.

There is power in choice. That's love.

Remember that okay?

Love and joy. In seeing you go. In watching you soar.

Amen.

# PART V

# Free Animal

# Chapter 40

# Bertie

They were passing north of Crete, the crew settling in for General Assembly, when the ship shuddered and slowed. Tubbs might have toppled from the diving board if Max weren't there to grab his arm. An alarm blared below deck. Audrey squeezed Bertie's hand. Tal's walkie-talkie burst with Uri's voice. His Hebrew sounded frantic.

"Fire!" Tal shouted, leaping from the pool.

"All hands to the lifeboats!" Tubbs bellowed.

Audrey moaned. Bertie guided her into a lifeboat and, with the help of Danny Noor, clipped her lifejacket snug. Some people lost their wits when dropped into the lap of crisis. Bertie was thankful to be in the opposite camp. Adrenaline gave her a cold, mechanical edge, even as a second alarm joined the first and she tasted the bitter fug of smoke and burning oil.

She touched Audrey's chin. "Breathe with me. Breathe."

She held eye contact, urging Audrey to mirror her inhalations.

"In and out, woman. There we go."

Then there was the third camp, the Maxes of the world, who wanted to help, but in the process only ratcheted up the anxiety. Max sat beside them in the lifeboat, wondering out loud if they'd been victim to Israeli sabotage. Probably a bomb. Bomb or infiltrator. What if the infiltrator had sabotaged the lifeboats, too?

Bertie elbowed Max's thigh.

The intercom crackled. It was Tubbs. "Situation under control. All crew return to General Assembly. We've got good news and bad."

The good news was that they had one functioning engine. As for the engine that went kablooey, Israeli sabotage wasn't to blame but the wine-dark sea. The ship had been designed for the Baltic. Tubbs suspected that the warmer waters of the Mediterranean may have overtaxed the cooling system. And here came the bad news: sailing on one engine was reckless. They had to dock for repairs. The nearest port was Athens.

The crew erupted in near-mutiny. Debt-ridden Greece would impound the ship and arrest Tubbs, people yelled, anything to keep its international creditors happy. Cyprus, on the other hand, as the sole non-NATO member of the EU, was free to offer the *A.R.C.* safe harbor and passage without fear of American economic revenge. Cyprus was only a day away. Why not push on?

"Because we might not make it on one engine." Tubbs's hands were smeared with soot and engine grease. "I won't put my crew in that kind of danger. I've already radioed us in."

Bertie and the crew deflated. There was nothing they could do. Within an hour, two Greek patrol boats appeared to escort the *A.R.C.* to port.

---

The Greeks arrested Tubbs. Disturbing the Sea. The crew couldn't visit him in detention, prohibited as they were from leaving the dock. They were stuck in the purgatory of international maritime law, which was the side berth of a naval pier, separated from the commercial port by cyclone fencing and two guards who smoked herculean quantities of cigarettes. Tugboat horns punctuated the air. Seagulls cawed incessantly.

"We protect you for your safety," said the representative from the Greek Foreign Ministry. Athens was unstable—a general strike, anti-austerity riots, student unrest—could they not smell the tear gas? Hear the rabble-rousers? The crew was merely being kept safe, the representative said. They could come and go to their boat. They could repair their engine. They could sunbathe. They were free to talk with the press.

"It's not free if it's through a fence." Bertie was part of the delegation meeting the representative on the dock. "You're violating international law."

"I'm merely following orders, Madam. May I suggest contacting your embassy?"

The representative smiled insincerely, for surely he knew that the crew had called the U.S. embassy, only to be told, rather undiplomatically, by an Assistant Deputy Section Chief, "Israel's our ally. What do you want us to do? Start a war?" Where else did they suppose the orders to arrest the Captain and detain the ship originated, if not from Washington?

The crew held an emergency General Assembly. Tensions ran high. The comm team had been busy blasting press releases, Max reported. The *A.R.C.* Home Front Committee was hammering sympathetic members of Congress. A Greek legal team was petitioning for the Captain's bail. Wheels were in motion. Not much else they could do but wait.

"Baloney," Bertie said, standing. "What would the Captain say?"

"*Find a broom and start sweeping.*"

In purgatory, they swept. They pumped toilets, refilled water tanks, polished sundeck railings. Tal and Uri, with the help of two Greek naval engineers whose loyalty to a good mechanical problem trumped loyalty to any flag, spent three days in the engine room amidst the *pop-spit-sizzle* of MIG welders. At General Assembly the following evening, they announced that the engine was back online. Tal pointed out that nothing was blocking their berth. If they were, theoretically, to power-down at night and, theoretically, unmoor quietly under the new moon and, theoretically, silently ride the tide out to international waters . . .

Only they couldn't abandon their captain.

Could they?

The crew voted unanimously that they could not.

Day four, five, six of purgatory.

Day seven, just after dawn, Bertie knocked on Max's cabin. Audrey had rediscovered sleep the moment they'd returned from the open sea. Bertie had not. Eyes closed, she saw razor wire, armed guards. She saw Araminta, imprisoned, half a world away.

Max opened the door with a yawn. "Hiya Bertie, what's up?"

"Just making sure you're taking care of yourself. Things being so hectic."

"I'm good. It's like Occupy, only we have beds. And it's not freezing. And every meal isn't pizza."

Bertie ran her hands along her pants.

Max yawned again, then frowned. "Everything okay?"

"I was just—if you had a moment, and it doesn't screw up your computers, could you help me make an online purchase?"

"What do you need?"

"My girls' album. Their new one. I'd like to contribute to their cause."

Max sat up, smacking their head on the top bunk.

"Oh my God, Bertie, we haven't checked in days! Why didn't you say something?"

Bertie hadn't dared to mention it—not to Audrey, not to anyone, certainly not with Tubbs in jail—but nearly a week had passed without a *Jailbreak* update and it knifed her chest not to know. Her girls could've very well raised bail. Araminta might be free.

"Personal matters have to take a backseat in times like these," Bertie said. "We've all been so busy. If it's any trouble at all, really, Max, don't bother. I can wait."

"*Bother?* Come on. Ara's probably out by now."

Max's face went blue in the glow of the phone. Bertie kneaded her hands in her lap. The fact of the matter was that she did feel proud. Proud of her girls, proud of herself. No secret of psychology that young girls who lose their father are prone to dependency issues. Bertie had done everything in her power to prevent that dependency from taking root. And look at them: her girls working together, organizing freedom from within prison. You couldn't ask for more.

But something was wrong.

Bertie saw it in Max's face, which turned from blue to pale. Max put a hand to their mouth, looked at Bertie, and buckled into tears. Bertie reached for the phone. Max pulled it back. Bertie had to physically wrest the phone from their hands. Then—

### Rock Musician Araminta Tayloe
### Dies in Prison, Officials Say

BOSTON—Araminta Tayloe, drummer and songwriter for the influential feminist punk band Jojo and the Twins, was found unresponsive in her maximum security cell where she was being held under protective custody, state prison officials said on Tuesday.

Staff at the Bogastow Correctional Institution found Tayloe in her cell at 6:05 a.m. on Tuesday, showing signs of drug overdose. She was taken to Leonard Morse hospital, where she was pronounced dead an hour later. "A definitive cause of death will not be established until toxicology results are confirmed," the state corrections commission said in a statement.

Tayloe, 36, was arrested in late July on alleged felony charges of conspiracy, possession, and aggravated assault. An effort to crowdfund her bail had grossed $32,550 at the time of her death, according to her band's fundraising website.

Tayloe and her twin sister were recipients of a Gold Record for their 2002 Grammy-nominated single "American Mosh." Described as "The most important band you've never heard of," by *Rolling Stone* magazine, Tayloe and her sister founded the pro-choice "Mosh for Women's Lives" movement, which originated in Boston and expanded to cities across the country. A week before her death, Tayloe published a statement on her band's website, "I am thankful for the opportunity to stay sober and focused, and grateful to our loyal fans during this difficult time."

—a violent hush overtook the cabin, the ship, Athens. The hum of the generators dropped. The distant honking of the tugboats dissolved. Max's sobbing vanished.

Bertie's mind went cold, sharp, clear.

Without waking Audrey, she collected her passport and purse. She marched off the ship and into the Aegean light. The guards held their cigarettes like sabers to halt her. She slipped through them like river water through rocks. They warned her they would shoot.

"Go ahead," she said. She was an old lady with nothing left to lose.

# Chapter 41

# Bertie

Not once in Bertie's legal career had she ever forced her clients to do anything they didn't agree to, a fact which the Massachusetts Bar had taken into consideration and swiftly discounted. The Bar was more interested in the trespassing, the breaking and entering, the aiding and abetting, the many "willful acts of moral turpitude" to which Bertie admitted without a whiff of repentance.

The hearings had taken place well after the hot supernova of the financial crisis, in which many of Bertie's clients were *homeless home-owners*, a capitalist koan made possible by subprime mortgages, big bank robo-signing, repeal of Glass-Steagall, and so on. Complex, but also very simple: Banks were foreclosing on families who had nowhere else to go. When some of these families came calling to the People's Law Center, their appeals going nowhere, Bertie advised them as she believed any decent lawyer should: *possession is nine-tenths of the law.*

In some cases (seven, documented) she'd arranged for and paid a locksmith to smooth the process of repossession. In other cases (three, documented) she'd done the job herself, showing up with bolt cutters, pry bar, sleeping bags, pizza, flashlights. Coloring books and juice boxes for the kids. She made squatting fun.

The Massachusetts Bar struck her name from the rolls of attorneys. After three decades of providing legal advice at MCI-Bogastow, her work there was forbidden. Now, as she stepped through the front doors and emptied her pockets, it was her first time back in two years. A young guard whom she didn't recognize patted her down and ran his hands through her hair. Six days had passed since Ara's death.

"Move ahead, Ma'am. We'll buzz you in when the ladies are ready."

She retucked her T-shirt. Her clothes still felt damp and briny from the Greek docks, the hours of airports and airplanes from Athens to London, London to Boston. She'd shared the butt of the plane with a Yemeni family. Two brothers, their wives and an indeterminate number of children who stampeded aisles, evaded flight attendants, scuttled over Bertie's lap, spilled milk. The brothers had worked as interpreters for the Green Berets, one told her. They were fleeing reprisal. That Bertie had abandoned the *A.R.C.* only to land on American soil with refugees after all was hardly a coincidence. She knew the world was teeming with the displaced and dispossessed. She saw their expressions in the airport bathroom mirror as she splashed water on her face after deplaning: exhausted, dazed, uprooted.

*My baby girl is dead.*

It felt impossible. But Bertie had flown this very route of grief before. She knew the sick, half-light dreaminess. The persistent nausea. The slow-cooking horror of wondering what she may have prevented. The maddening chitchat of well-meaning strangers.

"Business," she'd said, when the Yemeni brothers asked the reason for her travels.

She felt like a businesswoman. She did. Stepping into Boston's last page of summer, she felt cold, clear, calculating. Like walking through a cool blue mist.

Step One: Blue Line to Orange Line to Dorothy Day House, where she slipped inside to grab the van keys off the hook by the kitchen sink.

Step Two: Mass Pike west, where she coasted in the blind spot of an eighteen-wheeler for one calm second, inviting the truck to change lanes and flatten her against the Jersey barriers.

Step Three: Janice.

————

The buzzer rang. They embraced as they had so many times, only before they'd always met in the glassed-off lawyer room, never here in general visitation. Two women in green approached the table when she and Janice sat.

"Mrs. Tayloe, I'm so sorry," said one, a birthmark on her face. "Didn't know her long but your girl—"

"I lost my baby too!" blurted the other woman.

"Christ, Tara," said the first woman. "This isn't about you."

Janice shooed them. "Not now, girls. She's in shock."

Was she? In shock? Bertie didn't feel like she was in shock. But that was part of shock: You didn't feel it. You felt calm. Focused. The cool blue mist.

As soon as the two women left, Janice's shoulders bucked. "I'm so sorry, Bertie."

"Thank you." Bertie waited patiently as Janice cried, then took a centering breath and asked, "How are Emma and Josephine?"

Janice wiped her nose. "You haven't spoken to them?"

"I came straight here." After a pause she added, "I don't suspect they're eager to hear from me."

That Janice did not disagree told Bertie that her instinct was correct.

"Dean says they're okay," Janice said. "Grieving. Hanging in."

"Was there a service?"

"Something simple, he said. Just the girls." Janice dissolved into sobs. "Oh, Bertie. My release date is right around the corner . . . I had my head in the clouds. I should've kept her safe—I'd do another twenty-five to bring her back. You know that."

"I do," Bertie said.

Janice was a dear friend. Bertie regretted allowing so much time to pass without visiting. She'd been busy. Always busy. Busy helping those who needed love most. She patted Janice's hand. A guard stepped forward to reprimand, but another guard froze him with a look: *She's the mother, blockhead. She gets a pass.*

Janice hung her head and sobbed. Bertie grimaced. She remembered this feeling after Walt's death: the more upset others became, the less Bertie felt herself, as if the room held a finite mound of grief, and by the time she went to shovel her share, only scraps remained. The theft left her a little impatient.

"She had a disease, Janice. It was an accident. Nobody's blaming you."

Janice looked up. Her eyes skipped to the guards, then back to Bertie. "What?" Bertie said.

"Ara's roommate, she cleans Max. She found something." Janice's eyes welled. "I wanted to give you some time before you found out . . ."

"Found out what?"

"I don't allow drugs in here, Bertie. You *know* that."

Bertie leaned closer. "What are you saying? What happened?"

A baby laughed across the room. A can kerchunked down a vending machine. The microwave dinged.

Janice lowered her voice to a whisper. "It wasn't an accident."

## Chapter 42

# Bertie

Three days after her visit with Janice, the three-way mail began trickling into the Dorothy Day House. Marjorie Jevers, Bertie's old Law Center colleague, hadn't been willing to break the law—she wouldn't outright smuggle Ara's journal from the prison—but she *was* retired, bored, and impatient as ever with the slow plod of justice. So she met Bertie halfway, promising to forward along any confidential attorney-client correspondence that happened to arrive in her mailbox.

Two letters, five letters, eight.

One page per envelope, sent from different prisoners. The operation would take time, but Janice believed the precaution necessary to avoid Inner Perimeter suspicion.

Twelve letters, fourteen, fifteen.

Held to the window, the envelopes revealed the loops of Ara's words. Bertie remembered that heavy lodestone of despair, wishing Walt had left some written record, a last testament. But now that she had that very testament from her daughter, it glinted with an unexpected edge; whatever Bertie read, she'd never be able to unread.

She stacked the envelopes, unopened, on Audrey's dresser as they arrived.

Seventeen letters, nineteen, twenty-one.

She would've gladly distracted herself with chores, but the Dorothy Day House community had other ideas. The Catholic Workers split their time into thirds: one-third serving meals to Boston's homeless, one-third meeting in affinity groups to plan protests and actions, one-third personal time. For Bertie, the equation was now off. Athena wouldn't let her work the breakfast shift, insisting that she rest. Fanny and Dario offered to take her to Sunday Mass, but neglected to tell her about a march against a natural gas pipeline in West Roxbury. Mindy brought meals to her room. Their concern was imprisoning.

"They're just worried about you," Audrey said. "Let them be."

Audrey had called from the *A.R.C.* satellite phone, despite Bertie's insistence that surely there were more urgent demands for Max's precious bandwidth. Her voice came through crisp and glassy, none of the long-distance spit and hiss that had marked Walt's international calls. The *A.R.C.* was still detained in the docks, she reported. Tubbs still in jail. Athens still on strike. Might be some big news soon, but nothing she could discuss over the phone . . .

"Sounds exciting," Bertie said.

"It's boring as all hell and you know it. How are your girls holding up?"

"Grieving. Hanging in." Bertie repeated what Janice had told her. She couldn't bear to admit, even to Audrey, that she still hadn't spoken to her daughters.

"You're there for each other. That's what matters."

"Yes. It is."

"I'm still mad at you for leaving without telling me," Audrey said. "You know I would've come with."

"For what? There's nothing for you to do here."

"Bull. What would the Captain say?"

"They won't let me grab a broom, Audrey! I've tried."

"Then grab something else!"

Bertie took Audrey's advice, taking the keys to the van and weaving up Boylston toward Jamaica Plain. Josephine and Emma knew she was staying at the Dorothy Day House—Janice had told Dean. That they'd neither visited nor called was as relieving as it was painful. When Bertie flipped her blinker for the turnoff and pictured herself showing up announced—intruding upon their grief far too late—the scales tipped. She couldn't face her girls. Not so soon. Possibly never. In losing one daughter, she may have lost all three.

She hurtled past the turnoff. She merged onto the Mass Pike. Apparently she was pushing west. Apparently she was exiting for Bogastow. Apparently she was going home.

———

The van tires crunched over pinecones that littered the driveway. She parked by the front steps. The doors wore padlocks, so she walked around back and selected a hefty loaf from the stone wall. The lock to the cellar bulkhead snapped off with a clean, satisfying crack.

The cellar stairs led to the pantry, its empty shelves. She stood in her old kitchen, hands flat on the counter. She could see Emma, on the couch, strumming a guitar. Araminta, next to her, nose in a book. Josephine, on a stool to reach the stove, stirring macaroni into boiling water. She could feel the warmth of her girls. Their home.

Josephine, during the April weekend they packed up the house, had wasted no opportunity in highlighting what she saw as a rich irony: in helping other families break into their homes, Bertie had lost hers.

Bertie had only wanted to protect Araminta. Her sweet, sick girl who needed love the most. It wasn't her fault. It was a disease. A disease which nobody could have prevented, and which had cost them so much. A twenty-eight-day stay at a respectable rehabilitation center like New Pathways was nearly $40,000. Shocking, but what wouldn't a parent spend to save a child? Bertie told the girls they had plenty left in Walt's life-insurance fund. In truth, she'd used the fund as she'd always intended, on the girls' college tuition. To cover the New Pathways bill, Bertie needed a home equity loan. But recovery, as she had learned, is no straight path. Araminta had overdosed and nearly died. She needed more treatment. Another twenty-eight days. Another $40,000. Which Bertie didn't have, but what wouldn't a parent spend? She'd hardly dented the principal of her first home equity loan, and here she went, taking out a second. The only way to pay for both, along with the steep Bogastow property taxes, was by adjusting her salary to claim one hundred percent of her income. When the third letter of warning arrived from the IRS, the timing was unfortunate, her disbarment hearings underway. If she couldn't pay the banks or the Federal Government, she figured she might as well make a statement out of it.

War Tax Resisting was a worthy cause, as American as apple pie and the Boston Tea Party.

Even as Josephine slung her arrows, calling Bertie irresponsible, reckless, all manner of hurtful names, Bertie knew she would never share the truth. There was no good in burdening Araminta with the knowledge that she—her disease—had cost them the home. It wouldn't help her recovery. It wouldn't help anyone.

A floorboard popped upstairs, causing Bertie to jump. She'd been gripping the kitchen counter as if it were a railing on the *A.R.C.* She massaged her knuckles. She jangled the van keys in her pocket. She couldn't bear to return to the Dorothy Day House, their suffocating sympathy. She would've visited Janice, but visiting hours were long over. She wouldn't go anywhere, she decided. The stairs creaked as she padded up to the twins' old room. She lay down on the floor, where Araminta's bed had once been.

Cemeteries were such a criminal waste of money and space, second only to golf courses, Bertie believed. The dead were dead. They didn't need your love. You had to fight for the living. It was why she'd never gotten a headstone for Walt. But she had kept his ashes, and from time to time she'd sit with the cherrywood box. So perhaps there was some small comfort in a headstone. A focal point, to say what needed saying.

No. That was ridiculous. You might as well speak into the thin air.

So Bertie did.

"I'm sorry I left. I wish I didn't."

---

She woke in the velvet darkness with a headache that worsened on the return drive to Boston. Dario and Fanny were playing some complicated-looking boardgame in the common room when Bertie let herself in.

"Dinner's in the oven, Mama Bird," Fanny said. "Hope you're not sick of meatloaf. Mail's on the radiator."

Bertie skipped the meatloaf. Three more envelopes, forwarded from Marjorie. She was ready. Ready to touch something of her daughter's. Ready to hold her in her hands.

She locked herself in Audrey's room, opened all the envelopes, and began sorting the pages. From downstairs came the chopping of vegetables, the clatter of pots. Bertie took a breath. She was almost ready. She knelt on the floor and reached underneath the bed for the cherrywood box. She sat with it on the bed, and turned to the first page. She and Walt would read their daughter's final testament together.

*So my roommate Kyla has this theory on pain and the soul.*

The city light had diffused to a hazy glow by the time Bertie finished the journal. There had been no accidental overdose. Suicide, some would say. Not Bertie. She read murder. Her eyes throbbed red with it. Her hands trembled in her lap. Did the prison officials know? Or had the monster covered his tracks? Except he hadn't covered his tracks. Bertie was holding the proof. Ara had named him. The evidence would never hold up in court (it had inadmissibility all over it) but then again, Bertie's court days were finished. The antenna on the Prudential building blinked its warning through the window: red, red, red.

*Want to know what my mom __did__ teach me?*
*Never let the assholes get away with it.*

Bertie and her girls had never heard each other well. Grief, drugs, trauma, work. The many walls. But Araminta was speaking clearly to her now.

"Bertie, get down here! We just got news from Greece!"

Athena ran upstairs. She was knocking at Bertie's door.

"They bailed out the captain and escaped with the tide. They're sailing for Gaza! We're following the livestream. It's wild!"

"Be right there!" Bertie called, but she didn't move. The mind that had earned the highest score in the history of the Massachusetts Bar was shuffling the Rubik's Cube of Ara's last words.

*You have to show it. Action. That's what makes love concrete.*

Her sweet, sick girl, who had suffered most.
Who needed love the most.
Bertie held the pages to her face, inhaling any lingering trace.
You had to fight for the living.
Of course you did.
But you could also fight for the dead.

# Chapter 43

# Bertie

Bertie, over her career, had assembled a small roster of private investigators that generally played by the rules. Most never used warrantless wiretaps, or secretly taped witnesses, or impersonated detectives. DeMauro & Sons Investigative Services did. Finding Lieutenant Andrews's information, however, required no extralegal maneuvering, and less time than Bertie required to prep tomorrow's hashbrowns for the Dorothy Day House. She'd been shredding potatoes with Dario, when Charles DeMauro called back with those three magic words: "Got a pen?"

She grabbed a Costco receipt from the trash, and wrote down an address, vehicle type, color, and plate number.

"Want more?" Charles asked. "Names of the spouse and dependents?"

"No, this is fine. Thank you, dear."

She shredded the last potatoes, stashed the containers in the fridge, cleaned off the grater. She washed and dried her hands. She told Dario she was borrowing the van to check in on an old friend.

---

Lieutenant Blake Andrews lived in the right half of a newish duplex with white vertical siding and black window trim, one block uphill from a public running track and rec field. Bertie had only intended on a slow drive-by before dusk. Then she'd head back, avoiding as much night-driving as possible. That was the plan. But now, after navigating forty minutes of Mass Pike traffic and an *All Things Considered* repeat that she'd already heard on *Morning Edition*, her right foot grew a mind of its own, fully depressing the brake pedal in front of the duplex.

Plastic flowerpots lined three steps to a front porch where an orange tabby cat balanced on a railing, taking swipes at a limp American flag. An upstairs window flickered in TV blue. And a black pickup truck, backed into the driveway. Bertie checked the license plate. She double-checked. The numbers and letters matched what she'd scrawled on the Costco receipt.

The streetlights, along with the last blush of daylight, lit the scene like a movie set, making everything seem less than real. It felt both impossible, and yet completely logical, that he could be so close, perhaps in the upstairs room, watching TV, arms around his family. The man who'd killed her baby.

A downstairs light turned on, the cat leapt off the porch, and at the same moment a loud group of teens in athletic shorts turned the corner, jogging from the rec field, talking and laughing as they panted uphill. The confluence of events startled Bertie. She took her foot off the brake and tapped the gas a little too hard, jerking the van ahead.

One jogger glanced over. She smiled blankly at him and cursed her carelessness. This was the Dorothy Day House van. The last thing she wanted was to get the Catholic Workers involved.

She inched downhill, her palms leaving slicks of sweat on the steering wheel as she turned onto the main road. She had to drive back into the city and forget about all of this. She hadn't done anything wrong. But wasn't that the problem? Her entire life, she'd defended the powerless, but when had she fought the powerful head on? Made them pay for the misery they inflicted? She'd held corporations accountable, and governmental agencies, but the individuals who made the decisions? They got off, usually with promotions and bonuses. It seemed so painfully ineffectual now, the safe path she'd tread. She remembered convincing Walt not to go underground with Tess. What if they had joined the Weathermen? Fought with Janice? Would it have made any difference? Probably not. At least they could've said they tried.

*You have to show it. Action. That's what makes love concrete.*

Had Bertie ever made her love concrete?

# Chapter 44

# Bertie

She called in a favor so small it couldn't be turned down: she simply wanted her name on Roman Lang's visitor list. Roman's attorney, a public defender named Dickerson, had never worked directly with the People's Law Center, but he'd certainly heard of the organization, and was saddened to hear they'd closed. He'd always respected what they did, he told Bertie over the phone. He'd see what he could do.

Apparently, he'd done a lot, because not only was Bertie on the list when she arrived at the Middlesex jail, but a guard brought her to the deposition room rather than general visitation. Dickerson must have listed her as co-counsel. She hadn't mentioned her disbarment. She hoped he wouldn't suffer professionally.

"Hello, Roman."

Roman stood at attention, like a soldier. "Mrs. T."

He looked pale, haggard. His orange uniform bunched around his thick arms and chest. His head, shaved to the scalp when Bertie had last seen him, had grown a russet peach fuzz. A crust of sleep clung to the corner of an eye. Bertie had sat with hundreds of people in his condition, more than a few at this very table, in this very room. She knew he was battling exhaustion, depression, disbelief. That made two of them, she thought.

He stood, rooted in place, forcing himself to meet her eyes. "I'm so sorry, Mrs. T. I have no excuse."

She sat and nodded at his chair. "It's okay, dear. Sit with me. Please."

Dickerson had been the one to inform Roman of Araminta's passing, the lawyer had explained to Bertie. Because Ara had never been deposed, her death shifted Roman's legal situation in a favorable direction. No co-defendant to contradict his version of events. Though his client was less than thrilled at the development, he'd warned Bertie.

Roman ran a hand over the back of his neck. "I've been waiting for Josie and Emma to come in and rip me a new one. I know I deserve it. How are they holding up?"

"Grieving. Hanging in."

Roman lowered his head and punched himself one time, hard, on the chest. "Just give it to me, Mrs. T. I'm ready. Let me have it."

"Whenever you're done flagellating yourself, sit down and listen. I need your help."

"My help?"

She folded her hands in her lap. "You and I did not see eye to eye on much. I suspect we still don't. But we loved her." She met his eyes. "We cared for her, in our own ways."

Roman nodded. He squeezed his eyes shut and balled his hands into fists. Bertie had known him since his adolescent years. A friend of Araminta's. A polite young man. It wasn't until Araminta's assault, however, that Bertie understood how much Araminta had meant to him. A week after, Roman had appeared at the People's Law Center. He'd needed to speak with Bertie in private. Who'd done it? He wanted— *needed*—names.

Bertie wasn't a private investigator, she'd told him. Even if they had names, people were innocent until proven guilty. Most important, Araminta wished to move on, not involve the police or press charges, and although they might not agree with her decision, they had to respect the wishes of the victim.

"I'm not talking about pressing charges," Roman had said. "And Ara doesn't need to know."

Bertie had understood then exactly what he was offering, and his loyalty certainly helped to explain later, as the years rolled on, why she may have tolerated him more than Josie or Emma seemed to. It was true that Roman had enabled some of Araminta's worst habits, and they had their ridiculous two-month marriage, but Bertie firmly believed that her girl's disease would've pushed her elsewhere. Wasn't it better that she be with someone who'd protect her? Roman had saved her when she overdosed. He'd added precious months to her life, months in which the twins had moved home. Months that Bertie had cherished.

"I can't help now, Mrs. T, it's too late." Roman stood across the scuffed metal table. "She's dead. It's my fault and there's nothing I can do about it."

"You're wrong, dear. There is something you can do. So please stop feeling sorry for yourself and listen. Sit down. *Now*."

Roman sat.

Bertie, efficiently and without emotion, explained that Ara's death was no accident. She watched the numbness pass over Roman. Then anger. Then a great wash of what had to be relief, Bertie knew, because guilt was something you could only manhandle for so long. The moment you rested, there it went, sifting through your fingers like sand. But revenge? Revenge was hard, metallic, something solid you could wrap your hands around.

She asked him, directly.

He shifted in his chair. "You do know this is America?"

She shook her head. "I don't have time for all the regulatory riga-marole."

"Isn't that the point? Give you some time to think?"

"I've had plenty of time to think, dear. And I suspect you have, too."

Bertie knew that Roman probably thought of her as a soft and squishy liberal. But a lifetime ago, she'd asked DeMauro & Sons Investigative Services to quietly look into Ara's assault, and, if they happened to uncover any names, pass them along to one Roman Lang. Bertie hadn't known what had come of the investigation. She didn't want to know now. The important thing was that they were alike, she and Roman, and in more ways than people may have guessed.

"Alright, Mrs. T. Sure. I can help you with that."

# Chapter 45

# Bertie

She returned early the next morning, arriving moments before dawn to parallel park just off the main road, close to the track, but still within sight of the driveway. The track and rec field were a boon, all the early-risers walking laps. The steady foot and car traffic would make the elderly lady in the white cargo van that much less conspicuous. Bertie turned off the ignition and unbuckled her seat belt.

She'd driven out for two reasons. First, to fulfill the Dorothy Day House's weekly Costco run, and second, to be sure.

The black truck in the driveway was a match, but that didn't mean it was him. She needed a preponderance of evidence, which was why she'd come with a mason jar of mixed nuts, a bottle of water with lemon slices, and a breakfast sandwich, wrapped in foil and pleasantly warm on her lap. She was prepared for a stakeout of indefinite length. *Morning Edition* kept her company during the commute (a piece on substance use counseling, of all things), though Bertie now found herself glancing at the dashboard clock, impatient.

Two minutes before the hour rolled over, he stepped outside.

She didn't recognize him from the prison (she'd rarely interacted with Inner Perimeter) but she knew it was him. His short cop hair. His build. He swaggered to his truck, beeped it open, and slung himself in. She slumped in her seat as he pulled out.

She could've trailed him, but there was no need for the risk. Instead, she drove to Costco to push around a cruise ship of a shopping cart. Then, on her way back to the Mass Pike, the van brimming with the smell of cardboard and fresh onions, she detoured, parking in downtown Framingham and walking the mile to the prison. She was hot, sweating through her shirt, and wishing she'd worn a hat, when she arrived at the parking lot. The black truck would either be there, or it would not.

The truck was there, parked in a back corner.

She turned and walked out. Surely the prison had security cameras angled in every direction, Bertie thought, belatedly. She didn't care. She wasn't doing anything wrong. She wasn't trying to get away with anything.

# Chapter 46

# Bertie

For her third visit, she left the van keys on the hook in the Dorothy Day House kitchen. She'd hoped to slip out unnoticed, but Athena had woken early for some pre-breakfast-shift yoga, and happened to come in just as Bertie was leaving. Bertie explained she was stepping out for a morning walk before it got too hot. Athena said great, she needed some fresh air before inhaling grease and paprika for the next hour. "Gimme a sec to put down my stuff."

"Sorry dear," Bertie said, "I need to be alone to clear my mind."

Bertie stepped outside, wearing blue jeans, a clean T-shirt from the thrift bin (*Carroll Gardens Nanny Association*), sensible sneakers. A canvas *New Yorker* tote bag, heavy on her shoulder. She hadn't lied to Athena. She did need to clear her mind. If she extended a palm, she was trembling. She felt light-headed, giddy almost, from the cool, double-bladed edge of fear and fury. The man, Andrews, had been enjoying life as if nothing had happened. Watching TV with his family. Going to work. The prison hadn't suspended him. No disciplinary hearing, no investigation, no consequences. No justice.

She walked through the South End, then cut across a corner of the Boston Garden. She labored to keep her mind on the quiet beauty of the elms, the ironwork of the streetlamps, the pastels of the sunrise. The moment she let herself drift, she felt the thump of the tote bag against her ribs. Her breath would shorten, her pulse would quicken. She recentered.

The lightening blue of the sky.

The riotous green of the Garden.

The miracle of dawn.

Some overnight prankster had added detergent to the Copley Square fountain, leading to mountainous clouds of bubbles and shrieks from a toddler who'd declared war on the foam. Bertie met the eyes of the child's exhausted-looking caregiver and smiled, then walked into Back Bay Station, bought a commuter rail ticket in cash, and waited for the 6:10 outbound.

----

Eight stops later she was swinging her arms, walking with purpose as the municipal track came into view. The sun had crested the trees over the rec field. She turned onto his street. Her body hummed, hot with adrenaline. What if he had the day off? Or he'd left early? Or a child was home, sick? She walked uphill, hoping to see his black truck, and also hoping his driveway would be empty.

His driveway wasn't empty.

She walked by the truck, forcing herself not to look. A cat scampered over, the orange tabby from the other night. It followed her as she chugged uphill to the top of the block. A morning walker in purple leggings and a baggy sweatshirt waved from across the street. Bertie waved back. She leaned against a telephone pole. The tang of creosote wafted from the wood. An airplane contrail cut the morning blue like a scar. Her knees felt like they might give out. She felt sick.

The cat brushed against her ankles, meowing. Bertie crouched and ran a shaky hand across its back and tail. The cat had a tag: Rascal.

"Good kitty."

She looked downhill at the man's front porch. His door. She stood and reached into her tote bag, making sure everything was arranged just as Roman had instructed her in the deposition room.

The cat meowed again at Bertie's feet. She felt an extraordinary urge to pee. Three blue porta-potties dotted the edge of the rec field, but she didn't dare run down and risk missing him.

An eighteen-wheeler roared by the main road, brakes squealing.

A crow cawed out.

Rhombuses of sunlight inched across the sidewalk.

She petted the cat, maintaining her gaze on the front door. Seconds passed. Minutes? The fear crashed in waves. Agonizing, nauseating, then receding into a boredom so dense it rivaled third shift on the *A.R.C.*, before rising to a crest again.

The door had a pineapple knocker. The porch had a pair of roller-blades. The garden, well-tended, had two tomato plants, leaves sparkling with morning dew. A pleasant life. But Bertie refused to feel sorry for the man. She wouldn't humanize. Easy to imagine his life's deeds, and how the majority probably fell into the "good" category. He himself may have likely been abused, traumatized, wronged. But couldn't you say the same of anyone? Israeli settlers, Nazi doctors, elementary-school shooters? One thing to acknowledge messy human-ness. Another to overdose on empathy. Overdose on empathy and everyone's a victim at heart. No trespass too large for forgiveness. He'd killed Araminta.

*He murdered my girl.*

She ran her hand along the cat, its vertebrae a string of delicate pearls under her palm. She thought of Janice, who had been in a similar (but different) position in a bank lobby many years ago. She thought of Walt, if he would've encouraged her to turn the other cheek, or flip the table in the temple. She thought of Ronald Reagan, Henry Kissinger, George W. Bush. Her father and grandfather. Men she knew and didn't know, who'd taken and taken. Destroyed and destroyed. Who anchored her in the angry reefs of the past when every bone in her body hungered for the bright horizon.

An eternity passed. Her knees ached from crouching. She stood and wiped her palms on her jeans. The cat pressed against her legs, meowing for more. Bertie peeked into her tote bag to check everything again. Her mouth was dry. Stupid, forgetting to bring water. Stupid, all of this. What on earth was she thinking? This was crazy.

*Almost as crazy as doing nothing.*

Her stomach growled. "Quiet, you," she said, and then his front door opened and he stepped outside and all of Bertie's doubts self-immolated in the magnesium heat of panic.

She felt her feet moving beneath her, bringing her downhill. She floated toward him as he closed the door. He stepped off his porch and onto his driveway. He took out his keys. He beeped his truck. Bertie thought it impossible that he couldn't feel the thump of her heart from twenty yards away.

Ten yards.

Five.

She could keep walking. It wasn't too late—

"Ma'am? Are you okay?"

That sad fang of hope. How it must feel to be a man, that childish assumption of safety. To believe—*to know*—that you will be okay and get away with everything, without consequence, even as consequence stands at the edge of your driveway, sights all but drawn.

"Ma'am?"

He was looking directly at her, but he didn't see her, Bertie knew. He saw a flustered old lady. He pocketed his keys and took a concerned step. Square-jawed, thick-chested. He wore a tight white T-shirt, tucked into slacks. Over one shoulder he carried a dress shirt in dry-cleaning plastic. His prison uniform. He took another three steps toward her. She could see the stubble on his face. She could smell his aftershave. The cat ran from Bertie's feet to his.

"Ma'am? Are you lost? Do you need help?"

Bertie's hands were a pair of docked fish, floundering and gasping as she reached into her tote bag. Roman had told her to practice ahead of time, flipping the thumb safety off at the last moment, ensuring the chamber indicator shone red. She saw red now, as she pulled out the gun. The weapon shook in her hands like a conductor's baton, attempting to rein in the wild symphony of her heart.

Andrews blinked. His eyes grew huge. He hadn't seen her before, but he saw her now. He opened his mouth. "What the—"

The sound was astonishing. It feathered through her chest and bit a splintery chunk from the porch steps. He dropped, surprisingly fast for a man his size, and may have rolled underneath his truck had Roman not coached Bertie to squeeze, not jerk. Like dragging your trigger finger through peanut butter, Mrs. T. Two hands. Elbows shoulder height, slightly bent. Repeat. Slooow . . . smooth . . . slooow. Always in threes. Two to the chest, one to the head—"The Failure Drill," Roman had called it, and Bertie saw why: her second shot also went wild, puncturing the truck with a dull pock, but her third activated that dark magnet, tethering the man to the ground.

She lunged forward and squeezed another set into the bale of his body. And another. She had known her share of failure and would stand for no more.

Smoothly and slowly. Through peanut butter. *Slooow . . . smooth . . . slooow.*

Shiny exoskeletons skittered hot across the driveway.

The air, when she stopped, tasted bitter with ballistic fug. A steady background hum filled her ears, like power lines in the rain. His spotted heap lay half under the truck, feet extended.

Bertie swallowed, and the humming momentarily stopped. It was her ears that were ringing. Her hands sparked with arthritic hurt. He was supposed to have known. To have suffered. Bertie hadn't even had time to speak Araminta's name. It had happened too fast. Like partnership. And children. And career. And justice. The fields of life for which we dutifully plow the ground. Only the more she'd prepared her acres over the years, it seemed, the quicker the harvest. What to do now with the stubbled hills that remained?

Shouting. Doors slamming. A siren already coloring the distance. A woman in a gray sweat suit stood on the porch, pointing, screaming. A dog, somewhere, barking.

Bertie staggered to the curb and sat to examine the hot gun in her hands. She'd found the weapon exactly where Roman had sent her, in his basement drop ceiling, wrapped in plastic along with two others, a machine gun–looking thing and a shotgun, both cartoonishly large. Roman hadn't mentioned returning it. Perhaps he'd sensed that Bertie didn't expect to leave here today. But neither had she planned to stay.

The gun clicked dry. Dry against her scalp, dry against her teeth, dry against her chest. She thumbed the safety. Checked the indicator chamber. Dragged her finger through the peanut butter. Slow and smooth. But the thing was empty. Its job complete.

# Chapter 47

# Josie

The colony survived. Like leafcutter ants scrambling against the diluvial rains in the Nicaraguan neotropics: some individuals were lost, others damaged. The destruction, incalculable. But the colony endured the storm. Sisters, they soldiered on.

Josie saved herself by saving Emma. Emma made it easy. Not a drop of alcohol in fifteen years, and now drinking herself sick. She chased cruel men. She stayed out for days. She shuttered herself in the apartment for days. She lost weight, her period, a tooth. She buzzed her head. She'd lost her other half, and now she was halving herself again. She walked onto Jamaica Pond's early skim of ice. She palmed the baggie with Ara's unused heroin. She tested all the fragile centers. She saw Ara's face in the bathroom mirror and considered her duty, to follow. Only Josie wouldn't allow her to leave.

Josie couldn't lock Emma inside the apartment—she tried—but she could lock her arms around her in the bed they shared. She could make her tea, draw her hot baths, play her *Smiley Smile*. She could hound Emma at every opportunity, reminding her that she was loved. That she would be missed. Everything Josie believed she should have said to Ara. The force with which she should've held on.

She brought Emma home from the Centre Street bars.

She followed Emma onto slippery Jamaica Pond.

She broke in the bathroom door and scattered the line of heroin that Emma had prepared at the sink's edge; she held Emma on the tiled floor, rocking her as she sobbed.

"Let me go, Jojo. I want to go."

There, back against tub, sister in arms, Josie told her, "I didn't drop out of Stanford. I got kicked out." She gave an abbreviated version of what had happened. Her self-destruction under pressure, the shameful rush of relief when Emma had called.

Emma tilted her head. "You could've just told us."

"I was embarrassed. I still am. And I'm pregnant."

Emma lifted Josie's sweatshirt. A cold hand to her soft belly.

"Dean," Josie told her. "He doesn't know. Only you."

"What are you going to do?"

Josie, tipping soon into her second trimester and still undecided, decided now.

"This is half my DNA. That means its half yours, too. I'm going to need you, Em. I'll need you in five months, in five years, in fifteen years. I need you now."

She pressed Emma's hand again to her stomach and—a first for Josie—she asked for help.

———

Steps forward, leaps back.

First Emma was eating again. She was going for walks, returning with prenatal vitamins for Josie from the Yuppie Bodega. She nagged Josie to eat fiber, drink water, bounce on a yoga ball. But then Emma wouldn't get out of bed. She was slugging cough syrup to fall asleep. Whispering to the mirror, arguing with her reflection, leaving her twin a jeweled heap of broken glass in the sink.

Steps forward, leaps back.

*Jailbreak* hit number 10 on the Billboard Independent Albums chart. The one-two punch of Ara's death and the prison guard's murder had launched the album to new heights before it was even released. In the salacious weeks afterward, when headlines (first social media, then daytime TV, finally cable news) told of the fanboy guard, the prison diary, the vigilante mama bear who'd defended herself at her own murder trial, the waves of publicity acted as second-, third-, and fourth-stage booster rockets, sending *Jailbreak* stratospheric. Preorders topped 100,000. When Emma finally launched the EP—no label, just Emma and her workstation—the Awesong servers briefly crashed. "Free Animal" rose to 33 on the Billboard Hot 100.

The success was immense and entirely unenjoyable. Blood money. Back when Ara's diary arrived in the mail (no return address) the last pages were the most difficult: "Unburdened," Ara had written. Genetic altruism at its purest. The individual, sacrificing herself so the pack could endure.

*Fuck that*, the pack responded.

In Ara's name they donated to Mothers Against Mandatory Minimums, the Survivors' Resource Center, the Boston Bailout Project. An anonymous donation to secure three spots for Crystal, Ruby, and Gemma Johnson at the Berkshire Country Overnight Camp.

Day-to-day expenses aside (Thai food, iced oat milk lattes, kombucha) the sisters refused to benefit from Ara's death. Josie established a college fund for Mimi, who'd continued with their leafcutter trials. Mimi had been systematic in documenting the colony's regeneration. Josie threw her arms around the girl and sniffled back a few tears when Mimi shared her preliminary results.

"Um, we okay?" Mimi said.

"I just think you're amazing. You know that don't you?"

Josie registered Mimi for an expensive SAT prep course. She hired a tutor to help her apply for summer research internships at NASA, Harvard, MIT.

Still, Josie couldn't spend the money fast enough.

---

*Jailbreak* reached number 2 on the Billboard Independent Albums chart.

A 25,000 vinyl pressing sold out in advance.

An editor at W. W. Norton wanted to publish Ara's prison diary along with selections from her earlier journals.

A promoter for Coachella wanted Emma on the lineup.

A team of producers from Paramount called to discuss film rights: Mark Ruffalo and Rosario Dawson were still riding the buzz from the *A.R.C.*'s triumphant return (a highly emotional docking, 236 Syrian women and children marched from the ship to present themselves for asylum). Both actors were eager to use their Hollywood power for projects with substance. Funding was there if the Tayloe sisters wanted it.

What did the Tayloe sisters want?

They wanted their sister back.

They wanted to return her pound of flesh.

Josie, in particular, wanted to stop being angry. But angry she was.

She was angry when a day passed without mention of Ara, she was angry when anyone mentioned her too casually.

She was angry at the presumption of the fans who left flowers at the door, she was angry at the red and yellow bunches for wilting.

She was angry at three elderly women laughing in a booth at the Fountain, oblivious to those who'd never enjoy growing old with the people they loved.

She was angry at the wind for scattering Ara's ashes in the wrong direction during the small backyard ceremony at their old house.

She was angry at Emma for having Ara's face.

She was angry at Ara for refusing her help.

She was angry at Roman for helping in every wrong way.

She was angry at her adrenal cortex for the overproduction of cortisol.

She was angry at her father for dying.

She was angry at her fetus for forcing the challenge of motherhood, a subject in which she had zero credits and not one reputable thesis advisor.

She was angry at Bertie beyond words, beyond thought, beyond the scope of scientific notation.

Mostly she was angry at herself.

She was angry at herself for being so angry. She did not like this person she'd somehow become. This person she'd been for far too long.

Steps forward, leaps back.

———

A huge step forward when Janice completed her sentence and moved in that winter. The apartment should've felt crowded, yet Janice made more space, not less. She cooked hearty stews. She stocked the refrigerator. She brewed Josie an anti-nausea froth of brewer's yeast and raspberry leaf, a Clancy family recipe that, to Josie's surprise, worked. Janice did not mention Bertie. She did not ask Josie if she would invite Dean to move back in. She did not ask if they would co-parent, or what they might name the baby, though her every grandmotherly bone surely ached to know.

She slept on the pullout couch by the front door, prison-trained to float near the surface. When Emma tried slipping by, it was never quietly enough.

"Going out, hon?"

"Can't sleep."

Janice, throwing off her blanket, pulling on a jacket: "Oh goodie, me neither."

———

Emma and Janice grew close. Janice helped Emma back from the edge, and in return Emma helped Janice reintroduce herself to the Y chromosome, beginning with Fabio, their bachelor landlord whose loyalty to Apartment 3A Janice found endearing. Since the tragedy, as Fabio called it, he'd rescinded his eviction and reinstated Josie as the Butterfly & Reptile World's Director of Operations, whenever she was ready to return. When he stopped by with "gifts" from past tenants (a cashmere blanket, a space heater, a set of silverware), Emma would swoop in as wing-woman.

"Hey Fabio, did Janice tell you about the time she led a prison march to win back dessert?"

"Hey Fabio, what do you think of Janice's top?"

"Hey Fabio, you need to take Janice to *The Conjuring*. I can't watch that scary stuff."

Emma and Janice bundled up and went to brunch, the Centre Street Cinema, the conifer path through the Arboretum. Emma discovered on these winter strolls that she could talk to Janice openly. She didn't need to pretend to be her twin. She told Janice how she'd sabotaged Ara's safety, Ara's sobriety, Ara's life.

Janice listened patiently, for she knew better than most the treacherous path of self-forgiveness. She'd spent decades seeking to make amends with the family of a murdered police officer. Her final month at MCI-Bogastow had overlapped with Bertie's first. How many ways could a person say sorry? Janice had tried them all. She removed a mitten, took Emma's hand. The trick was expanding the world, not closing it, she said. Reaching out.

The message permeated the apartment, for Josie found herself doing the very thing she'd vowed against: She reached out to the Dorothy Day House and asked Audrey to arrange a visit to MCI-Bogastow. She had to see her mother.

———

Josie drove. Emma sat in the passenger seat. Six months had passed since she'd buzzed her head. Her hair had grown now to Ara's short length. She styled it like Ara, too, in the same faux-hawk fade. The likeness had the power to make Josie grateful or resentful, depending on her mood. Today, as they exited the Mass Pike and wove through the narrow Bogastow roads, gratitude led by a mile.

Emma, like Josie, had vowed to never again speak to their mother. But stress hormones weren't healthy for prenatal development, she said, so she'd come along to act as a human firewall. As they pulled into the prison parking lot, however, she leaned over and said to Josie, "What if we just ghost her? Give her a taste of her own medicine?"

Josie agreed it would feel good. Bertie was expecting them. To get her hopes up and not show? To estrange themselves as Bertie had with her own mother? "No. I want to start doing things differently."

"I know, I know," Emma groaned. "Me too."

Josie parked. She turned off the ignition. There stood the prison smokestack. The glinting razor wire. She reached for Emma's hand.

"You ready?"

"Showtime."

———

They claimed a table at the far end of the room, as far as possible from where they'd visited with Ara last summer. Josie rested her head on Emma's shoulder while they waited.

Emma rubbed Josie's belly. "How's baby?"

"Excited to get out."

"Me too." Emma looked around. "I don't care if she says she's sorry."

"I wouldn't worry about that."

"But I *want* her to be sorry."

A buzzer went off. Inmates funneled in. Bertie lurched from the rush, looking old and frantic, her hair brittle, the reed of her body adrift in the navy blue folds of her uniform. Josie swallowed an uninvited bubble of sympathy.

"Mom. Over here."

"Girls!"

Josie hadn't spoken to Bertie since the Griffinport docks. For Emma, it had been longer. When they had learned that she'd returned early from the *A.R.C.*, their thoughts were: *not early enough.* Ara was dead. That was before Bertie had killed the guard. An act so colossal it still floored Josie with wonder. Her mother never seemed to doubt that she could mold fate in her hands, shape it as she wished, and there was something inspiring in that. But Josie was also repulsed. The guard—a monster, to be sure—had a family, and what had Bertie done if not forge another link in the chain of loss and revenge? Mostly, though, Josie felt robbed. They were each responsible for Ara, but Bertie had skipped the hard work of repentance. In the game of atonement, she'd won: sentenced to life without parole. How could Josie ever compete with a sacrifice so ultimate?

By doing what they were doing right now, Josie reminded herself.

Vengeance was easy. What Josie was trying was harder: rerouting the heavy berm of evolution. This was the real work. This was why she was here.

They were the only visitors not to stand for hugs. Bertie sat across from them, adjusting her glasses, waving hello to other prisoners, fidgeting, looking everywhere except at Josie or Emma. "Yoo-hoo, Tori!" she sang to a woman by the vending machines. She lowered her voice. "I'm helping Tori sue D.O.C. for blood pressure medication. They're rationing, can you believe it? I'm running quite the legal clinic here. We won an injunction on overcrowding. I'm not allowed to practice, but what are they going to do? Sentence me to life?" She laughed a high-strung bark.

Josie squeezed Emma's hand under the table and asked slowly, as if speaking to a child, "Are you going to ask how we are? How we're doing? About Ara's service?"

Bertie flinched at Ara's name. "I would very much like to know, yes."

"Why are you acting so skittish?" Josie said, her voice like powdered sugar.

This was not why Josie had come—she did not *want* to make Bertie uncomfortable—but now that it was happening, she couldn't deny herself the dopamine.

"Who's skittish?"

"Mom, please. Cut the bullshit. You can't even look at us."

"That's ridiculous." Bertie made her case with a glance. As her eyes passed over Emma, the blood drained from her face. Josie was still getting used to it: looking at Emma and seeing Ara.

Bertie polished her glasses with a sleeve. "You're missing a tooth, dear."

"I sure am." Emma crossed her arms over her chest.

"And you've cut your hair."

"Okay, I can't do this." Emma pointed to Josie's stomach. "Aren't you going to say *anything* about the situation going on right here?"

"It's none of my business to pry—"

"This is your business, Mom." Josie rubbed her belly. "You're going to be a grandmother."

Bertie blinked a few times rapidly, and her eyes were shining, just like that.

"Do you have a name?"

"We're leaning toward Rose," Emma said.

"For Parks or Luxemburg?"

"*Rose*, Mom. Not Rosa."

"Rosie the Riveter!"

"No. Stop it," Josie said. "This baby isn't going to be named after anyone. They get to be whoever they want."

Bertie smiled. "I think that's a marvelous idea."

A guard sneezed loudly, cutting above the din.

"Gesundheit!" Bertie called out.

This tiny woman emptied a clip of hollow-point bullets into a human being, Josie reminded herself. She folded her hands on the shelf of her stomach, and, plainly as possible, said what she'd come to say.

"I'm angry at you, Mom. I'm so angry. I've been angry for a long time. But—"

"Me too!" Emma said, her voice trilling a high-C. "Maybe you feel good, killing him, but it doesn't bring Ara back. You could've helped when it mattered, and you didn't."

Bertie lowered her eyes.

"And you can't even say that you're sorry!" Emma yelled with a hiccup.

"Take a breath, Em," Josie said, a little startled to find herself in the frankly weird position of being the one to de-escalate a situation involving Bertie. The fractal nature of anger allowed for infinite replication—practically invited it. All you had to do was drop in and keep falling. Josie knew this too well. And she wanted to end the fall for good.

"We're angry, Mom, but we don't want to be. We want a relationship. A real one. We want to offer that. That means we're here for each other. And we share emotions, like normal human beings. It means we talk, for real. No more pretending that nothing bad has happened to our family. No more acting like the problems of the world mean ours don't count. No more sweeping everything under the rug. This baby is going to know about her aunt Ara. And her grandfather. And you. This baby is going to know exactly where they came from." She looked to Emma, who was nodding furiously in agreement. "If you want a relationship with us, Mom—if you want a relationship with your grandchild—those are our terms. It's time for this family to fucking evolve."

Bertie responded by putting her hands in her lap and bowing her head. A lightning bolt of pale scalp shone through the part of her thin, gray hair. Her thin shoulders rose and fell.

"Told you," Emma muttered. She signaled to a guard that they were ready. She stood to leave. Josie lifted herself out of her chair.

"Josephine. Emma. Wait."

Bertie removed her glasses. She wiped her eyes. "It wasn't fair, what happened with your father, you were so young . . . and your sister . . . you girls have suffered . . ."

"So have *you*, Mom!" Josie blurted. Her mother was a frail old woman who was going to die in this prison, as Ara had, and seeing this future so clearly cut deeply into the half-life of Josie's resentment. Entire decades shed.

"No, no, no," Bertie shook her head. "I've lived a privileged life."

"Come on, Mom," Josie insisted. "It's okay to admit—"

Bertie interrupted her by blowing her nose on a sleeve. "My goodness! Such a scene. I apologize."

Josie's mirror neurons were firing full blast, pressure mounting. She grabbed Bertie's hands and pressed them to her belly.

"No contact," said a guard.

Josie ignored him, squeezing her mother's sharp wrists.

Bertie searched Josie's face with wild eyes. "I hope you girls are very proud of yourselves. Your father—I just wish he could've seen the incredible women you've become."

Josie scrunched her face. "Oh, Mom."

"Tayloe, remove yourself from the visitor."

"Please, dude," Emma said to the guard. "Let us have a moment."

"No, he's right." Bertie sniffled. "You girls have eight million things to do. You have your lives to live. This isn't helpful for anyone. We should say goodbye."

But Josie wouldn't let go. And neither would Bertie. They held on.

The guard put a hand on Bertie's shoulder. "That was your last warning."

Emma tried to step between them. "Get your hands off her, man."

The guard tugged at Bertie and nodded at a second guard, who approached Emma. Yet Josie continued holding Bertie's hands to her stomach, because baby was kicking, kicking, kicking, almost as if stomping a beat.

Bertie yelled, a pained animal screech, as the guard wrenched her away. She twisted in his grip. Everyone in visitation was gaping. A third guard barged in. Bertie lunged, trying to break free. The guards picked her up like a child, and in two big steps, she was gone.

But her voice carried, before the door clanged behind her.

"Come back, girls! I want to tell you about your father. I want to be a grandmother! I want us to talk! I love you! I do!"

# Chapter 48

# Josie

For a lifelong biologist brimming with curiosity, Josie continued to seek surprisingly little data on her uterine biome. The truth was she was afraid. Afraid of deformity. Mutation. A split zygote. Double (*triple?!*) embryos. She was afraid of evolution. Two billion years ago, some hungry eukaryotic cell had engulfed a bacterium and evolved into the first mitochondria, the tiny engines of our bodies, and because mitochondrial DNA is passed down from eggs, not sperm, the very furnace of every human life derives exclusively from our mothers.

So really, when it came down to it, Josie was afraid of Bertie. She was afraid of becoming her mom. Passing down the same damaged instructions.

But Dean couldn't stand not knowing, and like any decent organizer, he could be a persistent pain in the ass when he wanted.

Dean had acted like a first responder after Ara's death, letting himself into the apartment (he never took the key off his ring) and asking how he could help. He could help by giving them space to grieve, Josie had said. He gave that space, only stopping by briefly with toilet paper, tissues, sandwiches from the Yuppie Bodega. He cleared their steps of melted candles and wilted flowers. He helped with the cleaning, hauling laundry to the basement washer. He folded T-shirts. He matched socks. And that was before Josie told him she was pregnant. Dean cried and whooped and cried more. Then he settled down and became the most devoted, fawning groupie in rock history. He bought groceries, offered to schedule doctor appointments. He worshipped Josie's third-trimester breasts, her stretch marks, her mermaid hair. He promised to drink less. Or he could stop altogether. Hell, he could stop right now.

---

Josie knew she should've been grateful, yet she watched herself snap at him for buying shampoo but forgetting conditioner, for washing Ara's *I Believe Anita Hill* sweatshirt, for suggesting she go to therapy, take a walk, sign up for childbirth classes. For excusing her every eruption as hormones. Her anger was a burnt kernel of corn, fossilizing to the pan of her heart, and it may have fused there permanently if Dean, one afternoon, hadn't snapped back.

He'd been trying to adjust Josie's pillows as she shifted on the couch, searching for a position that made her hips ache less. When he grazed her neck, she flinched.

"Your hands are freezing. Stop hovering. Go away."

Instead of apologizing, as usual, Dean cast off his halo and declared, just short of a yell, that it was time for them to talk a few fucking things out.

Emma glanced at Janice, who nodded at the front door. They rushed to pull on their coats.

Dean waited until they were gone, then told Josie not to worry; he wasn't going to propose again. He was just going to tell her how it was.

How it was: Bad shit happened. Welcome to life. Extremely unfair, extremely shitty shit. But that was no excuse to destroy the good. Dean had stuck by her through the worst, since they were kids. Yes, he'd abandon her one day, as would every living creature, but he was here now. She had to let people in! If she couldn't, if she continued to let the trauma of the past crayon away the present? Well then he was sincerely worried for her and their baby. Because it would never be simple. Never.

"I signed up for a parenting group by the way. I don't care if you're not going. I am. This baby's going to have a father." He reached for the doorknob. "I'll leave, but I'm not leaving."

Josie, waylaid by gratitude and grief and the work of making a human being, told him to stay.

"Why?" Dean said.

"Because." Josie swung her legs to the floor.

Dean crossed his arms. "I'm not talking about one foot in, one foot out. I'm done with that."

"I'm both feet in." She reached out to uncross his arms, standing up so they were face-to-face. She held his hands against her stomach. "The pack is all of us. I'm in, Dean. I'm all in."

---

Dean moved back in. Soon afterward, Josie caved under the pressure of his excitement and curiosity. During her twenty-nine-week checkup, the sonogram revealed what everyone said they already knew: a perfectly healthy baby girl.

"How about Harriet?" Emma said.

"I still like Rose," Josie said. "Sweet yet thorny."

They were drinking iced tea on the apartment porch. A man in a straw hat knelt in the community garden across the street, loosening the spring soil with a trowel. April branches budded tender greens.

Josie had observed another step forward in Emma, triggered by each grainy sonogram photo she stuck to the fridge. Emma could've afforded her own place, yet she chose to stay down the hall, in Josie's old room. Josie worried about her (her nightmares had tapered, would never disappear) but Emma insisted that, believe it or not, she slept better when she wasn't sharing the bed with someone who had to pee every five minutes.

Emma obsessed over mommy-to-be blogs, instructing Josie to drink constant fluids to counter constipation, chew apple slices to relieve heartburn, apply witch hazel to soothe hemorrhoids. She accompanied Josie to childbirth class when Dean was out facilitating a meeting. She brainstormed names.

"They say old-fashioned names are coming back."

"Yeah, like Rose," Josie said, watching the gardener, the packages of seeds at his side. "Or Dahlia. Or Violet."

"Or Black-Eyed Susan?" said Emma.

Josie laughed.

"What about Araminta?" said Emma.

"I thought about that," Josie said. "I still like Rose."

---

Monogamy did not require marriage, but UNITE HERE's health plan did. The only thing worse than dipping needlessly into the *Jailbreak* money was wasting it, and Josie's prenatal medical bills were snowballing. She and Dean made an appointment at the Middlesex County courthouse. The baby elbowed Josie's cervix as the officiant, a grinning older woman with a streak of purple in her hair, ran through the script like an auctioneer.

"Now go ahead and kiss the bride, good-looking, she ain't your girlfriend no more."

The marriage license was just a piece of paper. But it wasn't *just* a piece of paper.

Josie, on the drive home, ran her fingers over the raised golden seal and placed a hand on Dean's thigh and felt the heavy barge inside her tack, charting a slow change in course.

Hadn't she yearned since she was a girl to study life? And what was motherhood if not a great investigation of this very field? A lifelong study, if fortunate. She wouldn't be able to control for every variable or method, but she had notes, a little field experience on what worked (TV-free summers) and what didn't (silencing the past). And unlike her lonely days in the Nicaraguan rainforest, or Stanford, or the Carrizo Plain, she wouldn't be alone. She had Dean, her research colleague. If he stayed on, and stayed sober, great. If not, she had Emma and Janice. Josie would retain the role of primary investigator, no matter who came or went. This was, after all, her work.

She lowered the 4Runner's window. The cool spring air hissed against her outstretched hand. She'd insisted on no rings, no baby showers, no announcements, no fanfare, for celebrating without Ara was no celebration at all. But as the fresh air washed through the window and hit her like a bedsheet on the line, she understood why Bertie had kept so few family photos. She understood the half-assed birthdays and Christmases. She understood how her widowed mother had felt about graduations and gigs and weddings—not as celebrations, but daggers, painful reminders of who was missing. Josie put herself in Bertie's shoes, and then she kicked them off. She turned to Dean, who was smiling for no apparent reason.

"We have to stop at the Dollar Store. We need streamers. And balloons. We're having a party."

Every new generation represents an opportunity to reroute the tree of life. The unassailable advantage of horizontal gene transfer and natural selection. Evolution. Adaptation. Josie's spiraling stairways of DNA were similar to Bertie's, but they were not identical. She did not have to be like her mother. No natural law states that loss must harden. Loss, just as easily, can soften.

———

In honor of evolution, Josie and Dean threw a reception at the Butterfly & Reptile World. Mimi led the interns in hanging streamers between the monitor lizard tanks. The leafcutter ants painted highways of purple and yellow overhead, crocus and sunflower petals carried like parasols by the thousands. Emma was a one-woman wedding band: Otis Redding, Etta James, Janis Joplin. Fabio danced with Janice. Josie swung Dean in swooning circles. A trio of monarch butterflies fanned their stained-glass through the air.

———

In honor of evolution, Josie set up a weekly visit with her mother. Emma joined as often as she could. Conversation was awkward at first. Talk of the weather only got them so far. Then Emma suggested they think about their visits like a collaborative book. They could write whatever they wanted, whoever picked up the pen first. "What do you say, Mom? Want to start?"

"Start where?"

"Whatever interests you."

"Like what?"

"Like how did you and Dad meet?"

"What do you want to know? How was the weather? It was St. Augustine, it was hot, muggy——"

"Not the weather!" Emma and Josie said at the same time.

"What then?"

"Why were you there?"

"Martin Luther King was there. I'd always wanted to see him. Your father was working, taking pictures. He gave me his handkerchief when they started lobbing tear gas. He was very handsome. I'd snuck out and hitchhiked there. I was still in high school. Boy did I get it. You think I'm bad, you should've met my parents."

"What were they like?" asked Josie.

"Ha. You don't want to know."

"Yes we do, Mom. Tell us. Tell us everything."

———————

In honor of evolution, Josie called the university registrar at Stanford. She knew she could never go back—far too much time had passed—but she could request her transcripts and see about mastering out. Greater Boston was not the worst place to find yourself with a post-bachelor's degree in ecological and evolutionary biology. There were all the labs in Cambridge. Not to mention a college on every other block. She'd really enjoyed working with Mimi. Maybe she could continue to nurture the curiosity for life in others, wherever else it sought to bloom.

———————

In honor of evolution, Josie refused to hide the dead. She plastered the dead on every wall. Her dad, on the steps of their old house, striking a muscleman pose with baby Josie in his arms. Ara, behind her kit, costumed and smiling. Ara on the tour bus. A funny one of Ara squatting in a Kansas field, dress hiked, holding hands with Emma as they peed. Josie framed and hung them all. Spears to the gut. But the spears felt necessary. Sometimes the spears even felt good.

———————

Then one bright afternoon in late April, a dreamy piano progression woke Josie from a nap.

"Sounds great, Em," she said from bed.

Emma didn't hear. Emma was zeroed in, focused on her runs and fills. The apartment had been silent for so long. She was making music again.

Sometime later she crawled into Josie's bed. "I wrote a lullaby," she said, and stretched her headphones onto Josie's belly.

———————

Emma returned to the stage in May, teaming up with Carrie Brown-stein and Kathleen Hanna for a Survivors' Resource Center benefit at the Wilbur Theater. Josie was days, hours perhaps, from the contractions that would usher a new life into this old world. Until then, she would continue doing what she knew best: helping the colony. She was working the merch table. Janice and Dean were assisting. Dean had prepped a duffel bag, ready at arm's reach for the moment they needed to go to the hospital. He kept glancing at Josie. Touching her arm. She shook her head. Not yet. She didn't want to miss a second of Emma's show. The first live performance of *Jailbreak*. Ara's kit, painted stark white, blazed luminescent through the artificial fog. Emma wore boots, jumpsuit, gloves, sun hat—all black. She'd held it together for most of the show, but when Josie caught her eye through the lights and the artificial fog, Emma paused, mid-chorus. The band went on for another two beats before grinding to a halt.

"Sorry, everyone. I need a second. This is . . . sorry. I guess I'm a little emotional."

She nodded at the drummer to count them back in, and opened her mouth, ready to continue, but her face crumpled, and she choked out a sob. There was a moment of horrible silence in which Josie felt the world backsliding. They'd tried their best, but their best would never be enough—impossible without Ara. They couldn't do it.

But then someone from the audience yelled, "We love you, Emma!" and the crowd erupted in cheering, hooting, applause.

Josie threw one arm around Dean, and her other arm around Janice. Together with the theater, they filled their lungs and as one voice joined in, carrying Emma through the chorus, carrying them all:

*The pack is the nucleus*
*The pack is all of us*
*Family Loves*
*Family Kills*
*Free Animal*

# *Acknowledgments*

We human beings (like ants!) are one of the few truly social species on our planet, meaning we are pretty much useless on our own; everything we accomplish is thanks to the group, and that is absolutely true for this novel.

Thanks to the team at Atria Books, from Liz on copyediting, to Maudee and Holly on marketing and publicity, to Kyoko on design, to Libby and Lindsay at the helm. Thanks most of all to Sean deLone for the wise revision notes, the coaching and suggestions, and for keeping all the parts moving.

Thanks to Danielle Bukowski for representing and championing this book in all matters large and small.

Thanks to my fourth-grade class for helping to choose the cover. You kids are alright. ☺

Thanks to Jess Lamb, John Riley, and Will Urmston for honing Emma and Ara's musicality.

Thanks to Caleb Jacques and Matt Chatfield for your patience and expertise with all my inquiries about ecological, evolutionary, and molecular biology.

Thanks to Reena for help with the judicial and legal terminology. Thanks to my friends and early readers, Greg, Allison, Sophia, Katrina, Eric, Tom, Kat, and Christine.

Thanks to Hawthornden Castle for twenty-five uninterrupted days to get lost in this novel.

Thanks to every member of every Freedom Flotilla for the courage, love, and sacrifice required to sail in solidarity with the Palestinian people. You are some of the very best of our species.

Thanks to the Edinburgh Butterfly & Insect World for that most serendipitous afternoon, and to the charismatic megafauna who happened to be on duty to cheerfully answer each of my extremely specific questions.

Thanks to the public library of Belfast, Maine, for your small but mighty collection of insect books.

Thanks to Chris and Karen for the roof, coffee, bicycles, love, and support during my extended "residency" while beginning this novel.

Thanks to the MFA creative writing program at Rutgers University–Newark, and to the good people of New Jersey, for helping to fund my two years there.

Thanks to Ben for being such a great brother, from childhood into adulthood. It was no coincidence that sibling relationships were the heart of this book. I'm grateful to be going through life together.

Thanks to Mom and Dad for surrounding our childhood with books, magazines, newspapers, love, and encouragement. I wish all my students were so lucky.

Thanks, above all, to Lizzy, for bringing in the dough during the early years, for reading pages, for listening to me talk about these characters for a decade, for saying "go, go, go" that one dark winter when I was done, done, done. For the love. The pack can be as few as two.